"Hands down, the best mystery novel of the year. It might be the best mystery written in America in years. [This] book…packs a punch that left me breathlessly turning the pages."
—*Book Reporter*

"Another sure-fire winner…Reads like a collaboration between Henry Miller and Mickey Spillane."
—*Milwaukee Journal Sentinel*

"Expertly crafted in every way and ending with one of the most shocking…conclusions in recent memory."
—*Ellery Queen's Mystery Magazine*

"Reads like O. Henry run amok in McBain's 87th Precinct."
—*Ink19*

"Classic pulp."
—*Kevin Burton Smith, January Magazine*

"A wonderful chase from start to finish."
—*Charlie Stella*

"Excellent…terrific."
—*The Globe and Mail*

"Able to cut to the heart of a character or a situation with equal ease, he has a voice as unforgettable as his stories."
—*Billie Sue Mosiman*

"[Ardai] builds his tale slowly and really throws it into high gear in the emotional final chapters."
—*George Pelecanos*

"This guy's a gold mine," Borden said, jabbing with the back of his pen at the newest book to grace his desk. "He's the genuine article. Gold Medal wishes they could find a guy like this."

The book was titled I Robbed the Mob! and was credited to that most prolific of authors, Anonymous, but Tricia was as proud of it as if her name had been plastered all over the cover. The illustration showed a man in a heavy overcoat, his face hidden in shadows, advancing on a buxom woman in a torn blouse. What that had to do with robbing the Mob, Tricia had no idea. But Borden said it would sell books.

Beneath the title it said

Torn From the Headlines!
The Scandalous True Story of One Man's
LIFE in the UNDERWORLD!

"You know what Casper Citron said about us on his program yesterday?" Borden said. "He called the book reprehensible. Said we glorified crime. That's good for a thousand copies, easy. The thing's selling, Trixie. You did good—you and this guy you found." Borden grabbed his jacket from a hook on the back of the door, shrugged it on. "You think he really ripped off his boss?"

"Oh, I'm sure he wouldn't say it if it weren't true," Tricia said.

"Man," Borden said. "The guy has guts. I tell you, I wouldn't want to be in his shoes the day someone hands Nicolazzo a copy of the book."

It was at that moment that the frosted glass pane in Borden's door shattered...

FIFTY-*to*-ONE

by **Charles Ardai**

A HARD CASE CRIME NOVEL

A HARD CASE CRIME BOOK
(HCC-050)
December 2008

Published by

Dorchester Publishing Co., Inc.
200 Madison Avenue
New York, NY 10016

in collaboration with Winterfall LLC

ISBN 0-8439-5698-1
ISBN-13 978-0-8439-5968-0

Cover design by Cooley Design Lab

Typeset by Swordsmith Productions

The name "Hard Case Crime" and the Hard Case Crime logo
are trademarks of Winterfall LLC. Hard Case Crime books are
selected and edited by Charles Ardai.

Printed in the United States of America

Visit us on the web at www.HardCaseCrime.com

For Max Phillips,
Without whom

1.

Grifter's Game

The day she got the job dancing, they asked her what her name was and she told them the first thing that came to mind: Trixie. It wasn't her real name, of course, her sister had told her enough to know better than to give them her real name; but it was close enough that if someone called it out to her she wouldn't think they were calling someone else.

Her name was Tricia Heverstadt, Patricia Heverstadt. She was five foot one and weighed a hundred pounds soaking wet. She was pretty enough, but her body wouldn't make any man look at her twice—no bosom to speak of and nothing much in the way of hips. She had long legs for her frame, but what did that mean when your frame was as small as hers was? Her hair was brown, her eyes were brown, her skin was pale, her smile didn't shine. But she could move.

You put Tricia Heverstadt on a stage with a spotlight on her and a quartet pounding out some dance hall melody and you'd have yourself a show. Hell, forget the spotlight and the quartet. You put Tricia Heverstadt on the street in broad daylight, just walking along, and you'd see men's heads turn. It wasn't obvious just why. She wasn't beautiful. But when she moved, your eyes wanted to follow.

Coral Heverstadt, Tricia's older sister, had come to New York four years before, had gotten work in the chorus of a rooftop cabaret in Times Square, had written back home to Tricia in Aberdeen, South Dakota, telling how her feet ached and her shoulders chafed from the straps of the cigarette tray they made her carry around between performances, and how she couldn't get enough sleep because an hour after she finally made it home the garbage men were pulling up outside her window, making a racket. She wrote about the men, taking liberties in the club and whistling at her on the streets, and about one masher who walked out on her in the middle of a meal at Rosie O'Grady's when she shook her head no to the suggestion he whispered in her ear. She wrote about all this and signed her letters "Your struggling sister" but the day Tricia turned eighteen and her mother could no longer prevent her, she was on a train to New York.

She arrived at Grand Central Station and for a good fifteen minutes couldn't find her way out, just kept dragging her luggage in circles through its cavernous rooms and underground corridors, till finally a policeman pointed her toward the Vanderbilt Avenue exit. And as she headed off, the poor flatfoot's eyes followed her and he beat a little tattoo on his palm with his nightstick.

She had her sister's letters in a bundle in her purse, and she showed the return address to the cab driver at the head of the line. He heaved her two bags and her typewriter case into the trunk, ushered her into the back seat, slammed the door behind her, and took off down Lexington Avenue, aimed smack at the heart of Greenwich Village. At first Tricia didn't even notice the buildings speeding by outside, she was so taken with the pair of fold-down jump seats leaning up against the back of the driver's seat and the automatic taxi meter ticking away her fare. She didn't even mind watching the numbers rise, higher and higher. A taxi ride through New York City! It was an extravagance, a luxury, perhaps the last she'd enjoy for a good, long time; but she did enjoy it so. It felt as though her childhood in Aberdeen was dropping away from her at last with each city block they drove, with each expensive tick of the meter.

Coral greeted her at the door of the rooming house on Cornelia Street, hugged her and lifted her off her feet while the cab driver unloaded her luggage. Coral took after their mother, had the broad shoulders and muscular arms, and she picked up one heavy bag in each hand and carried them up the front steps without the slightest show of effort, chattering nervously as she went. It was lovely to see Tricia, it had been so *long*, what a wonderful idea, to drop by for a visit—how was mama? Tricia picked up the typewriter case and followed her sister up to the big glass door leading into the building's vestibule. "Mama's good," she said. "But Cory, I'm not here for a visit. I'm here for good." And then when Coral didn't respond, just stood there staring, she said, "I want to live in the city. I've moved here. To stay."

And the smile that had slowly been eroding on Coral's face as Tricia spoke fell all to pieces. "No," she said, putting the suitcases down on either side of her. "No, no...you come for a visit, Patty, you see the Empire State, you eat at Lindy's and you go right back home. You can't move here. You can't live here."

"Why not? You do."

That seemed to be a stumper. Coral Heverstadt heaved a sigh up from the depths of her abdomen. "I do lots of things, kiddo. You wouldn't want to do them. *I* wouldn't want you doing them, and mama sure as hell wouldn't."

"You mean dancing?"

"I don't mean dancing."

"Well, then what do you mean?"

Another sigh, long and plangent. "It would never work. What were you going to do for money?"

"I have some money," Tricia said, patting her purse. "I've been saving up for a while now. Maybe it won't last long, but it'll hold me for a month, I figure, and by then I'll have a job, and…I'll get by. I don't eat much." She smiled hopefully.

"And where were you planning to stay?"

The smile widened.

"No," Coral said. "Honey, no. I can't put you up. I— I just can't. Don't ask me why."

"Why?"

"Patty, listen to me. I live in one room. Bathroom's down the hall. There are ten other people on the same floor and in the morning you've got to fight the whole lot of them just to pee."

"That's okay. I can hold it."

"Patty, listen to me. I…don't live alone."

"Okay, so it's tight, I understand, but I wouldn't stay long. And it might even be fun, three girls in the big city—"

"Two girls," Coral said. "It'd be two girls."

"Two? But you said you don't live alone…" Tricia's hand leapt to her mouth. "Oh!"

"Yeah: Oh. So would you please just get yourself back on that train and go home to mama and tell her you saw me and everything was fine and you had a nice visit but now you're home to stay? Please?" She reached a hand out and ruffled Tricia's hair. "Please."

But Tricia didn't say anything. She couldn't. Her face was blank, her breathing slow. Comprehension was just beginning to break through.

"Please," her sister said again. "Go home." Coral held her eyes for a second, then turned, went inside, drew the door shut behind her. Through the glass, Tricia watched her retreat up the stairs.

Tricia set the typewriter case down beside her other

two bags. She looked around. The street was bustling, as every street in New York City seemed to be; but she might as well have been alone. She *was* alone.

In the first-floor window beside her head, a hand-lettered cardboard sign proclaimed "NO VACANCIES."

She felt a sob start climbing up inside her chest and a sense of panic gripped her, but she sensibly forced it down. This wasn't turning out the way she'd planned, but panicking wasn't going to make it better. So Coral wouldn't have her—fine. It was a big city, there were lots of places for a girl to stay. So she didn't happen to know any of them—fine. Fine. How hard could they be to find? She looked around her. Maybe one of these people would know, maybe this man coming toward her, with his nice panama hat and glasses and his white seersucker suit with the wide braces peeking out under his jacket.

He swept his hat off his head with one hand and offered the other to her to shake. "Miss, I'm sorry to bother you," he said in a rapid, delicate voice, "but I couldn't help overhearing your conversation, and you seemed as though you might be in need of some help—"

"Am I ever," Tricia said. "I was just trying to decide who I could ask for some."

"Well, if it's not too bold," the man said. He pulled a wallet from his pocket and took out a card with writing printed on one side. "It sounded as though you needed a place to stay. As it happens, my family owns a residential hotel for young women. A thoroughly respectable establishment, I assure you, and though generally we have no rooms available, as it happens just this morning one of our tenants moved out." He passed the card to her. In the center were the words THE KLONDIKE ARMS. Beneath this, it showed an address on Seventh Avenue and a telephone number, KL5-2703.

Tricia looked the man over. He looked to be in his

middle thirties. His suit was certainly nice enough, his hat as well, and his manner seemed, if not refined exactly, at least proper. His voice had a plummy Eastern Seaboard accent to it, the sort she associated with certain radio program hosts and movie actors, and the way he expressed himself was awfully formal. "Your family owns this hotel?" she asked.

He shrugged slightly, as if embarrassed to admit it. "It's one of several. But this is the only one where we allow unaccompanied young women to rent rooms. And the rules are quite strict—no men above the lobby after five, under any circumstances. No guests overnight. It's quite safe." He shook his head gently at her. "Not all your options would be. I don't want to frighten you, but this city can be dangerous for a girl in your situation."

"I'm sure it can," Tricia said, thinking of her sister's letters, thinking also of what she had just learned about Coral's living arrangements.

"There's just one thing," the man said, apologetically. "I can't be sure the room is still available. It was this morning—but it may have been rented since. There are so many young women in the city these days, and so few rooms."

"How can we find out?" Tricia said.

"I can phone my father and ask him—but if he says the room is still available, I'll need to be able to tell him you want it, so he'll take it off the market immediately. Otherwise…"

"What?"

"It could be available now and gone by the time you make it uptown."

"Surely your father would hold it," Tricia said, "if you told him I was on my way."

He shook his head ruefully. "You haven't met my father. He can't bear to turn down money. If I don't tell him I have a month's rent in my hands and that I'm on my way to the bank to deposit it right now, he'll gladly give the room away to the next woman who shows up at the front desk with cash in her hand. I'm sorry."

"Don't be," Tricia said, "I understand." She reached into her purse, found the small roll of bills she'd stashed there. An elastic band held the roll together and she worked it off now. "I can give you the money, that's not a problem. How much is it?"

He seemed embarrassed again. "It's one of our nicer rooms, I'm afraid. It rents for a dollar and a half a night. But," he hastened to add, "by the month it's just thirty-six dollars. And it comes with meals. Breakfast and dinner, anyway."

Well, that was something. She'd have to stretch to cover her other expenses, but with the food included in the monthly rate she could manage, for a while a least.

She handed over two ten dollar bills and two fives and then carefully counted out six ones.

"I'm going to be right over there," the man said, pointing at a telephone booth near the corner. "If he tells me the room's been rented, I'll bring the money back and see if I can help you find some other place to stay. But if the room's available, I'll tell him you'll take it."

"Thank you," Tricia said. She watched him run into the booth, pick up the receiver, wait while his call was put through, and then talk excitedly for a few moments. While he was doing that, she tucked the typewriter case under one arm and lifted the two suitcases, one in each hand, as Coral had. It was a struggle for her—she didn't have Coral's build or her strength—but she could manage it if she had to. By the time she'd wrestled the bags down to the sidewalk, the man was bounding back to her, a grin on his face.

"It's all set," he said. "But he says you have to get there

immediately, there's someone else looking the room over right now."

"Will you come with me?" Tricia said. "I hate to ask, but with all this to carry…"

"I wish I could," he said. "But he insists I deposit the money today, and the banks close at three. Perhaps I can put you in a taxi?"

She stiffened. "I'm afraid I can't afford—"

The man's eyes sparkled. "Here." He handed her back one of her dollar bills. "Don't tell the old man."

He stepped into the street and flagged down the first checker cab he saw, shoved her bags into the back seat and closed the door firmly once she was inside. She leaned on the open window, stuck her head out. "I can't tell you how much I appreciate your help," she said.

"It's no problem," the man said.

"It's funny," Tricia said, "I don't even know your name."

"It's Carter," he said, quickly enough. Then he seemed to have to pause to think for a second. "Carter Blandon." But before she could remark on the peculiarity of a man not remembering his own last name, the cab had already pulled away from the curb and was racing uptown.

The driver pulled up alongside the Klondike Arms, helped her out with her bags, gave her back two dimes in change from the dollar she presented and touched his cap in a casual salute when she returned one as a tip. Then he was gone and Tricia was left to maneuver her bags through the building's revolving door on her own.

It didn't *look* like any hotel she'd ever seen in the movies or on television, never mind the two they had back in Aberdeen. The lobby was dark and narrow; there was no place to sit; there were no bellboys pushing luggage carts, no potted plants for atmosphere, no concierge's desk, no registration window. Instead, there was only a

standing ashtray between a pair of elevator doors at the
room's far end and a large board on the wall, under glass.
Rows of metal letters behind the glass spelled out what
appeared to be the names of firms:

ACME NOTIONS & SUNDRIES	407
CATALONIA FOOTWEAR	213
EDMUND & EDMUND, IMPORTERS	902
GEO. CARMICHAEL, ATTORNEY-AT-LAW	1104
HARD CASE CRIME, INC.	315
HELGA MODELING AND DANCE	317
LERNER CASUAL WEAR	815

...and so on, through WHITEMAN AND SON, DDS in
404 and something merely called ZIEGLER in 1111.

Beside the board, screwed tightly to the wall, was an
angled metal dispenser containing a stack of business cards
for anyone to take. Tricia took one and compared it to the
one Carter Blandon had handed her. It was identical.

A residential hotel for unaccompanied young women?
This was an office building! And the worst sort, by all
appearances, the sort that rented tiny airless suites to
desperate businessmen and get-rich-quick schemers—
she knew the sort, she'd seen them often enough in the
movies, read about them in the two-bit crime novels they
sold in every drugstore.

The louse! The dirty...dirty...*rat!* To take a woman's
money like that, to pretend fellow-feeling and kindness
and generosity only as a pretense for stealing from her!
Tricia found the man's audacity breathtaking, literally—
she found she had to sit down on one of her suitcases and
make an effort to breathe. And now the feeling of panic
she'd quelled earlier returned, and the sob with it. She
was alone in New York City and very nearly penniless,
with three heavy bags and no place to stay and a sister

who had fallen into god only knew what sort of depravity—but not far enough into it that she was willing to share it with Tricia. Because the sad truth was, if she'd offered it to Tricia now, Tricia would have said yes. However bad things were in Coral's life, they could hardly be worse than Tricia's situation was right now.

She couldn't even return home as Coral had urged her to do—she didn't have the train fare.

She wiped her eyes on a handkerchief she retrieved from her purse, then got up and hefted her bags once more.

It was three in the afternoon and slowly but surely night was coming. She had to take care of herself—no one else was going to. With her free elbow she jabbed the elevator call button, and while she waited for the car to arrive she scanned through the building's list of tenants once more. A place to stay and a way to pay for it—that's what she needed. And the latter, at least, meant getting a job. Not a month from now—now.

She was no dentist, no lawyer, didn't know what a 'notion' or 'sundry' might be. Her knowledge of fashion was, as mama never hesitated to tell her, a disaster, and the only importing she'd ever done involved bringing herself from South Dakota to Manhattan.

But she could move.

When the elevator door slid open and the wizened operator on a stool inside drew back the metal accordion-fold gate, she lugged her bags inside, deposited them on the floor, and met his flinty stare with one of her own.

"Third floor," she said. "And step on it."

2.

Fade to Blonde

The hallway was, if possible, even shabbier than the lobby had been, the paint on the walls a tired olive green, the pebbled glass in most of the doorways dark. She passed doors labeled with faded gilt lettering and ones that weren't labeled at all, just hastily numbered with black paint. Green glass shades hung from the ceiling at intervals along the hall, but fewer than half the bulbs seemed to be working. A few of the doorways were illuminated, and one was propped open at the bottom with a brick. From inside she heard a radio quietly playing what sounded like Perry Como.

She looked back, but the elevator door had closed behind her.

After a stretch, the hallway branched, and a sign directed her to the left for 310-317, right for 318-325. She turned left.

310. 311. 312. Maintenance closet. 313.

Of course it had to be at the very end. Tricia's arms were getting sore, and she had to put her luggage down twice to rest them before she finally reached the door labeled 317. On the glass it said

MADAME HELGA
DANCERS, MODELS, CHANTEUSES, ETC.
"WE'VE GOT HER NUMBER!"

The glass was, against all odds, brightly lit. Tricia could even see shadows inside that looked like human silhouettes. She fixed her hair briefly and, glancing into her compact, traced a pinky along her lower lip to straighten the rouge she'd applied on the train. She looked a wreck, she thought. Her cheeks were flushed from exertion, her dress disarrayed, and the day's strain was telling around her eyes. But it wasn't as though the passage of still more time, never mind a night spent on the streets of New York, would make her look any better.

She put on the brightest smile she had and knocked briskly.

"G'way," a woman's voice called from inside, "audition's over!"

"I don't know what audition you mean," Tricia called back to her through the door. "I just got into the city and I'm looking for some work."

"What sort of work?" came the voice.

"What sort have you got?"

There was silence, and it stretched on a good long time.

Finally, the voice said, "Well, what do you do? Sing? Dance?"

"I can dance," Tricia said.

"What?"

She said it again, louder. "I can dance!"

"Well how do you expect me to see that through a closed door?"

Tricia tried the knob, cautiously pushed the door open. Inside was a big open room with a desk in the middle. A window on one wall had words lettered on it in reverse, so they could be read from the street outside. There was a wooden bench under the window and two young women were sitting there, folios of sheet music clutched in their hands. Behind the desk was a third young woman, only a year or two older than Tricia herself, wearing a black sheath dress with a bright red leather belt. Her hair neatly matched the belt.

"And you are?" the redhead asked.

"My name's...Trixie," Tricia said.

"Sure it is. Mine's Scarlett O'Hara. At least you're not another goddamn singer. No offense, girls." The girls on the bench didn't look offended. They looked terrified.

"So?" the redhead said. "Show me what you've got."

Tricia pulled her bags inside, shut the door, stepped up to the desk, then realized she had no idea what to do. "I'm not sure," she said, "exactly how this works."

"How it works? You show me your dancing, I tell you it's not good enough, and you take your pretty little keister back to Podunk, Wyoming or wherever the hell it is you came from. That's how it works."

"South Dakota," Tricia said icily. "Aberdeen, South Dakota. And if you've got your mind made up already, I don't see why I—"

At that moment, a buzzer sounded and a light lit up on the Bakelite intercom box beside the redhead's telephone. She thumbed a button.

A man's voice boomed from the loudspeaker. "It's gonna be Kitty. You can send the other one home."

"You heard him, girls," the redhead said. Both of the young women stood up, one looking elated, the other crushed. "Noon, tomorrow, Kitty, at Mizel's, they'll fit you for your gown. Sorry, Jean, better luck next time."

"You think so?" Jean said. "I've been waiting a long time for better luck."

The redhead shrugged. It was no problem of hers.

The two women filed out and the redhead turned her attention back to Tricia. "So, you gonna show me your dancing or what?"

But the buzzer interrupted again. "What?" the redhead asked the little box.

"We're gonna be here a couple hours more," the man said. "Order us some food, will you? Maybe some of that brisket from Lester's, and…what do you want, Robbie?"

Another man's voice, heavily accented, said "Brisket. What is that, beef?"

"Yeah," the first man said. "Make it two, Erin, and a couple of beers. Hey, listen, Erin, you know what else, Robbie's gonna need some girls to round out the number, can you ring up a few?"

"What kind of girls?" the redhead asked. "You want clotheshorses?"

"Jesus, no, they just stand there like coat racks. Get me some who know how to shake their little asses."

"When do you need 'em?"

"Yesterday."

The redhead looked up, released the button. "Can you shake your little ass, Wyoming?"

Tricia thought about walking out. She thought about it for all of two seconds. Then she nodded vigorously.

The redhead pushed the button again. "I've got someone here right now, says she can dance."

"Well, fine," the man said. "Send her in."

Tricia left her bags outside, walked through the door Erin held open for her. She put a little swing into her step, the sort she knew would win her a whistle on any street in downtown Aberdeen. The two men inside watched her approach. The younger one had a cigarette between his lips, a grey felt hat pushed back on his head, and his pulled-open necktie dangling halfway down his shirt. The other was nicely put together in a snappy suit and bowtie, his black hair slicked back, a pencil mustache punctuating his upper lip. This second man was swarthy, olive-skinned. He twirled a finger in the air in a gesture Tricia interpreted to mean "turn around."

Neither man whistled.

Tricia turned in place. She could be graceful, she could

be delicate—but she could also be earthy and sensual. She tried for a combination of the two. She saw their eyes following her, but couldn't read their reaction. She put together a couple of dance steps, something slow and languorous, something that looked like dancing even without any music to accompany it. She was tired and knew it probably showed, so she aimed for a sleepy-eyed strut that conveyed hints of opium dens and Oriental pleasure palaces. She raised one arm and ran the fingers of her other hand along it, down it, stroking slowly. She curled her fingers and twisted her neck, swept this way and that before them. Out of the corner of one eye she caught sight of the swarthy man nodding.

"What do you think?" the younger man said.

"She's good," he said. "She's good. How you say, very… romancing? Romantic. Very romantic. She make you want to kiss."

"Don't let your wife hear you talking like that."

"Or her uncle, eh?" The swarthy man stood, came up to Tricia, walked in a tight circle around her. "Not much up top," he said. "But put her in a nice dress, something satin, something bright…it could be okay, could be. Now, the hair…" He touched her hair, ran his thick fingers through it to her scalp. "This is not for Roberto Monge, this, this…plain, brown hair."

"No," the other man said. "Honey, you're gonna have to go blonde, or you know, red, like Erin—"

"Not red," Roberto said. "Blonde."

"Alright, blonde," he said. "You ever been blonde?"

Tricia, who'd spent the last minute mightily resisting the urge to slap Roberto's hand away, shook her head.

"You know how?"

"I'm sure there are instructions on the bottle," she said.

The man thumbed the intercom button on his desk. "Erin, I need you to get this girl's hair bleached."

Erin's voice came back in a crackle of static. "What, she can't do it herself?"

"We need her on stage tomorrow night. We can't take any chances something goes wrong."

Erin sighed. "You got it, Billy."

"Good." He turned back to Tricia. "Five nights a week, two shows a night, you'll be backing up Robbie's orchestra at the Sun. You know the Sun?"

She shook her head.

"See, Robbie? Not everyone knows who you are. Kid: It's a big nightclub on 49th Street near the river. Lots of swells go there. Broadway stars, Hollywood stars, big shots who want a nice time. They want to see something classy, not your low-down burlesque, you understand?"

She nodded.

"There'll be at least one or two other girls. You can work out a routine together, whatever Robbie wants. But nothing *too* sexy. We wouldn't want the place raided."

Roberto laughed.

"How much does it pay?" Tricia somehow worked up the nerve to ask.

"Pay?" the man said. "You want to get paid?" Then he chuckled at his little joke and Tricia's heart started beating again. "Five a night, sister. And you should be glad to get it. It's only that high because Robbie here's a generous man."

"I *am* glad to get it," Tricia said. "Believe me. You won't be sorry, Mister...?"

"Hoffman," the man said. "Billy Hoffman."

"Mr. Hoffman. Just one question, if I can, and I'm sorry if it's a little forward, but—is there any way I can get an advance on the first week's—"

"An advance?" Hoffman roared. "What do I look like, the Chase Manhattan bank?"

"It's just that I'm new in the city and don't have a place to stay..."

Hoffman rolled his eyes. He depressed the intercom button again. "Erin, is there any room at the chateau? For our newest dancer?"

"Am I going to have to cut up her food for her, too?" Erin said.

"Probably."

"She's little," Erin said. "We'll fit her in somewhere."

"So," Tricia asked, stepping out into the main room again, picking up her coat from where she'd left it draped over her bags, "what's this chateau Mr. Hoffman was talking about?"

"Oh, it's a gorgeous place," Erin said, "it's got fountains out front and big feather beds and a barn where we keep the animals—"

"Really?"

"Yeah, Wyoming, a big barn." Erin lifted the typewriter case, left the heavier bags for Tricia to carry. "You'll feel right at home."

"Is it far?"

"Not too far."

"Because I don't have the money for a cab ride, I'm sorry."

"That's okay," Erin said, "we're going to walk."

Tricia's face fell. "I don't know if I can make it."

"You'll make it." Erin held the front door open for her and followed her out into the corridor. Tricia started trudging in the direction of the elevator.

"Wrong way, kid. Come back."

Tricia looked around. What other way was there? But Erin was waiting, fists on her hips, tapping one foot against the threadbare carpet. So she came back.

Erin turned one of her hands palm-up and aimed it across the hall at one of the doors with no gilt lettering, just the number '316' painted on it. A light was on behind the glass, though not a very bright one, and now that she listened for it Tricia could hear some voices inside and a brief, high-pitched bray of laughter.

Erin knocked on the glass and a moment later the door swung inwards. A girl stood behind it in a half-slip and stockings, her hair up in curlers. She had one arm crossed over her breasts but let it drop when she saw there were only women there. She left the door standing open and padded back toward a cot in the corner where, Tricia saw, another girl was seated, painting polish on her toenails.

"Welcome to our chateau, kid," Erin said. "The modest one's Annabelle. She's a sweetheart. And Diane," she said, pointing at the girl doing her nails, "and Irene, and Lotty, and Rita." She pointed out the other girls as she ushered Tricia through the door. The office they stepped into was huge, obviously having been created by knocking down the walls between three or four smaller offices. There were standing floor screens here and there to divide the room up, but they didn't do much—a dozen army cots were ranked barracks-style in two uneven rows, and from where Tricia and Erin stood you could see most of the occupants, sitting on the cots or lying down or pacing having a smoke. The girls waved as Erin introduced them.

"There's Cristina—" a young Spanish girl looked up "—and Stella—" a brunette in men's pajamas nodded at them from the makeup table where she was covering a bruise on the side of her face with foundation "—and Marlene—" a dour-looking teenager raised one hand to her forehead in a sort of salute "—and, um, and…" Erin snapped her fingers twice, trying to remember the last girl's name.

"Joyce," the girl said, coming forward. She was almost six feet tall barefoot and had golden hair that poured halfway down her back. She was smoking a Pall Mall and held the pack out to Erin, who took one. "Who's this?"

"She calls herself Trixie," Erin said. "She's a dancer. She'll be staying with us a little while, so you girls make her feel welcome."

Joyce extended the cigarette pack in Tricia's direction. Tricia had to crane to look her in the face. "No thank you," she said. "I don't smoke." The pack hung there. "Thank you, though. Really. I appreciate it."

"A dancer, huh? Well, Trixie, the rest of us here are just models, so you'll be queen of the roost in no time."

"Oh, I don't think…"

"So, Trixie, you don't smoke, let's see…do you drink?"

Tricia shook her head no. "Not much. We had wine sometimes back home."

"Wine sometimes. That's pretty daring." Joyce reached out and stroked one finger along Tricia's cheek. "Is there anything else you don't do?"

"All right," Erin said, plucking Joyce's hand away, "leave the kid alone. She doesn't need you teaching her the feminine arts."

"Why, Erin," Joyce said, with a little drawl creeping into her voice, "I didn't realize. If I'd known you already had your hand in the honeypot I'd never have laid a finger on the child."

Erin took Tricia by the elbow, steered her to an empty cot. "Don't worry about Joyce. She's all talk. She's just glad she's not the new girl anymore."

"I heard that," Joyce called after them.

"Good," Erin called back. "Now, drop those bags and let's take care of your hair. You've really never had a dye job, a bleach job, anything?" Tricia shook her head. "That's okay, it's easy. You'll see. I've done it lots of times. I wasn't born this way." She primped her copper-colored hair, let it fall. "Hey, Rita, you still got that L'Oréal stuff your sister sent you?"

Rita dug through a footlocker next to her cot, found a

little container and brought it over. Her own hair was so
blond it was practically silver, which made a strange combination, Tricia thought, with her dark complexion.

Rita laid one hand on Tricia's arm. "It's good, trust me.
Just keep your eyes closed, 'cause this stuff really burns if
it gets in them."

Erin snatched the jar from Rita's hand and hustled
Tricia off through a doorway to a white-tiled office bathroom. "Thanks, beautiful," Erin called over her shoulder.

The bathroom was large, too, with three sinks and
three toilet stalls and, in the center, where a space had
been cleared and pipes rerouted to supply them, a pair of
bathtubs standing side by side on claw feet. There were
also two devices Tricia couldn't fathom, tall ceramic
troughs mounted vertically on the wall, with flush handles at the top like toilets. Erin saw her staring. "Never
mind about those, they're for boys. And maybe Joyce, if
she wants to try peeing standing up. Come over here."

One of the showers was in use—they could hear the
water going and someone soaping up behind the curtain.
The other was empty and off. Erin turned the two knobs
and a spray of water began. "Here, let's get you out of
that dress, this stuff'll ruin it."

Tricia hesitated, then began unbuttoning. She'd come
to New York because it wasn't Aberdeen, South Dakota,
because it was a place where you might find yourself
working for a nightclub full of Broadway stars and band-
leaders with slicked-back hair, where you might room
with a dozen girls you'd never met before and dye your
hair blonde and dance for a living. And if you were going
to come to New York good and proper, you had to leave
Aberdeen at the doorstep once and for all.

She was in her brassiere and panties in no time, head
held under the water, Erin roughly rinsing it, then patting it dry with a towel. While it dried, Erin stripped her

own dress off, swapped it for an old robe she found hanging behind the door, and started mixing the bleach. Then she had Tricia sit down on a hassock beside one of the sinks and tilt her head forward.

"Close your eyes, honey, and don't open 'em till I say so." Erin started applying the bleach from the back of her head forward, daubing it on in little smears. From time to time she'd tilt Tricia's head to one side or the other. She kept up a running monologue as she went. "...he'll dock you fifty cents a night for rooming here, but that's fair enough. Can't get a room for that price anywhere in this town. You're on your own for food, but nights you should be able to cadge some at the club and for breakfast there's always Lester's, where the rolls are fresh and he'll throw in coffee for free if he likes how you look."

"You think he'll like me?" Tricia said.

"Like you? When we're done, he'll leave his wife for you."

The bleach stung in a few places, just felt wet in others. It was strangely relaxing, though, to have someone working her way through your hair like this, and Tricia felt herself drifting off. She came to with a start when she heard the bathroom door fly open and slam against the wall.

"Hey, Erin," a voice said, "I'm not here. Understand?" A *man's* voice.

Tricia gasped, sat up, groped for the towel around her neck and used it to pat her eyes. Behind her, she heard a shower curtain pull to one side and the girl inside squealed, "Hey! What's the big idea?"

"Sh," the man said. "I'm not here, you didn't see me." Tricia heard him climb into the tub and then the curtain closed again.

"Who was that?" Tricia said, looking around, her eyes finally open and only stinging a little. "What's going on?"

Outside, they heard another door slam open and one

of the girls screamed. "You can't come in here!"

"Where is he?" A different male voice, this one angry.

"Just put your head back down," Erin said, "and keep your mouth shut."

But Tricia didn't. She watched as a broad-shouldered fellow in shirtsleeves bulled his way into the bathroom, trailing two of the girls behind him. He had a big, rectangular head with a buzz cut on top and craggy features. Looked about forty years old, with muscled forearms and clenched fists. Tricia stood up, held the towel draped inadequately in front of her. "Mister," she said, and she could feel her heart racing in her chest as he came toward her, "you shouldn't be in here. There are ladies present."

"Ladies?" the man said. "Where? I see some dames, a skirt or two, maybe a doll. I don't see any ladies."

"Then you're not looking very closely," Tricia said. "Now kindly leave."

"I'll leave, *lady*, when you hand over that scum-sucking lowlife who calls himself a book editor. I know he's in here."

"There's no one in here," Erin said. "Just us dolls."

The man wasn't paying attention. With the flat of his hand, he was slapping open the toilet stalls one by one, revealing no one inside. He peeked behind the bathroom door, where Erin's dress was hanging. Then he went up to the shower and yanked the curtain open.

The girl inside was dripping and naked. Her mouth dropped open and she ripped the curtain out of his hand, pulled it around her chest. With her other hand she slapped him across the face. It sounded like a gunshot but didn't seem to faze him in the slightest.

"Get out of here!"

"I'm sorry, ma'am," the man said, not sounding sorry so much as baffled. His prey seemed to have vanished and he didn't know how. He turned back to Tricia. "You're telling me you didn't see a man, a little shrimp of a guy, brown hair, about so tall—" he held up his hand well over Tricia's head—"come in here in the past five minutes?"

"I didn't see *anyone* come in here, until you did," Tricia said, which was true enough. "Now I need you to leave so I can wash this bleach out of my hair before it does some permanent damage. And—and—Rita there needs to get ready for an audition, and Lotty's got to change, and none of us are dressed to receive visitors and here you are, barging in…it's uncivilized. Now get out!"

He hesitated for a moment, seemed to be weighing a snappy comeback, but finally he just said, quietly, "You're absolutely right, ma'am. My beef's not with you. But if you see him," and here some of the fire returned to his voice, "I want you to let him know I'm not done with him. He can't imitate me and expect to get away with it. I'll find him, and when I do he'll be sorry he ever took me on in a fight. You tell him that!"

"And who should I tell him said it?" Tricia said.

"Who…?" He seemed affronted. "Just America's best-selling writer, doll. Tell him that. He'll know who."

And with that the man walked out, with one last glance at the bevy of young women around him in various stages of undress.

The woman in the shower let go of the curtain, turned off the water. She then drew back one foot and planted a kick in something soft lying in the bottom of the tub. They could all hear the dull thump as it landed. "Up," she said.

"Jesus, Milly," a voice said from inside the tub, "it's not enough that I'm half drowned down here? You have to kick me, too?"

She kicked him again. "Up."

Tricia watched as a man sat up inside the claw-foot bathtub, draped one waterlogged arm over each side. His

suit and shirt were completely soaked, and his hair was
plastered down over his forehead. The woman sharing
the tub with him, a handsome blonde who looked like
she'd been born that way, had her arms crossed and one
hip cocked. She didn't seem the least bit bashful. What
she seemed, mostly, was annoyed at having her shower
interrupted.

The man climbed out of the tub, slipping a little on
the pool of water that had collected on the floor beside it.
He pulled his hair out of his eyes, shook some more
water onto the floor, peeled off his jacket and dropped it
in a wet heap. His shirt was plastered to his chest and the
buckles of his wide suspenders gleamed wetly against it.
He looked around at the women in the room.

That was when Tricia got her first good look at his
face, and he at hers. They recognized each other in the
same instant.

She dropped the towel she was holding, strode up to
him in her underwear.

He said, "I can—"

Tricia cocked her arm back and swung. The punch connected on the point of his chin, his feet went slip-slip-slip
on the slick floor, and he fell backwards into the tub.

3.

Top of the Heap

"You're Carter Blandon! Your family owns a hotel! The
city can be dangerous for a girl like me! Tell me more,
why don't you?"

"Keep her away from me," the dripping man said,
having climbed out of the tub a second time. He was

keeping Tricia at arm's length, but she was pacing him, stepping forward each time he backed away.

"Where did your glasses go? Or were they all part of the act? Like that fancy accent you put on?"

"I don't know what you're talking about," the man said. "I've never worn glasses in my life." Tricia swung at him again and he ducked it. "Will somebody help me, please?"

"No way," Erin said. "We want to see how this one plays out. *Carter.*"

"Where's my money?" Tricia yelled.

"Gone," the man said. "It's gone. I spent it. All right? I spent it, every penny. To get my books out of hock before they went into a furnace. You would've done the same, I promise."

"You *promise?* You want me to tell everyone here what your promises are worth?"

"Oh, we know," Erin said. "We've heard them often enough."

"Listen to me, will you? Come on. Please. Let me explain." He sneezed. "I'm going to catch pneumonia. At least let me get into some dry clothes, okay?" He dropped his hands. "You might want to get into some yourself."

Tricia looked down at herself and remembered suddenly what she was wearing—or, more precisely, what she wasn't. Then her hand leaped to her head, where her hair was still slowly bleaching away. "Oh, no! Erin, we've got to wash this out—right?" She shot a glance at Blandon, or whatever his name really was. "Don't you dare set one foot out of this bathroom, do you understand me?"

"Be reasonable—what am I supposed to change into here? I've got another suit in my office. It's right across the hall. Erin can come with me, make sure I don't go anywhere. You come over when you're ready, I'll answer any questions you have. Okay?"

Tricia weighed her options. It didn't take long.

"Erin?"

"Sure, honey," the redhead said. "Go ahead and wash. I'll watch him for you."

"Which office?" Tricia said.

"Number 315," the man said. "Hard Case Crime."

Number 315 was a smaller office than Madame Helga's, just a single room with a single window and not too much light coming through it. Lettered on the glass it said HARD CASE CRIME BOOKS, and sure enough, the place was filled with books, shelves of them, stacks of them, and a handful spread out across the top of the wooden desk Blandon was sitting behind. Erin stood next to him, in her black dress once more, leaning one arm on his shoulder. He was in his shirtsleeves, with brown suspenders and a brown tie dotted with tiny red *fleurs-de-lis*, a brown fedora on his not yet completely dry hair.

"Have a seat," he said.

"That's all right," Tricia said, "I'll stand." Her own hair was not completely dry yet either and the new dress she'd unpacked had creases showing from the long train trip. She felt like a rube, a country girl facing down the slickest of city slickers, and it made her reluctant to give any quarter, any at all.

"I'm sorry about the money," Blandon said. "Believe it or not, I didn't like doing it. But I was desperate. If we don't have books to sell, we don't have a business, and my printer was threatening to destroy the lot if I didn't pay him at least a portion of what I owed."

"So you stole from me."

"Stole? You handed me your money, I didn't steal it. As I recall, you were standing on a New York City sidewalk, talking loudly about how much money you'd saved up. Lady, if I'm starving and you put a roast beef sandwich in front of me, I'm going to eat it and damn the consequences."

"So I'm a roast beef sandwich."

"In this metaphor, yes."

"And what do you think the police would call what you did?"

"They'd call it fraud and throw me behind bars for it. But that's just because they don't understand the realities of the modern business world. A small company like ours …thirty-five dollars can be the difference between life and death."

"What do you think it is to me?"

"An investment," he said. "And a smart investment, too. Think of it as buying a piece of New York's next great publishing company. Dell, Fawcett, Pocket Books… these are million-dollar operations. And why? Because of these." He lifted a couple of the skinny paperbacks from his desk, let them drop again. They looked like drugstore crime novels, the covers colorful and lurid and peppered with ladies in negligees and men with guns. Each book had an image of a yellow ribbon in the top left corner and one more on the spine. "Just twenty-five cents apiece, just five little nickels—but men have built castles on that foundation of nickels. They've built empires. And what have they got that I don't?"

"Ethics?" Erin said.

"Don't you believe it," Blandon said. "They've got no more ethics than a cat. They bite and claw and fight for every penny and if it takes a thumb in the eye or a knee in the groin to do it, that's what they deal out. It's every man for himself, winner take all. But for the winner who does take all, the one who comes out on top of the heap…" He fell silent, a dreamy look on his face. "And that's going to be me. That's going to be Hard Case Crime. We're going to come out on top."

"Even if you have to fight dirty to get there," Tricia said.

"That's right, sister. Even if. You see this book?" He picked out one of the books on his desk, held it out to her. The cover showed a nearly bare-breasted blonde dressed as Blind Justice, an old-fashioned scale in one hand and a bloody sword in the other. She was peeking out from under her blindfold at a couple of frightened-looking men. The title was *Eye The Jury* and in smaller type below that it said *A Mac Hatchet Mystery by Nicky Malone*.

"This was our first book, came out four months ago. That fellow who came after me in the bathroom? This is what he's all hot under the collar about. Just because I wrote a book ten years ago with a similar title about a guy named Mike Hammer. Am I imitating it? Damn right I am. His book sold millions of copies. Ours? So far we've shipped twelve thousand. Doesn't hurt Spillane at all. Guy hasn't written a book in six years, he's probably still raking it in. I guarantee our little book doesn't even make a dent in his income. But what it does do is get us started. At twenty-five cents apiece, twelve thousand copies are worth three thousand dollars, and half of that comes to us."

"So why did you need my thirty-five bucks?"

He shrugged, looked uncomfortable. "A copy shipped isn't a copy sold. And even when they do sell, the stores take their sweet time paying. And the printer gets his cut off the top. Then there's the warehouse and the trucking and the binding and the paper…"

"I'm sure," Tricia said, "and the author and the artist, too, but—"

Blandon blew a raspberry. "That's peanuts. Trucks and paper and printing—that's where the real money goes."

"Listen, Mr. Blandon," Tricia said, and then stopped. "Hold on, what's your real name? It's not Blandon, I'll bet."

He shook his head. "It's Borden. Like the milk. Charley Borden."

"Mr. Borden, then. I'm sorry to hear about your troubles. But we've all got troubles. And I'm happy to hear about your dreams, but we've all got those, too. I didn't set out to make an investment in your company, and it's not like you handed me a stock certificate back there on the sidewalk. What you did was lie to me and take my money. If I hadn't been lucky enough to get a job next door, I might've starved. You should be ashamed—"

"Of what? It's quite a good job you've gotten—yes, Erin told me. You're going to be dancing at Manhattan's premier nightspot. And would you ever have gotten that job if I hadn't given you the card for this building? Think about that. We both know you came to this city for a reason; I heard what you said to your sister. Well, I'd say you're well on your way to realizing *your* dream. And tell me, would you really be there this soon, this fast, if it hadn't been for me?" And he smiled, a big guileless smile with a little desperate twinkle in his eye.

Tricia wanted to tell him he was wrong. She wanted to slug him again, knock him off the straight-back chair he was sitting in and show him you didn't take advantage of a South Dakota girl, no sir. But there was just enough truth to what he said, and she was tired, and the cot across the hall was no feather bed but right now it was calling to her as if it were.

"All right, Mr. Borden. Here's my offer to you, you can take it or you can leave it. I didn't plan to invest thirty-five dollars in your company and I don't mean to do so now. So we'll call it a loan. You're going to pay it back to me, with interest, at the rate of five dollars a week. Let's say eight weeks instead of seven—that should cover it. If, at the end of eight weeks you haven't paid me in full, I'll go to the police and tell them what you did."

"They'll arrest you for usury," Borden said. "That's something like one hundred percent interest."

"Well, your other choice is that I can go to the police right now," Tricia said. "Take it or leave it, Mr. Borden."

He turned to Erin. "How old would you say she is? Our little usurer? Nineteen going on forty-five?"

Erin grinned. "I think you'd better agree to her terms, Charley, before she tightens the screws some more."

"All right," Borden said. "All right. I'll pay. But there's something you're going to do for me in return."

"What's that?" Tricia said.

"You're going to be working at the Sun, right? That's Sal Nicolazzo's joint." He fished around on his desk, found another book and tossed it to her. Tricia caught it. This one wasn't a Hard Case Crime title; it said *Gold Medal Book* in the upper left corner and *I, Mobster* across the top. The author was identified as "Anonymous."

"You're going to work for your money," Borden said. "You're going to keep your eyes and ears open, and you're going to bring back a story that'll sell a million copies."

4.
Little Girl Lost

The lights went down everywhere but on the little podium where Roberto Monge stood, baton in hand, and the men of his orchestra waited, poised for the downstroke, trombones and clarinets raised, lips puckered. Then the stroke, and music began to flow, like an undulating river, the percussionist in the corner adding a jungle beat by smacking the skins of a bongo. A spotlight splashed the center of the dance floor, so recently filled with swing-dancing couples, illuminating first the ankles, then the legs, then the spangled torso and cleavage and shoulders and beautifully made-up face of Miss Kitty Dufresne, looking so different now from the terrified girl on the bench in Madame Helga's office. She waited four beats and then launched into her song: *When they begin the beguine…it brings back the sound of music so tender…*

It was when Kitty stepped back and returned the microphone to its stand that Tricia and Cecilia came out from the wings on either side, each dressed in a flowing, feather-trimmed skirt and halter top, each swaying to the music. And Tricia looked different, too. Whatever had been left of the innocent eighteen-year-old girl from South Dakota was definitely gone now. Tricia was not only blonde but coiffed like a starlet out of a Hollywood musical. Her lips were pomegranate red, her eyebrows tweezed and shaped and accented with pencil, her eyelids powdered a sultry charcoal blue. Cecilia was the older of the two—by seven years, as she'd confided to Tricia in the dressing room they shared backstage—but when they were out on the floor, you couldn't tell. They might both have been twenty; they might both have been forty, or no age at all.

As the orchestra's playing swelled, they danced in tightening circles around one another, not touching, and then briefly with one another in a brisk imitation of a tango, first Cecilia leading, then Tricia. They ended with some side-by-side bump and grind moves as the orchestra changed tempos yet again, giving Cole Porter's music a jazzy sizzle. Nothing too naughty (Billy Hoffman had warned them, unnecessarily, that their clothes had to stay on), but they gave it all they had and the crowd applauded noisily.

The first night, Tricia had to concentrate on remembering the choreography, and didn't manage even so; there were some unseemly stumbles. But by the third night she had it down and by the end of the week, even while dancing the more strenuous parts of the routine she found herself paying more attention to the rapt faces in the audience than to her dancing, wondering what secrets each might hide, her mind returning to the meeting in Charley Borden's office.

She'd caught the book he'd thrown at her, *I, Mobster*. "What's this supposed to be?" she'd asked. The tag-line on the front cover said *The Confession of a Crime Czar*. And on the back it said,

> When we received the manuscript of this book in the office, we knew immediately we had something far out of the ordinary. We asked a prominent New York attorney to read the manuscript and arrange for the endorsement of a prominent judge, district attorney, or other high public official. Our friend, the lawyer, sent the manuscript back. "Too hot," he advised...

"It's *supposed* to be the true story of a mobster's life, from pinching candy as a kid up to running a criminal organization as an adult," Borden said. "That's what it's supposed to be. What it is, though, is pure, unadulterated malarkey, from the first page to the last. Probably written by some hack whose knowledge of crime is limited to the nights he's spent in a drunk tank for disorderly conduct. Not a word of it's true—not one. But how many copies did it sell? Go ahead, ask me."

"How many?" Tricia said.

"A lot," Borden said. "It sold a lot of copies. And now they've made a movie out of it, too, which is bound to sell some more." He leaned forward over his book-strewn desk. "But imagine how many they'd have sold if they'd had a true story that was actually true. A story from someone deep inside Sal Nicolazzo's outfit."

"This Nicolazzo is a mobster?" Tricia said.

"He's from Calabria, right next door to Sicily. What do you think?"

"I don't think every Italian's a mobster," Tricia said.

"Well, this one is. He runs illegal gambling joints up and down the east coast, two or three here in New York alone. People say there's cards and dice at the Sun, if you find the right room. And what better way to find it than from the inside?"

"So what you're saying is you want me to write you a book like this one," Tricia said.

"Who said anything about writing? More like taking dictation. You find the right person in the outfit and get him talking, all you'll need to do is copy down what he says."

"And you want me to do this for five dollars," Tricia said. "Not even. For the portion of my five dollars of interest that you feel is usury."

"Nah, forget that. You bring me a story, I'll pay a penny a word," Borden said. "The same as I pay the rest of our authors. Up to five hundred dollars, max, for a book. How you split it with the guy whose story you tell is up to you."

Tricia had smiled, thinking about the portable she'd been lugging around the city, the compact little Olympia SM3 DeLuxe with its two-tone ribbon, and about the half-ream of paper wedged inside the typewriter case, filled with all the short sketches she'd written during the endless train ride. Dancing wasn't her only ambition. She meant to visit the Algonquin Hotel, where Dorothy Parker and those other writers had congregated; she meant to write some Talk of the Town pieces for the *New Yorker*, perhaps about a country girl's impressions of the big city. She hadn't considered writing a story about mobsters, but…why not? For a penny a word, she'd give him all the story he could handle.

They'd shaken on it. "You're on," she'd told him.

But now here she was, deep inside, or as deep as a girl could get in one week, and so far there was no sign of illegal gambling, nothing to suggest anything untoward was going on at all. Sure, there were some men who loomed when they stood and whose tailored tuxedo jackets bulged suspiciously at the armpit. But those might be off-duty cops, hired to protect a rich man and his date for the evening—or even on-duty cops, for all she knew, casing the place for the same reason she was. There were some sideways glances she'd noticed from men as she left the floor at the end of her act, and once or twice a napkin pressed into her palm with a telephone or hotel room number written on it, but what girl didn't have that sort of thing happen, even if she wasn't dancing under a follow-spot in a halter top? It hardly made the Sun one of your worse dens of iniquity.

Nicolazzo himself (a brooding, heavy-browed man with what looked like a jagged scar along one cheek, judging by the newspaper photos she'd dug up at the library) so far hadn't shown his face in the club.

Taking off her makeup after the second show one night, Tricia asked Cecilia if she'd seen anything out of the ordinary.

"Like what?" Cecilia said. She was peeling off a set of fake eyelashes as she spoke.

"I don't know," Tricia said. "You hear stories about clubs like this. What goes on in the back rooms."

"Sure," Cecilia said. "The last place I worked, the boss lined all the girls up at the start of every week and he pointed—you, you, and you. And if you were one of the ones he pointed at you had to go back to his office with him, where he had this big fold-out couch, a Castro, you know? And if you didn't go, you were fired. And everyone knew it."

"Is that why you left?"

She nodded. "I haven't seen anything like that here. I mean, once in a while Robbie will give you a pat on the rear, but my god, if that's as far as it goes, I'll be on cloud nine."

"What about gambling?" Tricia said. "Or drugs? Anything like that?"

"Why? Have *you* seen anything, Trixie?"

"No," Tricia said. "You just hear stories."

Cecilia shrugged. "There's probably some of that. You get that sort of thing everywhere. My advice to you? Don't go looking for it. Keep your head down, do your job, collect your pay, and go home happy. What you don't know can't hurt you."

"Yeah, I guess you're right," Tricia said. "I was just wondering."

But Tricia had a second job to do. She had a book to write. And not having found any true crime to write about wasn't going to stand in her way. So she began to pound out a few pages a day, setting her Olympia up on the chateau's sole writing desk around two each afternoon, while most of the other girls were out on jobs, shooting covers for magazines or private stills for "collectors." The ones who didn't have any work watched her type with a mixture of idle curiosity and indifference, peering over her shoulder now and again but never long enough to read more than a few words. Which was just as well. If it got back to Borden that she was at work on something, he wouldn't be surprised—but he might be if he knew how often the story she was cooking up changed paths or a scene reached a dead end and needed to be scrapped and restarted, something that presumably would not have been the case if she'd just been, as he'd put it, taking dictation.

She read *I, Mobster* and some of the Hard Case Crime books and stole liberally from them, inventing a narrator who'd grown up in the slums and found opportunity in crime. She never gave him a name, just had other characters refer to him as "kid" or "buddy" or "hey, you." She figured she'd have them shift to calling him "mac" and then "mister" and then "sir" as he rose through the ranks. He came from Chicago to New York after the war, joined up with an old pro on a heist of grade-A beefsteaks (or was it a bank robbery? she went back and forth on this point), and ultimately became one of the senior soldiers working for a Sicilian crime family down on Mulberry Street…before finally getting lured away to work at the Sun by their chief rival, Sal Nicolazzo. And that's where the fun began in earnest, with her nameless hero getting his hands dirty in the world of illegal gambling and all the associated pleasures. She found it exciting to write about this fellow, imagining her way into his sinister, violent life, full of gunplay and brawls and round-heeled women who welcomed him into their arms. (These she based, one by one, on her roommates, not even bothering to change their names. None of them were big readers, and she felt confident they wouldn't sneak peeks at the growing manuscript she kept in the cardboard box beneath her cot.)

Whenever she found herself starved for an idea, she paid a quick afternoon visit to the public library and pored through old copies of the *New York Times* and the *Daily News*, hunting for stories about mobsters and their misdeeds. Eventually the steady diet of newspaper articles, all filled with juicy betrayals, gave her the idea to have her narrator grow sick of Nicolazzo's controlling hand and plan a robbery—a mammoth heist of his own operation that would involve opening the safe at the Sun and fleeing with a month's proceeds from the big man's casinos, tracks, and fight clubs. It was the sort of thing that, if it had ever really happened, Nicolazzo would of course hush up—a Mob boss clumsy enough to let himself get robbed by one of his subordinates?—and that, in turn, would account for the fact that the reading public had

never heard about it. The only difficult part was coming
up with a good plan for the heist—and for that she got
help from a couple of experts, two young fellows she
spotted bringing manuscripts to office 315 repeatedly
and trailed one day to the Red Baron, a dark little bar
down the block with propellers and pictures of biplanes
hanging on the walls.

"Gentlemen," she said, putting a little hip action into
her stride as she approached, "may I buy you a drink?"

"I didn't know this establishment was high-class enough
to maintain B-girls in the middle of the day," one of the
men said, a slightly chunky guy of maybe twenty with the
beginnings of a beard ambitiously darkening his cheeks.

"She's not asking you to buy her a drink, Larry," the
other said. He was clean-shaven, slight, slightly older.
"She's offering to buy you one. And me one, I believe."

"Then I'm hopelessly confused. Miss, don't you have it
backwards?"

Tricia hopped up on the stool beside them, put a dollar
on the bar. The place, having just opened at noon, was
empty aside from them and the bartender. "Not in the
slightest. I do want you to help me out, but not by buying
me drinks. I'll supply the alcohol, if you'll help me work
through a problem I have in a book I'm writing for Charley
Borden."

"A book!" Larry exclaimed, taking a beer from the bartender with a grateful nod. "Did you hear that, Don?
This young lady is writing a book. We have an authoress
in our midst. What sort of book is it, madam? Ah, no need
to answer that. If Borden's your publisher, it can only be
one of two things: a crime novel or a sex novel. And I
don't picture a nice girl like you writing pornography."

"Pornography?" Tricia said. "I thought he only published Hard Case Crime."

"That's all he writes on the window," Don said, "and it's

what he shows off on his desk. One of these days you might ask him about the books he keeps in his desk drawer."

"By authors such as we," Larry said. "Us? We or us?"

"Us," Don said.

"Us," Larry concurred. They clinked beer glasses.

"So you're not mystery writers?" she said, fighting to keep the disappointment out of her voice.

"Oh, we're that, too," Larry said. "We're every kind of writer."

"Except the well-paid kind," Don said. "For five hundred dollars we'll write mysteries, war stories, space operas, sex books. Hell, I wrote a travel guide to Berlin once for three hundred."

"And he'd never even been to Berlin," Larry said.

"Perfect," Tricia said. "You see, I'm writing a book about a mobster and it's supposed to be a true story. And I want to have him steal all the money out of his boss' safe and get away with it. But you have to figure the safe would be guarded, and...well, I've seen you two at the office, I know you've written several books for Mr. Borden, and I just thought maybe you'd have some thoughts about how it could be done. Something nice and clever, but not *too* clever—it's got to be plausible enough that readers could believe it really happened."

"And why," Larry said, "should we come up with a perfectly good plot and hand it over to you, when we could get a book out of it ourselves?"

"You're forgetting," Don said, "she's supplying the alcohol."

"Ah, yes," Larry said. "I was. That's fine then." He scratched at his beard. "Let's see. A robbery. What can you tell us about the place this guy's supposed to rob?"

So Tricia told them, told them everything she could think of from her weeks working at the Sun—about the layout and the staff and the schedule, about the parts of

the building she'd seen and the parts she hadn't, everything she'd read in the newspapers—and bit by bit a picture emerged. She told them about Nicolazzo, the various
charges against him, what she knew about his private life,
his family. They peppered her with questions and tossed
out one outlandish idea after another.

"What about a hot air balloon?" Larry said. "Finney
did that in *Five Against The House*."

"That's idiotic," Don said. "How about a submarine?"

And so it went, for four days in a row, from ten past
noon each day till the bar started filling up around three
or four and the boys' voices and their imaginations, no
matter how well lubricated along the way, finally gave
out. Tricia began to despair of getting anything for her
money except slightly high from beer fumes. But at the
end of the fourth afternoon, Don's eyes lit up and he said,
"I've got it!"

And he really had.

Tricia wrote as quickly as she could, typed till her fingers
ached.

Mornings, she slept in, recovering from the late-night
activities of the prior night at the Sun and appreciating
as she never had before the strain poor Coral had been
laboring under all this time. At least you couldn't hear
garbage trucks in the morning from the side of the
building the chateau was on; on the other hand, some of
the girls were restless sleepers, snoring or moaning or
talking in their sleep, and with a dozen in one room,
silence was hard to come by, even in the wee hours.

Afternoons, she worked on the book, sometimes getting so wrapped up in it that she had to race through her
shower and jump into her clothes willy-nilly or she'd have
been late for the first show at the club, which started at
the supper hour. Evenings she spent at the club, usually

staying till one or two AM, taking a late dinner in the kitchen with the waiters and musicians. Then there were her days off, when she sometimes didn't get out of her nightgown, just sat at the desk banging away from the time she woke up till the other girls threw pillows at her back and begged her to stop the racket.

In this way, her days passed, and her weeks, and eventually eight of them had gone by.

She was surprised, at the end of the eighth week, when Charley Borden, having avoided paying back a penny of the debt he owed her along the way, invited her into his office and, beaming with pride and the goodwill of a man who'd recently been fortunate enough to cash a check, handed her two twenty-dollar bills. "Now, what do you have to say about that?" he asked her grandly. "What do you think my promises are worth now?"

But she was not nearly as surprised by that as by the contents of the box she held tightly in her right hand, a stack of paper whose first page began with the words "Chapter 1" and whose last finished with "The End." She dropped it on Borden's desk.

"I say thank you. And," she said with a huge smile, "I say you owe me five hundred dollars more."

5.

Two for the Money

"This guy's a gold mine," Borden said, jabbing with the back of his pen at the newest book to grace his desk. Three months had passed since she'd turned the manuscript in. "He's the genuine article. Gold Medal *wishes* they could find a guy like this."

The book was titled *I Robbed the Mob!* and was credited to that most prolific of authors, Anonymous, but Tricia was as proud of it as if her name had been plastered all over the cover. The illustration showed a man in a heavy overcoat, his face hidden in shadows, advancing on a buxom woman in a torn blouse. What that had to do with robbing the Mob, Tricia had no idea. But Borden said it would sell books.

Beneath the title it said

Torn From the Headlines!
The Scandalous True Story of One Man's
LIFE in the UNDERWORLD!

"You know what Casper Citron said about us on his program yesterday?" Borden said. "He called the book reprehensible. Said we glorified crime. That's good for a thousand copies, easy."

"How many did you print?"

"Seventy thousand. But we're already going back to press. The thing's selling, Trixie. You did good—you and this guy you found." Borden grabbed his jacket from a hook on the back of the door, shrugged it on. "You think he really ripped off his boss?"

"Oh, I'm sure he wouldn't say it if it weren't true," Tricia said.

"Man," Borden said. "The guy has guts. I tell you, I wouldn't want to be in his shoes the day someone hands Nicolazzo a copy of the book."

It was at that moment that the frosted glass pane in Borden's door shattered.

Shards fell on the floor with a clatter. A fist reached through the newly formed opening, groped for a moment, found the doorknob and turned it. The door swung open.

There were two men at the door, but the first filled the doorway so thoroughly you could barely see the second standing behind him. The bigger of the men stood well north of six feet, Tricia judged, and the resemblance to Tor Johnson didn't end there. His face was round and pink, with no hair on it except for a pair of dense eyebrows overhanging deep-set eye sockets. Each of his fists looked like half a cinderblock, and the bloody scratches across the knuckles of the one he'd just shoved through the glass didn't seem to bother him at all. He wore a heavy overcoat. If his face had been in shadow, he'd have been a dead ringer for the man on the cover of the book.

The other man was smaller, only an inch or two bigger than Borden, but with much the same look about him as his hulking companion. There was something of the brute in his eyes, and if his knuckles weren't presently bleeding it was clear from all the pink scar tissue across them that they'd done their share of bleeding in the past.

"You Charley Borden?" the smaller man said.

"Me? Borden? No. Borden. No. Borden stepped out, just a moment ago."

"That's funny," the smaller man said, "there's no one in the hallway."

"Well, it was more than a *moment*. What would you say, honey, five minutes?" Tricia nodded mutely. "Five minutes. Said he had to go downstairs. Said we should wait for him. So we're, you know. Waiting."

The two men exchanged glances.

"My wife here's a painter," Borden said, "isn't that right, honey? And I'm a writer, and we came here to offer our services to Mr. Borden." He stuck out his hand. "Pleased to meet you. I'm Robert Ste—um—"

Damn it, Tricia thought. "Stephens," she said, just as Borden said, "Stevenson."

"—son," she said.

Borden said, "That's right, Robert Stevenson. And my wife. Louise. Say hello, Louise."

"Hello," Tricia said, with a little wave.

"You look like Borden," the smaller man said.

"Really? I don't think so. Do you think I look like him, honey?"

Tricia shrugged.

"How do you know what he looks like anyway?" Borden said. "It's not like he's a famous fashion plate or anything like that, he's just one of New York's more promising young editors…"

The big man took a creased photograph out of his coat pocket and unfolded it. It was a side-by-side mug shot, full-face on the left, profile on the right. In the photo, Borden's hair was mussed and one of his eyes was swollen shut; the sign he was holding up in his hands said

N.Y. COUNTY 013887
BORDEN—4/28/1950

"Oh, he was much younger then," Borden said. "Practically a kid. Looks completely different now. Wouldn't you say?"

"Absolutely," Tricia said. "For one thing, he doesn't have a black eye today. Yet."

"Oh, we're not here to hurt him, miss," the smaller man said, unconvincingly. "It's not Borden we're after. We're here for the money."

"What money?" Borden said.

"The money this fellow stole from us," the smaller man said, and he nudged the other man with his elbow. "Show them the book."

The big man stowed the mug shot in his pocket and took out a well-thumbed copy of *I Robbed the Mob!*, its spine cracked, its pages dog-eared. It pained Tricia to see it in such condition.

"This Mister Anonymous here," the smaller man said, pronouncing it like it was two names, *Ann an' Amos*, "is a turncoat and a rat. He took money that didn't belong to him from a man who'd never done anything but help him, and we're here to get it back."

"But that's impossible," Tricia said. "He's not—"

"He's not what, miss? Not a thief? Read the book. He admits he's been a thief all his life. Just this time he stole from the wrong person."

Tricia hadn't been about to say that he wasn't a thief. She'd been about to say he wasn't real. Which of course meant he couldn't have stolen anything from anyone. But in that case, what the hell were these two refugees from a Robert Mitchum picture doing here?

"So, Borden," the smaller man said, "you want to tell us who this guy is and where we can find him, and we'll be on our way?"

"I'd love to help you, gentlemen, but I'm really not Charley Borden. I'll be glad to give him a message, though, if you'd like to leave one."

The smaller man snapped his fingers at the bigger one, who walked over to Borden's desk, bent at the knees, tilted it forward slightly so he could get his fingers underneath and then turned it upside down. The telephone and the brass desk lamp went tumbling to the ground along with a pair of whiskey glasses and a rain of books. One of the drawers sprang open and more books spilled out. The one on top was titled *Hot-House Honey* and showed a lady wearing nothing but a gardenia behind one ear. She looked a lot like Rita.

"O-ho," the smaller man said, bending to pick it up. "You're a naughty boy, Borden."

"Stevenson," Borden said.

"Hit him," the smaller one said.

The big guy shot out a fist and caught Borden's lapels, pulled him close. He drew back his other fist like a piston.

"Hey," Erin said, "what's going on here?"

Tricia turned to see her standing in the doorway.

"What the hell are you doing?" Erin said.

"We're having a private conversation, miss," the smaller man said. "Run along."

"Call the cops," Borden shouted.

"Oh, I already did that," Erin said. "Soon as I heard the glass break. They'll be here any minute."

"That's unfortunate," the smaller man said, looking murderously at Erin. "I suppose we'll have to continue our conversation another time."

At a signal from his partner, the larger one released Borden's jacket, patted down the crumpled fabric.

"You'll give Borden our message, right?" the smaller one said. "Tell him Mr. Nicolazzo won't take no for an answer. Not twice."

Borden nodded. "I'll tell him."

"You do that. And ladies," the man said, "you might want to rethink the type of character you pal around with. It's not always...safe."

He fixed Erin with a stare that was full of unsavory implications.

"Hey," Borden said. "What about the desk?"

"What about it...Stevenson? You're telling us it's not your desk, what do you care?" The man tipped his hat at Tricia, his eyes narrowing for a moment as though he half recognized her; then he shook his head and backed out through the open door, slipping *Hot-House Honey* into his pocket on the way.

The big guy patted Borden twice on the cheek. "Think about it," he said, his voice like a gravel pit. He followed his partner out.

6.

The Confession

"Did you really call the police?" Tricia asked.

"Of course not," Erin said. "I just said that to make them scram. Last thing we need here is police."

"Why's that?"

"Never you mind," Erin said. "What'd you do to make those guys so mad, Charley?"

"They're book reviewers," he said. "The door-to-door variety."

"I'm so sorry," Tricia said. "This is all my fault."

"Nonsense," Borden said. "You mean because of the book? You just did what I told you to. If that weasel you got the story from ripped off Nicolazzo, how is that your fault? Look—" He fished around on the floor till he found a book with a toga-clad brunette on the cover, triremes sailing in the background. The title was *The Bedroom Secrets of Helen of Troy*. "You think Larry Block should apologize for the Trojan War? Or maybe Don Westlake should apologize to the Russkies." He dropped Helen of Troy on top of a book called *Communist Party Girls*. "The guy could've kept his mouth shut. He didn't have to talk to you. Now he'll get what's coming to him. It won't be pretty, but you know what? Better him than us." He bent and tried to set his desk upright again but was unable to budge it. He gave up, slapped his palms together as if he'd accomplished what he'd set out to do. "All we've got to do is give those two fellows the man's name and they won't bother us again."

"I can't do that," Tricia said.

Borden looked over at Erin, gave her a nervous little smile. He turned back to Tricia. "What do you mean you 'can't do that'?"

"I can't," Tricia said. "It isn't that I don't want to—I genuinely can't."

"Honey," Borden said, coming forward, "of course you can. You have to. Those guys weren't playing a game. Next time it'll be *me* they turn upside down and dump all over the floor."

"I know," Tricia said. "And it's all my fault."

"Forget about whose fault it is," Borden said. "Just give them the man's name."

"I told you, I *can't*."

"Why? Are you afraid of him, what he'll do to you? Or what—you feel bad being a snitch? Getting him in trouble? What?"

"No, no, it's nothing like that," Tricia said. "I mean, I *would* feel bad if someone had trusted me to keep his name secret and I…" She shook her head. "But that's not the point. I can't give you his name because he hasn't got one. There's no man. I made the whole thing up."

There was silence for a moment.

"Oh, come on," Borden said.

"I'm so sorry, I know you wanted a true story—"

"Come *on*," Borden said. "What do you take me for?"

"There's nothing going on at the Sun!" Tricia said. "There's nothing, I swear. I looked. I couldn't find one lousy poker game, one girl turning tricks. Well, okay, there was one—but she was doing it on her own and they fired her for it. Nicolazzo has never shown up once while I've been there—I'm not saying not often, I'm saying not once. I haven't seen any drugs, I haven't seen any guns. I haven't even seen any money, other than people paying their drink tabs and tipping the hat check girls."

"But it says right here," Borden said, picking up a copy of *I Robbed the Mob!*, "that Nicolazzo has a private suite in the back, with poker and craps games all night long—"

"I made it up—the whole thing, I made it up."

"The counting room with the stacks of hundred dollar bills—"

"The whole thing."

"Even the girl with the…?"

Tricia nodded. "Everything. Out of whole cloth." Her voice cracked. "Pure, unadulterated malarkey. I'm sorry."

"But then why," Borden said, "did those two goons just try to shake us down?"

"That's what I want to know!" Tricia said. "It doesn't make any sense. There never was any robbery. There wasn't any money stolen. There couldn't have been. I mean, I made it as realistic as I could—I based it on what I know about the place and what I've read in the newspapers—but everything about the robbery itself? I made it up. It never happened."

Borden looked at her sideways, started to say something, then lapsed into silence again.

"Maybe," Erin said, after the silence had stretched on long enough to become uncomfortable, "those two guys don't really work for Nicolazzo—but they'd like to. Maybe they're small timers, they read the book, they figured the robbery really happened, and they thought if they could find the man who stole the money from Nicolazzo they'd have an inside track to his affections—"

"Oh, sweet Jesus," Borden said, kicking a couple of books against the wall, "have you been *reading* these things again? I don't pay you to read, I pay you to answer the phones and keep the riffraff out."

"You hardly pay me to do that," Erin muttered.

"Wait a second," Tricia said. "I'm confused. *He* pays you? I thought you worked for Mr. Hoffman."

"Who do you think Mr. Hoffman works for?"

"Some woman named Madame Helga."

"Kid," Erin said, waving a hand in Borden's direction, "you're looking at Madame Helga. He's the Edmund of Edmund and Edmund, too."

"Ladies, ladies, if I can interrupt this little tea party," Borden said, "we've got a big problem here. There are men—large men, angry men—who would be happy to do me great physical harm if I don't give them a piece of information you're telling me I can't give them. This is not an acceptable situation."

"So what do you want me to do about it, *boss*?" Erin said. "I already gave you an idea and see what that got me. Last time I ever—"

"Trixie," Borden said, "Trixie, Trixie, Trixie, I'm asking you one more time, my hat in my hand—" he lifted his fedora off a peg on the wall, actually held it out toward her "—you've got to give me something here. Something I can use to get those apes off my back. Because if they came after me right now, I'd have no name to give them— other than yours."

Tricia blanched. "You wouldn't."

"I wouldn't *want* to," Borden corrected her. "But after I'd gone a few rounds with the big guy, who's to say what I would or wouldn't do?"

While they all stood there pondering that question, a knock came on what was left of the glass of the door.

Through the jagged hole they saw a blue sleeve with metal buttons at the cuff.

Then the sleeve went away and a face appeared in the hole. The skin was ruddy and pocked beneath the glossy bill of the man's uniform cap. "Hello?" the man said. "Is this the office of the Hard Case Crime book publishing company?"

Above the bill, the cap had a little metal insignia on it

that featured an eagle, a shield, and what looked like a frontiersman standing with a musket by his side—it was a little hard to make out all the details. But you didn't need to make them out to know what insignia it was.

"I thought you said you didn't call them," Tricia said.

"I didn't!" Erin said.

Borden put his hat on, swung the door open.

"Yes, this is Hard Case Crime," he said. "What can I do for you, officer?"

The man stepped inside. He was beefy and barrel-chested and he moved with the careless manner of an outdoorsman used to having plenty of room to swing his arms. You could picture him felling redwoods with an axe.

He doffed his cap, pointed with it at the overturned desk. "What happened here?"

"We're renovating," Borden said.

"I'll say," the policeman said. "Listen, I want to talk to the man in charge." He took a leather-covered pad from a clip on his belt, flipped through its pages till he found the one he wanted. "A mister Charles Borden." He shut the pad. "That you?"

"For variety's sake," Borden said, "let's say yes."

"And who are these two?" Pointing at Erin and Tricia.

"Colleagues of mine."

"I suppose that's all right then," the policeman said. "Just as well for you all to hear this. I need some information about one of your authors."

Tricia's heart fell.

"And which of our authors would that be," Borden said. "As if I didn't know already."

The policeman reached into his jacket pocket and pulled out a battered copy of *I Robbed the Mob!*.

"The one who stole three million dollars from Salvatore Nicolazzo last month," he said.

7.

Home Is the Sailor

"Funny story," Borden said. "That book isn't what you think it is. You probably think it's a true story, and I can certainly understand why, what with the word 'true' on the cover and all. But it isn't. It's actually a novel, same as all the other books we publish. One hundred percent fiction. Some of us just thought it would be," he took a deep breath, "amusing to present this one as if it had really happened." Borden smiled weakly. "But it didn't."

"Well, now, that *is* a funny story," the cop said. "Because someone did steal three million dollars from Sal Nicolazzo last month."

"Really," Borden said.

"Oh, yeah. Walked into the Sun after hours, made his way to the counting room, opened the safe, emptied it out, and got away with three million smackers, pretty much to the letter the way it's described in this fictional book of yours. Nicolazzo's managed to keep it under wraps, but we've got people on the inside and word is the big man's beside himself." He pointed to the desk again. "You want some help with that?"

"Sure," Borden said. "Why not." Together, he and the cop turned the desk over, set it on its stumpy legs again. Borden was breathing hard when they were done, but the exertion didn't seem to have bothered the cop at all.

"Mr. Borden," he said, "I've been doing this a lot of years. I know where renovations like these come from. They come from men with names that end in vowels."

"Like O'Malley?" Borden said, aiming a thumb at the nameplate pinned to the cop's jacket.

"Wiseass," O'Malley said. " 'Y' isn't a vowel."

"Sometimes it is."

"Well, the ones I'm talking about are your 'I's and your 'A's and your 'O's. Especially," he said emphatically, "your 'O's."

"You trying to say something, officer," Borden said, "or is this the Police Benevolent League's version of a cross-word puzzle?"

"All right, Borden. I'll make it plain, so that even a two-bit smut peddler like you can understand it. I think the men who did this to your office work for Nicolazzo, and unless you gave them what they wanted, I don't think they're through with you. Now, I want the same thing they do—but me, I don't put holes in people's doors, or in people. What I do is put people in holes. And I can put you in a deep one for a good long time if you don't come across with a name."

"Mother of mercy," Borden said. "What a day. O'Malley, I'm going to tell you something and you're not going to believe me, but it's going to be the god's honest truth. There's no name to give you. None. This book was not written by a man whose name ends with a vowel, or by one whose name ends with a consonant, or by any other sort of man. It was written by a sweet young girl with an overactive imagination and no more knowledge of gangsters than you have of ballet. If there was an actual robbery at the Sun it's a pure coincidence, and I'm sure Nicolazzo will figure that out soon enough. Now would you please leave us alone so we can clean the place up and go home?"

"I don't think you appreciate the position you're in," O'Malley said. "You think this guy is a run-of-the-mill heel? He's not. The man's a killer, Borden. He'd think no more about snuffing you than he'd think about blowing his nose. He's been convicted on fifteen federal racketeering charges and sentenced to three consecutive life terms. In principle, he can't even set foot in the United States or he'll be arrested on the spot."

"You're telling me this guy I'm supposed to be afraid of isn't even in this country?"

"Actually, I'm not telling you that," O'Malley said. "I'd have told you that for sure three weeks ago—he's been living for years on a yacht he keeps just outside U.S. coastal waters, where we can't touch him. Sails off for the open sea any time we come close. But that was before someone stole three million dollars from him.

"Word is, he's come home. We don't know when and we don't know where, other than he's somewhere in New York City. One of our sources says he was smuggled in in a pickle barrel. How do you like that? Another says he was brought in in the trunk of an automobile. Either way, it's a lot of trouble and discomfort and risk for him to have gone to, and it can't have put the man in a better mood. But he apparently felt it was worth it in order to find out who robbed him."

O'Malley slapped his copy of *I Robbed the Mob!* on the newly righted desk, where it had no competition for the attention of everyone in the room.

"And who do you think he's going to look to for the answer?"

Borden grimaced.

"The name, Borden. I don't care if it's a man or a woman or a newborn baby, I want a name. I've been after this son of a bitch for seven years, this is the best chance we've had in all that time of getting him, and I'm not leaving here without a name."

Tricia stepped forward. "I'll give you her name."

"Don't, Trixie," Borden said, but she ignored him.

"I'll give you her name, if you tell me what you're going to do with it."

"Do with it? I'm gonna find her and—" O'Malley halted, checking whatever it was he'd been about to say. He licked his lips. When he spoke again, it was more slowly and quietly and carefully. "I'm going to *talk* to her, and find out what she knows and how she learned it. Then I'm going to, to, um, keep an eye on her—so Nicolazzo can't get at her without our knowing about it. And then when he tries," he said, heating up again, "I'm going to put him away for the rest of his miserable life!"

"And you won't come after the woman who wrote this book," Tricia said.

"Come after her? Only to give her a medal," O'Malley said. "Anyone who helps us put Nicolazzo away deserves the key to the goddamn city. Excuse my French."

"You won't say she must've had something to do with the robbery," Tricia said. "You won't try to charge her with anything."

O'Malley seemed to be struggling to restrain his impatience, or maybe it was his temper. "What do we care if someone robs a crook like Nicolazzo?" he said. "It's dirty money to begin with. Let her have it."

"Maybe she doesn't have it," Tricia said.

"Fine," he said through clenched teeth. "Then let someone else have it, I don't care. Just as long as we get Nicolazzo."

"You swear," Tricia said.

"On my sainted mother's grave," O'Malley said. "Now, talk, lady."

"All right," Tricia said. She stiffened her spine and stood as straight as she could. "I wrote the book."

"*You* did," O'Malley said.

"That's right," Tricia said. "I did."

"Well," O'Malley said, slapping his cap back on his head, "that makes things easy. You're under arrest, lady."

"What?"

O'Malley whipped a pair of handcuffs off his belt with one hand and started drawing his service revolver from its holster with the other.

"But you said—" Tricia started.

"I don't remember saying anything," O'Malley said, or anyway he started to. He hadn't quite gotten the whole thing out when the brass desk lamp in Erin's hands collided with the back of his head.

8.

Kiss Her Goodbye

The big man sank to his knees and tipped forward, landing face-first on the carpet.

"Great," Borden said. "That's going to make us popular with the police."

"How popular were you before?" Erin said.

Borden took Tricia by the arm. "What the hell were you thinking, Trixie? Did you really think he was going to let you walk out of here after you told him you wrote a book detailing a three million dollar robbery?"

"He said—"

"He said," Borden scoffed. "If I said I'd step out that window and fly to Minnesota, would you buy tickets to see it?"

"No," Tricia said, "but he's a policeman and you're a liar."

"Well, kiddo, I think you've just had a valuable lesson in how honest New York's Finest are." Borden knelt beside

O'Malley on the floor, yanked the man's belt out of his pants and used it to bind his hands behind his back.

"Should we take his gun?" Erin said.

"Absolutely, that's a great idea. Because we're not in enough trouble as it is." Borden looked around the dark little room. "I really liked this office, too." Beneath him, O'Malley started groaning. His eyes were still closed, but how long would that last?

"Ladies, would you please wait for me outside in the hall?" Tricia and Erin stepped outside, shut the door behind them. Through the hole in the glass, Tricia saw Borden give O'Malley another clout with the heavy base of the lamp. O'Malley stopped groaning and lay still. A moment later, Borden joined them in the hallway.

"Is he dead?" Tricia asked.

"Just napping," Borden said. "Though he'll have a hell of a headache when he wakes up. Erin—will you let Billy know what happened?" Erin nodded. "Tell him I'll be working out of 902 till the heat's off, assuming it ever is. Now, Trixie: I need you to explain to me how this made-up robbery of yours could somehow actually have happened."

"I don't know," she said miserably.

"You're telling me you didn't steal three million dollars from the Sun," Borden said.

"Would she still be living here if she had?" Erin said.

"I need to hear it from her," Borden said. "Trixie, do you swear on your life—on your mother's life—on *my* life, that you didn't steal any money from the Sun?"

"Of course not," Tricia said. "What do you take me for?"

"I didn't take you for a novelist, and look how that turned out."

"I'm *not* a thief," Tricia said.

"All right, fine. If you didn't steal the money, someone else did. And if it happened the way you described in the book, it means whoever did it must've read the book."

"Thousands of people have read the book by now," Erin said. "Probably tens of thousands."

"Sure—by now. It's on every newsstand in America now. But a month ago? That would have been a bit harder, considering it hadn't been published yet. The question is, who could have read the book a month ago? Who had access to the manuscript?"

"The printer?" Erin said.

"Moe? Moe's seventy years old and walks with a cane."

"Any of the girls could have read it," Tricia said. "They all saw me working on it, and I just kept it in a box under my bed. But I didn't think any of them were interested—"

"Apparently one of them was," Borden said. He crossed the hallway. "Maybe more than one." He knocked briskly on the door to the chateau. "Everyone decent in there?" he called. "I'm coming in."

"Just a minute," a voice called back. It sounded like Rita.

"Come on, Charley," Erin said. "You really think one of the girls could pull off a heist like that? Forget about climbing eleven stories and opening a safe—just picture one of them trying to lug three million dollars around. How much would three million dollars even weigh?"

"Couple of tons, if it's pennies," Borden said. "Couple of ounces if it's diamonds. If we're talking about hundred dollar bills?" He thought for a second. "Maybe fifty, sixty pounds. I know men who couldn't carry that much and girls that could. Besides, who's to say our girl didn't have help? Any of them could've gotten a boyfriend involved in it." He knocked again, on the glass this time and louder. "Or a girlfriend."

An image of Joyce sprang into Tricia's mind—and Tricia knew Erin was thinking the same thing. Strapping, six-foot-tall Joyce, who from the first day had seemed so resentful of Tricia. She certainly could've carried fifty pounds if she had to.

Borden turned the knob, swung the door open. Rita was buttoning a blouse she'd obviously thrown on hastily —the buttons were one hole off all the way down. Annabelle was lying on her cot in a transparent nightie and slippers, blissfully unconcerned about being seen that way. The other cots were empty; from the bathroom came the sound of a shower running.

"Jeez," Rita said. "Can't a girl have a little privacy here?"

"No," Borden said. He strode over to the writing desk, where Tricia's typewriter was still set up. A small stack of pages next to it held her latest attempt at a short story. It hadn't been going very well, and she'd been on the verge of giving up on it and starting another book instead, maybe something about a rugged, two-fisted detective this time, or maybe an assassin, cruel but principled. She had no shortage of ideas, and the prospect of another five hundred dollars was a powerful incentive. But now that opportunity seemed to have shattered along with the glass across the hall.

"Which one's yours?" Borden asked.

Tricia pointed out her cot and he bent to look under it. He pulled out a box of manuscript pages labeled "I Robbed the Mob!" in his own handwriting. Her original title, which he'd crossed out, had been *Dark Temptation*.

Borden turned to Annabelle and Rita. "Girls, do either of you remember ever seeing anyone going through Trixie's things when she wasn't around?"

"Why?" Annabelle said. "Is something missing?"

"No," Erin said, "we're just trying to figure out who might have been reading Trixie's book."

"Her book?" Annabelle said, in a tone of voice that sounded roughly as puzzled as if she'd been asked which of her roommates had been riding Trixie's unicorn.

"Yes, her book," Borden said. "This thing." He opened the box, took out a batch of pages, waved them in the air.

"Did you ever see anyone other than Trixie reading it?"

Rita and Annabelle exchanged a glance.

"What is it, girls?" Borden said. "Spill."

"Couple of times, while you were out working, Trix, Joyce would pull it out, read from it out loud," Rita said. "She'd read a line or two and laugh, and some of the other girls would laugh along. I never did." After a second she added, "Annabelle, neither."

"You ever notice anyone paying particular attention when she did this?" Borden said.

"Sure, Stella," Rita said. "Back when she was here, she was always egging Joyce on to read more."

"Any particular part she seemed interested in?" Borden said.

"The part where the guy steals all the money? She got a real kick out of that."

Borden turned to Erin. "So, what happened to Stella? Why isn't she here anymore?"

"Nothing happened, Charley. She just moved out," Erin said. "Girls come, girls go—" She kissed her fingertips and blew it off in whatever direction girls go. "I didn't think anything of it."

"And when was this?" he said. "That she moved out?"

Erin shut her eyes, as if she didn't want to see Borden's reaction. "About a month ago," she said.

9.
361

Tricia and Erin waited till they were down on the sidewalk before discussing what they were going to do. No point in letting the elevator operator in on their plans, not when he was the first person O'Malley would grill upon regaining consciousness.

Before calling the elevator, Borden had run back into his office, stepped over O'Malley's prone form, and pulled two copies of a book called *Death Stalks a Bride* from one of the room's packed shelves. He'd torn the covers off both, handed one to each of Tricia and Erin, and tossed the remains of the two books on the floor. The cover showed a virginal brunette hiking up her wedding gown with both hands while running from a wild-eyed shirtless brute in overalls. The brute's face looked a little like Billy Hoffman's; the bride's was unmistakably Stella's.

"Call me immediately if you find her," Borden had said before opening the door to the fire stairs. "Erin knows the number. If it's busy, it just means I'm on the phone with Moe. I want to find out if there's anyone other than him who might have seen the manuscript over there."

"You sure it's safe for you to stay in the building?" Erin said.

"I'm not sure it's safe for me anywhere," he said and pounded upstairs.

Now Erin was pulling Tricia along toward the subway entrance.

"Where are we going?"

"Brooklyn."

"What's in Brooklyn?"

"Cheap rent," Erin said. "And plenty of bars. And what do you find where there's cheap rent and plentiful booze?"

"What?"

"Artists," Erin said.

"Stella's not an artist."

"No, Stella's a model. And who knows better where to find a model than artists?"

"I don't know," Tricia said. "If she's got three million

dollars now, I'm not sure she'd be modeling anymore."

"Neither am I," Erin said. "But if she is, the boys at 361 will know how to find her."

Between Knickerbocker Avenue and Irving, between Decatur Street to the northwest and the long, lonely stretches of cemetery grounds to the east, there's a desolate block where Cooper Avenue curves and quietly turns into Cooper Street—this, Erin said, was where they were going. They rode out on the BMT until it wouldn't take them any closer, decamping finally at an elevated station in the shadow of a stained and leaking water tower; and then they walked the rest of the way, the better part of a mile, sweating under the smothering blanket of late summer heat. By the time they arrived, the sun had hit its apex in the sky and begun its slow descent toward the distant skyscrapers of Manhattan. Tricia watched its progress with no little anxiety: When night fell, she was due back at the club, and she didn't know which would be more dangerous, showing up or not.

As they neared the end of the street they approached a building the likes of which Tricia had never seen outside of classroom filmstrips intended to teach the children of Aberdeen about the dangers of narcotics. The windows were dark with filth, the rain gutters dangled, the paint on the walls was peeling. Patches of scrubby grass grew from cracks in the paving stones out front. There were less leprous buildings on either side, but Tricia knew, somehow, that this was the one they were headed for even before the tarnished brass numerals "361" became visible on the front door.

"You're saying *artists* live here?" Tricia said, and Erin nodded. "Wouldn't you think they'd keep it looking a little nicer? Being artists, and all?"

"Have you got a lot to learn," Erin said.

The doorbell, when they pressed it, surprised Tricia not at all by being broken. Knocking didn't yield any better result until finally Erin began hammering the side of her fist against the door and shouted: "Rise and shine, boys! Rise and shine!"

"Easy, sister," a man with a mellow voice said, drawing the door away from her descending hand. "We can hear you. We're not deaf." He wore a tunic that covered him from neck to knees over faded dungarees and a pair of wooden sandals. His hair, longer than any Tricia had ever seen on a man, was tied back with a leather strap. Between two of his knuckles, a hand-rolled cigarette slowly burned while between the next two extended the narrow wooden shaft of a paintbrush. There were smears of bright red on the tunic that matched the still-wet color on the brush.

"Hi, there," Erin said. "Is Rudy around? Or Jim?"

"Everyone's in the back," the man said, "but if you wanted in on the session, you should've been here two hours ago."

"That's okay, we're not here to paint. We've just got a couple of questions for the boys."

"Questions?"

"Won't take but a minute," Erin said, and pushed past him. He let them go.

Erin led the way down a dark corridor lined with canvases, squares of painted Masonite and bent-wire sculptures.

"Did you think his cigarette smelled funny?" Tricia whispered.

"Hilarious," Erin said.

They passed through a kitchen whose sink was home to a stack of dishes crusted with the residue of a month's meals. The door to the back yard was open and Tricia saw five or six easels set up in a circle around a pair of models, a man straddling a tall bar stool and a woman sprawled backwards at his feet, one arm outstretched in front of her as though to ward off a blow.

The man in the tunic followed them out, took his place at the yard's one empty easel, tamped out his cigarette, slipped the butt behind one ear, and resumed painting.

Tricia followed Erin around the perimeter, glancing at each canvas as they passed. On the first, the man was a cowboy on a rearing horse, the woman a squaw about to be trampled. The next showed an eight-foot-tall metal man shooting bolts from his eyes and a spacewoman in a gold jumpsuit returning fire with her ray gun. The third showed a German soldier in a First World War uniform leaping into a trench; the woman was a resolute doughboy this time, bayonet fixed to spit the Boche when he landed. Each showed the pair from a different angle, of course, depending on where the painter was standing; no editor, art director, or reader would ever know the paintings came from a single sitting. But meanwhile the painters got to split one modeling fee, Tricia supposed.

Erin stopped, finally, beside a bear of a man in a denim smock, the pocket in the front erupting with a profusion of brushes, palette knives, and other implements. He dabbled the wide fan brush he was using in a jar of water, stuck it in the apron pocket, and said without turning, "Afternoon, Erin. What brings you to the hinterlands?"

"You know I always like seeing you, Rudy," Erin said. She looked over his canvas, which showed the woman on a heart-shaped mattress, naked and quite a bit bustier than the model was in life. The man in his picture was at the top of a stepladder, training a movie camera downwards. "Nice work. Is this for Charley?"

"He wishes," Rudy said. "I'll get five times as much for it from Hefner."

"Fair enough. Rudy, listen, there's someone I need to

find, a model. I thought you might know where she is. Stella Dane?"

"Stella Dane," Rudy said, scratching his chin with a thick and discolored fingernail. "Stella Dane. I remember her—I think. Was she the one I used on *The Big Blade*? Or was she *Death Rides the Rails*?"

Erin pulled out the cover of *Death Stalks a Bride*. "I don't know those two, but here's one Bob Maguire did of her."

"Oh, yeah, her. Sure. I painted her two, three times. We had her here for a session like this once. Jim, you remember Stella Dane?" A man across the way looked up, blinked twice, shrugged.

Tricia crossed to his easel, showed him her copy of the cover.

"Oh, sure, the tall girl," Jim said. "With the feet. She had these unusally long feet."

"Do you know where we could find her?" Erin said. "It's important."

"No idea," Jim said. And Rudy nodded.

"Let me see that," one of the other painters said, and Tricia brought the cover around to him. "Yeah, right—Stella. Isn't she the one who was talking the whole time about how she wanted to be in television? How she was really an actress and a singer and I don't know what-all else. Like maybe one of us would pull a record contract out of his back pocket if she kept talking about it. You remember Norm made her pose with a cigarette in her mouth just to shut her up?"

A couple of the others nodded.

"Any idea where she is now?" Tricia said

"Nope."

Tricia looked around the circle, saw heads shaking. Then a small voice said, "Excuse me?" They all looked down. From where she was lying on the ground, propped on one elbow, the squaw/spacewoman/doughboy said, "I think I know where she is."

"Keep your mouth closed, honey," one of the painters said. "I'm working on your face."

But Tricia darted over to the woman.

"Hey," the painter said, "get out of there, you're lousing up the pose."

"Just one second," Tricia said. Then, to the model, "Stella Dane, right? This girl?" She showed her the cover.

"Yeah, that's her," the model said. "I saw her just the other day."

"Where was this?" Tricia said.

"At the fights," she said. "In the basement at the Stars Club."

"She was in the audience?" Tricia said.

"No," the model said. "She was in the ring."

It took them a bit more than an hour to get back to Times Square and from there it was a short walk west to the Stars Club, a squat building in the shadow of the piers. It stood a scant quarter mile south of the Sun and though it was supposed to be independently owned, Tricia knew from the newspaper articles she'd read that Sal Nicolazzo was involved behind the scenes. He hadn't really gone out of his way to hide the connection—he also had a piece of one of the city's last remaining ten-cent-a-ticket dance halls, and a year ago he'd renamed it the Moon.

The doorman stationed outside the front door of the Stars looked like the least likely man in New York to be found wearing a top hat, but a top hat was what he was wearing. Beneath it he sported the crumpled face and cauliflower ears of a boxer who'd taken one too many trips to the mat. His fighting days looked to have ended around the time of Carnera, if not Dempsey, and he glared at anyone entering the building as though nursing a deep resentment that boxing attendance hadn't come to a halt the day he left the sport.

The lineup advertised on a card beside the door promoted three afternoon fights, the first already underway, Mick "the Brahmin Brawler" Brody against Jerry "the Jackhammer" Lamar. After that it was Norman "the Mountain" Peakes against Steve Curtis, who had no nickname, apparently, and then the headline bout, featuring former middleweight champ Bobo "the Hawaiian Swede" Olson, fresh out of a short-lived retirement, against Ramy "the Chemist" Farid. Those were the fights in the main arena on the ground floor. In a box at the bottom of the card there was also a mention of an exhibition bout in the basement, pitting a fighter called the Houston Hurricane against one called the Colorado Kid. Those two fighters conspicuously were identified only by their nicknames, not by name and not with photos. According to the girl out in Brooklyn there was a reason for it—the Houston Hurricane was one of the cover models from *Death Stalks a Bride*, and not the one in overalls.

"I'm surprised they let women box," Tricia said.

"They who? The boxing commissioner doesn't; the city of New York doesn't. But a lot of things go on behind closed doors that they don't allow."

Tricia aimed a thumb at the ex-pug, who was letting a well-dressed couple enter. "Looks like an open door to me."

"Just try getting past our friend there if he thinks you're an undercover cop, or an inspector."

"And what exactly is he going to think we are?"

"The two of us?" Erin said, putting one arm around Tricia's waist. "He's going to think we're girls who like watching other girls hit each other."

Erin tugged at Tricia to get her moving and whispered, "Put a little sex in it." The advice was superfluous; it didn't take guidance on Erin's part to make Tricia do the things that got heads swiveling. It wasn't something Tricia turned on and it wasn't something she could turn off. Cars that would've honked angrily at your typical New York jay-walker honked appreciatively instead. Passersby stopped passing, if they were of the male persuasion, and those with female companions were jerked promptly into motion again, departing with an involuntary glance back over one shoulder. The boxer at the door to the Stars Club didn't budge from his post, but his thick-veined eyes widened as they approached and his massive jaw swung down like a drawbridge.

"We're here for the fight," Erin said.

The boxer said, slowly, "Upstairs...or down?"

"What do you think?"

"I, I...look, I," the man said, and then started over. "They got a rule here. No ladies allowed unaccompanied, see?"

"Do we look unaccompanied?" Erin said. "I'm with her. And she's with me."

"But—"

Erin stepped forward, walked her index and middle fingers gently up the front of his too-tight jacket. "Or you could say we're both with you. If anyone asks. And no one's going to ask, will they?"

"I don't know—"

"Mister," Tricia said, "we're old friends of one of the fighters."

"Oh, yeah? Which one?"

"Stella Dane," Tricia said. "She and I used to live together. We...shared a room." It was true, Tricia told herself, only slightly ashamed of the deception. It wasn't her fault if the man leapt to conclusions.

Which he seemed to be doing, judging by the blush that reddened his ravaged cheeks. "You and she..."

"They were very close," Erin said. "Like family. You'd let a fighter's wife in, wouldn't you?"

"Sure," the boxer said. "But…"

"Well," Erin said, pulling the door beside him open, "then you should let my friend in."

The man shoved the door shut again, firmly, wagged an index finger at the two of them. "If anybody asks, I'm gonna say I didn't see you. You snuck by me. If there's any trouble, I'm not taking the fall for, for, for a coupla…"

"A couple of what?" Erin said, hands on hips.

"You know what," the boxer grumbled. "I don't need to say it."

"All right, then," Erin said.

Inside, a narrow staircase led down and a wide one led up. The wide one was better lit. From upstairs came the sound of feet slapping canvas, of wooden chairs sliding against a concrete floor, of men and women hooting and gasping. And of punches landing. Then a bell rang and you could hear a collective sigh—of relief, of despair, Tricia couldn't tell.

"Ladies and gentlemen…" came the amplified voice of a ring announcer. *"The winnah and still champeen… Jerry, the Jackhammer…"*

The voice faded as they began picking their way downstairs. Tricia held onto the railing and took care not to trip. She heard Erin's steps behind her. The basement ceiling was low and the lights hanging from it were all trained on the ring in the center of the room. There was an announcer here, too, and a microphone dangling at the level of his mouth, but the ring was empty otherwise, except for a stool in each corner and a metal pail beside it.

They made their way around the room, hugging the wall, murmuring apologies to the people they had to step past. The place was packed, all the rows of folding chairs filled and much of the standing room besides.

"Ladies and gentlemen," the announcer said, and the crowd hushed.

"You're about to witness something few have seen." His words echoed before fading out and he allowed them time to do so. "A battle in the squared circle unlike any you'll find anywhere else in this fair city. Now, some of you may have heard of fights down Texas way where ladies box like men—Buttrick and Kugler and all that jazz. And you've dismissed it as a passing fad. A bit of gulf madness. Like cockroach races, or those wrestling matches where a man goes up against a bear. But anyone who thinks that is mistaken. I'm here to tell you, it's nothing less than the future of this sweet science of ours.

"And we have here for you this afternoon two of the finest figures in the field…two fierce young fighters of the feminine fashion…in short, two women who will wow you with a demonstration of the distaff brand of brutal battery! Are you ready, I say are you ready, to meet the contenders?"

The crowd roared back in the affirmative, and a door opened just a few feet to Tricia's left. Three figures came out, a woman in a hooded satin robe followed close behind by two stocky cornermen. Stitched on the back of the robe in sequined letters half a foot high were the words HOUSTON HURRICANE. The woman held up her gloved fists as she passed and pushed the hood back. Her shoulder-length black hair was coiled up and pinned to the top of her head and there were some sort of marks on the side of her face—in the second before the three of them moved past, Tricia couldn't make out what they were. But it was Stella, all right. No question.

Stella made her way down a cleared path between the rows of chairs and then pulled herself up to the apron and climbed between the ropes. She shrugged the robe off her shoulders and took a few casual practice punches at an invisible opponent. Somewhere in the crowd some-one whistled loudly. Stella had on gray trunks and black canvas shoes with white laces up the front and white athletic socks; on top she was wearing a tight sleeveless jersey with her substantial bosom strapped down beneath it. In place of the placid expression Tricia was used to seeing from her when she was lounging around in her pajamas, Stella wore a steely, determined stare, and the narrow muscles of her arms stood out as she flexed them.

"Can you believe it," Tricia whispered to Erin, but turning, she saw that Erin was no longer standing beside her. She felt a tug on her shirt from behind her.

"Come on," Erin said, pulling her out into the aisle toward the still-open door.

"We can't go in there," Tricia whispered.

"Sure we can. We're like family." They ducked inside and took a hard right just as another robed and hooded fighter marched by, a trainer and a cutman trailing in her wake. The back of her robe said THE COLORADO KID. She was past before they could get a look at her face.

"What are we doing?" Tricia said.

"You're following me." Erin led her down the back-stage corridor, peeking in open doorways as they went, hurrying past one small office in which a radio was broad-casting the sixth inning of a ballgame out at Yankee Stadium.

At the end of the hall was a door labeled FIGHTERS ONLY. Erin turned the knob and went in.

There were two tables, one on either side of the room, each with a wide mirror against the wall surrounded by a border of bare light bulbs. A bank of lockers—four up, four down—stood on the far wall between the tables and a small older man with a tattoo of an anchor on his fore-arm stood before the lockers, a push-broom in one hand and a dustpan in the other. He'd swept together a small pile of cigarette butts on the floor and had a new one in the making between his lips.

"Hey," he said, looking up with the myopic stare of a man who needed glasses but was too embarrassed or stubborn to get them. "Who let you back here? This ain't Grand Central Station."

"Damn," Erin said, "and here's us looking for the train to Poughkeepsie. What's the matter, squinty? You don't recognize one of the greatest female fighters of our time?"

"Who? Her?"

"Yeah, her," Erin said. "This is Barbara Buttrick, the Mighty Atom of the Ring. Just flew in from Texas."

The guy walked up to them, gave Tricia a quick up-and-down glance. "Her?" he said again.

"She could punch you into next Tuesday," Erin said. "Want to show him, honey?"

"That's all right," Tricia mumbled. "Wouldn't want any sort of trouble."

"I thought Buttrick was a Brit. You don't sound like a Brit."

"She's tired," Erin said. "It was a long trip."

He narrowed his eyes, peered closely at Tricia. "She looks awful young."

"They all do in her family," Erin said. "Now, you want to leave us alone so she can change? Or were you hoping for a free peep show?"

He headed for the door, leaving his sweepings where they lay. As he went, he pitched his new butt onto the pile. "Ain't got much to show, has she?"

"Never mind him, honey," Erin said. "Probably prefers watching the men anyway."

"Some of 'em got bigger tits than her," the guy called over his shoulder.

"And bigger pricks than you," Erin said, but he'd swung the door shut, muttering.

"Do you think he believed you?" Tricia said, after a second.

"Sure," Erin said. "Why not? What else would we be doing here?"

"What *are* we doing here? Why not wait for her outside?"

"Where outside? There have got to be at least three exits from this building, maybe more. Besides, how long do you think we could stand on the sidewalk before somebody noticed?"

"So we're just going to wait here," Tricia said.

"No," Erin said, "we're not just going to wait. We're going to look through her things, see if we can find anything that—" Erin had been sifting through the various cans and jars on the nearer tabletop as she spoke, moving rolls of gauze and tape out of the way. She grabbed something from under one pile, held it up triumphantly. It was a copy of *I Robbed the Mob!*, the tassel of a bookmark lodged about three-quarters of the way in. Erin tossed it to Tricia. "How about that? She bought her own copy."

Tricia opened the book to the marked page. It was the start of Chapter 10. Her heart began to race. With a mixture of pride and dismay she read her own words on the page: *The afternoon of the heist was hot, as hot as hell, but I was wearing gloves and had my collar up...*

10.

Plunder of the Sun

The afternoon of the heist was hot, as hot as hell, but I was wearing gloves and had my collar up.

It was easier to keep my collar up than my spirits.

I'd done many bad things in my career, to many people,

but never anything like this. Today I'd be a rich man or a dead man—there was no in-between.

Mr. N kept his hands clean when it came to goings on at the Sun. You could walk around the place all day and if you didn't know where the secret rooms were you'd never find them. Entrance to his private suite was by invitation only. Money did change hands on the premises, but only between trusted old friends. If you were a member of the general public and wanted to play a hand of poker or put your paycheck down on a roll of the dice, or put a little something in your nose that didn't belong there, you had to go to one of Mr. N's other clubs. The Moon. The Stars. There were others. I don't think any of us knew what all of them were. Except maybe his accountants. Maybe.

Anyway, those other clubs were where the big bucks were made and lost. Made by Mr. N—lost by everybody else. That's where the cash flowed like water, and all in one direction. And once each day, after everyone closed up, each of those little streams flowed back to the main river. One by one, each of the clubs made a delivery to the Sun, handing over the lion's share of any ill-gotten gains they'd collected, minus only the thin sliver they were permitted to keep for themselves. Then, once each month, on the last Thursday of the month, the contents of the big safe at the Sun were trucked out to a secret spot where Mr. N kept his private stash. Except this month that wouldn't happen because when the truck showed up, the big safe would already have been emptied.

By me.

I pulled my coat tighter around myself, tugged my hat down lower on my brow.

All I had to do was get in, get out, and live to tell about it.

Which was like saying all I had to do was fly to the moon, drink the ocean and catch a bullet in my teeth.

But, hell. I had to try. After what he'd done to me, I owed him. I owed him big. He deserved to have this happen to him—and damn it, I deserved it, too.

I went over the plan in my mind as I turned onto 49th Street.

The first delivery of money each night took place at 2AM, and they kept coming until 9 or 10. The men on duty stayed in the counting room till noon, sometimes 1PM. By then they were tired and eager to call it a day, so they shut the safe, spun the big dial on the front to lock it, shut off the lights, locked the door of the counting room, and left the Sun in the care of the afternoon cleaning crew. Around 4PM the rest of the staff would start filtering in and at 6 the place would open for business and the whole cycle would start over again. But between 1 and 4, the only protection the place had was the cleaning crew. That and a pair of security guards sitting outside the locked front door, and one more in a little wooden booth on the street downstairs.

Three men. Mr. N figured he didn't need more security than that, and for all these years he'd been right. Because who in his right mind would try to rob Salvatore Nicolazzo?

Who.

Me.

I saw the security booth from half a block away, saw Roy Tucci sitting inside it, trying to look vigilant when, in fact, he was always on the point of nodding off. It wasn't an exciting job and the man was in his sixties. Besides which, the booth had no ventilation and the heat was brutal. Even with the door propped open, you'd cook in there.

But for once I didn't walk over and commiserate, the way I had so often before. Instead, I walked past on the far sidewalk, my pulled-up collar and pulled-down hat leaving little of my face for him to see or recognize. At the corner I crossed the street. The Sun occupied the top two floors of a twelve-story gray stone building and there was another building just like it next door—but not right next door. Wedged in between them was a narrow one-story building occupying the ground floor space of what was, above it, the airshaft that provided ventilation to the buildings on either side. All over town they rented out these little ground-floor spaces to one-man operations catering to the drop-in trade: shoe repair shops, locksmiths, places like that. This one was the shop of a glorified news peddler, offering candy out of a wooden tray and papers and magazines from a rack on the wall. There was a tiny counter inside with three wooden stools crammed in front of it, where you could get a soda on a hot day or a coffee on a cold one. For a nickel extra Jerry'd put a slug of something he called bourbon in the coffee, but it wasn't bourbon really and you were better off blowing the nickel on one of the dirty books he kept behind the counter.

When the coffee ran its course you could hold it till you got back to your office, wherever that was, or you could use the little toilet in a closet at the back. Jerry could be counted on to have his hands full opening coke bottles, breaking dollar bills for parking meters, and—this time of day—watching all the cute secretaries going by on their way back from lunch. So he didn't pay much attention when you went to use the can. Or when you came back.

Or when you didn't.

The toilet was filthy and dim, but not completely dark despite having no bulb overhead, and not completely airless, either. What there was overhead was a piece of frosted glass laced through with chicken wire. This piece of glass was hinged at one side and wedged open about an inch, letting in what little light and ventilation the room got.

I swung the lid of the toilet down, climbed onto the seat and then onto the tank, and pressed both hands—both *gloved* hands, I was taking no chances—against the glass. And shoved.

It took three tries before the hinge creaked open far enough for me to pull myself up through the opening. I used my heel to swing it shut again behind me. The surface of the roof was caked with bird droppings and piled with years of refuse thrown from windows higher up. Behind one such pile I saw a long-tailed rat eying me hungrily, its whiskers twitching. "You're on your own, friend," I told it.

I'd been up here once before, when casing the job, and I knew where the rain gutter was. It was a narrow pipe that ran the height of the building and you'd have to have been a Chinese acrobat to climb it if a pipe was all there was. But the pipe was clamped to the stone every three feet with a sturdy metal bracket and those brackets had just about enough room on either side to hold a carefully placed shoe-tip. There was also a bare inch or so of space between the pipe and the wall and I'd worn a girder-man's safety belt around my waist. I threaded the buckle behind the pipe and clicked its latch shut. I'd have to re-open and close it one-handed every three feet all the way up, but it was worth the extra effort. A fall from ten feet up might only break my leg—from fifty, it'd kill me for sure.

Or else leave me wishing it had, when my long-tailed friend came to feed.

I climbed.

Eleven stories may not seem like much when you're riding up in an elevator; even climbing stairs, it's no more than a good work-out. But let me tell you, climbing eleven stories one handhold and toehold at a time is agony. Your fingers seize up. Your calves start to ache. You want to let go, but you can't, not even for a moment, because what if the belt's not strong enough to hold you after all?

And four stories up, the windows start. Windows into offices, and unlike nightclubs, offices have people in them at two in the afternoon. You pray they'll be empty or if, when you glance in, they're not, you pray the people inside will leave quickly. Or if they don't, you pray they won't look your way.

And you keep climbing. Praying and climbing. And your fingers cry out with pain and stiffness, and your back and shoulders, and your ears from the tunneling wind of the airshaft around you, and your head's about to burst, and your bladder too because you didn't bother to actually *use* the toilet before climbing on top of it—and then you realize with a start that you've made it.

And then the real fun begins.

I reached into my jacket pocket and took out the fist-sized stone I'd picked up on the way downtown. No fancy devices for me. I smashed it into the window, used it to knock out some particularly nasty shards of glass, then dropped it down the airshaft. I had to grope for a second before I found the latch. Raising the window from the position I was in turned out to be harder than I'd expected, but once it was open I had no trouble climbing inside. I took a moment to let my eyes get used to the darkness of the room and my breathing return to normal. I flexed my fingers inside the gloves, tried to work out the kinks.

Then I made my way to the door.

The room I was in was the storage room behind the kitchen. Boxes of canned food and bottled beer were stacked from floor to ceiling, like in a warehouse. I pulled down one of the boxes and started taking bottles out of it, stacking them on the floor.

I carried the empty box with me into the kitchen.

Here, the remnants of the morning's work were tidied up: rows of metal pots and saucepans, washed and lined up face-down to dry; sacks of kitchen whites that were headed to the laundry because after a night of cooking they weren't so white anymore; wooden packing boxes like the one I was carrying, some broken down for disposal and others filled with empty bottles or other trash and stacked by the dumbwaiter for pick-up. I set the box down and tugged at the dumbwaiter rope till the little compartment surfaced, then tied the rope off so it couldn't go down again.

I listened at the swinging doors to the main dining room, heard the labored wheeze of a carpet sweeper being pushed back and forth, back and forth, back and forth. I knew the girl pushing it, a scarred twenty-year-old Belgian by the name of Heaven LaCroix whom all the other girls on the cleaning crew—bohunks and Slavs, every one of them, and none too attractive themselves—made a point of calling 'Heavy' to her face. So she was carrying a few pounds—what business was it of theirs? Looked like it was all muscle anyway, the sorts of labor they had her doing.

I glanced at her through the circular window in the kitchen door, then ducked when she turned in my direction. I'd figured she'd be finished with the dining room by now, but it looked like she still had plenty to go. I'd have to take the long way around.

Hefting the box, I picked my way to the far side of the kitchen, past the cold storage room where steaks and butter and ice were kept, past the grills and deep industrial sinks, past the trestle table where the dancers and musicians bolted their suppers between shows, to the door that led backstage. This door was locked overnight but everyone who worked at the Sun knew where the key was kept. I pried up the cover of the light switch with one fingernail, fished out the key, and used it to open the lock. The area beyond ran behind the orchestra platform and the dance floor, past the wings, and to a corridor that, during working hours, always had a man in it, someone to keep any straying patrons—or employees, for that matter —from straying too far. This time of day it was empty. I made my way to the far end.

And here I faced another locked door.

This was the one that counted.

It could all end here. Or it could all begin.

I knelt in front of the keyhole. From the inside pocket of my coat I took a rolled-up square of felt, cinched around the middle with twine. I drew the knot open and unrolled the cloth. It clanked lightly against the floor.

There were three narrow pockets, and from two of them I drew a machinist's hammer and a broad-edged chisel. The head of the hammer was a barrel-shaped slug of metal and heavy as hell. I wedged the chisel point into the groove where the shaft of the doorknob met the wooden surface of the door, then swung the hammer down, hard.

It took four blows before the knob came off. I paused after each, certain the clang of metal against metal had been heard. But this deep into the floor the place was silent and still. I went back to work like some ghostly blacksmith, hammering and pausing and hammering again in the darkness until the metal shaft bent and then snapped off, its counterpart falling to the floor on the other side of the door.

With the knob off, I had an opening into which I could insert the third of my tools, which I drew from its pocket now, a tapered hacksaw. Only its long, narrow nose could fit into the hole, but that was enough. I began the process of cutting a squared-off horseshoe shape into the wood around the latch.

I had a bad moment when the blade caught and I couldn't get it free. I was scared to pull too hard and maybe break the blade. For half a minute, while precious seconds ticked away, I knelt staring at it and did nothing. Then I began easing the blade slowly back and forth. After a tense minute I was able to dislodge it. I wiped my forehead on my sleeve. I started sawing again. Coming back at the same point from underneath, I was able to break through.

I was breathing heavily when the door finally swung open. The luminous dial of my wristwatch showed I'd taken almost an hour at my task. It was 3PM now and it wasn't unheard of for some of the staff to show up to work before 4. I had to move more quickly.

Or else—

Or else I'd be making the trip back down the airshaft without benefit of handholds and toeholds.

I picked up the broken halves of the doorknob, wrapped them up along with my tools in the felt square, and deposited the bundle in one corner of the empty box. Once inside the counting room, I closed the door and walked up to the safe.

It was the height of a man—a taller man than me. The dial was almost the size of a captain's wheel from an old schooner, only made of cast iron rather than wood. There were eight stubby metal arms you could use to turn the thing and numbers painted onto the rim in white, zero through 99. No hacksaw or chisel would get you into this beauty. Nothing short of knowing the combination would.

So it was a good thing that I did.

I turned the dial clockwise to 75.

Sal Nicolazzo—*Zio Nicolazzo*, as he liked to call himself, Uncle Nick—was a sentimental man. A mean bastard, sure, a vicious man, a gambler who'd wager on anything anytime, the bloodier the better—all true. But he fancied himself a good family man who took care of his own. He had family members by birth and marriage on his payroll and even the ones who didn't work for him he sent money to now and then, a little present when they needed it to keep them in the black.

I spun the dial back the other way to 23.

There was one relative, though, that he couldn't send presents to, except for flowers once a week, regular as clockwork, to dress her headstone. Her name had been Adelaide Barrone and she'd been his kid sister's younger daughter. Born in the U.S.A., served in the U.S. Army, died of malaria in North Africa in 1945. She'd been a WAC, and her dogtag number had been A-752344.

I turned the dial to 44.

The door to the safe swung open.

Sentimental bastard. I almost felt sorry for him.

Almost.

The dough was stacked neatly and it took me only ten minutes to transfer it to the box. I stopped when the box was full and the safe was empty, a happy coincidence. I didn't know how much I'd gotten. There'd be time to count it later.

If there was a later.

A grunt escaped my throat as I lifted the box. I felt a muscle spasm in my back, but didn't put it down again. No time. I could buy all the heating pads I wanted when I got home.

I retraced my steps as quickly as I could, one lurching step at a time.

Corridor. Backstage. Kitchen.

The dumbwaiter, bless it, was waiting where I'd left it. I slid the box inside, then unwound the rope holding it up and climbed in next to the box. It was a tight fit. Hand over hand, I let the rope play out and the dumbwaiter slowly descended. When we settled at the bottom of the shaft, I peeked through the closed door—lights off, no signs of movement—before raising it. I backed out, pulled the box out after me. Groped through the darkness till I found what I was looking for: one of the deep, fabric-sided carts the maintenance men used for bringing tools and supplies in and garbage and laundry out. The one I found was half full, which was perfect. With a mighty heave I lifted the box over and in, then rearranged the cart's prior contents to cover it up. I stripped off my coat and hat, balled them up, and shoved them down deep in the cart. Underneath I had on a khaki uniform that marked me as some sort of working stiff—I figured no one would ask precisely what sort. From inside my shirt I pulled a matching khaki cap, unfolded it, and tugged it down over my head, its bill hiding my eyes.

I pushed the cart out of the room, through a long, empty corridor, and up to the gate of the freight elevator. I knocked briskly on the metal gate and a few moments later it slid open, the tired-looking operator inside greeting me with a glazed look. I wheeled the cart inside. He reached for the handle to pull the gate shut again.

Just then, someone called, "Hey, you!"

My heart stopped. Simply stopped.

A man hustled up to the still-open elevator, dragging a lumpy sack behind him.

"You headed back to Jersey?" he said.

"That's right," I said.

"Can you take this with you?"

Without waiting for my answer, he swung his sack up and tossed it in my cart.

"Thanks, buddy," he said, and shuffled off.

"Next time," the elevator man said, "you guys get

everything ready *before* you make me come. Understand?"

"I'm sorry," I said.

"You're sorry, I'm sorry, everybody's sorry." He punched the freight car down to the basement. I stayed at the back of the car, where he'd have had to turn his head to look at me. He didn't bother.

When he opened the gate again, I pushed the cart out of the elevator, onto the rear loading dock and into the parking area behind the building. I half expected one of the security guards to be waiting for me. Or maybe Mr. N himself, disappointment in his eyes and a pistol in his fist.

But I made it to the street without seeing anyone I knew.

Whistling softly to myself, I wheeled the cart home.

11.

Branded Woman

"Trixie," Erin hissed, and then Tricia heard it, too: footsteps, coming toward the locker room. Tricia put the book down and darted over to where Erin was standing beside the door. When it opened, they'd be behind it.

It opened. They were behind it.

Two figures staggered in, one with the other's arm slung across his shoulders, Stella and her trainer. The trainer kicked the door shut without looking back and led her to the bench in front of the lockers. She sank onto it heavily and he started kneading her shoulders as she went at the laces of her glove with her teeth.

"Hello, Stella," Erin said.

Stella didn't move, just stopped biting at her laces. Her trainer turned around. He was a fireplug of a man, low and broad, and looked like he might have been an athlete once himself—not a boxer, maybe, but a wrestler, a weightlifter. "Excuse me," he said, "who are you?"

"We're friends of your fighter there."

"Is that true?" he asked Stella.

Stella slowly turned, brought her legs over to the other side of the bench, looked at them. Her face was bruised and there was a trail of blood under one nostril. And the marks on her cheek—looking at them now, Tricia thought they almost looked like letters, like a monogram in raised red welts.

Tricia ran to her. "My god, Stella, what happened to you?"

"I was in a fight," Stella said. "It's why the gloves, and trunks, and all."

"No, I mean your face. What is that?" She bent to look at the welts: a low, wide 'Z' next to an 'N.' In fact, it wasn't even two letters, it was the same letter twice, just turned sideways. And her blood ran cold as she realized the significance of those particular letters. ZN. *Zio Nicolazzo.*

"It should've been you, Trixie. Not me. You. You're the one knows who wrote the book."

"Nicolazzo did this to you?"

She turned to her trainer. "Could you leave us alone for a minute?"

"You sure you're okay?" he said.

"Yeah, I'm sure. Go on. I'm fine." He left reluctantly, watching from the door for a moment before letting it close. "Listen, kid," Stella said. "You need to know this. I gave you up. I didn't want to give the bastard anything, but…" She touched the padded tip of one glove to her cheek.

"You know how he did it?" she said. "He's got a ring with his initial on it, this big goddamn ring, and he held it over the flame from a cigarette lighter, a fancy gold

Zippo, and he said, 'You tell me which of my men betrayed me or you'll never work as a model again.' I told him I have no idea. They roughed me up a little, but Jesus, I've taken worse than that in my fights, and they knew it. So the ring. He said back in Italy, you'd use it to seal a letter, press it in hot wax. Leave your mark."

"Oh, god, Stella, I'm so sorry," Tricia said.

"Well, I'm just telling you, I talked. I told him everything I knew and some things I didn't. Anything to make him stop." Stella started biting at her laces again, finally got them loose, stripped off her gloves. Her hands were taped up underneath and the tape was dark with sweat.

"What exactly did you tell him?" Erin said.

"I told him I'd seen Trixie working on the book, that I'd read bits of it before it came out."

"That's it?"

"No." She turned to Trixie. "I said you were sleeping with the guy. That you told me you'd planned the robbery together."

"What?" Tricia exploded. "Why would you say that?"

"I had to say something. To make him stop."

"Did he?"

"Eventually."

"You shouldn't have lied," Tricia said.

"You try it sometime, having hot metal pressed into your face, and then tell me what I should or shouldn't have done."

"Why'd he even come after you? Why did he think you'd know anything about the robbery?"

"He had his men get copies of all of Charley's books, and they recognized me on some of the covers. I've been fighting here for a while, so they knew where to find me. And then, of course, they found the book in my locker."

"Yeah," Erin said, "we found it, too. You think maybe you'd want to get rid of it?"

"I wish I'd never seen it," Stella said. "I wish I'd never met any of you."

"Why'd you leave, Stella?" Tricia said. "A month ago. Right around the time of the robbery. Why'd you pick that time to move out?"

"What—*you* think I had something to do with it? Jesus Christ, after I took this because of you?" She was on her feet suddenly, aiming one taped hand at her scarred face. Tricia saw her fist clench and stepped back, out of range. Stella dropped her hands, disgusted. "Get out of here. Both of you."

"Not till you answer my question," Tricia said, trembling but hoping it didn't show. "We went through a lot to find you. We're not leaving without an answer."

"Why'd I move out? Look at me. This is what I look like after a fight—when I win. It's worse when I lose. Used to be I'd get a fight once a month, once every six weeks. Then about a month ago they offered me a regular gig, this whole 'Houston Hurricane,' 'Colorado Kid' thing. Good money, good hours, it's maybe a stepping stone to a stage gig what with all the Broadway types in the audience—but how many modeling jobs am I going to get with bruises like this? Or a split lip, or maybe a broken nose? It was either or. I had to make a choice."

"Did it occur to you," Erin said, "that maybe they gave you this regular gig because they wanted to keep closer tabs on you?"

"Not until last night," Stella said. "While they were doing this."

"This just happened last night?" Tricia said. "Why'd they wait that long?"

"What, you think they should've done it sooner?" Stella growled.

"I don't mean that, it's just…why didn't they?"

"Maybe Nicolazzo wasn't back in the city yet," Erin

said. "Or maybe they're getting desperate because no other leads have panned out. They must be pretty desperate to have sent those two goons to Charley's office."

"They got Charley?" Stella said.

"No, we chased them off."

"You got lucky, then. Nicolazzo's boys are awful mean. Charley'd crumble soon as they laid a finger on him. You, too," Stella said to Tricia. "They'd break you in two. Not sure about you, Erin. You might last a while."

"Thanks," Erin said. "I think."

"One more question," Tricia said, "then we'll go. Who else saw the book before it was published? Or did you tell anyone about it?"

"All the girls saw it. You left it lying around, for Christ's sake."

"Anyone else?"

"Well, Colleen—I told her. Don't ask me why. I just thought she might get a kick out of it. This was back before we got the regular gig."

"Who's Colleen?"

"Colleen King, the Colorado Kid. You might see her on the way out—she'll be the one coming to in the ring. She was one of Nicolazzo's taxi dancers before he put her in the fight game."

"Does Nicolazzo know you told her about the book?"

"Nicolazzo knows everything," Stella said. "Everything. I'm no pushover—but we've all got limits. I'll take it on my face if I have to, but when he started moving that ring south I sang like Mahalia Jackson."

Tricia nodded. What could you say to that? She walked to the door, Erin close behind. Stella watched them go.

"I'm sorry this happened," Tricia said, her hand on the knob. "I didn't mean for anyone to get hurt. I—" She stopped abruptly.

"What?" Stella said.

Tricia felt the knob turning under her hand. *Oh, no,* she said to herself. *Let it be the trainer coming back. Or Colleen King, coming in to peel her gloves off and change. Or Squinty, with his broom.*

But it wasn't.

12.

Dutch Uncle

"O-ho," said the smaller one, "look who's here." The larger one ground his knuckles together like a kid warming himself in front of a fire.

"We were just leaving," Erin said.

"I'm sure you were. You're not anymore, but I'm sure you were."

The big one reached inside his coat and brought out something wrapped in brown burlap.

"You can't keep us here," Tricia said.

"Who said anything about keeping you here?"

"You did," Tricia said. "You just said we're not leaving."

"What are you, a lawyer? I meant you're not leaving us." He snapped his fingers at his partner, who was untangling the burlap. "Bruno, come on, the boss is waiting."

Bruno finished pulling apart the wad of fabric, but there was nothing inside it—it was just burlap, all the way through. He walked up to Tricia, handed her a piece, then gave another to Erin and crammed the rest back in his deep coat pocket. "Put them on," he said in his gravel pit voice and mimed pulling something over his head.

Tricia saw the drawstring then, sticking out at the bottom, and realized it was a sack, the sort potatoes come in.

"I'm not putting a bag over my head," Erin said.

"If she doesn't," the other one said, "put it on her."

"What are you going to do to them?" Stella said.

"What business is it of yours?" the smaller man said. "You didn't have enough last night?"

Stella said nothing.

"That's better."

"People will be looking for us," Erin said.

"You mean your boss, Borden? You'll be seeing him soon enough."

So they'd gotten Charley after all. Tricia's heart sank.

"I mean the cops," Erin said. "We're wanted for assault. After you left, a cop named O'Malley tried to take her in—" she nodded toward Tricia "—and we knocked him out, tied him up. They're going to be looking for both of us. I don't know that you want to be seen in our company."

"Then it's a good thing you're going to have bags over your heads, isn't it? Now, quit talking and put 'em on." And he whipped out a revolver to emphasize his point. Reluctantly, Tricia opened her bag. She saw Erin doing the same.

The bag smelled musty and earthy as she pulled it over her head, as though it actually had held potatoes sometime recently. Through its coarse weave she could only see a hint of light. She felt a rough hand at her elbow, steering her toward the door.

"You really knocked out a cop?" she heard the smaller man say.

"Yeah," Erin said. Her voice was muffled. "We really did."

"With what?"

"Desk lamp."

"That brass one?" the man said. "Good for you."

He didn't say any more till they were in the car.

*

"All right, now you're going to go in and up two flights of stairs. You're going to keep the bag on till I tell you to take it off, understand?"

They'd been driving for the better part of an hour, making enough turns along the way that Tricia had no idea where they were. Which, presumably, was the point.

Something hard poked her in the side. "Understand?"

Tricia hadn't realized he was waiting for an answer from her. "Yes, I understand. Two flights of stairs, keep the bag on."

"Until what?"

"Until you say so."

"Good. Now, you."

Apparently he'd poked Erin, since she said, "Cut it out. I understand."

"No, for you the rules are different. You're going downstairs, to the cellar, where Bruno will keep an eye on you. You do whatever he tells you to. Understand?"

"Do I have a choice?"

"No."

"Well, then," Erin said.

"Hey, Mitch," came a low voice from the front seat, "where does he want them, out front or in the back?"

Tricia felt the leg pressed against hers in the back seat tense. Apparently Mitch didn't much mind them knowing Bruno's name but hadn't meant for them to know his.

"In the back," Mitch barked. "And keep your mouth shut from now on."

"What?" Bruno said. "Why?"

"You know what," Mitch said. "And you know why."

"I don't, Mitch—"

Tricia felt the man next to her lean forward, heard a slap of metal against flesh. The car swerved a little. Bruno kept his mouth shut from then on.

When the car drew to a stop, she was led out by the

elbow, across a stretch of what felt like gravel underfoot, and through a door that could've used a bit of oil on its hinges. On the way up the stairs inside, Tricia counted 37, 38, 39 steps and she was suddenly reminded of a movie she'd seen when she was a kid, at the local picture palace in Aberdeen. It was an old one, made before she was born, but she'd enjoyed it, people chasing each other around with guns, all sorts of peril and adventure. It had all seemed like so much fun then, when all she had to do was sit in the dark and watch it happen to people up on the screen. She'd never thought someday she'd be marched up a flight of stairs at gunpoint herself.

"Stop." Mitch walked around in front of her and she heard a door opening. "Okay." A hand at her shoulder pushed her forward. After she'd taken a few steps—onto a thick carpet, it felt like—he said, "You can take the bag off."

Tricia didn't wait to be told twice. She dropped the sack on the ground and took in big gulps of air as she looked around the room they were in. It was a sort of a library, with bookshelves running from the floor to the ceiling all the way around. The spines of the books were mostly dark leather with gold lettering, though a few looked newer, with paper dust jackets, and on one table she saw a disorderly stack of familiar-looking paperbacks. The one on top was *I Robbed the Mob!* and she winced when she saw its condition. The cover was bent back, several pages folded down or torn. Next to it she saw Stella staring up at her from the front of *The Crimson Cravat* by Bill Grewer. Someone had circled Stella's face in red ink.

"Young lady," a man's voice said, and Tricia hunted about for its source. She found it finally in a doorway off to one side, where a fat man stood wiping his hands on a towel. He was wearing a scarlet vest, a watch chain stretched across it like the equator on a globe. His shirt looked like silk, his hair like the sleek black coat of a wet seal. He tossed the hand towel onto a chair and came forward.

"Young lady," he said again, "I hope you don't think me rude, but let me tell you I am very disappointed in you. Very disappointed."

Tricia recognized him from the newspaper photos she'd seen, but only barely. The scar was there, the heavy brows—but his body had ballooned from years of luxurious shipboard living and his already swarthy skin was baked a deep, nut brown. He had on a medallion on a gold chain, glittering under his open shirt, and he had rings on three of his fingers. He looked like a portly pirate captain, she thought, lacking only the beard and eyepatch to complete the picture.

"Mr. Nicolazzo," Tricia said, "I'm sorry you—"

"Nick," he said. "Uncle Nick."

"Nick," she said.

"Uncle Nick," he said. "It's what everyone calls me."

"Okay, Uncle Nick. I'm sorry you—"

"Don't apologize. It makes you sound weak, like a little girl. Stand up for yourself. You're going to steal from powerful men like me, you've got to face the music like a grown-up."

"I didn't steal from you," Tricia said.

"Ah, that's even worse than apologizing. Lying, and so poorly too. Come, now, child, do you think your Uncle Nick is a fool? Is that what you're telling me?"

"No, sir. Not at all."

"Stand up straight."

She straightened, a sense of annoyance and embarrassment mingling with fear. She could see, as he waved his hands about, the backwards letter N protruding from the ring on his right index finger.

"I'm told I owe you something—Trixie, is it? I'm told audiences come to the Sun each night just to see you. Not to listen to Roberto's wretched music, not to see the other dancer—to see you. You've made me a good deal of money, with your dancing. I have been encouraged by my manager at the Sun not to harm you physically. I'd be stabbing myself in the pocketbook, if you take my meaning.

"But Trixie, you have been a bad girl. A very bad girl. You've cost me a good deal of money, and more than just money. There's also the respect of my peers, you've cost me that as well—and that's not the end of it either. As I believe you know, there was more than money in my safe the day of the break-in; and there is less than money in it now. This is not acceptable. What was taken I must have returned. If you refuse, I promise you, pocketbook or no pocketbook, you will suffer."

"Mr. Nic—" she started, but he raised a warning finger. "Uncle Nick. I don't know who robbed you. Honest, I don't know. I didn't even know till today that you had been robbed."

"Your friend Stella told me otherwise. Are you calling her a liar?"

"Absolutely," Tricia said. "But it's hardly her fault. I mean, with what you were doing to her."

"What I was doing? What *I* was doing?" He looked around incredulously, seeking a bit of justice in an unjust world. "My nightclub gets broken into and robbed, and I'm the one that's doing wrong? *Madonn'.*"

"You branded her on the cheek!"

"I let her off easy," he said. "Do not expect me to do the same for you."

"What do you want me to say? I can't tell you something I don't know."

"Very simple," Nicolazzo said. "Who was it? Which of

my men seduced you into helping him rob me, and then
had the *palle* to write a book about it? You'll notice I'm
giving you the benefit of the doubt—I am assuming *you*
didn't seduce *him* into doing it."

"Nobody seduced anyone," Tricia said. "I had nothing
to do with the robbery. Nothing."

He picked up the paperback, waved it at her. "But
somebody told you this story."

"No," Tricia said. "I just made it up—all of it, out of
my imagination. None of it really happened. None of it
was supposed to, anyway."

"But it did happen," Nicolazzo said. "Just the way it's
described in here: the broken window, the chiseled doorknob, the sawn-open door, the missing cart. And the
empty safe. For heaven's sake, child, if you made it all up,
how could you possibly know the combination to my
safe?"

"You mean it was right?" Tricia said, and he glared at
her. "I just guessed! I'd read the *Daily News* article about
your sister and her daughters and the flowers every week
for the one who died, and I needed a combination for the
safe, and I just thought, well, what would I choose if I
were him?"

"That's preposterous," Nicolazzo said. "You should be
ashamed of yourself, concocting such an absurd story."

"It's the truth."

He waved a hand in Mitch's direction. "Bring one of
them up here," he said. Then to Tricia: "We will see how
long you continue to lie when the life of someone you
care about is at stake."

Mitch left the room. She heard him stomp down the
stairs, then the creak of the door, then a few minutes later
two sets of footsteps returning. When they reached the
top she expected to see Erin or Charley come marching
out, hands raised, but instead it was Roberto Monge, his

wrists tied behind his back, stumbling as Mitch prodded him with his gun.

"Ah, Roberto," Nicolazzo said, patting the bandleader on the side of his face. "Pretty soon they'll be waiting for you at the club. For both of you. What will they do when you don't show up? Elect another bandleader? Maybe Joey with the clarinet? Or Hugo with the drums?"

Monge didn't reply. His skin was pale and Tricia saw sweat beading at his hairline. His eyes kept darting over to her, then back at Nicolazzo.

"Robbie. Robbie. Did you do this thing to me? You and your little dancer?"

"No—no, Uncle Nick," Monge said. His voice was shaking. "She is nothing to me, this one. You know I love my wife."

"Your wife," Nicolazzo said. "She was my niece before she was your wife, Robbie. And maybe you love her, maybe not, but your little *minchia*, she likes to wander, no? Maybe I should get a knife, cut her off, so she can wander far away?"

Monge was shaking his head. "You don't have to do that."

"I don't have to," Nicolazzo said, "but maybe I should."

"I haven't touched another woman in three years, I swear it!"

But Nicolazzo had already turned his attention back to Tricia. "Is this the one? Did you devise this robbery with him?"

"I barely even know him," Tricia said. "I do a dance number twice a night for his band, that's it."

"If that's so," Nicolazzo said, reaching into his pants pocket and drawing out a bit of polished black wood with metal caps at either end, "you won't mind seeing him bleed a little bit." He pressed one of the studs along its length and a spring-loaded stiletto blade shot out.

"Of course I mind," Tricia said. "You can't do that."

"I can't? Ah, but you know I can, I see it in your eyes. Good girl. I make you a deal: You tell me who robbed me and if it's not him, I let him go."

"I told you, I don't know."

Mitch gripped Monge by the elbows and Nicolazzo drew the blade lightly against his chin. A thin line of blood formed.

"Stop it!" Tricia said.

"Tell me who did it," Nicolazzo said, "and I'll stop."

"All right," Tricia said desperately. She pointed at Mitch. "He did it. Mitch did. With Bruno. They did it together. It was them. I didn't want to tell you with him in the room, but it was the two of them."

"Boss, it's not true—" Mitch said.

"Of course not," Nicolazzo told him. To Tricia he said, "Enough. I lose patience. You'll tell me what I want to know or say goodbye to your boyfriend here." He nicked Robbie again, beneath the ear this time.

"He's not my boyfriend!"

"Who robbed me?"

"I don't know!"

"You don't believe I will do it," Nicolazzo said. "It's too bad. Next time you will." He looked in the doomed man's eyes. *"Stronzo.* I've wanted to do this since the wedding." And switching to an overhand grip, he buried the blade in Monge's chest.

"No," Tricia shouted, and ran to him, but Nicolazzo grabbed her, his arms like steel bands around her chest, his bulk an impassable obstacle. Mitch let Monge's body down slowly to the floor, where his blood spilled onto a circular throw rug that almost looked as if it had been put there for the purpose of catching it. He pulled the knife out of Monge's shuddering chest, wiped it off with a handkerchief, and made it disappear inside his jacket.

"Now we send you down to the cellar, to think," Nicolazzo said, his breath hot against her face. "You think
carefully for your old Uncle, eh? You come back with
answers, my dear, or more of your friends will die. You
don't want that, do you?"

Tricia felt her stomach heave. How had everything
gone so terribly wrong?

Nicolazzo pushed her into Mitch's arms. "Take her
downstairs," he said. "Put her in with the boxer, not with
Borden or the other girl. I don't want them hatching any
schemes together." He wiped his palms against the seat
of his pants. "Then come back and—" he waved a hand at
his employee's body, at the bloody rug "—clean this up."

"Yes, sir," Mitch said.

Nicolazzo raised a finger and wagged it in stern cor-
rection. "What's this 'sir'?" he said. "Yes, *Uncle.*"

13.

The Colorado Kid

The boxer, Tricia thought as Mitch led her downstairs,
the burlap sack over her head once more. That's what
he'd said: Put her in with the boxer. It wouldn't be Stella
—it had to be the other one, this Colleen King. The
Colorado Kid. Another innocent, dragged into this for no
reason. Unless, of course—

Unless she was the one who had robbed the place.
Unless she'd pumped Stella for information about the
book and decided to carry out the heist she'd heard described. But how could that be? Anyone who thought the
book was a true story would have thought the robbery
had already taken place—and anyone who thought it was

fiction would have no reason to think the plan would actually work. Especially the combination to the safe. Who would risk everything on the remote possibility that a made-up combination might just possibly be correct? Of course, it apparently had been. But no one could have counted on that. And you don't risk your life on a guess.

Tricia heard a key going into a lock and the cylinder turning, then the hammer of a gun being drawn back. "Miss King," Mitch called out, "I'm coming in. I'm bringing you a roommate. I've also got a gun. If you're not at least five feet away when I open this door, I'll shoot you dead, do we understand each other?"

A woman's voice came through the door: "Yes."

"All right. Just step back, keep your distance, and no one'll get hurt." Tricia heard the door swing open. "That's good, like that. With your hands up, please."

From the other end of the room, the woman said something that was a little hard for Tricia to make out, the sound muffled by the sack. It sounded like, "Who is she?"

"Girl named Trixie," Mitch said. "No one you know. She's a friend of your sparring partner." He touched Tricia on the shoulder. "You can take the bag off when you hear the door close."

Tricia waited till she heard the latch click into place, then turned and ran to the door, tearing off the bag as she went. She tried the knob. Already locked. She rattled it, tugged at it, rammed the door with her shoulder. Nothing.

"Don't bother," the other woman said, from behind her. "I've tried, and I'm bigger than you are." The voice was improbably familiar, and when, after a second, she realized why, Tricia's blood ran cold. It couldn't be.

Tricia turned to face her.

They stared at each other, dumbstruck. The other

woman (the *Colorado* Kid? why not Nebraska, at least?) stood up from the bunk where she'd been sitting, came forward into the light. "Patty?" she said.

"Cory?" Tricia said.

14.

The Girl With the Long Green Heart

Coral Heverstadt, Tricia's older sister, had been born the year before Alfred Hitchcock made his movie *The 39 Steps* and been gone by the time Tricia found herself sitting in the dark in the Aberdeen Cinerama watching it. She'd lasted at home two years longer than Tricia, moving out the day of her twentieth birthday rather than her eighteenth. She'd been better made for rural life, with her wide, powerful legs and muscular frame. She could push a loaded barrow through mud half a foot deep or lift a hundred-pound bag of feed, if not barehanded then with the assistance only of a pair of heavy work gloves, and so had found work reliably on the farms on the outskirts of town. Tricia, at fourteen, still child-small and fencerail-thin, had looked up to her with an admiration bordering on awe.

Her odd jobs had meant Coral always had some cash in her pocket—not much, perhaps, but enough to treat her kid sister to lunch or a movie or a treat from the drugstore, with its spinning wire racks of brightly colored novels. She'd enjoyed the feel of folding money under her fingers, the freedom it imparted—to do what she wanted, to go where she wanted. But the amount you could make for pushing barrows and lifting feed bags was limited. A few dollars here, a few there. She wanted more. And so she began a quest for more remunerative employment, finding work as a waitress, a bar hostess, a day-shift worker at the 3M plant running the machine that wound the Scotch tape onto those little spools. In each of these roles, she confided to Tricia as they lay in their beds at night in the room they shared, she found herself the center of a certain amount of attention—male attention, to put a finer point on it. Coral took after their mother and was big all over, not just her muscles but her feminine parts, and the local farmboys and mill workers and 3M middle managers gazed at her appreciatively as she approached and longingly as she passed.

These were men with wives at home and families, but they also had money in the bank—not the farmboys so much, but the middle managers for sure—and not just the drugstore-treat variety either. They had dough, in the vernacular of the paperback novels Tricia devoured so eagerly—cabbage, lettuce, mazuma, the long green. And they spent it on her happily. They took her out for meals, bought her gifts, once even paid for an overnight business trip to Sioux Falls. And in return they expected, well...to hear Coral tell it, never anything worse than a kiss or a hug, maybe gave her a pinch now and then, but she sternly told them off if they made any advances less proper than that. Anyway, that's what she told her sister at the time, and it was the picture she continued to paint of her experiences in her letters back home after she left the Great Prairie for the Big Apple. She was a good girl, if occasionally put upon by a certain predatory type of male, and well equipped to handle herself, thank you very much.

So when, precisely, had she become a lady boxer?

Coral sank back onto the thinly padded bunk beside her sister and told the rest of the story.

Some of the pinches had actually been pokes, and not all of them with a finger, either; at age twenty-one, on her own in New York City, she'd found herself in the family way, and she could only conceal her growing belly beneath the cigarette tray she wore at her job for so long. They fired her when they found out—what else could she expect?—and she found herself struggling at once both with morning sickness and a fast-declining balance in her bank account.

So she went to the man who'd knocked her up—no use for nicer language than that, it's what he'd done—and told him she'd pay a visit to his fiancée, the daughter of a powerful and unforgiving man, if he didn't restock her account on the double and keep it filled for the duration. It wasn't blackmail, she felt; it was just collecting what she was due. A man should pay for his own child.

That child, Arthur Lyle Heverstadt, came howling into the world on January 4, 1955, in the middle of a terrible snowstorm that snarled traffic on the way to the hospital. She gave birth, in fact, in the frigid back seat of a checker cab, the driver—who kept repeating that he'd been a medic at Guadalcanal—helping with the delivery from the folded-down jumpseat beside her.

"Not really," Tricia said, interrupting her sister at this improbable juncture. "You didn't really have a baby in the back of a taxicab, did you?"

Coral nodded. "It sounds worse than it was. He got me to St. Vincent's eventually, and the baby was fine. He's three now, Artie. Almost four."

"Artie."

"He's the sweetest child, Patty."

"And that's the man you live with," Tricia said. "The one you couldn't tell me about the day I came to town. The reason you didn't let me stay with you, not even for one night."

"I didn't want you to know," Coral said. "I didn't want mama to know."

"I wouldn't have told her."

"You say that now," Coral said.

"Who watches him while you're working? Who's with him now?"

"A couple of other girls who live there. They help me out and I give them a few bucks when I can."

Tricia nodded slowly. "And you became a boxer how?"

Coral shrugged. "A baby has to eat. His mother, too. I took the work I could get. I'm not eighteen anymore, Patty. I'm not twenty-one. I'll be twenty-five next year, I've had a kid, and there's a new crop of bright young things each year for the men in this town to look at."

"Like me, you mean."

"Like you," Coral said. "Look at you, blonde as anything. What'd he call you? Trixie?"

"It was your idea, giving a fake name," Tricia said. "*Colleen.*"

"The two of us," Coral said softly. "If mama could see us now."

"I still don't understand how you ended up…like this. I thought you were working as a dancer."

"I was—I worked at a club called the Moon run by a man named Nicolazzo."

"Uncle Nick," Tricia said.

"You know him?"

"I'm sorry to say I do," Tricia said. "I work for him too. At the Sun."

"No—really? Doing what? Dancing?" Tricia nodded. "That's funny. I worked there for a while, but only after hours. Cleaning." Coral brushed her hair out of her face, uncovering a darkening bruise on one cheek. "Well, I'm sure dancing at the Sun's a whole other story. At the Moon it was horrible."

"Worse than getting punched in the face?"

"Oh, yeah," Coral said. "Much. On your feet for hours at a stretch every night. Every sort of man pressing up against you, thinking you're his for a handful of dimes. I'd rather take a punch any day."

"So Nicolazzo made you a fighter," Tricia said. "And now he thinks you robbed him."

"He does?"

"Either that or he thinks you know who did. That's why he's got you here. It's why he's got me. And he just killed a man for less. I saw him do it."

Coral sank her head into her hands. "Patty," she said, after a moment, "I need you to promise me something. If you get out of this and I don't, you'll take Artie back home to Aberdeen."

"Don't even talk like that."

"I've got to," Coral said.

"No."

"I do," Coral said. "You see, Nicolazzo's right. I did rob him."

"What are you talking about?" Tricia said. "What do you mean you…Cory, why would you do that?"

"Stella told me about this book she'd seen. That gave me the idea," Coral said. "I didn't seriously plan to do it. But all that money—you know what I could do with a tenth part of that much money? You know the clothes and things I could buy for Artie? For me?"

"But stealing from a man like Nicolazzo—"

"I know, I know." She wiped the back of one hand against her eye. "It was stupid. But you know, it came in baby steps. There was an opening on the cleaning crew at the Sun. So I asked if I could do a couple afternoons a week, and they said yes. And there I am, washing the dishes and cleaning the carpets, and I can't stop thinking about that book. The big safe in the back, like Stella described it. I didn't want to think about it, but you spend a couple of hours polishing floors and your mind starts to wander."

"Cory…"

"No, listen. I was thinking about it but I wasn't going to do anything—it was just something to daydream about. But then one day I'm working there and I hear some banging. You know, hammering. And my first thought is, It's maintenance, they're fixing something. But my second thought is, This is like that book. Maybe someone's breaking in. And part of me is thinking, I'd better stay away. But the other part's thinking, Why? Maybe this is my one big chance." She reached out for Tricia's hands, held them in her lap. "So I finish up what I'm doing and start hunting around, where I heard the sound coming from, and when I get there what do you think I find? There's a door standing open with the knob cut out and sure enough the safe's there, and its door's open, too. And the thing's been emptied!"

"Emptied?" Tricia said. "Then someone else robbed him, not you."

"Well," Coral said. "Not completely emptied. There was a box in the very back, a flat leather box in the corner. It was dark. Whoever'd been there before me must have missed it."

"And you took it?"

"It was small," Coral said, squeezing Tricia's hands tight enough that it hurt. "I didn't even look inside till I got it home. I just grabbed it and ran."

"And what was in it?"

Before Coral could answer, they both heard the key in the lock, then the click of a gun being armed. "Ladies," Mitch said through the door, "I'm coming in."

15.

The Gutter and the Grave

"What was in it?" Tricia whispered. "Coral, quick!"

"Pictures," Coral whispered back.

"Ladies?" Mitch called. "Make some sound so I know you hear me."

"We hear you," Tricia shouted. "And we're nowhere near the door." Then in a low voice to Coral, "What sort of pictures? You mean like dirty pictures?"

"Not the way you mean," Coral whispered, her words all rushing together. "It was dead people, murdered, lying in the street. There was one where they shot a man outside a bar, he was lying in the gutter, must've had fifteen bullet holes in him. And you could see who shot him. They were standing over him with their guns out."

"You recognize who they were?"

"Yeah, one of them was—"

But the door had swung open and Mitch had walked in, gun extended before him in one hand. "What are you girls gossiping about?"

"Nothing," Tricia said.

"Get over here," Mitch said, "pick that up," gesturing toward the sack lying on the floor, "and put it on. He wants to see you again."

Tricia stood. "It was good to meet you, Colleen," she said. "I hope to see you fight someday when this is all over."

Coral didn't say anything. Tricia pulled the bag on and followed Mitch out the door.

*

Upstairs, when the bag came off, Tricia found herself looking at Charley Borden. He gave her a wan smile. His hands were tied behind him and his hair was disheveled. He had on a vest and pinstriped pants, but the suit jacket that went with them was nowhere to be seen. Strewn on the ground at his feet were the contents of his pockets: a leather wallet, a comb, some coins, a pack of playing cards, some keys on a metal ring.

Nicolazzo paced in a little circle between them, a few steps forward and a few back, saying nothing, just glaring at each of them in turn. In one hand he held his stiletto, playing idly with the blade, springing it out and pulling it back in. There wasn't a trace of blood on it that Tricia could see, or on the circular patch of carpet where the throw rug had been.

"So, my dear," Nicolazzo said, "have you decided to tell me what you know, or shall we have another round of mumblety-peg?"

"You can save your breath," Borden said. "She doesn't know anything."

"My friend, it's your breath you should be worried about conserving, not mine." Nicolazzo held the blade up to Borden's throat and turned to Tricia. "So? What have you got to say?"

"I don't know where your money is," Tricia said, "or who took it. That's the plain truth."

"I'm sorry to hear that," Nicolazzo said.

"But I do know," Tricia continued, and her voice only trembled a little as she said it, "what else was stolen from your safe."

Nicolazzo's eyes narrowed.

"It's photographs, isn't it?" Tricia said, her mind clicking along, trying to make sense of what Coral had told her. A man lying in the gutter, dead. Other men standing over him with guns—one of whom Coral had recognized. Coral, who'd worked for Nicolazzo and so would have known some of Uncle Nick's other employees. "Incriminating photographs," she said. "The sort you'd keep in your safe in case you ever needed to use them, but that you otherwise wouldn't want anyone else ever to see. Photos of your own men—something you can hold over their heads to keep them in line, maybe?" Off to one side, she saw Mitch shift uncomfortably.

"Trixie," Borden said in a strained little voice, trying hard not to touch the blade hovering below his chin. "You're a very imaginative girl, but maybe this isn't the time to be dreaming up the plot for your next book—"

"Quiet, you," Nicolazzo said. Then to Tricia: "Go on."

"If these pictures wound up in the hands of the police, it would be bad for you. If they wound up in the hands of your rivals, it might be even worse."

"Never mind that," Nicolazzo said. "Where are they?"

"If you let us go—all of us—I'll find them and I'll bring them to you."

"I don't like that idea," Nicolazzo said. "I don't like it at all. If I let you all go, what incentive would you have to come back? No. I think maybe it's better if I do a little work right now on this young fellow here. Perhaps I should take the skin off him one inch at a time, till you tell me what I want to know."

"May I say something?" Borden said.

"Hush," Nicolazzo said. "You're a little apple, waiting to be peeled. Little apples do not talk."

"If you touch him," Tricia said, "I'll never tell you anything."

"Do you really think so? Do you really think you will be able to stand there and watch him suffer when it's

entirely in your power to put an end to it? When all you
have to do is utter a few words—a location, an address—
and the man's pain stops?"

"How do I know you won't just kill him then? And me,
too, while you're at it."

"Because, my dear, I always keep my bargains. I am a
man of my word. Ask anyone. Salvatore Nicolazzo has
never welshed on any deal in his life. Million dollars on a
wager? I pay off. If I lose. And collect if I win. That's the
way it works in my world. If you don't have your word,
you've got nothing."

"And I have your word," Tricia said.

"You have my word. That I will not harm either of you
if you return my stolen property to me. The photos *and*
the money. And that I will if you do not."

Tricia looked at Borden, straining to keep his head
back, away from the knife, and at Nicolazzo, holding it
there carelessly, loosely, but with the same avid look on
his face that he'd had before using that very blade to end
another man's life. She thought about her sister down in
the cellar, and about Erin—and about herself.

"The money I can't promise," she said, "but I'm pretty
sure the photos are on Cornelia Street. I don't know exactly where—but I'm confident I can find them, and
when I do I'll bring them to you. That's the best I can
offer." She stepped forward bravely, hands on her hips.
"Now let him go."

"Go? No, I won't do that. He and I will wait here for
you. We'll—" He glanced about, bent down, and picked
up the deck of cards from the floor. He closed the stiletto
and slipped it into his pocket. "We'll occupy ourselves
with a little game. You play cards, do you, Mr. Borden? A
bit of rummy, perhaps? Or canasta? You can play it with
two, I'll show you how." To Tricia he said, "But come
back quickly, my dear. Or I'll grow impatient with canasta

and teach him another game I like. It's called 'Fifty-to-One.' Those are the odds, you see. The odds against."

"Against winning?" Borden said, clearly relieved no longer to have a switchblade quivering at his neck.

"Against surviving," Nicolazzo said, and all the blood that had returned to Borden's cheeks drained away again.

Nicolazzo snapped his fingers at Mitch. "You—go with her. Make sure she doesn't try anything funny. And get rid of the stiff while you're at it."

"Yes, boss," Mitch said.

A plump finger rose admonishingly.

"Uncle Nick," Mitch said. "Excuse me."

Nicolazzo smiled. "Now Mr. Borden," he said, "would you like the first deal or shall I?"

16.
Night Walker

Mitch pulled the bag off her head as they crossed the 59th Street Bridge into Manhattan. He left it lying on the front seat between them.

"So we were in Queens?" Tricia asked after taking a few deep breaths to clear her head of the burlap smell. She didn't turn to look at Mitch. She watched the New York skyline rush toward them through the windshield instead.

"Never mind where we were," Mitch said. "The less you know, the better."

"How can you work for a man like that?" Tricia said.

Mitch shrugged, held the wheel steady. "He's not a bad sort. Most of the time."

"He just killed a man!"

"So?" Mitch honked and swerved around a station wagon that was going too slowly for his taste. "Guy was no prize. Cheated on his wife. Played lousy music."

Tricia didn't answer. It wasn't lousy music. But that hardly seemed like the point most worth arguing about right now.

"I never did anything to him," Tricia said finally. "Charley and Erin didn't, and god knows Cor—Colleen didn't."

"Yeah?" Mitch said. "That's not what it sounded like to me."

"What do you mean?"

Mitch raised his eyebrows, let them fall, kept his eyes on the road. "Sounded to me like she did plenty. Little leather box, and all."

"Were you listening? At the door?"

"Could be," Mitch said.

Tricia pinched the bridge of her nose between her fingers. She could feel the beginnings of a bad headache.

"You heard everything?"

"You think your sister really had her baby in a taxi, or she was just pulling your leg?"

"So why didn't you say anything to your boss? To Uncle Nick?"

He shrugged again. "I would've, if I'd had to. I was waiting to see what you'd do."

"What I'd do."

"Would you offer to go get the photos. I knew he wouldn't let you go alone."

"And you wanted to be with me…why?"

"Think about it," Mitch said.

"The photos," Tricia said. "Incriminating photos of his own men. Are some of them photos of you?"

"Could be," Mitch said.

Something dawned on Tricia. "You're the one. The one she recognized."

"Saw it in her eyes as soon as I picked her up in the ring," Mitch said. "I was saying to myself, how the hell does this twist know me? I never saw her before in my life. Well."

"And you want, what, when we get the pictures you'll take yours out before we give them to Nicolazzo? Won't that be a little obvious?"

"We'll take a few out. Not just mine."

"That's fine for you," Tricia said. "But what about me and my friends? He'll say I'm holding out on him, that I welshed on our deal."

"Just tell him that's all you found," Mitch said.

"He'll kill us!"

"You?" Mitch said. "With how well you dance? He won't kill you."

"My sister—"

"Why would he want to lose a good fighter?" Mitch said. "She brings in a decent gate."

"But Charley and Erin—"

He shrugged once more. "You can't have everything."

"I'm not going to let him hurt them," Tricia said.

"The man lost three million dollars. He's got to hurt someone."

"What if I tell him you made me give you the photos of you," Tricia said.

"I'd say you were lying," Mitch said, "and that he should beat the truth out of you."

They were nearing the end of the bridge, slowing as they approached the turn-off for Second Avenue.

"But there's no reason it needs to come to that," Mitch said, flipping on his turn signal. "You've got nothing to gain by—hey!"

Tricia had been inching her fingers toward the door handle and now had turned and in one swift movement tugged up the door lock, unlatched the door, and dived out onto the macadam. She fell on her shoulder and rolled twice, narrowly missing being run over by the station wagon behind them. The other driver leaned on his horn angrily and a few more cars joined in. She saw the door of Mitch's car still swinging open. The car came squealing to a halt.

She got up, ran to the concrete barrier at the side of the bridge. A few yards away she would've been looking down a hundred feet at the cold and unforgiving surface of the East River, but here it was just a twenty foot drop to the 60th Street underpass. She climbed onto the barrier, turned, and let herself down carefully, dangling by her fingertips before allowing herself to drop. For a second she was falling through the air. Then she hit the sidewalk and sprawled backwards onto her rump. Looking up she saw Mitch's face appear above the barrier. The honking had become a full-on chorus, drivers angry at this wiseacre who'd left his car standing in the exit lane, blocking their way.

"Get back here," Mitch shouted, aiming a long arm down at her, finger extended like Uncle Sam. He started to climb over the barrier and she scrambled to her feet, ready to run—then she saw a hand appear at Mitch's shoulder, a wooden nightstick protruding from it.

"Mister," came the cop's voice, shouting to be heard over the cacophony, "what do you think you're doing?"

"My—my wife, officer, she just—she jumped over—"

Tricia ducked under one of the bridge's huge concrete stanchions.

"I don't see anyone," the cop said a moment later.

"But she just…"

"You been drinking, mister? Let's see that car of yours."

Tricia couldn't hear Mitch's response as the two of them walked away. But she thought about that car of his. If she had any luck, the cop would ask to look in the trunk. *Get rid of the stiff*, Nicolazzo had said. Robbie hadn't been in the back seat; he had to be somewhere.

Come on, she said to herself, you're New York's finest, look in the goddamn trunk.

She dusted off her palms and started walking, fast as she could, first west to Second Avenue and then south toward her sister's place downtown. She had no money for a taxi, not even for a subway. And she had four miles to walk. At least with the sun down, the heat wasn't so powerful. She opened the top button of her dress. Let a little air in.

Much of the city was shutting down for the night, shopkeepers dragging cartons and signs in from the sidewalk, pulling down metal gates over their plate glass windows. The bars on either side of the avenue, conversely, were coming to life, strains of jukebox music pouring out each time one of their doors swung open, neon lights blinking on overhead.

There was life on the street—pedestrians and loafers, men in their undershirts and trousers taking an evening smoke on the stoop of their apartment buildings, cars motoring by at a casual pace. This was a neighborhood of four- and five-story brick buildings inhabited by working men and women, restaurant staff and seamstresses, dockworkers and laundry workers, Irish mostly; and those as were still out of doors gave her the eye as she passed, one or two of the men whistling low, one throwing her a loud kiss. She was used to it, and most nights it wouldn't have bothered her, but tonight it added to her feeling of straining toward a goal and not making progress, like she was walking through sand or mud or in a dream. Cornelia Street was far away, in the city's lower reaches, and here she was walking through a darkening forest of hungry-eyed men with bare arms and puckered lips. The El had run here once, she knew, its metal tracks casting the whole of the avenue into darkness; and though it had been demolished nearly twenty years back, as night fell it was almost as if you were still walking under its shadow, listening with half an ear for the clattering roar of ghost cars overhead.

As she passed 49th Street, a man fell into step beside her; she glanced and for a moment was relieved to see the blue of his uniform—but only for a moment.

"You all right, miss?" the flatfoot said.

"Yes, sir," Tricia said. She tried to keep her voice even, her head down.

"This isn't a neighborhood for a girl to go walking alone."

"I'm just a couple of blocks from home," Tricia said, resisting the urge to walk faster, to try to get away. How many more steps would she get before he took a good look at her face and recognized her from the bulletin O'Malley must have circulated? When would he put out a hand and stop her, leaving her the choice of running for it or heading off to jail?

She felt a trail of perspiration forming along her spine and prayed it didn't show.

"I'm fine—thank you," Tricia said. "You don't need to walk with me."

He stopped, and against every impulse urging her on, she stopped as well, tried to appear casual, at ease, not twitch under his stare.

Had she gone too far? Should she apologize? She was on the verge of doing so when the policeman tipped his cap to her and said, "All right, miss. Have it your way." He fell behind as she walked on. She glanced back and saw him peering into a parked car, going on with his rounds.

Thank you, she whispered to herself, for blind policemen, thank you. Only please let the one on the bridge have been more observant.

The streets passed, one by one, and her legs grew sore from exertion, but she didn't stop, didn't even slow, didn't dare. Somewhere down by Washington Square Park, a three-year-old boy was waiting for his mother to come home; and a box of photographs that could send who knew how many men to jail was sitting out on a table or hidden behind the public toilet tank down the hall or waiting in the dust under the bed. If the cops had let Mitch go—and they might have, they easily might have— he'd be heading down there as well, and faster than she could hope to make it. He didn't have an address, but Cornelia Street was only one block long, maybe a dozen buildings on either side—he didn't need an address, just time enough to canvass them all. And he surely had money with him; and he had a car; and his gun, he had that, too.

Oh, please, she thought, please let them at least have found his gun. Let them have locked him up tight, and no phone call back to Uncle Nick in Queens, not yet.

But Tricia had limited confidence in the value of prayers. So she walked, fast as she could, through the night.

17.

A Touch of Death

The lights were on in all the second- and third-story windows, and in one or two of the storefronts besides: a pagoda-roofed restaurant on the corner of Cornelia and Bleecker, a 24-hour laundry halfway down the block. Tricia made her way to the grey stone building near West 4th where the taxi from the train station had dropped her off what felt like such a long time ago. The hand-lettered

NO VACANCIES sign was still—or again—in the window by the front door. She looked around for Mitch, or Bruno, or anyone of comparable appearance, but there was no one in sight. Except for a collarless dog sniffing at one of the sidewalk's scrawny trees, the block was empty.

Which either meant she was in time or that she was too late.

Tricia leaned on the buzzer till she could hear footsteps approaching from the other side and didn't release it until she heard the cover slide away from the peephole. She stepped back so the person looking out could see more than the top of her head.

"I'm Colleen King's sister," she said. "Trixie…Trixie King."

"Not here," came a woman's voice, accented as much from cigarette smoke as from what sounded like some sort of Eastern European upbringing.

"I know, I was just with her, she asked me to come by, give something to her son. To Artie." When there was no response, she added, "Please, I've walked a long way."

Whether that was what did it she'd never know—but the locks turned and the door swung open. Behind it a woman no taller than Tricia but quite a bit older stood in a flower-print wrapper, hairnet over a tangle of grey curls, slippers on her feet. She had the doorknob in one hand, the burning stub of a Marlboro between the knuckles of the other.

"You sister?" She drew deeply on the cigarette, consuming half its remaining length in one pull. "She look nothing like you."

"She takes after our mother," Tricia said. "May I go up to her room?"

"You have key?"

Tricia nodded, hoping the woman wouldn't ask her to produce it.

"Okay," the woman said. "Is 3D, like Duck. But child is in 3F. Like Fox."

"Thank you," Tricia said, wondering what sort of zoo-based primer the woman had used when learning English. She made her way to the staircase in the corner of the room. The woman retreated to a doorway near the foot of the stairs where she smoked the remnant of her cigarette and watched Tricia climb with a look on her face that seemed caught halfway between suspicion and apathy.

When she reached the third floor, Tricia went from door to door, scanning the heavy brass letters screwed into the wood—'A' like Alligator, 'B' like Bat. She tried the knob at D-like-Duck, but it was locked. 'F' was across the hall and she knocked briskly.

"Sh," a voice came, a husky whisper. "You'll wake him." The knob gently turned and the door swung slowly ajar, a soft creak escaping from the hinges despite all the care to avoid it. A scarred face appeared in the opening, the pink and white of old burns on both plump cheeks and across her chin. It was a face Tricia recognized from the Sun, from one of the times she'd visited the club early to scope it out while plotting Chapter 10. Tricia had even put her in the chapter, given her a little cameo to address the lousy treatment she'd seen her bear at the hands of the other girls on the cleaning crew.

"Heaven," Tricia said. "I didn't know you lived here."

"What are you doing here, then?" Heaven LaCroix spoke English with only the faintest hint of a Belgian accent, having come over on a refugee ship at age seven. She stood just half a head taller than Tricia but she was as broad across the shoulders as Coral; she had the arms, too, thick and muscled.

"It's a long story," Tricia said, "and it's probably going to sound crazy to you, but I'm Colleen's sister—I know, we don't look anything alike. But it's true. And she's in trouble. I need to get into her room, get something she left there. You've got a key, right? You must, if you take care of Artie."

"Now hold on," Heaven said, stepping out into the hallway and pulling the door shut behind her. She was wearing a heavy robe, something frilly peeking out at the collar, like she'd been in bed when Tricia knocked. "I don't know you, except that you dance for a living and ask a lot of questions. That time you came by, I almost got in trouble myself, you kept me so long with your questions."

"I'm sorry, Heaven, I was just new and curious about a lot of things."

"I'll say." Heaven crossed her arms over her chest. "Now you want to get into my friend's room and you've got a story about how you're her sister, but how am I supposed to know that's so? You could be anybody. You could be working for Mrs. Barrone, for all I know."

"I don't know anyone named Barrone," Tricia said, though she realized as she said it that it wasn't true: Nicolazzo's sister had married a man named Barrone, had raised two daughters also named Barrone: the unfortunate Adelaide, victim of a malarial fever in North Africa, and her older sister...Renata? Tricia thought that's what she'd read in the *News*. Something like Renata, anyway.

"I'd show you my birth certificate if I had it," Tricia said, "but I don't. I don't have anything on me other than what you see. All I can tell you is that the man who runs the Sun has Colleen locked up right now because he thinks she stole something from him and he wants it back. He let me out to come here and get it. If I don't bring it back to him in the next hour or so, he's going to hurt her real bad, maybe even kill her. You want her son to grow up without a mother?"

"You're really something," Heaven said, "you know that? Even if I believed you I still couldn't let you rummage around Colleen's room, taking things, without her telling me it's okay."

"She can't tell you," Tricia said, "she's locked in a cellar somewhere in Queens."

"Where?"

Tricia sighed. "I don't know exactly. Somewhere just the other side of the river."

"Well, if you don't know exactly, how're you going to get whatever it is you want to get from Colleen's room back to her?"

It was one hell of a good question and it stopped Tricia in her tracks. Without Mitch, she had no way back.

She opened her mouth to answer, not sure what she was going to say—but before she could get a word out, a pounding came at the front door, loud enough that they heard it two stories up. Tricia crept to the staircase, listened over the banister as the woman downstairs opened the door.

"Excuse me, ma'am," came a man's voice, "but have you seen a young woman come by tonight, about so tall, blonde hair—"

Tricia stepped back from the staircase. Try to look at the bright side, she said to herself. At least now you have a way back.

"Quick," she whispered, and tugged Heaven with her toward Coral's room. "You've got to let me in. That's one of the men who's holding Colleen." And when she didn't budge, "Heaven, he's got a gun." They heard heavy steps on the stairs, coming up. "A gun, Heaven. He'll kill us both."

"No he won't," Heaven said. "You just keep calm."

Mitch's head emerged above the top step, then his shoulders and his torso and, held at the level of his waist, his clenched gun hand. The barrel of his revolver was pointing directly at them.

"You think you're clever, don't you," he said to Tricia. Then, to Heaven, who was standing in front of her, "Out of the way, Scarface."

"You put that gun down, mister," Heaven said, "and we can talk about this like civilized people."

Mitch raised his gun till it was aimed directly at her head. She didn't flinch, just looked sad, dug her hands into the pockets of her robe. "I'm sorry, mister," she said.

"That's all right," Mitch said, "just go back in your room and forget you saw anything."

"No, I'm sorry for what I have to do," Heaven said and, pulling a Luger from the pocket of her robe, shot him twice in the chest.

18.

Say It With Bullets

Four or five things happened then, all at once, it seemed: A child's voice rose behind the door of 3-F, wailing like a police car siren; doors swung open up and down the hall, then shut again when the people behind them saw Mitch tumble forward, his gun striking the floor and discharging, sending a bullet speeding at ankle level into the far wall; Heaven grabbed up Mitch's gun and stowed it with her own in the pocket of her robe; and more footsteps began pounding up the stairs, two or three people's worth.

"Here," Heaven said, and unlocked the door to 3-D. She shoved it open with the heel of one hand and stepped back. "Get him in there, close the door, stay inside. Don't take anything. I've got to see to Artie."

Slightly dazed, Tricia lugged Mitch's body into the room, left it lying beside a potted plant and a stack of old magazines. She had to bend his knees to get the door to close. It looked uncomfortable, but the man was past complaining.

Staying in the room wasn't much of an option. There was a trail of blood outside leading right to this door—she could hardly expect to hide here. But at least while she was here she could look for what she'd come to find.

There was an icebox in one corner of the room and a small chest of drawers in another. She opened each of these in turn and found no leather box and no photos. A vaguely rectangular object in the icebox turned out to be the re-frozen remnants of a Swanson TV dinner. (There was no TV in the room, Tricia noted—but then 98 cents for the dinner was a lot easier to scrape together than the 98 dollars it would cost for a television set to eat it in front of.) The drawers held blouses and skirts and scanties with labels from Orbach's; they held a necklace and ear-ring set with plastic beads that didn't look much like pearls but were clearly supposed to; they held a slim bible and a New York City telephone book. But no box, no photos.

Tricia riffled quickly through the pages of the bible and the phone book and then, one by one, the magazines. There were footsteps outside and a babble of voices and some knocking on doors, Coral's and others. She ignored it all. She got down on her hands and knees and peered under the bed—nothing. She pulled up the coverlet and the sheet under it, stripped the cases off the pillows, lifted the corners of the mattress. What else? What else? There was a tiny, shallow closet that took just a minute to search thoroughly. A night table with some makeup on it. A rug with no suspicious bulges showing. She lifted it anyway, let it drop. Damn it, where would Coral have left the box?

There was one window in the room, shaded by vene-

tian blinds and a curtain, and she pulled the latter and
raised the former. Outside, a rusted fire escape led up
and down. On the windowsill behind the curtain Tricia
spotted a metal key ring with a pair of keys on it, together
with a plastic disk embossed with the name and address
of a local garage: ROYAL AUTO STORAGE (TUNEUPS—
REPAIRS—SUPPLIES—24 HOURS). Which made no
sense—what would a single woman living in Manhattan
need with a car? And where would someone who couldn't
afford a TV set find the money to buy one?

The knocking at the door was louder now, and the
landlady's voice called out, "The police has been called,
young lady. You better open door."

What Tricia opened was the window. Pocketing the key
ring, she climbed out onto the fire escape, taking a second
to draw the curtain, lower the blinds behind her, and pull
the window down as far as she could from the outside.

A choice loomed. Up or down? The sound of a police
siren coming around the corner decided it for her: Down
would put her right in the path of their headlights.

Tricia shot up the metal steps, one hand to her hip to
keep the keys from jingling in the pocket of her dress.
She thought about Heaven as she went, still trying to
digest what had happened. Where had the gun come
from? You heard about people bringing trophies back
from the war, and a German gun, well, that could certainly have been someone's trophy. But this one hadn't
just been polished up and left on a shelf, it had been
loaded and ready. This was clearly a tool, not a conversation piece, and what's more, Heaven must've had it close
at hand, to be able to jam it in her pocket when a knock
came out of the blue. What other secrets was she hiding?
Hell—had she been working at the Sun the same afternoon Coral nabbed the box out of Nicolazzo's safe?
Somebody had taken the money—and Tricia could cer-

tainly see Heaven LaCroix lugging fifty or sixty pounds without breaking a sweat.

But she'd seemed so decent—

Yeah, said a little voice in Tricia's head, she seemed decent until she shot a man dead in front of you.

But that was self-defense—

Yeah, said the voice. Still.

Tricia reached the top of the fire escape and climbed the narrow metal ladder leading up from there to the roof of the building. She threw one leg over the edge of the cornice. Before she could follow it with the other she heard an amplified voice from the street below.

"You! Freeze!"

She hesitated a moment, half on the ladder, half on the roof, her dress up around her thighs. Glancing back and down, she saw a pair of policemen, hunched behind their open car doors, guns drawn and pointing up toward her. One had a bullhorn in his other hand.

"Come on down, lady, nice and easy, we don't want to have to shoot you."

Well, that was all well and good, since Tricia didn't want to be shot. But she didn't want to be arrested either, particularly now that the charges against her had presumably escalated from assaulting a police officer to manslaughter. She heaved her other leg up and over and an instant later heard bullets splintering the stone of the wall the ladder was anchored to.

Well, that was one way to send the message that they meant business.

Staying on her hands and knees, she crawled past a huge ventilation fan in a dented tin housing, crossing to the rear of the building. The wall separating this building from the next one over was barely a separation at all, just a few rows of bricks that Tricia went over like a champion high-jumper. She didn't hear any more gunshots, at least, so she took a chance and rose from her knees, scampering across the next roof in a low crouch, a little like Groucho Marx if Groucho Marx had been running for his life across a tenement roof.

Another low wall, past it another roof—but now Tricia was running out of buildings and pretty soon would have to find some way down. The current roof was covered with tarpaper and stank from the tar, still tacky from a day in the sun. A little shed marked the top of the stairwell and Tricia wrenched the door open, listened for footsteps before starting to descend. She only heard her own until she reached the second floor landing, at which point her steps were joined by the sound of another pair, coming up. She darted out into the second floor corridor and started trying all the apartment doorknobs, one by one. The third one she tried turned, and she stepped inside as the service door to the stairwell sprang open, banging against the far wall.

She looked around desperately. This apartment did have a television set and it was on, showing the tail end of an *Ellery Queen* episode. All the lamps in the place were burning. Whoever lived here clearly had just stepped out for a minute, perhaps to pick up his laundry in the basement or a pack of cigarettes around the corner. Or maybe he was in the bathroom and would appear any moment—

The knock at the door was brisk and professional, not an assault on the wood the way Mitch's had been at the rooming house. A peek out the peephole showed a policeman in full regalia—but not, she thought, one of the pair who'd been shooting at her. Tricia took a deep breath. How would Borden do it? she asked herself.

She opened the door.

19.

Witness to Myself

"Oh, officer, I'm so glad to see you, it was terrible," Tricia said, reaching out to grip the policeman's hands tightly in her own. "This woman came by, just a minute ago, all wild-eyed and upset. She asked me to let her in, but I said no, I couldn't, my husband's not home and I couldn't let a stranger in. Who is she? What has she done?"

The officer, whose nameplate said LENAHAN, drew his hands back and took the regulation notepad off his belt. He was a young man, maybe two, three years older than Tricia, and she could see in his eyes that he still had the impulse to comfort, to ease suffering. How many cops had that impulse, Tricia wondered. Most of them, probably, the year they joined the force; none of them, probably, a few years later.

"It's okay, ma'am," Lenahan said, "we've got half a dozen men from the Sixth on the scene and more on their way. She's not going to escape."

"Oh, good," Tricia said. "That's a relief."

"Just stay inside and if anyone comes to your door other than a policeman, don't open it, understand?"

Tricia nodded. She understood.

"Now, what can you tell us about this woman—how tall would you say she was?"

"Oh, taller than me," Tricia said, "maybe your height." The cop was nearly six feet.

"What color hair?"

"Brown," Tricia said. "Light brown, like, um, hazelnut."

"Hazelnut," Lenahan said, and wrote it in his book. "Eyes?"

"I didn't notice, I'm sorry."

"That's okay. How much would you say she weighed?"

"I don't know. More than me. She was quite large in the—in the chest, if you know what I mean." She dipped her eyes demurely.

"In the chest," Lenahan said as he wrote.

"Oh, and officer, she had a limp, like maybe one leg was shorter than the other."

"Or maybe one of our men winged her with one of his shots," Lenahan speculated.

"Sure. Maybe," Tricia said, and thought of Mitch. *Could be*, he'd have said. *Could be*.

"Anything else you noticed? This is very helpful."

Tricia tried to think of something else she might have noticed. "Her ears—there was something funny about them. Really long earlobes."

"Oh, yeah?" Lenahan's hand hung above his pad, not writing.

What? Was that too much? "Well, I don't know," Tricia said. "They looked long to me. But I only got a quick look."

He wrote it down. "And what was she wearing? I have it here she's in a blue dress and, um, wide-heeled pumps."

"Oh, no, I wouldn't say blue, more like grey, actually."

A new voice emerged behind her: "Would you? Grey? Didn't you think it was closer to navy?"

She turned, saw a young man in his shirtsleeves, wiping his hands on a paper towel. She smiled at him hopefully, tried to send a signal without being too obvious about it. *Please, mister, play along.*

He smiled back at her.

"Or teal?" he said, coming forward. He dropped the crumpled paper towel on a side table.

"Sure, teal," Tricia said.

"I thought you said your husband wasn't home," Lenahan said.

"Oh, he's not. This is my cousin. Jim. Jim, this is Officer Lenahan of the Sixth Precinct."

Cousin Jim reached out a hand, shook Lenahan's when he extended it.

"Pleased to meet you, Officer Lenahan," he said. "I've never seen this woman before in my life."

20.

Bust

Lenahan had her in cuffs before she could even voice a protest, hands behind her back. He patted her down, apologizing for it first, but doing it all the same. She hadn't imagined that the first time she'd let a man touch her all over would be like this. Even when handcuffs were involved, it somehow seemed so much sexier in the books she'd read.

"Hazelnut," Lenahan muttered as he swiftly went up her left leg and down her right, pat pat pat. "Large in the chest." He streaked his fingertips along her shoulder blades and down her spine. "Excuse me," he said as he felt her backside, her hips, around in front. "It'd be better if I had a matron here to do this, but I don't, and we're required to search suspects thoroughly."

"What do you think I could hide down there, a gun?" Tricia said, and he blushed—for a moment he actually blushed.

"It may sound foolish to you, miss, but they teach us in the academy about women who've concealed more than you might think."

"Doesn't sound foolish, just painful."

"Well, there you go. Good thing you didn't do it, then. Come on." He guided her by the shoulder toward the stairs and they descended to the ground floor together.

"What are you going to do with me?"

"I'm going to hand you off to a senior officer," Lenahan said. "He's going to take you to central booking and get you processed. I'm sure they'll make it as quick and painless as they can."

"And then," Tricia said, "you'll lock me up?"

"You're a wanted fugitive, miss. You'll be a guest of the state till your case is resolved."

Tricia thought of Charley and Erin and Coral, trapped with Nicolazzo, not to mention with Bruno. How long before Nicolazzo lost his patience and began taking it out on them? How long before he heard about Mitch?

"Officer," Tricia said, "I need to talk to someone before you lock me up—my sister is in serious danger, she's being held captive by a fugitive much worse than me—"

"Miss, please," Lenahan said. "You'll have your chance to tell your story, I promise."

"But not in time! Please, he's going to kill her—"

Lenahan nodded politely, but he wasn't listening. He'd been snookered by her once; he wasn't going to fall for it again.

He walked her out through the building's front door, down a few steps to the sidewalk and over toward a police car parked at an angle to the curb. There was a crowd in the street, cops and ordinary citizens attracted by the sound of gunfire. Down the block she saw Coral's building, where the biggest mass of people was.

A figure came toward them out of a narrow alleyway between buildings, a policeman with captain's bars on his jacket and his cap pulled down low. The jacket hung a little loose on him, Tricia thought, like he'd lost weight recently; funny, the things you think about at a time like this.

He strode up to Lenahan, put one hand out to stop him. "Nice going, officer," he said in a broad Bronx accent. "I'll take it from here."

"Captain," Tricia said, "you've got to listen to me, my sister's life is in danger—"

"Shut up," the captain said. And when she kept talking he turned to face her, raised his cap for a second and drew a finger along his lips. "Zip it."

She dropped silent in the middle of her sentence.

"She's the one we're looking for," Lenahan said, "I'm sure of it. I caught her in an apartment she'd broken into—"

"That's excellent police work," the captain said. "I'll make sure you're recognized for it. Now hand her over. I'll take full responsibility."

"Thank you, sir. My name's Lenahan, sir, Bill Lenahan."

"All right, Lenahan. You'll get a commendation for this." He reached out for Tricia's arm.

"Is there anything else you need, Captain…" Lenahan leaned forward to look at the captain's nameplate, but it was half covered by his jacket's lapel. "Captain…?"

"Um," the captain said.

Tricia bent to peer under the lapel. "Clohessy," she read.

"Clohessy," the captain said.

"Is there anything…?" Lenahan said, looking only slightly more puzzled than he had when Tricia had told him about the long earlobes.

"Yes, there is," said Captain Clohessy, pulling Tricia out of Lenahan's grasp. "I want you to go over there," he pointed toward the big crowd, "find Sergeant Mulvaney, and tell him I'm taking the suspect downtown."

"Downtown, sir?"

"That's right, downtown. Oh, and Lenahan, let me use your car." He held out a hand for the keys.

"My car, sir?"

"Yes. I can't get mine out, just look at that mob."

"Yes, sir." Lenahan found his car keys and handed them over. The captain snatched them and Lenahan turned to go find Sergeant Mulvaney. "Oh, Lenahan," the captain said, and Lenahan turned back.

"Sir?"

The captain waved at the cars nearest to them. "Which one…?"

"This one, sir," Lenahan said, patting the nearest on the hood.

"Of course," the captain said, and unlocked the door. "Thank you. That's all." And when Lenahan didn't depart, "What are you waiting for?"

"Sir!" Lenahan spun on his heel and dived into the throng, looking for a police sergeant Tricia firmly believed existed only in the realm of imagination.

"My god," she said, but the captain held up a finger in warning.

"In the car." He opened the rear door of the police cruiser and Tricia slid in. Then he climbed behind the wheel, cranked the ignition, backed out, and made the turn onto West 4th.

Tricia waited to speak till she saw Washington Square Park racing past the windows.

"So where's Captain Clohessy?" she finally said.

"Never fear. He's sleeping peacefully, right where I left him."

"And how did you manage to get away from Uncle Nick?"

"It's a funny story," Borden replied.

21.
Straight Cut

Nicolazzo smiled narrowly as he walked Borden to a pair of overstuffed, leather-upholstered armchairs on either side of a glass-topped oval table. He pulled the stiletto, sprang the blade, stepped behind Borden's back, and for a moment Borden feared the worst. But all Nicolazzo used the blade on was the rope holding his hands together, sawing away until it dropped to the ground. Borden rubbed his wrists and when Nicolazzo gestured for him to do so, sat.

"So you're the one published the book," Nicolazzo said.

"What book?" Borden said.

"What book. Very good." Nicolazzo opened the cardboard box the playing cards were in, set it aside, shuffled. "They warned me you were a *rompiculo*." He slid the deck across the table. "Cut."

Borden split the deck in half, set the top half over to the right of the bottom. Nicolazzo reassembled the deck, shuffled again.

"Why would you publish a book like this, revealing a man's private concerns?"

"For money," Borden said.

Nicolazzo nodded. That was reasoning he could understand, could appreciate. "Why not just come to me? I might have paid you not to publish it."

"It's not just this book," Borden said. "I publish one book that's a hit, it puts the whole line on the map."

"I might have paid you not to publish the whole line."

"Or you might have killed me," Borden said. "Saved yourself some money."

"I might kill you now," Nicolazzo said.

"The horse is out of the barn now," Borden said. "What good would killing me now do?"

"Maybe it would just make me feel better," Nicolazzo said. "Maybe it would keep some other *farabutto* from screwing with me next time."

"What's a *farabutto*?"

"You," Nicolazzo said. "You're a *farabutto*. And—" he glanced at his watch "—for the next fifty minutes or so, you're a live *farabutto*. After that…" He raised his shoulders expressively, let them fall. "So, canasta? Rummy? Or you like something simpler?"

"Simple is always nice," Borden said.

Nicolazzo slapped the cards down. "Straight cut. High card wins."

"How much?" Borden said.

"How much can you afford? Hundred bucks a point?"

Borden, who couldn't afford one buck a point, said, "Sure." He divided the deck into two parts, roughly equal.

Nicolazzo pushed the top two cards off the bottom half with a plump index finger. "Choose," he said.

Borden looked at the backs of the two cards, scrutinized them as though the intricate pattern could reveal something to him about what was on the other side. Finally he flipped one face up. Two of diamonds.

Nicolazzo turned over the other card. Seven of clubs. "You owe me five hundred dollars."

"I thought you said one hundred," Borden said.

"One hundred a point. Seven minus two is five points. Five hundred. Do you disagree?"

Borden shook his head. Nicolazzo gathered up the cards, shuffled again, slapped them down. "Cut," he said.

Borden cut, Nicolazzo slid two cards forward, and

Borden turned over the jack of hearts. Nicolazzo turned over the queen of hearts. "One point," Nicolazzo said. "That's one hundred dollars. For a total of six hundred. Double or nothing?"

"What the hell," Borden said. "Double or nothing."

Half an hour later, Borden was forty thousand dollars in the hole and still plunging, no bottom in sight.

"At this rate," Borden said, "you'll have your three million back before the night's out."

"That assumes you have three million to lose," Nicolazzo said, "which I'm betting you don't."

"You're right about that," Borden said. "But what if I told you I knew who did?"

"My three million?"

"Your three million."

Nicolazzo pushed the deck toward him. Borden cut it and Nicolazzo fingered off two cards. By this point, they could do it without talking, without even paying much attention. Borden turned over the four of clubs, Nicolazzo the nine of spades. Eighty thousand.

"Quite the losing streak," Nicolazzo said. "You haven't gotten one right yet."

Borden shrugged. "Happens."

"So," Nicolazzo said, "where's my money?"

"You may find this surprising," Borden said, "but I don't keep eighty thousand dollars in my wallet."

"Not that money," Nicolazzo said. "The three million dollars this Judas took from me."

"Ah, yes. That money." Borden fingered the cards thoughtfully. "Well, I may not be winning right now, but I'm sure you'll agree I don't owe you that much quite yet."

Nicolazzo leaned forward across the table, glared at Borden ominously. "Where's my money? You don't want to play games with me."

"I thought you liked games," Borden said. "Canasta and all."

"If you don't tell me right now—"

"I'll tell you what I'll do," Borden said. "Let's cut for it. Make a little wager. Three million dollars if you win."

"You're not serious."

"Why not?" Borden said.

Nicolazzo thought about it. "And if you win?"

"I walk out of here right now," Borden said, "and you don't stop me. You don't touch me. You don't get that bruiser of yours to stop me and you don't send him after me. I win and we're even. I don't owe you the eighty thousand, I don't owe you anything." Charley leaned in, matched Nicolazzo stare for stare. "Or are you scared to risk that much on a hand of cards?"

Nicolazzo raised a meaty fist, shook it at Borden. "Salvatore Nicolazzo," he said in a strangled voice, "is not afraid of any bet."

Borden pushed the cards toward him. "Then shuffle, big man."

Nicolazzo snatched up the cards, violently riffled them together. It sounded like a string of firecrackers going off. "All right, Borden," he said. "All right. But we play my game now. No more straight cut. We play Fifty-to-One, eh?"

"You give your word on the stakes?" Borden said.

"Absolutely. If you win, you walk out of here. But you won't win. And if you don't win, you'll tell me where my money is, and you'll tell me who took it, or I will cut your hands and feet off, I'll take your eyes out, I'll feed you your *coglioni*, and then, when you beg me on your knees to kill you, I will kindly and lovingly slit your throat. Do we understand each other, Mr. Borden?"

Borden swallowed, nodded.

"So." Nicolazzo set the cards down gently, squared up

the edges of the deck. He flipped the top card face up. It was the four of spades. He set it aside. He looked at Borden, waited with a vicious and self-satisfied smile on his face.

"What do I do?" Borden said.

"It's very simple, Borden," Nicolazzo said. He tapped his index finger on the back of the topmost card on the deck. "You just tell me what this card is."

"What do you mean what that card is?" Borden said. "How am I supposed to know? That's ridiculous."

"It's not ridiculous," Nicolazzo said. "You've got fifty chances to be wrong, one chance to be right. Fifty-to-one. Now name your card."

Borden stared at the deck.

"I'm waiting," Nicolazzo said.

Borden stared some more.

"Say *something*, Borden."

"Six of diamonds," Borden said.

Nicolazzo shoved the top card forward, dug a thumbnail under it, flipped it over.

Both men stared at it.

Borden smiled weakly.

"Fare un bidone—" Nicolazzo sputtered.

Borden stood, walked quickly to the door.

22.

Lemons Never Lie

"You just *left* them there?" Tricia said. "Erin and Coral, with Nicolazzo fuming like that—"

Borden glanced at her in the rear-view mirror. "You think it'd be better if I was still locked up with them?"

"Maybe," Tricia said.

"And who's this 'Coral'?"

"My sister."

"Your sister," Borden said.

"Yes. And god only knows what he's doing to her right now, and to Erin, thanks to you."

"He'd be doing it to me, too, if I were there," Borden said. "This way we at least have a chance."

"You took an awful risk," Tricia said, "using marked cards. That's what you did, isn't it?"

"You don't believe I just got lucky?"

"No, and Nicolazzo shouldn't either. You went through how many straight cuts with him and didn't guess right even once? That's as improbable as if you'd guessed right every time. He should have been tipped off by that alone."

Borden thought about it. "You're right," he said. "I should've given myself one or two."

"How long till he figures it out? You know he's not going to feel obliged to keep his word once he does. And now he thinks you know where his money is!"

"All true," Borden said, "but at least I'm here and not there, and he's there and not here, and I got you out of the bind you were in, so you know, I'd say we're not doing too bad."

"I'm handcuffed in the back seat of a stolen police car," Tricia said, "driving god knows where, you're wanted for assaulting *two* policemen now and impersonating one of them, I'm probably wanted for murder—"

"Murder?"

"Mitch," Tricia said, "got shot. I didn't do it. But they think I did—that's what all the cops were there for. And now one of the most bloodthirsty gangsters on the east coast is gunning for us both. That's your idea of not doing too bad?"

"Could be worse," Borden said.

The car's police-band radio, which had been alternating between static and background chatter all the way from Cornelia Street, broke in on them now with a loud announcement: *"All cars, all cars, respond immediately; stolen police vehicle V-J-1-3-9, that's Victor-Jason-1-3-9, spotted going north on First Avenue, use extreme caution, suspects armed and dangerous—"*

"That's us, isn't it?" Tricia said.

"Unless someone else stole a cop car and is joyriding right behind us."

"What are you going to do?"

"I don't know," Borden said.

"Well, you'd better think of something."

"Me? I got us this far, why don't you think of something now?"

Tricia was about to spit back a nasty response when she did, in fact, think of something. "Hold on," she said, and twisted around in the back seat, trying to get her arms around to her side and her dress shifted over so the pocket was within reach. It felt like her shoulders were coming out of their sockets and when the car bumped over a deep pothole the jolt was excruciating. But she kept straining, groping, reaching till her fingers closed on the key ring.

"What are you doing back there?" Borden said, glancing in the mirror again.

"We need to go to…15th Street and Avenue C," she said, reading off the little disk. "But not in this car. Pull over somewhere and we'll go the rest of the way on foot."

"What's there?"

"Other cars," Tricia said, "less conspicuous than this one. Maybe even one we won't have to steal."

"Oh, yeah? Whose?"

"Coral's," Tricia said. "Now just pull over somewhere. And I hope that uniform you grabbed has a pair of handcuff keys on it."

Borden made a hard right onto a side street, swerved over to the curb, left the car parked in front of a fire hydrant. He came around to the back, opened the door and helped Tricia out. Her dress was twisted and crumpled and the two top buttons were gone, leaving a fair expanse showing of what would have been cleavage on a bigger woman. Borden politely pretended not to notice. He had a pair of stubby metal keys ready in his fist and used one to release her from the cuffs Lenahan had cinched on her. She rotated her wrists to get the blood flowing again while Borden tossed the cuffs and keys and his cap and jacket through the car window and onto the front seat.

He left the engine running. "Maybe someone else will steal it and drive it away," he said optimistically, and Tricia breathed a silent prayer that someone would. They needed all the help they could get.

They ran. A couple of blocks east, they spotted the sign for Royal's. It rose, illuminated, above a fenced-in compound filled end-to-end with automobiles. As they got closer, it became increasingly obvious that the garage doubled as a used car lot. The cars were not, for the most part, in good condition—some had visible dents in their hoods or side doors, some were missing hubcaps or headlights, one had a spiderweb of cracks radiating out from a hole in the windshield. But at least the cardboard signs propped on the hoods asked for commensurately modest prices.

And true to the "24 HOURS" claim, the place was open. Tricia waved to catch the eye of the sullen, pear-shaped man stationed by the gate.

"Can you help us find a car?" Tricia asked him, struggling to catch her breath. Glancing back over her shoulder she didn't see anyone in pursuit. Not yet, anyway.

The man unplugged the earpiece of a little transistor Sony from his ear. "What kind you thinking about?"

"Sorry—we're not here to buy. It's my sister's car. I'm just picking it up."

The minimal light of interest that had kindled in his eyes went out. "Keys," he said.

Tricia handed them over. The guy pointed with one pinky at a tiny number impressed into the top rim of each key. "Nineteen H," he said, and Tricia thought, *like Horse*. "That's in the garage." He stretched an arm toward a long, low bunker at the far end of the lot.

"Thank you," Tricia said, but he'd already returned to listening to his program on the radio.

The garage door was open. Just inside, a man with a cap of black hair and a pencil moustache sat behind a wooden desk, flipping pages in this week's issue of *Look* and listening to Norman Vincent Peale on a little Sony of his own. He flicked it off when he saw them approach.

"Ah, the happy couple," the man said, springing to his feet. "Sir, madam. Looking for a starter, a budget or economy car, to get you through that tough first year? Then you're in the right place, let me tell you."

"We're not—" Tricia said, but he waved away her objection before she could even finish uttering it, a habit you got the sense he'd formed long ago, as a sort of survival instinct.

"Please, allow me. I won't try to sell you anything, you needn't worry. Consider me a friend. I'll show you some of the options you have and then if you decide to buy elsewhere, well, you'll have my blessing." He nudged Charley with a companionable elbow. "I don't say it will happen—you won't find a lower price at Schultz's or Greenpoint Ford or, well, anywhere else—but if you decide you prefer to pay more for less, well, that's every man's privilege."

Somewhere in the distance—but not far enough in the distance—a police siren wailed.

"Friend," Charley said, "it's a fine spiel, but save it for the rubes. We're just picking up. Give him the keys, Trixie."

Tricia handed them over, pointed at the little 19-H.

The man's face fell. "Are you quite sure? Even if it's not why you came, while you're here, why not give a thought to—"

"No," Borden said. "Just the car."

"All right. I can see you're a serious man who knows what he wants. I'll bring you the car. But while I'm gone I'll leave you with this thought: In the modern marriage, one car just isn't enough. The lady needs her own—"

"I'm sorry," Borden said, "we're in a bit of a hurry here."

"Well, then, why don't you walk with me? It'll save you some time, and who knows what might catch the lady's eye along the way?"

He placed a feather-light hand at the small of Tricia's back and steered them down a narrow aisle between two tightly packed rows of cars, junkers one and all.

"Now there's a nice Pontiac Streamliner, only ten years old, fewer miles on her than you might think," he said as they passed a decrepit hulk with rust stains the size of dinner plates and a crooked rear bumper.

"No," Borden said.

"Perhaps madam would enjoy the freedom of a fine Ford coupe, like this one with its Flathead V8 engine," the man said, waving at a ragtop whose top literally was in rags.

"No," Borden said.

"Madam," the man said, turning to Tricia, "couldn't you see yourself behind the wheel of—"

"No," Borden said. He pointed to a sign on the wall that said 'D'. "Which way is 'H'?"

The man heaved a deep sigh. Positive thinking only went so far, apparently. "This way," he said.

Tricia couldn't avoid a growing feeling of despair. Seeing all these terrible cars filled her with dread as to what they'd find when they finally got to Coral's. Of course Coral wouldn't have been able to afford anything better—no surprise there. But there were limits. Would the thing even run?

"I see a look of concern in your eyes, madam," the man said, launching one last desperate sally. "Is it perhaps that you fear you're missing out on a great opportunity?"

"Honestly, mister," Tricia said, "meaning no offence, I'm just trying to understand why every car here is in such awful condition."

"Madam," the man said, pulling himself up to his not-too-impressive full height and smoothing back his hair with one hand. "Anyone can sell you a car that looks clean and new and pristine—there's nothing to it. But what does the outer surface tell you about how a machine will run, about what's going on under the hood? Absolutely nothing. Many a fine-looking automobile hides flaws you won't discover till you get it home, and then, well, it's too late, isn't it? We are honest dealers, madam: we put all our cards on the table. Our cars may not look like much and they won't win races—they're more *lemons* than *Le Mans*, if you will. But at least with us you know what you're getting, and at a fair price, too." He shook his head ruefully. "Appearances may deceive, madam. Lemons never lie."

"That's…that's absurd," Tricia sputtered. "You're saying your cars are better because they look just as lousy as they run…?"

By this point Borden had gone ahead and they heard a low whistle from the next row over. "Now that's my kind of lemon," he called. "Kid, get over here."

Rounding the corner, Tricia saw him standing next to a sleek, shiny, new Mark III Lincoln Continental. Not a mark on it.

The salesman followed and when he saw the car his face drained of all color. "Let me see those keys." He read off the number on the keys and grimaced as if making a connection for the first time. "No. No no no. This can't be. That's Miss King's car."

"Yes, that's right," Tricia said brightly, "Colleen King. That's my sister. I'm picking it up for her."

"But—but—" the man said. "Royal gave it to her. He's very particular. He wouldn't want us to let it out into anyone else's hands."

"Royal?" Tricia said.

"The owner here. The boss. It used to be his personal car—he drove it every day."

"But you're saying he gave it to her," Tricia said. "It's hers now."

"Yes, but—"

"And she asked me to bring it to her. She gave me the keys," Tricia said. The man was shaking his head. "Why don't we ask Royal? I'm sure he'll understand."

"We can't do that," he said. "He's not here. Royal's been away the past month—I don't know when he'll be back."

"Well, how's he going to feel," Tricia said, "when he does come back, if he finds out you stopped me from doing what Colleen asked?"

He twitched like an animal caught in a trap.

Finally he threw up his hands, slapped the keys into

Tricia's waiting palm. "It's your neck, lady," he said. "You've got the keys, you do what you want. But let me tell you something. You do *not* want to mess with Royal Barrone."

"Barrone?" Tricia said.

"It's your neck," the man repeated and hightailed it out of sight.

23.

The Last Quarry

While Borden drove, first onto the F.D.R. and then north along the rim of Manhattan, Tricia straightened her hair in the lighted fold-down mirror on the passenger side. The ride was smooth and silent, the seats plush and supple. It hardly felt like they were moving, yet outside the windows the world swept past in a blur.

"Where are we going?" she said, touching a fingertip to the corner of her mouth to fix a spot where her rouge had smeared.

"Who cares?" Borden said. "Anywhere's better than where we were."

"You know how to get us back to Nicolazzo's place?"

"Sure, corner of Van Dam and Greenpoint, near the cemetery. But why would we go there?"

"My sister's there," Tricia said. "So's Erin. You want to get them out, don't you?"

"Sure," Borden said, with all the conviction of a soldier told to exit the nice, comfortable foxhole he's been cowering in. "But driving up to the front door with no plan and no resources is not a way to get them out. It's just a way to get us captured, too."

"Fine. So where are we going?"

"How about finding this Barrone? He obviously likes your sister, if he gave her this car; and the way that guy acted back there, Barrone must pull some weight. Maybe he'll help us."

"Yeah, but, see, that makes no sense," Tricia said. "If he's who I think he is, he'd have no reason to like Coral, and every reason to like Nicolazzo."

"Why's that? Who is he?"

"Nicolazzo's brother-in-law."

Borden drove on in silence for a while.

"His brother-in-law," he said.

"Yes."

"Nicolazzo's—"

"Brother-in-law. His sister married a man named Barrone. Who else could it be?"

"There's probably more than one Barrone in New York City," Borden said.

"Probably."

"But you think this one's the same one…"

"Don't you?"

Borden reluctantly nodded. "So what's Barrone's connection with…what's your sister's name anyway, Coral or Colleen?"

"What's your name, Carter or Charley?"

"Touché," Borden said. "Let's just call her Colleen, then. What's Colleen's connection to Barrone?"

"I'd have said there isn't one," Tricia said, "except that when I went to her apartment, the neighbor who watches her son accused me of working for Mrs. Barrone. Made it pretty clear that Mrs. Barrone, at least, is no friend of Colleen's."

"Aha," Borden said. "The mister is, the missus isn't—classic case of hot pants in the Barrone household?"

Tricia considered this. "Wouldn't be the first one. Robbie Monge was married to the Barrones' daughter, and he was unfaithful—that's what Nicolazzo said, anyway. Before he killed him."

"Runs in the family, then. Like father, like son-in-law."

"But why my sister? How would Barrone even have known her?"

"You said she worked at Nicolazzo's clubs," Borden said. "If Barrone's part of the family, he'd probably have shown up from time to time—maybe he even has some sort of role in them, owns a piece or something. Not hard to imagine them meeting."

"And then…"

"Exactly. And then. Like Cole Porter wrote. Birds do it, bees do it."

Tricia shuddered. "He must be sixty years old!"

"What, you think you won't want company in bed any more when you're sixty?" Borden looked over at her, and she hoped that in the darkness he couldn't see she was blushing. She was grateful when he turned back to the road.

"I see," he said. "There hasn't been a Mister Trixie yet, has there."

"I've had plenty of boyfriends," Tricia said. "Back home."

"I'm sure—to share malteds with at the soda shoppe, hold hands at the drive-in. It's okay. I understand. Things don't move quite as fast in South Dakota."

"I'll have you know," Tricia said, coldly, "things move plenty fast in South Dakota. Boys have more hands there than a wall of clocks. Coral had to—*Colleen* had to beat 'em off with a stick."

"Oh, is that what she used?" Borden said, and Tricia felt herself blushing again.

"There's no need to be vulgar, Mr. Borden," Tricia said.

"Charley," Borden said. "Call me Charley. Everything

we've been through together, we should be on a first-name basis."

Tricia looked down at her hands. "Tricia," she said.

"Tricia," Charley said, as they tooled along the highway at a whisper. "Pleased to meet you."

He reached out a hand and patted hers, and for the first time in a long time she felt a bit of relief, a trace— just a trace—of comfort. She wasn't in this alone.

But the moment passed. Charley took his hand away and said, "So. Barrone. Where are we going to find him?"

"Don't look at me," Tricia said. "I don't know."

"Well, this *is* the man's car. There's got to be something in here that'll give us an address. Check the glovebox, why don't you. Maybe he's got the papers for the car in there. Or *something* with his address on it."

Tricia unlatched the glove compartment, swung it open, and a little light inside flickered on. She started sorting through the contents. "He does have some papers, let's see…here's a map…a brochure…two ballpoint pens …a writing tablet…a—"

"What?" Charley said, after she'd been silent for a bit. "What else?"

"Pull over," Tricia said.

"What? Why? Here?"

"Pull over," she said again, and when he turned to look she held up a slim leather box filled with photographs.

In the wan light from the dashboard, from the illuminated mirror, and from the glove compartment, the two of them flipped through the photos. There were somewhere between twenty and thirty of them—closer to thirty, Tricia thought. Each was a stark black-and-white image, and each showed a combination of people—some vertical, some horizontal; some living, some dead. Halfway down the stack she found two that included Mitch. In one he

was holding a knife, maybe the very stiletto she'd seen
him pocket earlier that night; if not, one much like it. The
man at his feet had bled copiously, though in black and
white you couldn't quite tell where the blood ended and
the dark tile floor began.

In one she saw Robbie, and though he wasn't holding
a weapon himself what he was holding was nearly as bad:
He held another man's arms behind his back, much as
Mitch had held his, and the man he was holding was
coming to a similar bad end. The circle of life.

Each photo had a date inscribed by hand on the back,
along with a location: *Umberto's*, *Central Park Boathouse*,
Corner Mulberry & Hester. Each had names: *Monge*,
Mitchell, *Paulie Lips*. And on each, one of the names was
crossed out. On one, two names were crossed out, and
turning it over Tricia saw a pair of dead bodies on the
front, a man and a woman caught naked in what looked
like a basement rec room. She felt her stomach rebel,
forced herself to fight her rising gorge.

Several of the photos had the name *Barrone* written
on them, and in those the man holding a gun in the pictures was tall and chiseled, skin pockmarked, close-set
eyes cold. In fairness, he didn't look his age—even in the
later-dated photos he looked like he could be forty, not
sixty. But he didn't look like a man you'd want your sister
to take to bed all the same.

"Jesus," Charley said, after Barrone had made his fifth
fatal appearance. "This is not your average garage owner."

"Maybe there's an explanation—"

"Of course there's an explanation. Your sister's boyfriend is a hit man. That's the explanation."

They kept turning over the photos, one by one, images
of bad men and worse, hunters and their prey.

Then they got to the end.

The last photo—the very last one—dated just a little

over a month ago—showed the scene Coral had described:
a dead man in a gutter, several live ones standing over
him. One of them was Mitch. The tall man with the chiseled features was in this photo, too, and his name was on
the back. But it had been the last hunt for him and he'd
been the final quarry.

Because he was the man in the gutter, and on the back
it said ~~Barrone~~.

24.

The Guns of Heaven

"I guess we know why he's been away for the past month,"
Charley said.

Tricia put the photos back into the box, put the lid back
on, and slid it into the pocket of her dress.

"And I guess that rules out finding him," Charley said.
"He's not exactly in a position to help us."

Tricia put her head back against the seat, closed her
eyes. She felt like crying. These were killers—real killers,
not the fun sort you read about in books. They killed
without remorse, without hesitation, over and over; they
even killed their own. And took pictures to remember it
by. What chance did she and Charley stand against them?
What chance did Erin and Coral have?

"What do you want to do?" Charley said. "Now that
we've got the photos, we've got something to trade. We
could head out to Queens, try to make a deal. Or, Tricia,"
he said, "*I* could take the photos out to Queens and you
could get on a train back to South Dakota. They wouldn't
look for you there. You could go back to your old life,
pretend you never met me, pretend none of this ever

happened. Maybe that'd be the smartest. What do you say?"

Tricia opened her eyes, pinned him with her stare. "I say we need guns."

They drove off the highway and back into the heart of the city. At the all-night drugstore in the lobby of the Warwick, Charley went to the counter to coax a sandwich and a coke out of the counterman, while Tricia worked the payphone in the corner. On the way in, Charley had asked her where she proposed to find guns at eleven on a Saturday night in the middle of New York City. "Do you know any gunsmiths that keep night hours on weekends? Because I don't. I don't know any gunsmiths, period."

"I don't know any gunsmiths either," Tricia said, "but I know a woman who's got at least two guns."

"Who?"

"Just get your sandwich, I'll be back in a minute."

She'd gone to the payphone, hunted through the heavy phone book hanging from a wire, found no "Heaven" or "H" on the page for "LaCroix," struck out again looking for Coral under both "King" and "Heverstadt." Finally she just rang up the operator and gave her the address of the rooming house itself.

"Oh, is that where all the excitement was?" the operator said with a girlish squeal. "Down on Cornelia Street? I just heard about it on the radio!"

"Yeah, very exciting," Tricia said. "People getting shot. Nothing more exciting than that."

"Well, you don't have to be a grouch about it," the operator said. The phone on the other end started ringing.

As it rang, Tricia found herself thinking, *Can you trust Heaven? Are you sure?* But Coral had trusted her; that had to count for something. And what choice did she have anyway?

It took half a dozen rings before a familiar Eastern European voice answered. "Hello?"

"I'm calling for Heaven LaCroix," Tricia said.

"Not here," the landlady said. "You call back later. Is madhouse."

"Please," Tricia said quickly, before the woman could hang up, "I know she's there, she's taking care of a little boy, she wouldn't have left him alone. Please. Just put her on the phone."

"Who *is* this?" the landlady said, and you could almost hear her eyes narrowing.

"A friend of hers. It's very important—"

The landlady's voice dropped to a whisper. "You the girl came by earlier, ran out after shooting."

"I didn't shoot anyone—"

"No," the woman whispered, "I know, Heaven tell me. But the police, they say you do, they wait for you. Don't come back."

"I won't," Tricia said. "But I need to talk to Heaven. Could you please get her on the phone?"

"I get." Tricia heard her set the receiver down. Then the sound of footsteps departing. There was a murmur of voices in the background. Boarders? Or cops? Both, probably.

Before the footsteps returned, Tricia heard her dime fall into the phone's innards and she deposited another from the handful of change Charley had given her.

Eventually, the footsteps came back—two pairs of them. "Hello?" It was a different accent this time, very light, almost Dutch-sounding.

"Heaven," Tricia said. "Don't say my name, don't give any sign that it's me."

"Okay," Heaven said.

"I'm safe—but I need your help."

"Okay," she said again, though this time it sounded like a question.

"I'm going to get Colleen out from where she's being held, I have someone with me, but we're dealing with some very dangerous men and can't go in barehanded. I need to borrow your guns, Heaven—yours and the one you took from Mitch, the guy in the hallway."

"Who's that on the phone?" a voice asked. "Hey—miss, I'm asking you a question."

"My sister," Heaven said, "calling from Limbourg. I'll just be a minute." Then, to Tricia, "Dear Clara, I'm so glad to hear you're moving to New York. I do think I can help you find work, yes. You know weekends I work at a club called the Stars, right? After the last match, cleaning up—usually starting one-thirty, two in the morning. I bet they'd have work for you, too." Her voice rose. "We'll ask them when you come, Clara. Next month."

"I hear you," Tricia said. "I'll be there tonight. One-thirty."

"How's mother, Clara?"

"I'm going to hang up now."

"Oh, good, good."

Tricia set the phone back in its cradle, hoped the call hadn't been traced, hoped the operator hadn't listened in. But just in case—

She returned to the counter, lifted one of Charley's arms. "We'd better go."

"Can't you sit for a minute to eat," he said through a mouthful of turkey and lettuce. "I got one for you."

"We'll take it with us," she said.

He grabbed the two sandwiches, one whole and one partly eaten, wrapped them in a paper napkin, dipped for one last pull at his coke.

"Now," Tricia said.

"I'm coming, I'm coming." Outside, on the street, he asked, "What's the rush? Your friend with the guns?"

"No, she won't be ready for another two hours. I just didn't like how nosy the operator was getting. She seemed a little too interested in what was happening down on Cornelia Street."

"You think she called the cops?"

"I don't want to find out."

They rounded the corner to the side street where they'd parked the Lincoln, then backed away when they saw a policeman bending over beside it, hands on his knees, trying to see in through the driver's side window.

"Easy come, easy go," Charley muttered.

They walked briskly through the combination of pitch-black and bright-as-day that is New York City as midnight approaches. After a couple of blocks, Tricia found herself flagging, falling behind. "Do you know any place we can go for a couple of hours?" she said. "I'm beat."

"I know some places we *can't* go. The office. The Sun, the Stars. Cornelia Street. Queens. This city's starting to feel awful small."

She chose not to mention that they'd be going to one of those very places when 1:30 rolled around. "Come on, Charley, you're a resourceful man. Where would you go if you didn't want to be found for a few hours?"

He thought for a bit, then took her arm. "I know a place."

Half a mile downtown and a few blocks west, just off Times Square, Charley led her up a flight of stairs and knocked on a heavy wooden door. A panel slid open speakeasy-style and a pair of eyes looked out at them. "Borden!" a voice called out. "Haven't see you in dog's years!"

"Mike," Charley said when the door swung wide, revealing a man in an undershirt and apron, dishtowel in one hand and a pair of shot glasses in the other. "This is…Trixie, Mike. A friend of mine. We've got an appointment in two hours, need to be off the street in the meantime."

"No problem," Mike said, and ushered them into a quiet, dark room where a handful of men sat drinking. No one looked up, no one said anything to them. "What's your thirst?"

"No drinking for us tonight, Mike," Charley said. "What we really need is a good hour's sleep. The back room occupied?"

"No," Mike said, "just some things of mine I can clear out."

"Leave 'em," Charley said. "We're not particular."

Mike took them to the room, where Tricia had to step over a man-sized duffel bag and a pile of newspapers and pawnshop tickets to get to the low mattress on the other side. There was an armchair, too, though it looked none too comfortable.

"You'll tell me what this was all about, right," Mike said, "when it's all over?"

"If I'm in talking condition, you'll be the first I tell."

"Knock in an hour?"

"Give us ninety minutes," Borden said.

"You got it." Mike swung the door shut.

"Go ahead," Charley said, and waved at the mattress. He lowered himself into the chair. "Lie down."

Tricia did, pulled up a thin blanket over her. She kicked off her shoes and instantly felt better. She looked at Charley, who was twisting to find a comfortable angle in the chair.

"Hey, Borden," she said and lifted the blanket. He looked up. "There's room here for two."

"You're not worried I'll offend your virtue?" Charley said.

"Two hours from now, I'll have a loaded gun in my hands," Tricia said. "I'm sure you'll be a perfect gentleman until then. Now lie down and get some sleep."

"Yes, ma'am," Charley said.

25.
The Last Match

She didn't intend to wind up in his arms, but that's where she found herself when the knocking at the door awakened them. It felt nice, she had to admit. Secure. Even if it was a false sense of security—and lord knows it was—there was something to be said for having a strong pair of arms around you. Or even a not-so-strong pair like Charley's.

But it was moot, since she didn't have it anymore. Charley had leapt up, shooting from a deep sleep to fully awake like toast from a toaster. He'd said nothing about how they'd found themselves, and she'd gone along with his silence. Just as well not to add one more complication to a situation that was already, not to put too fine a point on it, a goddamn mess.

While she splashed some cold water on her face and gargled a mouthful of Listerine in the little bathroom across the hall, Tricia tried to decide whether getting ninety minutes of sleep was a blessing or a curse. She felt less sore but more groggy. Take your pick.

"If anyone asks, Mike," Charley was saying when she returned from the bathroom, "you haven't seen us. That's for your sake, not ours. Well, not just ours, anyway."

"That's okay," Mike said. "You know me. I never see anything. It's how I stay in business."

"Good man."

"How do you know him?" Tricia asked, when they were down on the sidewalk again.

"Who? Mike? He's an old, old friend. Known him longer than…well, probably longer than anyone. We were in reform school together."

"Reform school?"

"There's a lot you don't know about me," Charley said. "Bet you never would've guessed I was in reform school."

"No, actually I would have guessed that," Tricia said. "I just wouldn't have guessed you had any old friends."

"Ouch," Charley said. "You'd think you'd be nicer to me after we spent the night together."

"We didn't spend the night, we spent ninety minutes."

"Still and all," Charley said. He reached into his pocket, pulled out an apple and something wrapped in a napkin. He held the apple out to her. "A present from Mike." She took it. He unwrapped the last remaining bites of his sandwich. "So, where are we meeting this friend of yours?"

Through a mouthful of Granny Smith she said, "The Stars Club."

"That's funny," Charley said, "it almost sounded like you said 'The Stars Club.'"

She swallowed. "I did. Heaven will meet us there after the last match ends. She works there nights."

Charley stopped walking. "Are you out of your mind? Tricia, we can't go there. Nicolazzo owns the place. He could *be* there, for all we know. And even if he's not, he's certainly got people there, they know what you look like, they'll recognize you as soon as you walk up to the front door."

"So we won't go to the front door," Tricia said, thinking of Erin saying, *There have got to be at least three exits from this building, maybe more*. Three ways out meant three ways in.

She walked on for a few steps, saw Charley still standing where she'd left him. "You coming? Or are you leaving me to do it alone? Because I will. Come or don't, it's up to you, but I'm going." She didn't wait for an answer, just walked off, and it took half a block before Charley caught up with her.

"Damn it, Tricia, I don't want you to get hurt."

"You mean you don't want *you* to get hurt," Tricia said.

"That, too."

"Well, I don't see that we have a choice, Charley. We need to get Coral and Erin, and we need weapons to do that, and the one person who can give us what we need is at the Stars Club. So that's where we're going."

They walked the rest of the way in silence. Charley threw out the napkin when he'd finished his sandwich and Tricia did the same with the apple core a block later. Empty-handed, they made their way to the rear of the building the Stars Club was located in. They searched along the unlighted brick wall for the outlines of a service entrance and did find one metal door, but it was locked. There were two narrow windows, but both were covered with formidable iron grillwork so that even if opening them had been possible it would have been no use.

Rounding the corner, they saw a side door swing open and ducked back into the shadows as a group of people spilled out. At least two of them looked like fighters, taller and bulkier than the rest and muscular even under their coats. The rest looked like trainers, managers, miscellaneous hangers-on. There was lots of laughter and high-spirited talk about what after-hours bar would still be serving at 2AM, and then some about how it wasn't really 2AM yet, was it, and how no, it wasn't, but it would be by the time they made it to the nearest bar. As the last of them exited the building, the door slowly began to swing shut.

"We've got to—" Tricia started to say, then realized she wasn't saying it to anyone, since Charley wasn't beside her any longer.

She saw him, then, darting out into the midst of the little crowd. "Gents! Gents! Coming through!" He patted one of the big men on the back. "Hey, nice work tonight. Nice work. Give it to him, right?" He caught the closing door with one hand before it could shut. "Is Barney in there? Never mind, I'll find him." And before anyone could say anything he was inside and had pulled the door closed behind him.

"Barney?" one of the men asked. "Who's Barney?" Another shrugged and a third stepped out into the empty street with an arm upraised to hail a cab. When none came, the lot of them shuffled in a group toward the corner where Tricia was standing. She backed up into an alcove, hoping the shadow would cover her.

"Hey, look what we've got here," one of the fighters said and pointed toward her as they passed. "Looking for company, honey?"

"Come on, bruiser," one of the smaller types said, and Tricia realized with a start that it was the janitor, the one with the squint. "Keep it in your pants." She pressed her back hard against the wall, her chin against her chest. He looked right at her, tipped his hat in her direction. "Sorry, sister, he didn't mean nothing."

Thank god for myopia, she thought.

When the last of them had gone and the sound of their loud conversation had dwindled in the distance, Tricia ducked out of the alcove and sprinted to the side door where Charley had gone in. She knocked. "Open up," she said, "it's—"

The door opened and Charley pulled her inside, a

finger to his lips. They were at the top of a staircase and Charley led her down to its foot.

From somewhere not too far away, she heard a punch land and the sound of a tired crowd that could barely rouse itself from its torpor to cheer. Another punch landed, and another, and then came a heavier sound, a body hitting the canvas. "Huh-*one!* Aaa-*two!* Thuh-*ree!*" the ref counted, but he got no further than the 'F' in "Four" before the felled fighter apparently righted himself. The crowd mumbled a desultory blend of approval and disdain. Then a bell rang and there were scattered groans from people in the audience who wanted the fight to be over, already.

Charley pulled Tricia down the long, T-shaped corridor. Though all but one of the ceiling lights were off now, she recognized it from before: they were behind the arena, near the changing rooms. She had to figure the cleaning crew would be based somewhere around here. But it was a big place. Hell, there were other floors entirely. Maybe they stashed the cleaning crew on one of those.

"So?" Charley whispered in her ear. "Where's your friend?"

Then he stiffened and stepped away from her slowly, his arms rising, palms out. "Hold on," he said, "don't shoot, I'm not armed."

"Of course you're not," Heaven said, stepping out of the shadows. She had a gun pressed between Charley's shoulderblades and she held it there while she steered him over to face the wall. "That's why you're here. Is this the person helping you?" she asked Tricia.

"Yes," Tricia said.

"You might want to reconsider," Heaven said, "just how much help he's likely to be."

"You think you could put the gun down now?" Charley

said, but she didn't. Tricia saw it was the Luger, the gun that had killed Mitch.

"If I could get the drop on you so easily, the people who have Colleen will, too. They're professionals. I'm just someone who knows how to take care of myself." She finally took the gun away from Charley's spine, lowered it. "You don't seem to be either."

"We've done okay so far," Charley said, bristling.

"Heaven," Tricia said, "thank you for coming. Did you bring both of them?"

Heaven nodded and took the other gun out from the pocket of the windbreaker she was wearing. She handed both guns to Tricia. They were heavier than Tricia expected.

"They're fully loaded," Heaven said. "But when they're done, they're done. That's all the bullets I had."

"Thank you," Tricia said. "I can't tell you—"

"Don't tell me. Just go. I can't be seen with you."

"Who's with Artie now?" Tricia said.

"Malwa. A Ukrainian girl. He'll be fine. Now, go."

"No," said a deep voice from further down the corridor, "you stay right where you are." A hulking shape moved toward them. The gun held in one of his hands came into view before his face did, but eventually his face followed.

"Bruno," Tricia said.

"Drop the guns," Bruno said. "The boss said to bring you in alive if I can, but I can shoot you if I need to."

"Kill him," Heaven said. "That's what they're for—use them!"

"Quiet," Bruno said, and his rumbling bass voice made the word sound like a commandment. "Now put the guns down."

"You, too, son," said a nasal voice from the other end of the corridor, where (Tricia saw, turning) several men were clattering down the stairs she and Charley had used just minutes before. "Drop it. You too, Borden. You're all under arrest."

And as this new figure stepped from darkness into light Tricia saw it was O'Malley, his nose bandaged and his face bruised. He had his police service revolver outstretched and two patrolmen behind him had theirs out, too.

"I don't even have a gun," Charley said.

"Well, put down whatever you've got, all of you."

Tricia lowered her hands and bent to put the guns on the floor. Bruno seemed to be weighing his options.

From the other side of the wall, then, the bell sounded and a second later a massive punch connected. The crowd, roused from its stupor, roared; you could hear chairs tip over as people rose to their feet.

And Tricia took the opportunity to raise one of the guns she'd been about to put down and, aiming well over everyone's heads, fired it.

She'd only meant it as a distraction, a warning shot, a ploy out of sheer desperation; she couldn't have hit the ceiling light if she'd aimed at it, not in a million years. But she hadn't aimed at it and now it winked out with a tinkle of shattering glass.

Hearing the gunshot, the audience screamed and stampeded; from the ring came the sound of the bell being rung repeatedly in a futile effort to restore order.

From somewhere in the darkness, O'Malley shouted, "Nobody move!"

Someone grabbed Tricia's arm and in the chaos she didn't know if it was friend or foe until Charley said, his breath warm in her ear, "This way."

She ran beside him down what she guessed was the middle branch of the 'T', one gun in each fist, her legs aching and her breath short.

"Do you know where we're going?" she gasped.

"Nope," Charley said.

This arm of the corridor dead-ended at a doorway and, barreling through it, they almost toppled down the stairway just inside. They were in the basement, but apparently the place had a sub-basement, since the barely illuminated steps were inviting them further down.

Charley slammed the door behind them and locked it. Instants later, they heard the knob rattle and a fist pound against the door's surface. Charley held out his hand for one of the guns and Tricia passed him the Luger. He fired a round into the door below the knob, scaring off the person on the other side at least for a moment and maybe—Tricia hoped—jamming the lock mechanism in the bargain.

Of course, while that might keep their pursuers out it also left them only one way to go, since this room was where the stairs began. There was no up—only down. Which struck Tricia as an apt metaphor for their entire situation.

Side by side, guns held tightly in their sweating fists, they started to descend.

26.

Grave Descend

The stairs turned twice at little square landings, but there were no doors at either, no way to go but further down. The only light came from low-wattage bulbs hanging overhead in metal cages, and few enough of them that there were stretches where Tricia couldn't see a thing. In an act of what she first thought of as unaccountable bravery Charley led the way, walking in front of her into the unknown; but then she thought about the known they were walking away from and his eagerness made more sense.

"Do you see anything?" she said.

"Sh," he said.

In the faintest whisper she could manage she said, "Well? Do you?"

"No."

"Be careful," she said.

"That's good advice," he muttered. "I'll keep it in mind."

He stopped suddenly and she collided with his back. The gun fortunately didn't go off.

"Door," he whispered.

"Can you open it?"

She heard a knob turn. Charley leaned into the door with his shoulder, gently eased it open.

Past it, the light was slightly better, but only slightly. A long tunnel extended perhaps twenty yards before curving out of sight. It looked a little like a subway tunnel except for the absence of rails along the bottom. Instead the ground looked to be dirt—hard-packed earth, uneven and pitted, as though dug by hand.

They stepped inside, closed the door behind them, and Charley swung a metal bar down to latch it shut.

"What is this?" Tricia said. "An old bootlegging tunnel? Some sort of secret escape tunnel?"

"You know something," Charley said, "you read too many books."

"Well what do *you* think it is?"

"Oh, I'm not saying you're wrong. I'm just saying you read too many books." He started off down the tunnel and she followed.

"What's that supposed to mean?"

He crept cautiously through the tunnel's curve, gun

held high, finger tight on the trigger. They came out into another straight stretch. There was no one in sight, but he didn't lower the gun. "You say 'bootlegging tunnel' like it's something romantic. It's not romantic. It's ugly. It's people stealing from each other, cutting each other's throats. There are probably people buried down here, you know—nice romantic bootleggers who fell out of favor with Uncle Nick." He kicked at the dirt underfoot. "We're probably walking on their graves."

"That's horrible."

"It's the real world, kid. It's not like you read about in paperbacks."

"You mean like the ones you publish, Charley?"

"I mean like the one you wrote," he said. "Bang-bang stuff, where the blood all washes off by the final scene and the bad guys all wear black."

"You liked it well enough when I wrote it," Tricia said.

"Sure. I just don't like living the real-world version."

"You think I do?"

They walked on at as fast a pace as they could manage, the tunnel stretching out more or less endlessly in front of them.

"I'm sorry, Charley," Tricia said. "Okay? I shouldn't have done it. I shouldn't have written the book."

"Ah, hell," Charley said. "I shouldn't have asked you to."

"You didn't ask me to make things up."

"No," Charley said. "But all you did was make them up. I'm the one that published it."

"You thought it was all true," Tricia said.

"And that makes it better? Would you tell me what the hell I was thinking, deciding to publish the actual secrets of an actual mobster?"

"That you'd sell a lot of books."

"Yep. That's what I was thinking, all right."

"And you will," Tricia said.

"Maybe the profits will pay for a nice headstone," Charley said.

"Only if we get out of this tunnel," Tricia said. "They bury us down here, we don't get a headstone."

They both walked faster after that.

By the time they reached the far end of the tunnel, Tricia figured they must have walked a good quarter of a mile, maybe more. How anyone had been able to dig a tunnel under the streets of Manhattan that ran at least five blocks she couldn't fathom. Unless this was a much older tunnel even than Prohibition—maybe, she thought, the tunnel came first and the buildings were built around it.

The room at the far end had wooden crates stacked against the walls and a folding card table in the center. It had no chairs and no people, though, and the one door in the room was closed and barred. The question was what they'd find when they opened it.

"They know we're here," Charley said. "They must. There's nowhere else we can be. The only thing we can hope is that we made it faster than they could because they were busy dealing with the cops."

"And that none of them had the chance to telephone ahead," Tricia said, "to tell someone to be here when we came out."

"Yeah," Charley said. "That, too."

He hesitated, counted *three, two, one* with his fingers, and in a rush of movement raised the metal bar, pulled the door open, and stepped through it gun-first. There was no one on the other side.

"Well, that's a relief," he said.

"We're not out yet."

They raced up the staircase they found, cousin to the one in the basement of the Stars Club. At the top another door waited. When Charley started the bit with his fingers again, Tricia just pushed it open and walked out into the basement of the Sun.

Off to one side she saw the freight elevator and two of the fabric-sided carts the maintenance staff used to wheel supplies in and out—the same sort she'd had her unnamed thief use to escape with the loot in her book. The same sort the real thief had used, too, apparently.

She heard sounds from the loading dock outside: running feet, then hands at the metal gate, trying to raise it. Tricia went to the freight elevator door, banged on it with the flat of her palm. From the loading dock came the rattle of a padlock. "Come on, come on," came a muffled voice. "Who has a key?"

Tricia rapped on the elevator door again, kept pounding until it slid open. The operator stuck his head out, barking, "What are you doing, banging away—"

She put her gun in his face and he quieted down. When he saw Charley leveling a gun at him too, he meekly put his hands up.

"I were you, I wouldn't rob this place," he said. "We got hit just a month ago and the people in charge are out for blood."

"We're not here to rob the place," Tricia said. "Just take us upstairs."

Out on the loading dock, a gunshot went off like a cherry bomb and what Tricia had to assume were padlock fragments rained against the metal gate.

She stepped into the elevator. "Up."

The operator pulled the door closed and worked the lever to start the car. Heavy chains clanked overhead and they started to rise.

"How far?" he said.

"All the way," Tricia said.

"Is that smart?" Charley said. "Why not just go to the lobby?"

"Because it's almost two AM, Charley," Tricia said, "and at two AM people from Nicolazzo's other clubs start showing up in the lobby, delivering the night's take. Some of them are probably there already. With armed bodyguards. Not to mention the man in the security booth out front."

"But if we go up to the club," Charley said, "how are we going to get out…?"

Tricia watched the little metal arrow above the door travel to the end of its arc. "What, you didn't read my book?"

At the top floor, they left the operator tied hand and foot with his belt and Charley's necktie; a handkerchief they found in the man's back pocket served for a gag. They turned the elevator off. Let the boys in the basement holler for it. That'd buy a few minutes at least.

They followed the hallway to a pair of swinging doors and pushed through, finding themselves in the kitchen, where a sloe-eyed saxophonist sat nuzzling a tall glass of something amber. A woman setting dishes in one of the sinks looked up when they entered: Cecilia, still wearing her costume from their dance number, which she'd presumably had to turn into a solo. "Trixie! What happened to you? Where were you?"

"It's a long story, Cecilia," Tricia said, hurrying past, "I'm sorry I let you down tonight."

"Robbie didn't show up either. Do you know where he is?"

Probably still in the trunk of Mitch's car, wherever that was. "No," Tricia said. "Listen, we've got to go. If anyone asks, you didn't see us. It's for your own good, trust me." She realized as she said it that it was the same thing Charley had told Mike. Well, it was doubly true for her. Cecilia certainly didn't need a 'ZN' added to her cheek.

"Will you be here tomorrow?" Cecilia asked.

"I don't think so," Tricia called over her shoulder.

"That lady's sure in a hurry," the saxophonist said to no one in particular.

They burst through the door to the storeroom, rushed down the crowded aisle between two tall metal shelves. The window at the end was closed; the glass was unbroken. Tricia tried to open it but couldn't. "Charley, you try," Tricia said.

"I'm not climbing eleven stories down the side of a building," Charley said.

"Then open the window so I can," Tricia said. "And when he gets here, say hello to Uncle Nick for me."

Charley gave her a murderous stare, spat on each of his palms, planted his feet and tried to wrench the window up. When his first try failed, he gave two more heaves, grimacing furiously each time. The third, true to form, was the charm. Tricia, meanwhile, slipped the gun into the pocket of her dress, next to the box of photos. It was a tight fit, even though she'd kept the smaller of the guns for herself.

"Okay." She stuck her head out the window, looked down, wished she hadn't. Not that she could see much in the dead of night, but the little she could see didn't make her want to climb out on the window ledge.

She climbed out on the window ledge.

Charley gripped her legs with both hands. Holding on tight to the window frame with her left hand, she fished for the rain gutter with her right. Her fingertips brushed it twice before she was able to get a good grip.

"Okay," she said. "Let go."

"You sure?" Charley said. He sounded dubious.

"Yes." Stretching out one leg to the side, she found the nearest of the metal brackets that anchored the pipe to the wall and when she felt reasonably secure putting her weight on it, she brought her other hand and leg over.

"Nothing to it," she said, or tried to, but her teeth were chattering too much and she gave up.

"You think it can hold both of us at once?" Charley said.

She would've shrugged but didn't want to chance it. Instead, she started carefully inching her right leg along the pipe, feeling for the next bracket down. It was too far beneath her, especially with her legs constrained by the way she was dressed. (*Slacks,* she thought. *Why couldn't I have worn a nice pair of slacks?*) But she knew the bracket was there, just inches below her toes. So holding tight to the pipe with both hands and both knees and thinking of all the trees she'd climbed as young girl in Aberdeen, she let herself slide slowly—slowly!—down to the bracket. She rested there for a moment, flexed her fingers slightly, then tightened her grip and let herself down to the next one.

As she went, she kept her eyes focused on the bricks immediately before her. This was about feeling her way, not seeing where she was going. Slide; stop. Slide; stop.

Down had to be easier than up, at least. That's what she kept telling herself. But her hands had already started to hurt. Her chest, too, from tension and the drumbeat of her racing heart. She chanced a look up, saw Charley's legs and posterior a few feet above her. He was on the pipe too, now. Once again she found herself with nowhere to go but down.

I'll never tell another lie as long as I live. I swear it. I'll never write another book about gangsters. Only friendly, happy subjects, like trips to the beach and picking flowers. I promise. Just let me not die here in this airshaft. Let me make it down. Please.

Slide. Stop. Deep breath. Slide. Stop.

"You know something?" Charley's voice was weak; she imagined she could hear his teeth chattering too. "It's not eleven floors." He let himself down to the next bracket above her head, made sure of his footing. "It's only ten."

"What?" Tricia managed to say.

"We only have to make it to the *roof* of that news peddler's place," Charley said. "That's the second floor. So we're only going ten floors, not eleven. And," he added with a hopeful tone, "a fall from just one floor up probably wouldn't kill us. So it's really only nine that we have to worry about. And," he said, "we must be at least halfway there already."

"Charley," she said.

"Yes?"

"Shut up and climb."

Two stories later, Tricia lost her grip. Her left hand, sweaty and tired, slipped off the pipe. She felt herself tilting backwards, her feet losing their purchase on the bracket. Desperately, she tried to wedge her entire right arm between the pipe and the wall, but thin as it was, it wouldn't fit. She scrabbled with her feet, tried to hold on with just one hand, but found herself falling. She meant to scream, but somehow nothing came out, and as she fell she only had time to think, *So, this is it.*

Then she hit, and though the breath was badly knocked out of her, she was somewhat astonished to find that the life wasn't. She lay where she'd landed, flat on her back, just eight or nine feet below where she'd lost hold of the pipe.

"Tricia!" Charley called. "What happened? Are you okay?" When she didn't answer, he looked down. "Oh, thank god." He quickly slid the rest of the way to the bottom. "You see? We *were* more than halfway."

Looking up at him from where she lay, she nodded very slightly and concentrated on breathing in and out.

"Come on," Charley said, inching over to the chicken wire-laced window above the toilet. "It looks like there's a light on."

27.

The Peddler

Tricia forced herself to get up, brushed off her hands and the seat of her dress, which was smeared now with god only knew what. The smell here was dismal, and though she'd made up the rat for the chapter in the book, she didn't doubt that there were various sorts of vermin here, biding their time in the darkness.

While Charley pried open the window and let himself down, Tricia checked her pocket. The gun and the photos were still there. The gun hadn't even gone off and shot her in the thigh, and for that small miracle she was thankful. She limped over to the skylight, where Charley's arms were sticking out, reaching up for her. She let him lower her down, and they stood together in the tiny bathroom.

There *was* a light on, not here in this little closet of a room, but outside—you could see it leaking through around the door. Tricia tried to remember, from her many nights at the Sun, whether she'd ever seen this place open at 2AM—she didn't think so. How many people could possibly want a newspaper or a coffee at 2AM?

There was nothing to do about it, though. They couldn't stay in here much longer. For one thing, their entrance had probably been heard. And even if it hadn't, if there were people outside someone would eventually come in to use the toilet, and then what would they say?

Charley grabbed a handful of the coarse brown paper towels the owner had set out and, wiping his hands, pushed the door open.

"Gentlemen," he said. Tricia followed him out. There were two men in the small space, a heavyset character, gray at the temples, sitting at the counter with a mug in front of him, and a skinny one standing behind it, wearing his usual canvas apron, the pocket in front loaded down with coins. The door to the street was closed, a shade drawn over the glass. Charley seemed to be deciding, for a moment, whether to bolt or stay—were they safer in here or out on the sidewalk? Finally he went to one of the two empty stools, motioned Tricia to the other.

The men stared at them. They both seemed to have been caught in mid-sentence.

"Jerry," Tricia said to the man in the apron, "this is my friend Charley. Charley, Jerry. Jerry's always very nice to me any time I come in."

"How'd you get in there, Trixie?" Jerry said nervously. "You weren't there ten minutes ago."

Tricia shrugged. There was no good answer, and why give a bad one?

"You don't mind," Charley said, "we'd both do well with a cup of coffee." He dug a few coins out of his pocket, dropped them on the counter.

"Actually," Jerry said, his eyes darting toward his other customer.

"Actually," the customer said, turning on his stool to face them, "we were transacting some private business, and I don't like being interrupted." He reached inside his suit jacket as though to pull out a wallet or change purse, but what he came out with was a gun. And here they were, Tricia and Charley, both of them with their hard-won armament tucked away safely in their pockets.

"Now who are you," the heavyset man said, "and what were you doing spying on us?"

"Spying?" Charley said. "Nothing of the sort. We were just…well, you know. Using the room." He bent toward

Tricia, kissed her lightly on the neck. Startled, she jumped a little. She felt a blush shoot up her cheeks.

"But how did you get *in* there?" Jerry said, still stuck on the logistics like a kid working out a magic trick.

"I work next door, on the third floor," Charley said. "At the big theatrical agency, you know the one I mean. And we just…climbed out the window, came down."

"Why?" Jerry said. "Why would you want to do it in my bathroom? If you like bathrooms, don't you have one in your office?"

"It's not as private," Charley began, but the man with the gun waved him to silence.

"That's all right, Jerry," the man said, "they're just lying to you. There's only one reason they'd be here, and you know what it is. Sal's always liked to keep an eye on me, and I guess he's gotten suspicious of you, too."

"She does work for him," Jerry said. "Told me she's a dancer."

"I *am* a dancer," Tricia said.

"Sure," the man with the gun said. "And he's your partner, and you do your best dancing in toilets. Don't play me for a sap. What's Sal paying you to be his eyes and ears?"

"Nothing!" Tricia said.

"So you do it for free? Jerry here charges Sal seventy bucks a month, and half the information he sells him you could get for nothing on the street." And when Tricia registered surprise, he said, "What? You thought Jerry pays his rent peddling candy and papers at a nickel a throw? You can peddle information for a lot more. More than it's worth, sometimes."

"Don't say that, Mr. B," Jerry said, "I give good value—"

"We don't work for Nicolazzo," Charley said. "We never met him before today."

"Shut up," Mr. B said. "The lot of you." To Charley he

said, "Of course you never met him before, the man lives on a goddamn boat. Doesn't mean you don't work for him. I work for him. Jerry works for him. We all work for Uncle Nick." He said it with unconcealed disgust—something Tricia feared meant he had no intention of letting them leave the room alive.

She looked more closely at his face. She'd never seen him before—she was certain of that. But there was something familiar about him and she suddenly realized what it was. "Mr. B," she said. "Does that stand for Barrone?"

The big man looked over at Jerry. "Listen to that. 'Does it stand for Barrone?' You do a fine innocent act, sister. You should be an actress, not a dancer."

"No, really," Tricia said, "does it?"

"Why? What are you going to tell me if I say yes?"

"That I've got something you're going to want to see. Or maybe you won't want to see it, but you ought to."

"And what's that?"

"Some pictures," Tricia said. "Out of Mr. Nicolazzo's safe."

The bluff, hectoring expression vanished from the big man's face. He was deadly serious now. "Where are these pictures?"

"In my pocket," Tricia said. "I'll give them to you."

"Slowly," he said, and she eased the leather box out of her pocket, slid it to him across the counter.

"You can look at all of them," Tricia said, "but the one you'll want to see is the last one."

"Open it," he told Jerry, and he kept his gun trained on Tricia and Charley while Jerry lifted off the lid of the box and spread its contents out over the counter.

"Aw, jeez," Jerry said when he got to the last picture. Mr. B looked down at it. He didn't say anything, but his hand shook and Tricia wondered whether he was going to shoot them all.

"Mr. Barrone," Tricia said, "I'm so sorry about Royal. Was he your brother?"

"What are you talking about? *I'm* Royal Barrone. That's Frankie. That's my son."

"You say you got these from Sal's safe?" Barrone said.

"I didn't," Tricia said, "my sister did. I think you know her—Colleen King?" His eyes narrowed and he nodded as though, bit by bit, he was putting things together. "She told me she found them in the safe after someone else broke in and stole all the money. But Nicolazzo thinks she took the money, too, or at least knows who did, and he's holding her somewhere in Queens, along with a friend of ours. Charley just got away a few hours ago. I barely got away myself."

"I see," Barrone said. He turned to Jerry. "And what do you know about all this?"

Jerry was backing away from the counter, although in the narrow space there wasn't far for him to go. He was shaking his head, the loose skin under his chin quivering. "Nothing, Mr. B, honest."

"Don't give me that, Jerry. You hear everything. You must've heard something about this."

"Sure, I hear things, but half of it's just talk—"

"How about the other half?"

"Like I was saying before—I hear Sal's rounding up everyone who might've had anything to do with the robbery, no matter how remote. He even grabbed the guy published that book, you know, the one talked about the robbery…" He looked over at Charley. "Word is, this guy took him at Fifty-to-One, walked out the front door. This was a couple of hours ago."

Charley smiled weakly.

"What about Frankie?" Barrone said. "What do you hear about Frankie?"

"Nothing," Jerry mumbled.

"Jerry, how much do I pay you? Not Sal—me. How much? Now answer my goddamn question."

Jerry sounded like the words were being pulled out of him with pincers. "Frankie was asking for more," he said, "that's what I hear. More money. And when Sal said no, he threatened to walk. Pictures or no pictures. Said he'd take what he knew to the cops. If he went down, he'd take Sal with him."

"And why didn't you tell me this before?"

"I didn't want—I didn't want you to be mad at me," Jerry said.

"Goddamn Frankie," Barrone whispered. "Never listened. Never knew how to keep his mouth shut." He waved the gun at Charley. "You. Take that gun out of your pocket, slide it over here. Yes, I can see it, I'm not blind. You, too, sister. I'm keeping them and we're going for a little ride." Tricia and Charley reluctantly handed over the guns they'd gone to such trouble to obtain.

"You," Barrone said to Jerry, as he packed the photos back into the box one-handed. "If you ever lie to me again—no, listen. If you ever lie to me again, or hold out on me, I'm going to kill you. Do we understand each other? Right through the head, with this gun here, I'm going to shoot you. If you lie to me. Is that okay with you, Jerry? Yeah?" Jerry was nodding wildly. Yes, absolutely, Mr. B, shoot me, that's fine.

Barrone dropped the box of photos into his jacket pocket.

"You're lucky that they're *not* spies for Sal, because if they were I'd have to kill all three of you. You're no use to me, Jerry, if Sal knows about you."

"He doesn't," Jerry said. "I'd never tell no one. Only people know are you, me...and now them, I guess."

"Oh, we'd never tell anyone either," Charley said, and

Tricia shook her head in agreement. "Why would we? You want it in writing, we'll—"

"Get up," Barrone said. He grabbed their guns, waved them toward the door.

Charley and Tricia got up. She glanced back at Jerry, who had a half-apologetic look on his face. *Sorry*, it said, *but better you than me*.

Outside, there was a long black limo waiting at the curb.

"Open the door."

Charley complied.

"Now get in."

They climbed into the car, found seats along what seemed to be a six-foot-long banquette while Barrone climbed in after them, sat on the shorter crosswise seat at the end. He slammed the door shut. "Eddie," he called, "take us to Fulton Street." The car started up.

"Now," Barrone said, "let's hear what you know about my brother-in-law."

28.
Lucky At Cards

It didn't take long, since Charley didn't know much and Tricia had decided she'd be a better listener than Frankie and keep her mouth shut.

"You've seen the book, right?" Charley said. "Well, that's what I know. Nothing more, nothing less, just what I read in there."

"You working with the cops?" Barrone said.

"Pfff." Charley blew a half-hearted raspberry. "Only if by 'working with' you mean 'wanted for assault and battery by.' There are two cops wearing bandages because of me, and that's just the past day's worth. I have a police record going back to 1950."

"He does," Tricia said. "I saw the mug shot."

"Oh, a mug shot," Barrone said. "You must be some sort of big-time criminal."

"I wouldn't say big time," Charley said. "But then I wouldn't say criminal either. I'd just say the cops don't see the merit in everything I do."

"Well, that's the cops for you," Barrone said. He rotated his gun to point at Tricia. "And you're Colleen's sister?" She nodded hopefully. "You know your sister's been squeezing me for months now?"

Tricia's face fell. "Squeezing?"

"First she wanted the car," Barrone said. "Then it was money. Then it was introductions to people I know in the fight business. Or else."

"I'm sure she didn't mean to—"

"Oh, she knew exactly what she was doing, and she meant every word."

"I think you're wrong, Mr. Barrone. My sister's a good person. She's not some sort of…blackmailer."

"Some sort of blackmailer is exactly what she is." The gun rotated back to Charley. "And you. Did you really take Sal at Fifty-to-One?"

"We played a hand," Charley said. "I got lucky."

"I don't buy that. No one gets lucky at Fifty-to-One."

"One in fifty people should," Charley said. "If you think about it."

"You don't leave something like that to luck," Barrone said, "not when your life's at stake. If you beat him at his game, you had a way to beat him. What's the trick?"

"No trick," Charley said.

"What's the goddamn trick?"

"No trick," Charley insisted.

"My son," Barrone said, "hasn't been seen for a month. Now I find out he's dead. The man who killed him likes playing an insane little game with his enemies that I've never heard of anyone surviving—except you. The way things are going, I may find myself playing that game before too much longer, and if there's a way to beat it, I want to know what it is." As he spoke, Barrone dug into a little well in the armrest beside him, dropped one item after another on the seat—a balled-up handkerchief, a couple of cellophane-wrapped hard candies, a corkscrew. Finally he came up with a pack of cards. "Now show me how the hell you did it," he said.

"I wish I could," Charley said. "Believe me, nothing would make me happier. But I can't."

"How about this," Barrone said, flicking the top card off the pack with his thumb. It landed on the seat next to him. Four of clubs. "Tell me what the next card is or I'll blow your girlfriend's brains out."

Tricia blanched as Barrone's gun swung toward her once more. The barrel gaped between her eyes. Such a big opening for such a small fistful of metal. She wanted to run, but where? She couldn't even make it to the door, never mind through it, before he could pull the trigger.

"Her?" Charley said, affecting a desperate little laugh. "She's not my girlfriend. She's just some girl who came to audition today. We're casting for the new Comden and Green revue—"

"—and you take all the girls who come in for auditions to the toilet for a little fun."

"Absolutely. Every one I can," Charley said. "Wouldn't you? Love 'em and leave 'em, that's me."

"Nice try," Barrone said. "But I saw her face when you kissed her. I see your face now. She's not just 'some girl' to you." He cocked the gun. "So I say again, name the next card, or I'll ventilate her."

"Charley!" Tricia said.

"All right," Charley said. "All right. I'll tell you. The cards we were playing with were marked—a mechanic's deck. I had them on me when Nicolazzo grabbed me. I was just lucky he used my cards instead of a deck of his own. That's the big secret. Now leave her alone. Shoot me if you've got to shoot somebody."

"Okay," Barrone said, swinging his gun around.

"No, wait, wait—I said 'if.' *If* you have to shoot somebody." Charley put up his hands as though they might repel bullets. "But why would you have to shoot anybody? Least of all us. You could get life for that, if they didn't put you in the chair. We're not worth it."

"That's a point," Barrone said.

"We're not even worth the stain on the upholstery," Charley said.

"That's a point, too," Barrone said.

"We're not even worth the *bullets* it would take," Charley said.

"Don't sell yourself short," Barrone said. "You're worth the bullets."

"The point is," Charley said, "the person you really want is Nicolazzo, right? Well, that's just fine with us— we don't have any love for the man ourselves. In fact, we were getting ready to go after him—it's what we got the guns for, the ones you took away from us. If you want to do something smart, why not let us finish what we started? Give us back the guns and we'll get rid of him for you."

Tricia gave him the sort of look you'd give to a relative who'd suddenly proposed skinny-dipping in the fountain in front of the Plaza Hotel.

"You?" Barrone said. "With your mug shot and your marked cards and your fumbling around in toilets? Sal would eat you for breakfast."

"Yeah? Seems to me he had the chance and here we are, still uneaten."

"You said yourself, you got lucky."

"So maybe we'll get lucky again," Charley said. "Or maybe not, maybe we'll fail, but if so you're no worse off—if he kills us we're just as dead as if you did it, and at least that way it's one less pair of murders you have to answer for."

"What if he doesn't kill you? What if he captures you, makes you talk, and you tell him about me to save your rotten life?"

"You think he'd believe us?" Charley said. "Or do you think he'd believe we were just making things up to save our rotten lives?"

Baronne seemed to be mulling it over. His finger was still on the trigger, though.

"And that's if we fail," Charley said. "But maybe we won't fail. Maybe we'll succeed. Right? It could happen. And then…"

"And then what?"

"And then whatever you want," Charley said. "You can move up, take his place. You can stop being a lackey, running a tenth-rate used car lot while he's hobnobbing with stars at swanky nightclubs. You're the man's brother-in-law, aren't you? You're married to his sister. When do you get what you're due? Well, we can help you get it. But only," Charley said, emphasizing the critical point, "if you don't shoot us."

Barrone thought about it for a while, during which time Tricia felt sweat running down her back and sides in rivulets. She'd never been this frightened in her life, not even when she'd been climbing down the rain gutter from twelve stories up. The widening stains on Charley's shirt suggested he was feeling some anxiety himself.

After letting them stew a while, Barrone lowered his

gun, released the hammer. "You'd have made a good salesman, Borden. If you *do* things half as well as you talk about them, maybe you've got a chance." He shook his head. "Maybe. But never forget you're one wrong step away from a bullet in the back."

"Trust me," Charley said, "that's not the sort of thing I'm likely to forget."

In the seat beside him, Tricia started breathing again.

Barrone sat back, slipped his gun inside his jacket. "Marked cards," he said. "You little sneak." He waved the deck at Charley. "Want to see how you would've done with a straight deck?"

Charley said, "Not really."

"Come on," Barrone said. "Just for a lark."

"Fine," Charley said, staring at the back of the top-most card. "Six of diamonds."

Barrone thumbed the card in Charley's direction. "Let's see."

Charley reached out, turned the card over. Two of spades.

"You're a lucky man," Barrone said.

"Sometimes," Charley said. "Just not at cards."

29.
Robbie's Wife

The car pulled to a stop at Fulton Street, near where the Fish Market would be opening for business in just a few hours. Already there were trucks pulling in and off-loading crates that stank of fresh catches and seawater. The driver came around and opened the door. Barrone gestured for them to get out first. He followed, wincing as he got to his feet. He was not a young man and was carrying a lot of weight on those not-young knees.

"Come upstairs," he said.

"If it's all the same to you," Charley said, "we'd just as soon be on our way—"

"I said come upstairs," Barrone said.

"Why?"

"You want your guns back, for one thing, and I'm not handing them to you loaded. Apart from that—have you gotten a look at yourself?" He grabbed hold of the back of Charley's neck, steered him over to one of the limo's side-view mirrors. Tricia followed. Charley fingered the stubble on his chin as though surprised to discover it there. "You can't go after Sal looking like a bum and smelling worse—not if you want to have a serious chance to get close to him. You need a bath, you need a shave. And you need some sleep—look at your eyes. I've seen smaller bags on a Pullman car." He snapped his fingers at the driver, a young man who looked like he'd grow up to be Barrone's shape if he lived long enough. "Eddie, clear out the room on the top floor." The driver nodded, headed off.

"Mr. Barrone," Tricia said, "it isn't that I'm not grateful—I'd dearly love a good night's sleep. But my sister's in trouble *now*. We can't just leave her in Nicolazzo's hands while we lie down and take a nap. We've lost enough time as it is."

"All due respect—Trixie, is it?" Barrone said. "If Sal wanted Colleen dead, she's dead already. If she's alive now, she'll still be alive in five, six hours."

"You sure it's not that you'd prefer her dead," Tricia said, "because she's been squeezing you?"

"What, for a few bucks and a car? I don't like it, but I don't want her dead for it." Barrone waved an arm at her. "Anyway, look at you. You'd be no use to her the way you are now. You can barely stand up."

Since 2004, **HARD CASE CRIME** has brought readers the finest in hard-boiled crime fiction, from yesterday's and today's best writers.

In honor of the publication of our 50th title, we're proud to present this gallery of our first 50 covers.

If you haven't read all of these fine novels, you can order any you're missing by calling 1-800-481-9191. You'll find a checklist on the last page for your convenience.

—Charles Ardai
Editor

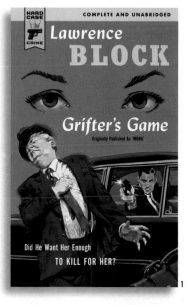

KISS HER GOODBYE

Allan Guthrie

8

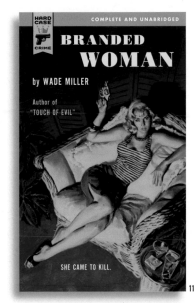

BRANDED WOMAN

by WADE MILLER

Author of "TOUCH OF EVIL"

SHE CAME TO KILL.

11

DONALD E. WESTLAKE

361

9

**DAVID DODGE
PLUNDER OF THE SUN**

10

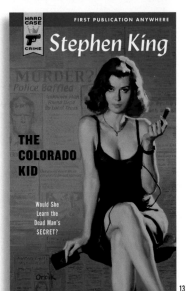

Stephen King

MURDER?
Police Baffled

THE COLORADO KID

Would She Learn the Dead Man's SECRET?

13

DUTCH UNCLE

PETER PAVIA

12

HARD CASE CRIME

COMPLETE AND UNABRIDGED

Lawrence
BLOCK
The
GIRL
with the
*She Had
A Grifter's Soul.*
**LONG
GREEN
HEART**

14

HARD CASE CRIME

COMPLETE AND UNABRIDGED

THEY WERE ON THE RUN... FROM A DEAD MAN!

**NIGHT
WALKER**

**DONALD
HAMILTON**
Bestselling Creator
of Matt Helm

16

HARD CASE CRIME

COMPLETE AND UNABRIDGED

CHARLES WILLIAMS

A Beauty On A Burglary
...JUST ENDED
AS A NIGHTMARE!

A Touch of Death

17

HARD CASE CRIME

COMPLETE AND UNABRIDGED

Mystery Writers of America Grandmaster

ED McBAIN

"ED McBAIN
IS A MASTER."
—NEWSWEEK

**The Gutter
and the Grave**

15

HARD CASE CRIME

FIRST PUBLICATION IN 50 YEARS

When It's Time To Say Goodbye...

**SAY IT WITH
BULLETS**

By **RICHARD POWELL**
Author of *A Shot In The Dark*

18

HARD CASE CRIME

FIRST PUBLICATION ANYWHERE

**WITNESS
TO MYSELF**

By **SEYMOUR SHUBIN**

New York Times
Bestselling Author

HE KNEW HE WAS GUILTY... BUT OF WHAT?

19

FIRST PUBLICATION ANYWHERE

by KEN BRUEN and JASON STARR

SECRETS CAN KILL

BUST

20

HARD CASE CRIME

COMPLETE AND UNABRIDGED

DONALD E. WESTLAKE Writing As

Richard Stark

LEMONS NEVER LIE

"Whatever Stark writes, I read."
— ELMORE LEONARD

22

COMPLETE AND UNABRIDGED

MADISON SMARTT BELL

Straight Cut

SHE WAS A PAWN IN THEIR DEADLY GAME...

21

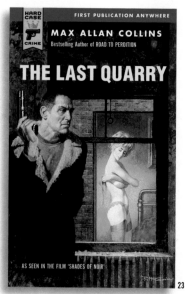

HARD CASE CRIME

FIRST PUBLICATION ANYWHERE

MAX ALLAN COLLINS

Bestselling Author of ROAD TO PERDITION

THE LAST QUARRY

AS SEEN IN THE FILM 'SHADES OF NOIR'

23

COMPLETE AND UNABRIDGED

The Guns of Heaven

PETE HAMILL

24

NEVER BEFORE PUBLISHED!

DAVID DODGE

THE LAST MATCH

25

HARD CASE CRIME

COMPLETE AND UNABRIDGED

JOHN LANGE

SOMETHING'S
GOING DOWN
OFF THE COAST
OF JAMAICA...

Nominated For
the Edgar® Award

**GRAVE
DESCEND**

26

COMPLETE AND UNABRIDGED

The Peddler

Richard S. Prather

HE SOLD THEIR BODIES
—AND HIS SOUL

27

FIRST PUBLICATION IN ALMOST 40 YEARS!

Lawrence
BLOCK

Lucky at Cards

He handled cards like a master.
BUT COULD HE HANDLE HER?

28

HARD CASE CRIME

FIRST PUBLICATION ANYWHERE

"Come on, J——," Steve
dares with an ——, she
said. The pale ——was playing
another Sinatra song.
"Go ahead," Jack, ROBie
said, "Warm ——up because
I think, at that moment
I could have —— bed him."

**ROBBIE'S
WIFE**

THE NEW NOVEL BY RUSSELL HILL

29

HARD CASE CRIME

COMPLETE AND UNABRIDGED

DAVID GOODIS
Author of "Dark Passage"

The WOUNDED
and the SLAIN

Was She His Savior—
or His Betrayer?

31

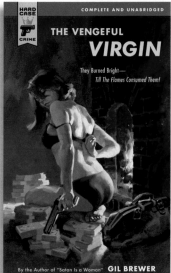

HARD CASE CRIME

COMPLETE AND UNABRIDGED

**THE VENGEFUL
VIRGIN**

They Burned Bright—
Till The Flames Consumed Them!

By the Author of "Satan Is a Woman" **GIL BREWER**

30

32

33

34

35

36

37

38

39

40

HARD CASE CRIME

JOHN LANGE
Best-Selling Author of DRUG ZEROED

ZERO COOL
THE HEAT IS ON

41

HARD CASE CRIME

TWO COMPLETE NOVELS!

SPIDERWEB
ROBERT BLOCH

SHOOTING STAR
ROBERT BLOCH

Robert Bloch

SHOOTING STAR

42

HARD CASE CRIME

COMPLETE AND UNABRIDGED

THE MURDERER VINE

SHEPARD RIFKIN

43

HARD CASE CRIME

COMPLETE AND UNABRIDGED

STEVE FISHER

NO HOUSE LIMIT

45

HARD CASE CRIME

FIRST PUBLICATION IN 50 YEARS

BABY MOLL

By John Farris

writing as "Jack Farris"

46

HARD CASE CRIME

FIRST PUBLICATION ANYWHERE

KEN BRUEN and JASON STARR
Award-Winning Authors of Bust and Slide

THE MAX
GREED... AND DANGEROUS!

47

HARD CASE CRIME

FIRST PUBLICATION ANYWHERE

THE FIRST QUARRY

MAX ALLAN COLLINS

48

HARD CASE CRIME

FIRST PUBLICATION IN OVER 35 YEARS!

DONALD E. WESTLAKE

EVEN A NEW YORK CABBIE CAN GET TAKEN FOR A RIDE...

SOMEBODY OWES ME MONEY

44

49

50

✓ CHECKLIST

It was true enough. She was listing like a tree in loose soil.

"Now for the last time," Barrone said. "Come upstairs. Or would you rather do it at gunpoint?"

"No, no," Charley said. "We'll come."

Inside, the building was spare, obviously less a home than a headquarters. There was a kitchen on the first floor, but it was full of burly men with empty shoulder holsters, some downing beers as they read the newspaper, some running oil-stained cloths through the pulled-apart mechanisms of their guns. The rooms Tricia and Charley passed as they climbed the stairs were under-furnished— a sectional sofa in one corner, a bare table in another. There was, Tricia thought, no woman's touch; which made sense, since as far as she could see, there were no women.

Barrone stopped climbing after two floors. He leaned on the banister and watched as they continued without him. "Go ahead," he said. "There's a bathroom on the top floor. Eddie should've put out a razor for you. We'll talk strategy in the morning."

When he'd dropped out of sight at last, Tricia leaned in close to Charley and whispered. "What the hell are we doing? We're *working* for him now?"

"We're breathing," Charley said. "One thing at a time."

"But he expects us to kill Nicolazzo for him. We can't do that!"

"You don't know what you can do till you try," Charley said.

Tricia's feet felt like stones and her head felt even heavier. Just keeping her eyelids open was an effort. "We're not killers, Charley," she said. "I'm not, anyway."

"The police think you are."

"So I might as well be? Is that what you're saying?"

"I don't know what I'm saying. I'm too tired to think."

They turned the last corner and made their way up the

final half-flight of stairs. The floor they came out on was a little better decorated than downstairs, with floral wallpaper and moldings up by the stamped-tin ceiling. An open door at one end of the short corridor led to a bathroom and Tricia could hear water running into a tub. Through the door at the other end she saw the corner of a bed. *Halfway between two bales of hay and unable to choose, the donkey starved to death.* That wouldn't be her fate. Let Charley take the bath; she'd sleep first.

She staggered into the bedroom. Eddie was there, loaded down with an armful of blankets and stripped-off bed linens, and there was a woman in there, too, loading another few pieces onto the pile. She was tall and thin and looked to be in her middle thirties, with the close-set eyes and narrow axe-blade of a nose that stamped her as one of the Barrone clan. She gave Eddie a little shove toward the door and he headed out with a glance back at her; he seemed a little moony-eyed, Tricia thought.

"Go on," the woman said, and a few seconds later they heard him tromping down the stairs.

Charley came in quietly beside Tricia. The woman, who'd paid Tricia no attention whatsoever, eyed him up and down with considerably more interest.

"Scruffy, aintcha?" She wet her lips with the tip of her tongue. "You're papa's new pet? Eddie told me he'd picked up some strays."

"You're Mr. Barrone's daughter?" Tricia said.

"Among other things," she said, not taking her eyes off Charley.

Tricia scoured her memory for the daughter's name, the surviving daughter—the dead one was Adelaide, she remembered that. "Renata," she said. "Right?"

"Points to the little lady," Renata said—to Charley. "She might win herself a kewpie doll yet."

"And you're married to—" Tricia caught herself.

"Robbie Monge, that's right," Renata said, brightening. "The famous bandleader. Read about us in Hedda's column, did you?"

"Among other places," Tricia said. She didn't like this woman, she decided. Didn't like her at all, and wouldn't have liked her even if she hadn't been sizing Charley up like a dressmaker eyeing a bolt of satin.

"Why no ring?" Charley said, nodding toward her hand.

She lifted the hand, stared at it as though noticing for the first time the absence of a wedding band. "I wore one for a while," she said. "It made my finger itch."

And she tilted her face down to give him an up-from-under stare straight off the cover of *Real Confessions*.

"Awful nice to have met you," Tricia said, emphasizing the *awful* more than the *nice*. "But we're pretty tired and we've got an early day. Maybe you could let us get some sleep?"

Renata didn't take her eyes off Charley. "What is she," Renata asked, "your kid sister? Or just your kid?"

Tricia's mouth dropped open, but Charley put a hand on her arm before she could say anything. "Mrs. Monge, Trixie's right, we really do need to get some sleep. If you wouldn't mind…?"

"Oh, I wouldn't mind," Renata said. "I wouldn't mind at all." On her way out the door she patted Tricia's forehead. "Pleasant dreams, honey."

The door clicked shut behind her.

"What a hussy!" Tricia fumed. "She's a married woman!"

"Didn't you tell me she's a widow?" Charley said.

"Yeah, but she doesn't know that," Tricia said.

"How do you know she doesn't?" Charley said.

"If she does, that's even worse," Tricia said. "Her husband's not even buried yet—"

"Robbie didn't sound like a prize himself," Charley said. "Anyway, that's not the point."

"Oh? What's the point, then?"

"The point is she's Barrone's daughter, and we might need her help. We certainly don't need to get into a fight with her."

"I wouldn't say a fight's what she wants to get into with you," Tricia said. "You might want to check the tub before you climb in."

Charley wearily slid his suspenders off his shoulders, began undoing his cuffs. "Her cozying up to us isn't the worst thing that could happen, Tricia."

"Us? She's not cozying up to *us*."

"So?" Charley said. "One of us is better than neither. We need every advantage we can get."

He was right, of course—she knew he was right. Still. "Go take your bath," she said. She pulled off her shoes one by one, threw them at the armchair in the corner. She slung herself backwards across the bed, let her eyes close. "And don't wake me when you come back."

"Then move over," Charley said, "so I won't have to."

"I think maybe you should take the chair this time," she said.

"Swell," Charley muttered and headed toward the sound of pouring water.

30.

The Vengeful Virgin

When the first rays of sunlight through the blinds prodded her awake, Charley wasn't in the bed; he wasn't in the chair either. His shoes were on the floor, next to hers— he'd left the four of them lined up, side by side. She saw his pants draped over the arm of the chair. Her dress, which she'd stripped off and left in a heap on the floor with her underwear, was missing, and in its place was a folded robe. It was too large for her, but she put it on and managed to walk down the hall to the bathroom in it without tripping.

The hallway lights were off and the house was silent. She rapped gently on the bathroom door and prepared to whisper his name, but it swung open under the impact of her knuckles. There was no one inside—but there were her dress and her intimates, hanging from the shower rod and almost dry. Charley's shirt and undershirt were hanging beside them. She looked at the seat of the dress. The stain from where she'd landed on Jerry's roof hadn't come out, not completely, but it was faint enough now that you wouldn't notice if you didn't know to look for it; and the smell, at least, was gone.

She got washed at the sink like she'd done for years on cold mornings in Aberdeen: a splash of water, a streak of soap, some more water, vigorous toweling. She brushed her hair back, briefly inspecting the dark roots that had started to show at her scalp. Would she dye it again? If she got out of this mess, would she stay blonde? Or would she go back to the old brown of Aberdeen, quiet and unexciting but safe? It was tempting—to not be Trixie any longer, just Patricia Heverstadt once again, attracting glances as she walked down the street but not bullets. Yet she wondered whether this temptation was like the bargains she'd found herself making while climbing down the rain gutter, the sort you might contemplate in a dire moment but that you'd never go through with in the end.

She pushed the question out of her mind. First things first. Finding Charley (maybe he was in the kitchen, grabbing some breakfast?), finding the guns (would Barrone really let them have them back?), and then finding Nicolazzo and Erin and Coral (the corner of Van Dam and Greenpoint, wasn't that what Charley had said?).

She pulled the dress on over her head, buttoned it up as far as the missing buttons would permit, drew on her stockings, then padded back toward the bedroom for her shoes. There was one other room on the floor—one other door anyway, halfway down the hall—and she went slowly as she passed it, trying to make as little noise as possible.

She needn't have bothered. She heard a throaty chuckle from within, a creaking of springs. Then a woman's voice, coaxing: "C'mon, beautiful. Ain't you slept enough?" More creaking followed. The people inside weren't listening to anything going on in the hall.

Tricia moved on. Then stopped dead when she heard a voice, muffled by the door, say, "I really need to go." It was Charley's voice.

"What's the hurry?" Renata asked. "It's early still."

"We've got a long day coming up," Charley said.

"That's not all you've got coming up," she said.

"Renata, let go. Please. Stop that."

"Oh, but you like it," she said. "I can tell."

"I like it fine," Charley said, "but I need to go."

"I'll show you what you need," Renata said, and whatever response Charley had been about to give was stifled under a barrage of laughter and kisses.

There was a keyhole in the door, but Tricia didn't stoop to looking through it. She continued on to the bedroom, grabbed her shoes, hesitated, then dug a handful of money out of the pocket of Charley's pants, transferred it to her own.

You need every advantage you can get? Well, Charley, so do I.

Holding her shoes in one hand, she slipped silently down the stairs. She put the shoes on when she reached the ground floor.

Love 'em and leave 'em, that's me. Every one I can.
You certainly couldn't say the man hadn't been up front; he
told you right out what a creep he was. The problem was,
even when he made it clear he was lying you couldn't
believe him.

She remembered Barrone denying it, saying, *She's not
just 'some girl' to you.*

Yeah, well.

She entered the kitchen, empty now except for Eddie,
who either was the earliest riser in the house or had
stayed up all night. He sat at a circular table with a cardboard cereal box and an empty bowl, plus the pair of guns
Barrone had taken from them, the Luger and Heaven's
smaller gun, the one Tricia had been carrying. Two piles
of bullets were lying on the tabletop between them.

"Miss," he said.

"It's Trixie, Eddie. You can call me Trixie. We're going
to be working together, after all."

"Okay," he said. "Trixie."

"Listen," she said, thinking, all right, I've found Charley,
I've found the guns, now it's time to get on with it. She had
a brief twinge of remorse, but she stifled it. Coral wasn't
going to have to wait till mister love 'em and leave 'em
got around to leaving this one.

"Listen," she said again. "Renata was asking for you
just now."

"Really?" The poor boy's eyes lit up.

"Mm-hm. She said to ask you to come up. Just go quietly. And," Tricia said, "don't knock. Just let yourself in."

"Really?"

"Mm-hm."

He was halfway out of his seat before he looked back
at the table. "I don't know…I don't think Mr. Barrone
would want me to leave you here with the guns, Trixie."

"Well, I don't think Renata would want me coming up

to the room with you. It sounded like she was looking forward to having some privacy with you."

"Privacy," he said.

"Look, the guns are empty, right?" He nodded. "Fine. Then here—" Tricia swept the bullets up in her hands and held them out to Eddie, who cupped his palms to receive them. "Now I can't do anything. And you can go enjoy yourself."

Eddie jammed the bullets in his pockets and hastened to the door. "Thanks, Trixie. You're a pal."

"Have fun, Eddie," she said.

When she heard his step on the stairs, Tricia picked up the Luger. She tried loading it with the one bullet she'd managed to hold out, clamped between her palm and the base of her thumb. It didn't fit, so she grabbed the other gun, tried loading it into that one. It clicked neatly into place.

One bullet wasn't much. But it would have to be enough.

From upstairs she heard a commotion. Someone was shouting. Doors were opening on other floors. It was time to go.

She hustled to the front door and down the five stone steps to the street.

Subway…subway…she looked around hastily to orient herself then headed off to the west.

I'm coming, Cory, she thought.

And Charley? She thought of him, too, as she went, thought with a little regret of what he'd be facing now at Eddie's hands, and Renata's, and Mr. Barrone's, if he wasn't able to talk his way out of it. But hell, he'd be able to talk his way out of it. Maybe not before picking up a few bruises, but—

You made your bed, Charley, Tricia thought. I hope she was worth it.

31.

The Wounded and the Slain

She rode the train, rattling and shaking and nearly empty, out to Queens Plaza, where she begged a map from the token booth clerk in the station. She unfolded it and took a minute to find Van Dam Street. It looked like half a mile to get there, another mile or so before it crossed Greenpoint Avenue. She thought about splurging and blowing some of Charley's money on a taxi, but on a Sunday morning in Queens you were as likely to see a circus caravan pass as an empty cab. She didn't see either and started walking.

She did pass a small grocery store whose owner was letting down the awning with a long metal hand-crank. She stopped inside and picked up a couple of buttered rolls and a coke—not much of a breakfast, but she wolfed it down and kept going.

In the pocket of her dress, the gun—lighter now, with just the one bullet—felt like a brick, weighing her down. She wondered if she'd actually have the guts to use it. To stand in front of a man, the way Heaven had, the way Nicolazzo had, and end his life with a movement of her hand, a flick of a finger.

If her own life depended on it, she supposed she could, or if Coral's did. But if it didn't? Or if it wasn't clear?

She thought with a shiver of the dead men she'd seen since this began—more in one day than she'd seen in her previous 18 years, if you counted the ones in the photos, and a tie even if you just counted the ones slain before her eyes. And there was a big difference between seeing her father or granddad laid out in their best suits, hair carefully brushed and cheeks touched with makeup, a preacher by their side, the church choir singing hymns, and seeing a man's blood spill out of him onto the floor. Dead was dead—but the polite, quiet death of a funeral ceremony was worlds apart from the loud report of a gunshot, the acrid tang of powder in the air, or the snick of a blade unfolding and the desperate groan when it met flesh.

She wished she could get it out of her mind, but as she made her way toward Nicolazzo's hideout the images kept coming came back to her, the dead men and their near cousins, the ones who'd survived the recent events but not unscathed: Stella with her branded cheek; O'Malley with his bandaged face; Clohessy in the alley where Charley had left him, bearing who knew what sort of wound. It frightened her to think of the blood that had been shed, the pain suffered, and all because of her— because of the book she'd written, the men she'd spurred into action. And women, too. Her own sister, a thief. *Stella told me about this book she'd seen*, Coral had said. *That gave me the idea.*

She had to make things right. She had to. Somehow.

She reached Van Dam, followed it south toward the huge green sward of Calvary Cemetery. It wasn't the same size as the mammoth burial plots down by where the artists lived in Brooklyn, not quite; but it was plenty large and it loomed in the distance, a wholly unneeded reminder of mortality. *Bring me your dead*, it seemed to Tricia to be saying. *Bring all you want. We've got room for more.*

She counted blocks, referred to her map, drew near. When she reached the intersection, she didn't recognize any of the buildings, but why should she? She'd had a bag

over her head coming and going. But in this neighborhood of narrow, wedge-shaped blocks, only one corner
could properly be called the corner of Van Dam and
Greenpoint, and only one building could properly be said
to be on that corner. And it looked about right: There was
a front way and a back way in, there was gravel in the
rear, and there were several stories, enough to require a
staircase with 39 steps. The windows were shuttered
from the outside and, where she could see between the
shutters, curtained on the inside. As you'd expect—a
man who had to smuggle himself ashore in a pickle barrel
wouldn't take any chances with his privacy. There were
no sounds coming from the building, which might mean
anything or nothing. Tricia couldn't see any lights on
inside, but she wasn't sure she'd be able to in the daytime
even if they were on.

She circled the building, trying to divine the best way
in. Front door, back door? Neither seemed great. A half-
height window into the cellar held more promise. Using a
stick she found on the ground for leverage, Tricia forced
the shutters open, then squatted and peered inside.
There were curtains here, too, but enough space sepa-
rated them that she could see a sliver of the room. By
angling herself this way and that she could make out that
there was no one inside. She tried to open the window,
straining the way Charley had at the Sun (only without
spitting on her hands first—she didn't see how that would
help). When it didn't budge, she took out the gun and,
holding it by the barrel, swung it against the glass.

The pane cracked and pieces tinkled to the floor inside.
Tricia ducked out of sight. A few moments later she cautiously crept back, looked in. There was still no one there.
She wormed her arm in through the hole, avoiding the
jagged edges, and felt around the frame. Sure enough,
the window was locked. She unlocked it. It went up

smoothly after that and she dropped through it to the cellar floor.

Glass crunching slightly underfoot, she made her way to the door of the room where she and Coral had been held. "Cory," she whispered. She tried the knob. The door swung open.

"Cory?"

The room was dark. She groped for the cord to the hanging light and switched it on. Coral wasn't there; no one was. The bunk in the back was empty.

Was she upstairs? Tricia wondered. Were they all upstairs, putting Coral through some horrible ordeal, trying to get out of her some secret she didn't possess or information she didn't know? Tricia listened for some sign that this might be going on. She heard nothing, but it gave her little comfort. They might have gagged her. She might be unconscious. She might, as Barrone had said, already be dead.

Tricia knew she had to find out, had to go upstairs, had to face whatever was waiting for her there. But she was glad for any excuse to put it off, even just for a minute. So she went to the far side of the room, to the bunk where Coral had been sitting when Mitch had shoved Tricia in, the bunk where they'd sat together while Coral told her story. She hunted around the foot of the bunk, felt underneath it, looking for she didn't know what. A message, she supposed. Some sign that Coral had been here. She knew she'd have tried to leave one for Coral if their positions had been reversed.

Conscious of the time slipping away—someone could come downstairs at any moment, and of course Barrone could also show up at any moment, with or without Charley in tow; they must have figured out by now where she'd gone—Tricia pulled the bunk away from the wall. And there, scratched into the brick with a nail or a stone or in any event *something* with a sharp edge, were a dozen words made up of ragged, angular, hastily formed letters:

GARAGE 15 ST AVE C
19H GLOVE COMPMT
MORE AT MOON, LCKR22

Tricia pushed the bunk back. More at Moon, Locker 22. 'Moon' had to mean Nicolazzo's club, of course, the dime-a-dance place Coral had worked at before she took up boxing. But more what? More photographs? Of whom?

Tricia backed out of the room, held the gun firmly before her, took off the safety, and climbed the stairs. At each landing she spun left and right, gun before her, solitary bullet at the ready, but no one appeared. The building really was completely silent, and dark, and by the time she made it to the top she knew there was a good reason for it.

The place was empty—abandoned. Nicolazzo had hared off to another location, one she couldn't even begin to guess at. And he'd taken Erin and Coral with him, in whatever condition his interrogations had left them.

At least that was the hopeful possibility. The alternative was that he'd buried them here. That was the big question, really: Were they among the wounded or the slain?

Don't you touch them, you bastard, Tricia thought as she headed down to the street. Don't you dare touch them.

It felt more like a prayer than a threat and she kept repeating it to herself as she raced back toward the subway station, putting out of her mind the possibility that maybe he already had.

A block away from Queens Plaza she saw a limo heading toward her, pulling off the lower level of the 59th Street Bridge. Startled, she found herself frozen in place, unable even to turn away, but it passed without slowing, without the man on the other side of the open driver's-side window even giving her a glance.

She glanced at him, though. Eddie. Sporting what looked, as he sped past, like a black eye.

Charley's handiwork? she wondered. Or Renata's?

Tricia heard her train pulling in then and ran for it.

Let Eddie and his passenger discover what she already had, that Nicolazzo was nowhere to be found—that he'd flown the coop, probably as soon as Charley had walked out the door without anything to prevent him from seeing where he was. Let them exercise themselves trying to find him. She had a lead to follow, however tenuous.

Like Gleason used to say, she thought. To the moon, Alice. Straight to the Moon.

32.

Blackmailer

Unlike the Sun, which famously crowned a midtown office building, or the Stars, which filled a two-story bunker of its own near the waterfront, the Moon almost invisibly occupied the second story of a squat Garment District tenement, sandwiched between a buttons-and-trimmings wholesaler on the ground floor and a battery of one- and two-man tailoring shops on the third. There was no night-club banner flapping from a flagpole here, no doorman in livery to usher you inside (or to keep you out, for that matter). There was a front door and a staircase and, in one of the second floor windows, a neon image winking from full moon to crescent and back again, twenty-four hours a day.

On the sidewalk, wiry men heaved wheeled metal racks loaded down with dresses on hangers, one rack in each hand, while others scurried alongside, lettering tags on the run with swipes of a grease pencil. Even on a Sunday morning, the neighborhood was buzzing, in part to make up for the day many houses lost on Saturday (when the Millinery Center Synagogue on 38th was perhaps the busiest building in the neighborhood) and in part to prepare for the onslaught of orders that would roar in Monday morning.

Tricia picked her way through the chaos, stepping up into doorways or down into the gutter as necessary to allow men in an even greater hurry than she was to pass. She knew where the club was—it was no secret. The *Times* and the *News* had both written about it. But she'd never had reason to go herself. It was widely known to be a place only men frequented, and mostly a certain type of man: an older man, perhaps, or one burdened with some minor deformity; the halt, the lame; the shy, the scared, the slow of tongue, the foreign accented; those men whose appetite for female company, in short, exceeded their ability to procure any for themselves absent a fistful of tickets and a roster of women whose job it was to not notice the defects in their dancing partners.

It wasn't prostitution, though of course you heard stories; and many a feel was copped in the name of close dancing. That Coral had passed her first years in New York working here saddened Tricia. She'd pictured her sister headlining in a rooftop revue, or at least enlivening the chorus, not letting herself be tooled around a dance floor by a succession of sweaty-handed romeos with a buck to spare.

But better that than where she was now. Better a lifetime of sweaty embraces under dim lights than the deadly attentions of a man like Nicolazzo.

Tricia climbed to the second floor, where she found the club's door wedged open with a doorstop. The music playing sounded languorous and soporific, almost as if the record player were set at too slow a speed. Connie Francis' voice came on, asking who's sorry now, and the two women working at the moment went round and round with their charges in time to her plaintive query. Two other women seated on chairs against the wall looked up when Tricia walked in, then looked down again when they saw her. No trade here, just competition.

A man in dungarees and a button-down shirt came over, quickly taking Tricia's measure as he approached. She recognized him from one of Nicolazzo's photos—this was Paulie Lips, recognizable at a glance from the prominence not just of his lips but the entire lower portion of his face, which culminated in a shovel-shaped jaw with a darkening shadow of stubble just below the skin.

He had the self-confident walk and attitude of a man in charge and gave the impression of being the manager here. Tricia could see his eyes darting about her person, noting her wrinkled dress, the missing buttons, the perspiration on her forehead and under her arms, the circles under her eyes. A job seeker, he must've been thinking; and perhaps if there'd been more business to go around he'd have entertained the notion or at least strung her along, but Tricia could see he was getting ready to send her on her way.

She didn't give him the chance. "Hey, are you Paulie?" she said. He stopped, looked at her more closely. "My sister used to work here, and she left something she asked me to pick up. In her locker."

"Oh?" he said, taken aback. "Who's your sister?"

"Colleen King."

A smile unfolded on his face but it had all the sincerity of a Halloween mask. "Colleen," he said. "That would make you Patty, right?" He took her hand and squeezed it. "I guess she mentioned me?" He didn't wait for her to answer. "So, what, you just get into town?" His voice dropped and he edged closer. "Do you need anything? Some money? You look a little…"

"I'm fine," Tricia said. "I just need to get into my sister's locker."

"Actually," Paulie said, "she doesn't have a locker here anymore. You have to work here to have a locker, and she doesn't. Hasn't for a good long time. Think she's, ah, boxing now. You know." He playfully threw a few punches in the air. "Though she still comes by now and again to chew the fat with her old friends. Isn't that right girls?" The two seated women nodded when he directed the question at them, though it wasn't clear they knew just what they were agreeing with, or much cared.

"Maybe it's not her locker, then," Tricia said, "but it's *a* locker, and she told me to come here and empty it out for her. Locker 22?"

Paulie's smile grew more strained. "She told you that?" he said. "Locker 22?"

"She left me a note," Tricia said.

"Can I see it?"

"I'm afraid not," Tricia said. "I don't have it with me."

Paulie shook his head in an unconvincing pantomime of helplessness. His palms turned up and his eyebrows rose along with them. "Sorry to say, you got some wires crossed somewhere. The lockers here only go up to 20. Maybe ask your sister to come by, she and I can figure it out—"

"I can't," Tricia said. "She's…not available."

"Well, when she's available again, have her call me. We'll work it out. Maybe the three of us can get together for a drink sometime—"

He must've felt the barrel of the gun poking into his

gut then, through the fabric of her dress pocket, because his face fell. He looked confused first and then fear crept into his expression. "Are you serious?" he said, his voice low. "You think you can pull a gun on me in my own place?"

"I don't think anything," Tricia said. "I've done it. Now take me to locker 22, Paulie, or I swear to god you won't live to hear the end of this song."

Connie Francis' voice drawled on in the sudden silence between them.

Could she really do it? Could she pull the trigger in cold blood, leave this man sprawled and dying on his well-worn parquet? She doubted it—not least of all because it would mean using up her only bullet. But she made an effort to keep this from showing on her face. To look at her, you'd have thought her a hardened jailbird.

Paulie bristled with hostility. He was bigger than she was—but the gun more than evened up the sides. "Follow me," he said and led her through the long, narrow room to a curtained-off section in the back. The walls were lined with lockers and the numbers on them, Tricia saw, went up to 28.

"Are you even her sister?" Paulie asked.

"I don't see why you'd believe me," Tricia said, "but I am."

"And she really told you to come here."

"She left word I could find something in locker 22."

"She didn't tell you what?"

"She didn't have the time to go into much detail," Tricia said.

He stopped in front of 22 with one hand on the lock. "Why didn't she have the time?"

"Just open the locker."

"What if I told you I don't have the key?"

"I'd shoot you," Tricia said, "and take the key out of your pocket."

"Just asking," Paulie said. He pulled out a ring of keys, opened the padlock, and stepped aside.

Tricia drew the gun out of her pocket, leveled it at him, used it to shoo him back a few more steps. She opened the locker door without taking her eyes off him, then swiftly shot a glance inside. There were several stacks of papers—mainly letters, it looked like, along with a pile of photographs and a telegram or two.

"What is all this stuff?" Tricia said. "And don't say you don't know."

"Colleen called it her nest egg," Paulie said.

Tricia reached in, grabbed the first batch of photos off the top, thumbed through them one by one. A couple slipped onto the floor. She didn't pick them up.

Coral was in most of the pictures, though not all. She was younger in them—these dated back a few years, clearly, maybe to when she'd first come to New York or a little after. She'd been even prettier then and her figure had looked terrific, even in candid shots like these with their bad lighting and blurred portions where one of the subjects had moved as the shutter closed. There was a man in each of the photos, not the same one every time. By and large their figures didn't look as fine as Coral's, but like her they seemed not at all bashful about showing them off, at least in what they'd clearly thought was the privacy of a bedroom. They were the sort of photos you could be arrested for taking, or selling, or sending through the mails, and she felt her cheeks reddening as she looked at them. She stuffed them in her pocket, waved the gun at Paulie. "What are you looking at?" she snarled. "You just stay there and don't move."

"Calm down, lady," he said. "I'm not doing anything."

She reached into the locker again, grabbed a handful of the letters. They were on onionskin, carbon copies of letters whose originals had been written in ballpoint pen.

The handwriting was Coral's.

She glanced down at the first letter and up again at Paulie, reading it in snatches so she could keep an eye on him.

Dearest Royal—Artie is growing up so quickly! You'd be proud of him. He'll be a real Barrone man someday— commanding and virile, like his father. But Royal, he needs so much, and money's so very tight. Even a small amount would help…

She peeled back the top sheet with her thumb, crumpling it slightly.

Robbie, the next one down began. *Artie's growing up so quickly! You'd be proud of him. He's going to be a real Monge man someday—strong and talented, like his father. He's a growing boy, though, and needs so much. I hate to ask you to help, but money's tight…*

She waved the letters at Paulie, who looked more miserable than terrified now, like a magician caught with his hand up his sleeve.

"Just how many fathers did this kid have?" Tricia said.

"One," Paulie said, with a measure of defensiveness in his voice. "And you're looking at him."

33.
Songs of Innocence

"You…?"

"Me," Paulie Lips said. "He's my kid." He patted himself on the side of the face and this time the smile that emerged seemed genuine. "If you'd ever seen him, you'd know. He's got his poppa's chin. The poor boy."

"And what was your part in all…this?"

"Someone had to take the pictures," Paulie said.

"You watched her go to bed with all these other men? With Monge and Barrone?" Tricia said. "The mother of your child?"

"She wasn't the mother of my child yet. Not in most of them, anyway."

"How can you live with yourself?" Tricia said. "That's disgusting."

His face darkened into a scowl. "Put down the gun and say that."

"So you're bigger than me, so what. Doesn't make it less disgusting."

"What do you want?" Paulie said. "To stand there and insult me? Well, the gun gives you that privilege. But don't push me too far. I could take it away from you, you know."

"You could try," Tricia said.

They faced each other down. It felt to Tricia like a scene from the circus, the lion tamer in the cage with a tiger on one barrel and a lion on the next and nothing in his hand but a little wooden chair and a whip.

"I'm taking all this stuff with me," Tricia said. "Colleen wanted me to have it. She's in bad trouble and must've figured it could help. If you care about her at all, you won't try to stop me."

"What sort of trouble?"

"Your boss, Nicolazzo," she said. "You probably heard he was robbed. Hell, maybe you were in on the robbery. Maybe you both were."

"Uh-uh," he said. "No way. We're not thieves."

"Just blackmailers."

"That's right," Paulie said. "There's a difference. Being guilty of the one doesn't mean you're guilty of the other."

"Sure," Tricia said. "You're the picture of innocence."

"I didn't say that."

"Well, someone took three million dollars from Nicolazzo's safe and he's decided Colleen knows something about it. Maybe he doesn't think the distinction between blackmailer and thief is so crystal clear."

"He wouldn't know about the blackmail," Paulie said. "We never tried tapping him."

"Well, that's something, anyway. But he's still holding Colleen."

"And how will having this stuff help get her out?"

"I don't know," Tricia admitted. "But if Colleen thought it would, there must be a reason. Maybe there's something in here that could be used against Nicolazzo, or something she thinks might point to the real thief. Or at least something that points to where Nicolazzo might have taken her."

"You don't even know where she is?"

"Not right this moment, no," Tricia said. "But I'll find her."

Paulie's stare could've cut glass. "You'd better," he said.

"Does that mean you're going to help me?"

"It means I'm going to forget you pulled a gun on me," Paulie said.

"You'll do more than that," Tricia said. "Get a bag."

She left with an old Gladstone bag in one hand, packed with the contents of the locker. The bag shielded the gun in her other hand from view as she walked out, Paulie walking before her. She wasn't taking any chances.

As soon as she'd reached the sidewalk and sent Paulie back up, she flagged down a cab. Paulie might let her go, as he'd promised—but he might also sneak back down and try to follow her, or think he was being cute by staying put himself but sending someone else after her, maybe one of his dancers; they certainly had time on their hands. Or he might telephone any of a number of people to tell

them where she was. There were too many bad possibili-
ties and she was determined to be far away before any of
them materialized.

The press of people running back and forth in the
street made progress slow for a few blocks, but before
long things cleared up and they had a clear run up Sixth
Avenue to 44th Street.

She paid the cabbie at the corner, walked the rest of the
way only after he'd driven off. She climbed the stairs and
knocked on the door and didn't wait for the panel to slide
open before saying, "It's Trixie, Mike. Are you in there?"

The door opened. Mike stood behind it, apron smeared
and stained, looking much as he had the night before.
The bar behind him looked much the same as well, except
that instead of several solitary drinkers with their backs
to her, hunched over their glasses, Tricia only saw one.
She wondered if he was a holdover from last night or the
sort that liked to get an early start on his drinking Sunday
mornings.

"I'm sorry to bother you, Mike, but I need a place to
go through some things in private." She dropped the
Gladstone and it landed heavily on the floor, raising a puff
of dust. "Any chance I could use the back room? Twenty,
thirty minutes should be plenty."

"In private?" said a familiar voice. "I wouldn't think you
knew the meaning."

And turning on his barstool, Charley favored her with a
baleful stare out of the one of his eyes that wasn't swollen
shut.

"My god, Charley," Tricia said, her hand leaping to her
mouth.

He took a swallow from the tumbler of whiskey in his
hand. "You should see the other guy," he said.

"I think I did," she said, "if you mean Eddie. But you
look a lot worse."

"Thanks," Charley said, getting down off his stool and limping toward her. His voice was thick with drink. "That's what I needed to hear."

"I didn't mean for them to—"

"What did you think was going to happen? Eddie'd barge in and we'd have ourselves a merry little *ménage a trois*?"

"Charley!"

"If that's what gets your motor turning, honey, you could've just walked in and joined us yourself. Ah, but I forget, you're a sweet young thing and cannot leave your mother."

"Charley," Tricia said, "I didn't want you to get hurt"— but of course this wasn't true and she knew it. Part of her had badly wanted him to get hurt. But she hadn't envisioned it…like this. "What did you think you were doing, going to that, that…creature's bed—"

"Rather than the chair you so kindly left me," Charley said. "Oh, come off it, Tricia. You know what I was doing, and you know I was right to do it. I wasn't *enjoying* myself, I was trying to find a way to get us out of there."

Sure. And Paulie Lips was no thief, oh no, not him— just a blackmailer. Men! Singing their little songs of innocence. Could they possibly think they were convincing anyone?

"Charley," Tricia said frostily, "the way out of there was not hidden inside Renata Barrone's panties. *I* found a way out, and it didn't involve sleeping with anyone."

"Lucky you," he said. He handed the tumbler to Mike, then unbuttoned several buttons on his shirt, reached inside, and pulled out the leather box of photographs. "But you didn't get these, did you?"

"How…?"

He spread his arms and made a little unsteady bow. He really was quite drunk.

"A gentleman never kisses and tells," he said.

"*Renata* got them for you?"

"No," he admitted, "I grabbed them on my way out, saw them sitting on Barrone's dresser—but still. The point is I have them. Now, where's my thank you? Where's my 'I'm sorry, Charley, I'll never do it again?' Huh? Tricia?"

"I think you ought to get some sleep," Tricia said. Taking him by the arm, she tugged him toward the back room. "We can talk about it when you've sobered up."

"Ah, sleep and sobriety," Charley mumbled. "You see, Mike, she does care about me. You were wrong when you said all those scurrilous things about her."

Mike said, "I didn't—"

"No, I guess you didn't, it must've been me." Charley leaned heavily on Tricia, his boozy breath just inches from her nose, his bruised flesh a rainbow of purple and yellow. "You do care," he said, "don't you?"

She brushed something out of her eye—a reaction to the whiskey fumes he was breathing on her, she told herself, nothing more. "Go to sleep, Charley," she said. "You'll feel better when you wake up."

"I'll feel like hell when I wake up," he mumbled.

"Well, *I'll* feel better," she said. "Do it for me."

She deposited him heavily on the mattress and went back for the bag. By the time she returned, he was snoring.

While he was out cold, she went through all the material in the bag. There was a great deal of it. Coral had been putting the pinch on five men in all, some of them for years; six if you counted Paulie. He really seemed to believe he was the father of her child—but who's to say the others didn't? And Tricia had a feeling Coral had been hitting him up for more than just locker room space.

Thinking of Paulie as another of Coral's marks helped answer a question that had been nagging Tricia: If Coral

kept all her other incriminating materials in the locker at
the Moon, why had she kept Nicolazzo's box of photos in
the glove compartment of the car she'd extorted from
Barrone? The only answer that made sense was that
Coral had wanted to make sure Paulie didn't find them,
couldn't destroy them—especially the one he'd have been
most likely to destroy, the photo of himself. Which suggested that Coral had wanted to have something on him.

Of course, maybe she just liked having something on
everyone she knew.

Barrone, meanwhile, was a bit of a puzzle himself. If it
was his son who had died a month ago, not him, where
had Royal been for the past month? On an assignment
for Nicolazzo? Or lying low somewhere, to keep away
from Nicolazzo?

And Renata—what was she doing holed up in the old
man's headquarters downtown instead of living at home
with her husband? Or, if she and Robbie had been on the
outs (made her finger itch, indeed), why wasn't she living
at her parents' house, or some place of her own…some-
where, anywhere, that wasn't a Lower East Side boy's
club filled with gunmen and criminals?

But the big question wasn't Paulie or Barrone or
Renata—it was Nicolazzo. One question, of course, was
who had broken into his safe and taken the money out,
and Tricia had a feeling she'd need to answer it before
this was all over. But more urgently, where would the
man have gone with his hostages when his location on
Van Dam Street was blown?

Tricia scoured every letter, every photograph, looking
for a clue and finally she found one, near the bottom of
the pile. It was in a note Barrone had sent to Coral, dated
a year earlier:

Can't meet you in the city, it said, *that's final. N wants
us all out at his place at the track while he's waiting out*

the investigation. O'Malley's getting too damn close to play games. I'll call you with a location and you'll come out there if you want your goddam money.

And penciled in the margin, in Coral's handwriting, was the information she'd presumably copied down when he'd called: *AQUEDUCT, STABLE 8, STALL 3.*

Charley stirred, turned over on his side. He didn't wake.

Tricia took the leather box from the corner of the mattress and slipped it into her pocket beneath the gun. One way or the other she'd be prepared.

She stepped out into the hallway.

"How's he doing?" Mike asked.

"Sleeping," Tricia said. "Probably the best thing for him." She made her way to the front of the bar.

"What should I tell him when he wakes up?"

"Tell him I said to stay here. That I'll be back as soon as I can."

"And if he asks where you went?"

"Tell him you don't know. It'll be the truth."

"Are you sure it's smart to go off on your own like this?" Mike said.

"No," Tricia said, and went.

34.

Fright

If you want to get your money's worth from a New York City subway ride, you'll do as the song says and take the A train, whether it's to Sugar Hill way up in Harlem or to Rockaway Beach way down in Queens. It's a thirty mile ride from one end to the other, the longest you can take,

and it'll occupy the better part of two hours if you let it. If
you get tired before it's over or don't want to spring for
the extra fifteen-cent fare that kicks in right before you
hit the beach, you can trade the promise of sun and sand
for a day of playing the ponies at the Aqueduct Race
Track in lovely South Ozone Park. Or at least you could
before the State Racing Commission turned over control
of the track to the newly formed "New York Racing
Association" in 1955. One of the first things the new association did was to shut down the Big A and launch a reno-
vation project that promised to deliver to gamblers the
most modern racetrack of the Atomic Age. Almost three
years and thirty million dollars later, the project wasn't
finished and the track was still shuttered, though plenty
of pockets had gotten handsome new linings along the
way. Mostly in nearby Ozone Park, which was South
Ozone Park with redwood instead of aluminum siding on
the walls but just as much garlic in the marinara sauce.

Tricia watched the construction site loom as she climbed
toward it from the subway station.

One problem with a 200-acre racetrack, of course, is
that even when you've shut it down you can't shut it down
—you can stop racing horses there, but just try to keep
people out. Even if you fenced the thing in, curious neighborhood kids would find a pair of diagonal cutters and
make their way inside on a dare. And the construction
crew at the Aqueduct hadn't bothered with a fence,
relying instead on the low walls and shrubbery already in
place to keep people out.

Which made it pretty easy for Tricia to enter. The track
was surrounded on three sides by huge empty parking
lots, all converging on an entry gate to the main building,
which looked like it was destined to be a combination
clubhouse for high rollers and grandstand for the rank-
and-file. The first two stories had been constructed and

girders poking out the top showed it was due to keep climbing for at least a few stories more. There was a giant crane standing immobile by the side of the building, its steel cable dangling with a weighted ball at the end to keep it from swinging free. As you'd expect on a Sunday, no one was sitting in the cab of the crane or walking along the girders. At first glance, no one seemed to be on the grounds at all, though Tricia had to assume there was at least some security staff around, maybe making their rounds on the other side of the lot.

Past the torn-up dirt of the racetrack itself, Tricia saw the dozen wooden buildings of the stable area and she headed over with what she feared was an excessive sense of purpose. Knowing where Barrone had met Coral once a year earlier wasn't the same as knowing where Nicolazzo was holding her today. But what she did know was that there was a precedent for Nicolazzo going to ground here, and like the proverbial drunk with his missing keys, Tricia figured she had to start searching where the light was best.

Tricia had to squeeze past a turnstile to get into the main area. She hiked around mounds of dirt and piles of cinderblocks, large spools with thick metal wire coiled around them, pallets filled with sacks of cement baking in the sun. The old, wooden stable buildings stood at the Belt Parkway end of the property and she headed toward them. These would be demolished sometime soon, presumably, but they hadn't been yet, suggesting that some, at least, were still in use. Perhaps to store tools and supplies, perhaps to stall the horses that would have been housed on premises had the track still been in operation—even if they were doing all their racing at other tracks now, they had to live somewhere, and it wasn't as though there were a lot of farms in the middle of New York.

She took the gun out of her pocket, found a comfortable position for it in her palm, and crept up to the nearest of the long, barn-like buildings. Listening at the door, she heard snuffling and neighing inside, then a man's voice saying something she couldn't make out. So she wasn't alone. Just as well to know for sure.

Staying close to the walls, keeping to the shadows as much as possible and walking softly, she went on to the next building. This time she heard nothing at the door. She continued to a third, lower building, where she heard the ring of metal against metal, and she imagined a burly smith hammering a horseshoe, the sort you might find in an illustrated Longfellow. She peeked inside through a space between two boards, but couldn't see anything. It was too dark within, too bright outside.

The taller buildings resumed and she scurried past several of them, scanning the numbers painted beside each door as she went: 4, 5, 6. At the door to Stable 8, she paused to listen, heard no sign of people inside, and carefully slid the door open on its rollers, just wide enough to admit her if she squeezed through sideways. She slipped in through the opening, dragged the door shut behind her.

It took a moment for her eyes to adjust to the darkness. There were stalls along both sides of an open central passage. The roof was high enough overhead that she couldn't make it out. The only light came through cracks and crevices in the walls, plus one small, high window on the far end that threw a single spot of daylight on the straw-strewn floor. Two long banks of electric lights were turned off, and Tricia wasn't about to turn them on.

She passed along the row of stalls on one side, most of them empty. Halfway down she saw a silver horse, a filly two heads taller than her, with fine white hair criss-crossing over her forehead like a lace veil. The filly nickered as Tricia went by. In a wooden rack beside the stall a cardboard placard said *Spiderweb* and beneath this, on a chalkboard hanging from a nail, were supplied a dozen lines of information in a crabbed cursive handwriting: the horse's feeding schedule, her training history, her ownership. Tricia peered close to make out this last. Spiderweb was owned by an outfit called the Nickels Group. Nickels—Nicolazzo? Maybe. Tricia moved on.

The only other horse on this side was a red roan stallion named *Make A Wish*, also credited to the Nickels Group. She moved to the opposite side and found two more: *Braddock's Bane* and *Shooting Star*. Four Nickels. One more, she thought, and you'd have a quarter. Or a quarterhorse.

Come on, Tricia. Don't get loopy.

She made her way back to the entrance and was about to slide the door open again when she heard a sound outside: footsteps, heavy tramping ones, two men at least, and they were approaching quickly, almost at a run. She glanced around, looking for a place to conceal herself if they came in, but there was nothing—not so much as a bale of hay she could crouch behind, just the stalls themselves, and the nearest one was occupied.

The footsteps stopped directly outside the door and she heard a voice bark, "Where is she? Where did you say you saw her?"

Tricia's heart stopped. She felt the weight of the gun in her hand, the pressure of the trigger against her finger. At least two men—and she had just the one bullet.

"She was right here, goin' from building to building," came a voice Tricia recognized with dread as Bruno's. "Right here," he said again.

Tricia heard the door's rollers creak and shift in their track, saw the crack of daylight at the door's edge begin widening. There was no time to think. She turned, ran to the chest-high door of the stall behind her and, climbing on the groom's stool beside it, pushed herself over the top. She toppled onto the ground beside Shooting Star, a tall black horse with a deep chest and white markings on his lower legs. The horse shifted nervously and neighed as she gathered herself and brushed urine-scented straw off her knees. At the risk of being seen, she stood up, held one hand to the horse's cheek and the other to his neck, and stroked gently, whispering, "Sh...sh..." She thought back to childhood and the first stable she'd ever been in, just outside Aberdeen, one Coral had taken her to when she'd been little. The horses had frightened her then. It wasn't the horses that frightened her now.

Shooting Star whinnied and Tricia redoubled her efforts to calm him. The door, meanwhile, had slid open to its full width, letting in a wide slash of sunlight that fell across the floor like a guillotine blade. Through the open top portion of the stall door, Tricia could see a long shadow step forward, one arm bent at the elbow and holding a pistol before it. She dropped back to a crouch. She heard the man go by, followed a moment later by a second.

Tricia inched over to the corner of the stall beside the door and then, with her back pressed against the wall, stood once more. There was a wide wooden post here at the border between this stall and the next that topped out around seven feet, and standing behind it she was fairly sure they couldn't see her. She'd stopped whispering to the horse once the men came in and now she was too far away to stroke him, but from her hiding place in the corner she held him with her eyes, and though it felt foolish she raised one index finger to her lips. Would it help? Who could say? But Shooting Star stared back and stayed quiet. All Tricia could hear were the steps of the men as they walked to the far end of the barn and came back—that, and the thudding of her pulse in her ears.

"Hey," one of the men called, the one who wasn't Bruno. His back was to her at the moment—both men's were. "We know you're in here. We won't hurt you if you come out." The false friendliness in his voice was chilling. He made almost no effort at all to sound as though he meant it.

Tricia tried to breathe as shallowly as possible, making no sound. She raised the gun, shrank into the shadow.

"Come on," the man said, "don't make us do this the hard way. You're just going to make us mad."

When they got no response, Bruno said, "Maybe it was the next stable over."

"You said this one."

"I thought it was this one," Bruno said, "but maybe it was the next."

"Well, why don't you go look there then." The other man sounded annoyed. "If she's here, I'll flush her out. If you see her, yell."

"Okay," Bruno said. Then: "Remember, she's got a gun now."

"You really think I'd forget that?" the other man said. "Now get over there."

"Okay," Bruno said again, and Tricia heard him leaving.

Remember, she's got a gun—well, of course Bruno would know that. But now the other guy did, too, which was a shame. On the positive side, the odds had just improved: There was now only one man here, which lined up better with the one bullet. Except that the sound of a gunshot would surely bring Bruno running right back in…

"I'll count to three," the remaining man said, his voice fading as he paced further away and then growing louder as he returned. "If you're not out here by the time I reach three…" He stopped pacing and his voice grew darker, nastier. "Let's just say you'll be sorry. We understand each other, right? Uncle Nick wants you alive—but that leaves me plenty of options. *Plenty.* You've only gotten a little taste so far."

Tricia stood in the darkness, shaking. There was a part of her that wanted to step out, gun blazing, take this man down before he knew what hit him. But could she hit him? It was far from certain. She'd fired guns before, every kid in South Dakota did, but not for a while now, and not in a darkened barn, and never at a target that was armed and ready to shoot back.

Meanwhile, there was another part of her that wanted to surrender—drop the gun, step out with her hands up, tell the guy she had Nicolazzo's photos and demand that he take her to him unharmed, untouched. It might work. It might. But it might not. And even if it did, then what? Nicolazzo would have his pictures back and she'd have no gun and no way out, nor any way to help Coral get out.

"If you're in here," the man bellowed, "I'm going to find you. You can't get away."

Tricia heard the door to one of the stalls—it sounded far enough away to be the one on the other end—swing open and slam against the stable wall. A few footsteps, then another door swung and slammed, this one a little nearer. "There's nowhere you can hide. Don't you understand that?"

She understood. She understood it fine.

At the rate he was going, he'd reach her end of the row in seconds—thirty seconds? Forty-five? And then she'd be forced to make a decision. A terrible decision with terrible consequences, whichever way she decided it.

Another door slammed and she heard the man leap into the newly opened stall with a loud *"Hah!"* A moment later he stepped out again.

"You are making me *very* angry," he said, and he certainly sounded it. Almost to himself, he added, "I'm gonna make you hurt real bad." Less a threat than a promise.

He was just two stalls away now.

Tricia tried to will her right hand to stop shaking. She steadied it with her left, held the gun between both, fit both index fingers inside the trigger guard. Her breath was coming fast now, and she could hardly believe he couldn't hear it, that and the pounding of her heart. It was a cacophony to her. Shooting Star whinnied beside her—he probably smells the fear on me, Tricia thought, and why not? I must stink of it.

"Shut up, you nag," the man said. He stopped at the stall beside Tricia's, put his hand on the door latch.

He yanked it open, let the door swing free, and began another exclamation—*Hah!* or *Huh!* or something of that sort—but just what it was Tricia would never find out since from inside the stall came the explosion of a gunshot and the man fell backwards clutching his chest.

35.

Kill Now, Pay Later

Shooting Star reared up and bucked wildly; the other three horses sounded like they were doing the same. Dodging the horse's flailing hooves, Tricia flung herself at the door to the stall, scrabbled up and over and landed in a heap on the ground. She saw the man lying there, blood pooling around him, just a few feet away. From the open stall a figure came forward, gun in hand—

"Don't shoot!" Tricia screamed and swung her hands up, thinking too late that maybe she should have dropped her gun first. That would've made for a more convincing surrender. But instead of blasting her, the figure lowered its own gun.

"Trixie?" Erin said. "Is that you?"

"Erin?" Tricia said. "How did you—never mind, you'll tell me later. We've got to get out of here before Bruno comes back."

"Hold on," Erin said, and bending over the fallen man, calmly put another pair of bullets into him. Judging by his lack of any reaction, they were superfluous; but judging by the clicking of Erin's gun she would gladly have given him more if she hadn't run out of bullets. "There," she said, to the corpse. "How's that for a little taste?"

"Jesus, Erin!" Tricia stood up, pulled at Erin's arm. "Come—"

But Bruno was filling the doorway now, silhouetted in the light from outside. They ducked to either side as a twin-barreled shotgun gun swung up and spat flame at them. The hammering of the horses' hooves against the stall doors echoed like a further fusillade.

Bruno ran between them to where his fellow gunman lay. "What did you do?" he shouted, swinging his shotgun back around, trying to find them in the shadows. With his other hand he pulled a second gun from his belt, a handgun. "If you…if you killed him, you'll pay for it!"

"Probably," Tricia heard Erin say, "but not today." Then came the sound of a door being unlatched and swinging open, followed by a half-ton of angry horse erupting from the stall.

Tricia felt a hand on her arm, pulling her toward the entrance, saw Bruno, illuminated by brief flashes of gunfire, shooting point-blank into the horse's pale brown torso but making not the slightest dent in his momentum. She saw Bruno go down, still firing, saw Braddock's Bane tumble onto him; then Erin pulled her out into daylight and they both began running at full speed, arms and legs pumping hard, toward the front gate in the distance.

"There!" someone behind them shouted, and a pair of gunshots chased them across the gravel walk and onto the track. Tricia expected a bullet to catch her at any instant.

"You! Stop!"

More shots whizzed by, one tearing up the dirt by their feet and spattering clods against their shins.

The turnstile seemed very far off. And past it was the largest of the parking lots—nothing but blank concrete there, nothing to hide behind: not trees, not cars, nothing. If they could make it through the lot to the sidewalk they'd have a better chance, but even there...

And that was assuming they made it to and through the turnstile. Doing so would require them to get past this no man's land in the center of the track, half planted with trees and shrubs, half empty soil. On the barren side, Tricia saw an earth grader standing silent and un-helpful; on the other, a paddock where a track walker with remarkably bad timing was trying to keep the bay stallion he'd brought out for a trot from running each time a gunshot split the air.

Erin, meanwhile, was falling behind—she didn't have the benefit of dancing two shows a night to build up her stamina and endurance, not to mention the lingering effects of whatever mistreatment she'd suffered at the hands of Nicolazzo and the gunman she'd put down back in the stable.

"Can you make it?" Tricia said.

"Do I have a choice?" Erin said. She stumbled and almost fell, but she caught and righted herself, kept going.

Behind them, Tricia heard the pounding of feet, the heavy breathing and cursing of their pursuers. There were at least three of them, maybe four, and no more than forty yards away.

"Is there a car somewhere?" Tricia said. "Something we could use…?"

"Just that thing," Erin said, jerking her head toward the grader. "If you know how to jumpstart it."

She didn't—but glancing over the opposite way, Tricia had another thought. She angled off to the left, running along a line of low bushes.

"Trixie! It's—it's longer that way—"

It was. But it also intersected the paddock where the walker was working, with some success, to calm his horse. He looked up as they burst in on him.

"We need that horse," Tricia said, gesturing with her gun. His mouth opened, but before he could say anything she grabbed the reins out of his hands and hoisted herself up onto the horse's back, bunching her dress around her waist, modesty be damned. She kept the gun trained on the man with her other hand.

Erin tried to follow but slipped off the horse's side on her first attempt. The men chasing after them were shouting now, just twenty yards away and closing. One of them sent a bullet at them through the trees. Tricia heard a branch crack and fall. The horse squealed and jerked to one side; it was all Tricia could do to keep him from bolting.

"Erin, quick!" She reached down one arm and Erin caught it, almost pulled Tricia off, but grabbing hold of the horse's mane with her other hand and kicking wildly with her feet she finally managed to sling herself belly-first across the horse's back. She snaked one arm around Tricia's waist, held on tight. Tricia kneed the horse in the sides, cracked the reins, shouted—"*Yah!*"—and the horse burst forward, delighted to be doing what it did best and to be doing it in a direction that took it away from the men with guns.

The horse pounded across the dirt, over the track, his sides heaving and hooves thundering. When he came to the low concrete wall separating the track area from the parking lot, he leapt it smoothly, landing with a jarring jolt that almost unseated them both. But Tricia held onto the reins and Erin, now upright at last, held onto Tricia, and the horse went *clopclopclop* across the asphalt and onto Rockaway Boulevard.

36.
Slide

Cars swerved, honking, out of their path. Pedestrians, too, made way as the horse loudly approached, its metal shoes echoing against the pavement. This was one of the main shopping thoroughfares in this part of Queens and Sunday afternoon was prime shopping time. There was no shortage of people to goggle at Tricia and Erin as they galloped past.

Several ran for street-corner phone booths, leaving Tricia wondering how long they had before more than just the attention of passersby was directed their way. They'd left the men at the track far behind, but it wasn't as though Nicolazzo's men were the only ones interested in getting their hands on her. And riding a racehorse down Rockaway Boulevard was as fine a way to attract the attention of the others as any Tricia could imagine.

They sped along the avenue, attracting stares and gasps. One little girl on the sidewalk raised her arm and pointed, only to have her mother slap her hand down and yank her protectively out of the way. The girl started bawling, but at the pace they were going Tricia could only hear it for a few seconds.

The police sirens, when they came, were louder and lasted longer. One cruiser slid in behind them as they crossed 103rd Avenue, but they lost him by taking a sharp left against the traffic onto 102nd Road and then racing through a gas station parking lot and the scruffy back yards of three low brick homes. Another cop car picked up the chase when they hit Eldert Lane, the driver shouting at them through his bullhorn to pull over. "We'll shoot if you don't stop," came the amplified voice.

Tricia could feel the horse tiring under her, felt its ragged breaths, its slowing pace. They wouldn't be able to go a whole lot farther even if the cops didn't shoot. But Erin urged her on. "Don't," Erin said. "We've got to shake them."

"Where?" Tricia shouted back, her voice getting lost in the wind. But she tugged on the reins, turning the horse off the main road, and they vanished once more into the maze of yards and passages behind and between buildings.

"We'll have to stop soon," Tricia shouted and she felt Erin nodding against her back.

"You know where Jamaica Avenue is?" Erin said.

"No," Tricia said.

"Up by all those cemeteries? Mount Cypress, Mount Lebanon, you know."

She didn't know. But somehow Tricia wasn't surprised to find herself racing toward yet another cemetery. There seemed to be no getting away from them. New York was peppered with good places to lie down and have a final rest, to go with all the reasons you might need to.

"Just keep going, you'll hit it," Erin said.

"Why there?" Tricia shouted.

"We can ride into the cemetery," Erin said. "The cops can't drive in. They'd smash up all the graves. They'd never do it."

"How far is it?"

"Not much farther."

"How much?"

"I don't know, eight blocks? Nine?"

"Great," Tricia said and urged the horse on.

It turned out to be twelve blocks. By the time they reached the elevated tracks marking the end of the road, Tricia could feel the horse trembling from exertion and the unaccustomed weight they'd made him carry, like running a race with two jockeys. They sped under the high metal beams as a row of subway cars clattered by overhead, then through the wide-open front gate of a place identified by a large but tasteful sign as *Mount Hope*. Tricia was willing to take the name as a good omen. Better, at least, as death-related gateways went, than *Abandon Hope*.

A steep hill just inside the gate led to a cluster of mausoleum buildings at the top. The horse strained to climb it at a decent canter.

As they neared the top, Erin said, "We should get off here, quick. Let him keep going. Just slide off."

"What do you mean 'slide off'? You can't just slide off a moving horse."

"We don't want him to stop," Erin said. "We need them to keep chasing him."

"They'll see we aren't on him," Tricia said.

"Not right away. Now slide off. Slide!"

Tricia felt Erin tilting behind her, felt gravity take hold. The sweat on the horse's sides contributed its part and she felt herself accelerating toward the ground—which

was still going by at a considerable clip. She hadn't been
able to scream when she fell from the rain gutter, but she
screamed now, and Erin joined her. It didn't last: Col-
liding with the ground knocked the wind out of them.
For an instant, all Tricia could see were the horse's hooves
raising and lowering like angled pistons just inches away
from her head—but then they were a foot away, and then
a yard, and then the horse was off in the distance, gal-
loping to freedom among the tombstones.

The police sirens, meanwhile, had grown louder as the
hoofbeats faded. A pair of cars squealed to a halt at the
bottom of the hill. Tricia glanced around, saw Erin beside
her doing the same. There wasn't much here: the stone
mausoleums, whose doors presumably were locked; a
narrow footpath, winding off into the heart of the cemetery; another path, leading down the hill; a plot of graves,
mostly old and overgrown, though one was freshly dug
and covered with a tarpaulin, presumably for a burial
later today.

Tricia and Erin looked at each other, gave each other
a chance to object or to propose a better idea. Instead,
they nodded simultaneously, then scampered on hands
and knees toward the grave, lifted the side of the tarp,
and slid under it. Carefully, they let themselves down
into the hole. The tarp settled back into place.

Moments later, they heard the police arrive. They saw
shadows through the tarp, heard sounds of men arguing,
walking this way and that overhead, complaining. A radio
crackled with static followed by the voice of someone
back in the stationhouse issuing orders. Tricia couldn't
quite hear what they were but made out a few incredu-
lous-sounding words, "horse" chief among them.

The cops departed a moment later, no doubt following
the horse's tracks. Tricia reached above her to push the
tarp back, but Erin raised one palm in a gesture that

meant *Wait*. The caution did make a certain amount of sense—what if the cops had left a man or two behind to search the area?

So they waited. It was cool and damp standing in the grave. Surprisingly, it wasn't unpleasant. A bit of light filtered in through the tarp, the fabric tinting it a lush shade of green. Being off the horse gave Tricia the opportunity to flex her legs, strained from straddling the animal's shoulders. She hadn't ridden like that in years and her thighs had taken a pounding. She saw Erin doing the same, bending her knees in the limited space the grave afforded and massaging her lower back with one hand.

When a few minutes had passed without any further voices or tumult overhead (it felt like more than a few minutes, but Tricia figured everything felt longer when you were standing in a grave), Erin knelt and put her hands out in a cupped position. Tricia set one foot into them and Erin hefted her toward the tarp.

Tricia yanked the fabric to one side and popped her head out of the grave. Behind her, she heard a sharp intake of breath.

She pulled herself out of the hole and scrambled to her feet. A small man in a surplice stood at graveside, a prayer book open in his hands; beside him, an old woman in black, a veil lowered over her face, dipped a gloved hand below the veil to bring a handkerchief to her eyes. Beside her was a slightly younger woman. Her eyes, prominent to begin with, looked positively ready to leave their sockets.

Tricia bent down, extended an arm, and helped Erin out of the hole.

"Inspection," Tricia said, by way of explanation, and Erin nodded. They both wiped their palms off on their sides.

"Everything's in order," Erin said.

"Good drainage," Tricia said.

"Solid foundation," Erin said.

"Up to code," Tricia said.

"Carry on," Erin said, nodding to the priest.

"Thank you so much," the old woman said, "for taking the trouble. Calvin would be so grateful."

Feeling like a heel, Tricia led the way past a wheeled gurney holding a coffin and off into the graveyard's crowded interior.

37.
Dead Street

As soon as they were out of sight of the hilltop, Tricia said, "We have to go back."

"Back? What are you talking about? Back where?"

"Wherever they were holding you," Tricia said. "And Coral. Colleen. My sister—the fighter?" Erin's face showed no sign of recognition. "The Colorado Kid, remember?"

"That's your *sister*?"

"It's a long story," Tricia said. "But yes, she's my sister. And we've got to—"

"All we've got to do is get out of here. There's no point in going back. I'm sure they're not there anymore. They hustled us out of the other place as soon as Charley got out—now that I've escaped, you can bet they're gone from this one."

She was right, of course. But Tricia's heart fell at the prospect of having to figure out where Nicolazzo might hole up next. Would Coral have been able to leave her another message, scratched on another wall in another basement cell? It was too much to hope for.

"How *did* you escape?" Tricia asked.

"That's kind of a long story, too," Erin said. She kept walking swiftly, picking a path between gravestones and along the edges of the tree-lined lawns.

"You got a gun somehow," Tricia said.

"That's right. I got a gun somehow."

"You don't want to talk about it?"

"No," Erin said, "and you don't want to hear about it. It'd turn your hair white, Wyoming. Better than that bleach we used."

"That bad?"

Erin nodded. Looking her over, Tricia couldn't see any particular signs—no marks on her face, for instance. But what did that mean? Tricia let the subject drop, tried not to think about what Nicolazzo's men might be doing to Coral right now. At least there were two fewer of them now. That was something.

"Is Charley okay?" Erin asked.

"So-so," Tricia said. And when Erin looked alarmed, "Oh, he's safe. He just had a…run-in, with someone who works for this mobster we met."

"For Nicolazzo?"

"No, Barrone."

"Barrone?"

"Long story."

They were making their way now through a rough, un-tamed bit of wilderness, the border between two abutting cemeteries. It felt a little like one of those black-and-white spy movies, crossing from Hungary into Austria under cover of darkness, only without the darkness, and without the zither music.

"Where are we going?" Tricia said.

"Best chance of catching a ride around here's on Dead Street," Erin said, and Tricia gave her a blank look. "Never heard it called that?" Tricia shook her head. "The Interborough Parkway—between Cypress and Forest Parkway it runs right through the cemetery. Blame Robert Moses. Twenty-some years ago he came along and said, 'What we need here's a highway, a nice four-lane highway.' "

"In the middle of a cemetery?"

"This is Robert Moses we're talking about. Where he wants a highway, he gets a highway," Erin said. "They had to dig up hundreds of graves, move the bodies…you really never heard about this? What do they teach you in Wyoming, anyway?"

"South Dakota."

"South Dakota," Erin conceded. She looked around. "Not too much farther."

"Good," Tricia said.

"When we were kids," Erin said, "the story was they didn't move all the bodies, just paved over some of them. If your parents drove along Dead Street, you wouldn't roll down your window. You ever walked it or rode a bike, you held your breath."

"You grew up in this area?"

"Oh, yeah," Erin said. "Woodhaven born and bred. Me and George Gershwin."

"Is *he* buried here?"

Erin sneered. "This place is for the working classes, honey. I'm sure he's got a fine plot upstate somewhere, or maybe in Hollywood, with a lovely view, and not of a highway, either."

Up ahead, a steep embankment led to a low concrete wall. The sound of cars rushing by came through from the other side.

"What if the cops are waiting for us?" Tricia asked in a low voice.

"Then we find another grave to go stand in till they go away."

They crept up to the wall, keeping their heads down as

they went. Erin peeked over the top and Tricia felt a sudden wave of anxiety. She reached toward her pocket, where the gun lay. But before she could get to it, Erin stood, waved Tricia up. "We're alone."

Tricia let her hand drop. Her fingers, she noticed, were trembling.

They made their way onto the shoulder of the highway. Traffic was light, just a car every thirty seconds or so, drivers zooming from west to east at top speed. Maybe trying to cover the length of Dead Street without taking a breath.

In one of the lulls, they crossed to the other side.

"Now what?" Tricia said.

"You never hitchhiked, Trixie? Back in that small town of yours?"

"Sure, but it's different in a small town—"

"It's no different," Erin said. "Just show a little leg." She gave Tricia a nudge toward the traffic. "You showed plenty when we were on that horse."

Tricia felt foolish standing on the side of the road, one hip cocked, thumb extended in imitation of countless stranded movie heroines; but she did it. After the third car passed them by, Erin joined her, unbuttoning a few buttons on the front of her dress and throwing back her shoulders.

The next car that passed slowed down and tootled its horn as it went by, but it didn't stop.

"Thanks a lot," Erin shouted. She opened a few more buttons, bent forward so more of her bosom spilled out.

"Erin!" Tricia said.

"No time to be a shrinking violet," Erin said. "I'd take it off if it would get us a ride."

But that proved unnecessary. A white Pontiac convertible with a chrome dart running along the side drew to a stop, throwing up a little cloud of dust. The driver was a man in his middle forties, corpulent and sunburned, driving with one hand on the wheel and the other arm extended over the back of the empty passenger seat beside him.

"Car broke down, girls?" he said, eyeing the two of them over the top of his black-framed sunglasses.

"That's right," Erin said, leaning on the side of the car. "We need to get back to Manhattan."

"Ah," the man said. "That's a shame. A real shame." He tore his gaze away from her cleavage with some difficulty. "I'm headed to Bensonhurst. Much as I'd enjoy your company…" He made a movement toward the steering wheel and Tricia saw his foot inch toward the gas. He gestured with his chin at Erin, who was still leaning on the door. "If you don't mind…?"

"Lucy," Erin said, and it took Tricia a moment to realize Erin meant her, "why don't you show the man what you've got in your pocket?"

"The pict—" Tricia said, and then: "Oh." She took out the gun, aimed it at the driver, whose face fell. He looked ten years older suddenly.

"We need to get back to Manhattan," Erin said. "You want to drive us, or would you rather get out here so we can drive ourselves? Or would you prefer the third option?"

"What's that?" the man said nervously.

"They call it Dead Street for a reason," Erin said, and smiled.

For a moment it looked like the man might stomp the gas and peel away, but he must've figured his chances of outrunning a bullet weren't good enough to risk it.

Grudgingly he said, "Get in." And to Tricia, "Please, just be careful with that thing."

"Don't worry about Lucy," Erin said. "She's a crack shot. Steadiest hands in the east."

"That right," the man said.

"Oh, yeah," Erin said. "Took home three medals for marksmanship. Isn't that right, Lucy?" Tricia didn't say anything, just concentrated on keeping the steadiest hands in the east from shaking while she climbed into the car.

"She's modest," Erin said. "But deadly. So drive carefully."

He drove very carefully.

Half a mile down the road, they saw a bay stallion grazing at the side of the highway. Two cops were beside it, one talking into a radio.

Erin and Tricia both turned slightly in their seats to face away from the policemen.

"Keep your hands on the wheel," Erin said, "and your mouth shut."

"What are you," the driver muttered, "car thieves or horse thieves?"

"Now, now," Erin said. "No reason a girl can't be both."

38.

Deadly Beloved

They pulled to a stop in the shadow of the Williamsburg Bridge. "Don't look back," Tricia said, the first words yet that she'd spoken to the driver, and she said them in the most menacing tone she could muster. She kept one hand in her pocket as she climbed out of the car, then hastened with Erin to the subway the instant the Pontiac sped out of sight.

Would the driver stop at the nearest police station and report them or just count himself lucky and hurry off to whatever he was late for in Bensonhurst? No way to know, and it was best not to take any chances.

The Times Square station was crowded when they arrived there and Tricia briefly lost sight of Erin on the way out. They found each other on the street.

"I left Charley in a bar near here," Tricia said, "a sort of after-hours place run by a guy named—"

"Mike?" Erin said. Tricia nodded. "I know Mike. He's okay."

"He was very decent to us," Tricia said. "Let us use his back room."

Erin gave her a funny look. "You and Charley? You used Mike's back room?"

"Yes. We needed some sleep. Only managed to get an hour or so, but…"

"I bet you did," Erin said. "I didn't think you had it in you, kid. Or that he had it in you. I guess I shouldn't underestimate Charley."

Tricia found herself blushing furiously. "We just slept there," she said. "Nothing else."

"Save it for the folks back home," Erin said. "I know better. Charley took me to Mike's back room once, too."

"I'm telling you, nothing happened!"

"Well, if that's true," Erin said, making the turn onto 44th Street, "I'm sorry for you. You missed something fine."

Tricia found herself wondering, from the look on Erin's face, whether maybe she had.

They climbed the stairs to Mike's place, knocked on the door, knocked again when no answer came. After another minute, footsteps approached, the panel slid open, and then Mike opened the door. "Did Charley find you?" Mike said breathlessly.

"What do you mean did he find me?" Tricia said.

"When he woke up and saw that you were gone, he

was pretty sore. Mostly with me. Wanted to know why I let you go off by yourself."

"What were you supposed to do, physically restrain me?"

"That's exactly what I asked him. He said yes, physically restrain you. If that's what it took."

"So where is he?"

"He went through all those papers you left here—the photos and letters and so on, and he found this." Mike picked up Royal Barrone's note from the bar. There was Coral's handwriting, in the margin: *AQUEDUCT, STABLE 8, STALL 3*. "He asked if that's where you'd gone. I said I didn't know. He went anyway."

"When was this?"

"Maybe an hour after you left? Hour and a half?"

"And you haven't heard from him since?" Erin said.

Mike shook his head. He led them over to the bar, walked behind it, took out two glasses unasked and filled them with beer from a tap. "I'm sorry, Erin. I shouldn't have let him go."

"That's right," Erin said. "You should've physically restrained him."

"You think he's in trouble?"

"Yes," Erin said.

"But he'll get out of it," Mike said. "He always does."

"You just keep telling yourself that," Erin said. "If it makes you feel better."

Tricia, meanwhile, was trying to think who would have been waiting for Charley at the track when he arrived— Nicolazzo's men? Or the police?

"We've got to go back, Erin," Tricia said. "Now we really do."

"No way," Erin said. "You think Charley would want us to put ourselves in danger?"

"I think he'd want us to get him out of there," Tricia

said, "just like he came for me when the police tried to arrest me downtown."

"Get him out of where?" Erin said. "We don't even know where he is."

"I've been calling around," Mike said. "That's why I couldn't come right away when you knocked—I was on the phone. He hasn't been arrested. I've got friends on the force who'd know it if he had."

"You might think that's good news, Mike," Tricia said, "but arrested's probably the better of the alternatives right now."

"I'm just saying, he's not in police custody. That's all I know."

"Well, he's in *someone's* custody," Tricia said. "Or he'd be back here already. Or at least he'd have called."

The phone on the wall behind the bar chose that moment to ring.

They all looked at each other. Mike reached out an arm, lifted the receiver the way a ranger might pick up a snake.

"Mike? Mike?" came a tiny voice. "Say something, Mike, I can't talk for long."

"Charley?" Mike said, bringing the receiver to one ear but keeping it tilted away from his head so they could all hear.

"Listen, if you see Tricia or Erin, tell them I'm fine, don't let them know—"

"We're right here," Erin shouted.

"Oh," came the voice. "Well. I'm fine."

"Stop it," Tricia said. "We're going to come get you."

"Don't," Charley said. "You'll just get yourself killed. Let Mike. He's got experience."

"Where are you?" Mike said.

"On the waterfront," Charley said, "somewhere near the Gowanus. They're putting me on a diet of treacle this evening."

"On what?"

"A diet of treacle," Charley said. "It's a boat. That's its name: *A Diet of Treacle*. Mike, are you there?"

"I'm here."

"Nicolazzo's here, too. I think we're going to meet his yacht off the coast."

"Is Coral there?" Tricia said.

"I don't know, I haven't seen her. I'm sorry. Mike? Listen, you've got to come get me before the third race at Belmont. They're just staying long enough to pick up the purse from that race and then they're gone. It's at—ah, jeez, I've got to go, he's coming to." And the phone went *click*.

Mike replaced the handset on its hooks, reached beneath the bar for a telephone book. He flipped to the back where the maps were printed. He didn't say anything, and neither did Tricia or Erin. It didn't feel like there was anything to say, or any time to say it.

Mike ran his finger along the coastline of Brooklyn till he found the piers by the Gowanus Expressway, jutting provocatively at New Jersey across the water. He flipped back through the business listings, looking for something. It took a while for him to find it. When he finally did, he reached for the phone—but before he could lift it, it rang again.

"Hello?" he answered.

A different voice this time, deeper and bearing a familiar accent.

"Put the girl on," said Uncle Nick.

"What girl?"

"Hold on," he said, and then they heard the unmistakable sound of a punch landing, someone going *oof*. Then Nicolazzo returned. "Now: Put the girl on."

"Which—" Mike started to ask, but Tricia shouted, "I'm here!"

"Good. Thank you. It isn't so much to ask, a little courtesy, is it?"

"How'd you get this number?" Mike said.

"Your friend here was kind enough to supply it," Nicolazzo said. "We only had to break one of his fingers."

Erin erupted, tears suddenly in her eyes, "If you hurt him again—"

"Yes? If I hurt him, then what? You'll hurt me? Please. Don't be foolish. Now, put the other girl back on."

"I'm here," Tricia said.

"Get closer to the phone or speak up, young lady. I can barely hear you."

"I'm *here*," Tricia said.

"All right. So." Nicolazzo cleared his throat. "I know you have my pictures. I also know who took my money and then bragged to you about how he did so."

"You do?" Tricia said.

"Oh, yes. I received a visit earlier today from my beloved niece, and she brought the *voltagabanna* with her."

"Who?"

"As if you don't know. I have to say, young Edward denied it most convincingly, right up to the end. But he did finally confess. At the very end."

Tricia could barely speak. She thought of Eddie with his black eye, racing past her in Queens. When they found the building empty, he must have driven on to the shuttered racetrack, Renata surely having known about that hideout from when her father had used it the year before. Tricia pictured it, Eddie driving furiously and unknowingly to his own death, Renata urging him on from the back seat.

"You killed him?" Tricia said. She said it quietly, but Nicolazzo heard her.

"No, of course not," Nicolazzo said, and Tricia let out a relieved breath. But then he continued: "My beloved niece did. She really wanted to do it herself. Seemed to bear the boy some ill will."

At this, Tricia felt herself start to shake. She remembered the look on Eddie's face just before he headed upstairs. *Thanks, Trixie*, he'd said. *You're a pal.*

If I'd been a pal, Eddie, I'd have put a bullet in you right then and there. Would've been kinder.

"What do you want?" Tricia said, in a dead voice.

"What do you think? I want my pictures and I want my money. And according to Eddie, he left both with you."

"With me?"

"That's what he said. With his dying breath. A man's not going to lie with his dying breath, now is he?"

"This one did," Tricia said.

"Please. I'm not a fool. You have what I want. If you give it to me, I'll let your friend here go. You, too. I know you're not the one who took it from me, you're not the thief. You just let this man use you. There's no reason you need to suffer."

No, no reason. But you'll make me suffer anyway if you get your hands on me, won't you? Your promises notwithstanding.

But playing along seemed to be the only thing to do. Playing along and playing for time.

"Fine," Tricia said. "I'll do it. But I need some time."

"How much time?"

Tricia looked over at Mike, who held up six fingers. "Till six," she said, but Mike shook his head furiously, mouthed *Six hours*. "...in the morning," she finished. Mike thought about it, shrugged, nodded.

"That's too late," Nicolazzo said. "It has to be today."

"It's Sunday afternoon," Tricia said. "The banks aren't open."

"You put my money in a bank?"

"Safe deposit box," Tricia said.

"And this bank opens before six in the morning?"

"Yes," Tricia said. "It does."

"What kind of bank opens before six in the morning?"

"Mine," Tricia said, coldly.

Nicolazzo was silent for a bit, then she heard the muffled sounds of a conversation in the background. He came back on the line. "Fine. Six. You'll be picked up by two men and brought to me. You'll get a call at this number telling you where. Be there, with my money *and* my photographs, and no police, or your friend here will suffer more than a broken finger." Nicolazzo paused to punch Charley again. It sounded like a boxer socking a heavy bag. "Your sister, too. Oh, yes, I know that's who she is. I know a good deal, Miss Heverstadt. Of Aberdeen, South Dakota. That's right, isn't it? Hmm?" He paused, but Tricia couldn't have answered him if she wanted to, her throat having constricted to the width of a pencil. "Don't cross me, young lady. I'm not such a nice man when I'm crossed."

Nicolazzo broke the connection.

"What are we going to do?" Erin said.

"I'm going to find where they're holding him," Mike said. "You're going to stay here and wait for that phone call."

"That's right, Erin," Tricia said. "We need you here."

"*Both* of you are going to stay here," Mike said. "You heard what Charley said. You can't come with me."

"Who said anything about coming with you?" Tricia asked. "I've got to go get that money."

"You know where it is?" Erin said.

"I have an idea," Tricia said.

39.

A Diet of Treacle

Mike telephoned Volker's from the street and was relieved to find them open. They were the only business he knew in the neighborhood, an importer of German beers that had somehow kept plying its trade all through Prohibition and two wars against the Fatherland. Damned if he knew how they'd pulled that off, what palms they'd had to grease, what lies they'd had to tell, what business they'd had to pretend to be in. But there they were, celebrating their fiftieth year in the same location, according to the brass plaque by the entryway.

This stretch of the Gowanus area of Brooklyn stank, not just of industry and trash and too many people in too close a space, but of fermentation and hops, since in addition to whatever spills and leaks Volker's produced on a daily basis there was, right next door, a one-time leatherwork factory that had more recently been turned into a brewery. The painted brick wall still said JAS. PORTER— SADDLES, RIDING GEAR, &C. — FOUNDED 1870, but the smell said something else altogether.

Volker's eldest son, Adolphe—and speaking of saddles, could his father possibly have saddled the poor boy with a more unfortunate name?—greeted Mike at the door, pinning his hand in the iron grip of one who spent all day every day lifting barrels off ships and onto trucks. "Marie tells me you were coming. Is there anything the matter with our shippings?" He'd been born here; there was no reason for his English to be less than perfect. But it was, and slightly accented, too, as if he'd taken over more than just his father's business when the old man died.

"Not at all," Mike said. "You're on time every time. I just need a favor."

"What is it, Michael? Anything, for one customer of ours."

"I'm looking for a boat that's down here somewhere. Its name's *A Diet of Treacle*. Does that ring any bells?"

"Diet of tree-kill?" Adolphe scrunched up his forehead in thought. "Not a bell," he said. "Not a one. But someone here might know." He walked down onto the floor and called out something in German to the brawny workers moving crates stacked five-high on metal hand-trucks. Mike saw a few shrugs, some heads shaken from side to side. One man said something, though, and Mike looked to Adolphe for a translation.

"He says he does not know this boat himself but suggests you ask at Biro's down the block. Many shipping folk can be found there."

"Thank you," Mike said. And to the man who'd made the suggestion: *"Danke."* It was all the German he remembered from his time on the front.

Outside in the sun again, Mike scanned the block for a sign that would point him in the right direction. He spotted one swaying in the wind, a wooden shingle with the word "Biro" painted on it in faded letters over a sketch of a bull standing in what looked like a pool of blood. He approached a little cautiously, half expecting to walk into an abattoir, but Biro's turned out to be a saloon. The walls were lined with wine bottles, the labels incoherent to any but one of Mr. Biro's fellow Magyars.

"That one's called 'Bull's Blood,' " said a voice behind Mike's left shoulder. "Specialty of the house. It's from a town called Eger. You have heard of Eger?"

"No," Mike said, "but I'll try a glass." He laid a ten

dollar bill on the bar. "You can keep the change if you answer a question for me."

"That must be some question," said the man, a compact fellow with a broad face and a florid mustache. Mr. Biro, presumably.

"We'll see," Mike said. "You ever hear of a boat called *A Diet of Treacle*?"

Biro snatched the bill, made it vanish into the pocket of his vest quick as a dog swallowing a scrap of meat. "Mr. Kraus got a telephone call about it just a few minutes ago. You can talk to him over there." He pointed to a table in a shadowy corner where a white-haired man sat alone. "I bring your wine."

"Mr. Kraus?" Mike said, extending one hand as he approached. The old man looked up from where he sat, stooped, over a half-empty glass. There was a telephone beside the glass, its cord dangling beneath the table.

The man straightened as much as he could, which wasn't very much. "Yes?"

"My name's Mike Hanlon. I'm trying to find a boat called *A Diet of Treacle*. I was told to see you."

"You were told right," Mr. Kraus said. His voice was soft and he had a wet sort of lisp, as if his dentures hadn't been fitted quite right. "It's my boat. I imagine you're curious why I gave it that name."

Mike wasn't, particularly, and more importantly felt the urgency of Charley's situation weighing on him—but he figured saying he wasn't interested was no way to gain the man's confidence. "Of course," he said, sitting down. A hand appeared over his shoulder and set a glass of red wine before him. He sipped it. It was nothing special.

Mr. Kraus said, "My first name is Dorman. Dorman Kraus. In school, the other boys called me Dormouse. Like in *Alice In Wonderland*."

"And...?"

"Are you not a reader, Mr. Hanlon?" Kraus said. "The Mad Hatter's tea party. The Dormouse tells a story about three girls who live on a diet of treacle."

"Sure," Mike said unconvincingly, "that makes perfect sense."

"What did you want to know about my boat, Mr. Hanlon?"

"Do you ever rent it out?"

"Certainly not."

"That's odd," Mike said, "because I understand someone is making a trip in it this evening."

"Nonsense," said Mr. Kraus.

"What was the phone call you got about it?"

"Who says I got a phone call about it?"

"Biro."

"He's wrong."

Mike dug a ten dollar bill out of his pocket and slid it across the table. Mr. Kraus stared at it.

"I don't need to know much," Mike said. "Just where you dock the boat. That'll be plenty."

"It might be too much."

"How so?" Mike said.

"I may be an old man," Kraus said, "but I look forward to living a few years still. Why should I risk that for ten lousy dollars?"

"Another man's life is at stake, too. A friend of mine. A young man, who should have more than a few years ahead of him. He won't if you don't help me."

"This is not my concern," Kraus said.

Mike set a second ten dollar bill on top of the first.

Kraus took out a pocket watch, stared at its face, wound its stem, returned it to his pocket. "It is starting to concern me somewhat more," he said.

"But not enough?"

"Not quite."

A third sawbuck joined the other two. Krauss neat-
ened up their edges, folded the bills in two and then in
two again, set his palm down over them. "Come with me,"
he said and slowly, painfully stood. He took two teetering
steps away from the table with the aid of a cane. "Will you
take my arm? I don't walk very well anymore."

"You don't have to walk," Mike said. "Just tell me where
it is and I'll go there myself."

"No," Kraus said. "I'll take you there. Or you can have
your money back." When Mike hesitated, Kraus said,
"Those are my terms."

Mike reluctantly took his arm, walked with him to the
door. On the sidewalk outside, Kraus looked at his watch
again, then set off at a snail's pace in the direction of the
water.

They walked up First Avenue, pausing repeatedly to let
Kraus rest and catch what little remained of his breath.
In this fashion, they passed warehouses and slips and a
cavernous import-export arcade where traders of various
sorts maintained one-man booths and fanned themselves
to combat the stifling heat. At the pier off 57th Street, a
tugboat labored valiantly to pull an overladen barge out
of its dock. At 53rd, the pier was walled off and Mike
could only see the upper decks of the two ships tied up
there.

When Kraus halted for the third or fourth time in one
block, Mike considered abandoning him and continuing
his search by brute force, hunting down every boat one
by one. But there were too many—too many boats, too
many buildings, too many blocks. He could spend the
next three hours at it and not see them all. And what if
the *Treacle* was docked behind one of the waterfront's
locked gates?

Between 50th Street and 47th, the piers were overgrown with grass and weeds, but a profusion of boats still

stood at them, bobbing gently, while others rode at anchor just off some the longer outcroppings of the shore. Mike scanned the hulls, looking for any names longer than a word or two. "How much farther?" he asked. And, each time they came to a pier, "Is this the one?" But Kraus just shook his head, kept his gaze trained on the ground, and concentrated on putting one frail leg in front of the other.

Only when they reached the far end of the avenue did Kraus take one last look at his watch and say, "All right."

"Where's the boat?" Mike said, staring at the empty pier they were approaching.

"There," Kraus said, and pointed out toward the horizon. There was a ship in the middle distance, chugging swiftly toward the open water. It wasn't so far that Mike couldn't make out figures on her deck. One of them looked like it might be Charley.

Mike rounded on the old man, had to restrain himself from picking him up bodily by the lapels and shaking him. "You knew," he said accusingly. "You—that's why all the time with the watch. Jesus Christ. I bet you can probably walk just fine."

"Sadly, no," Kraus said.

"But you can do better than creeping along like this, can't you? You were making sure they had time to get away!"

"You said all you wanted to know was where I dock the boat," Kraus said. "Well, now you know. I dock it here. You got what you paid for."

"But why...why would they leave now? I thought they weren't going to leave till tonight—" Mike closed his eyes. "They changed their plans, didn't they. That's what the phone call was—telling you they were leaving early. As long as they're collecting the money from Tricia tomorrow morning, they can pick up the purse from the race then, too."

"I don't know what you're talking about," Kraus said. "And I don't want to know. I'm going back now. You don't have to walk with me."

"Walk with you?" Mike growled. "I ought to throw you in the goddamn bay."

"Don't you dare," Kraus said. "I'll scream if you touch me. You'll have the police on you so fast, young man, you won't know what hit you."

"You know something," Mike said, "it'd almost—

40.

Money Shot

—be worth it,' I told him." Mike shook his head. "But of course it wouldn't have been. It would've been a disaster. So I left him there and grabbed the first train back." He swallowed the shot of whiskey he'd poured himself from the row of bottles on his back bar. "I hope you had better luck."

"Not exactly," Tricia said.

"So you didn't find the money?" Erin said.

"Do you see three million dollars on me?"

"What happened?" Mike said. "Where did you go?"

"To Fulton Street," Tricia said.

The brownstone was where she'd left it, looking much the way it had at dawn. She watched from across the street as men entered and departed, one by one or in pairs. She didn't recognize any of them. The limousine wasn't parked out front or, the one time she circled the block to peek at the building from the rear, out back either. There were some cars along the curb, but no way to know whether they belonged to Barrone and his men or to the neighbors.

The curtains were drawn in the windows all the way up, except for one room at the top where the window was open. It was too high up for Tricia to see in, though.

She thought about walking up the stone steps and ringing the doorbell, trying to talk her way in, but it wasn't hard to imagine more ways that could turn out badly than well. So she waited, and she watched.

Renata came out twenty minutes later. She was by herself, Tricia was happy to see, wearing a patterned sundress in red and white and cat's eye sunglasses with her hair pinned up. She looked a bit like an actress trying to go incognito. Tricia fell into step behind her. She kept half a block back, kept other pedestrians between them, but at the same time kept an eye on Renata, watched to see where she'd go. And when she stopped outside a dressmaker's window to light a cigarette, Tricia took the opportunity to come up behind her and plant the nose of her gun in the small of Renata's back.

"Don't turn around," Tricia said.

"Ah, Tricia," Renata said, flipping her lighter closed and replacing it in the clutch purse she was carrying. "You think I didn't know you were there?" She didn't turn, didn't look back over her shoulder, but they could each see the other's face reflected in the darkened store window beside them. "I spotted you the moment I stepped outside."

"I don't believe you," Tricia said. "If you had, you'd never have let me get the drop on you."

"Drop? What drop?" Renata laughed. "You dumb cluck. There are three men watching us right now who'll shoot you the moment I give the signal."

"Oh, yeah? What's the signal?"

She wagged the cigarette between her fingers. "I drop this on the sidewalk. Grind it out under my toe. It'll be the last thing you see. Unless you walk away right now."

"I can pull this trigger before they get me."

"I doubt it," Renata said. She didn't seem nervous at all. She took a long pull on the cigarette, exhaled a mouthful of smoke. "Not going? All right. Have it your way. What do you want?" She raised the cigarette. "You don't have much time left."

"The money," Tricia said. "Where is it?"

"What money?"

"The money you took from your uncle's safe. The three million dollars."

Now Renata began to laugh in earnest, really laugh, so hard her shoulders shook from it. "Oh, god. That's rich. You think I took it."

"Yes, I do," Tricia said. "You took your uncle's money, and then spent the past month holed up in your father's headquarters for protection. I don't know if you planned it together or you did it on your own, but he must know about it now because he's been keeping out of sight too— lying low with you for the past month, trying to keep you safe. That went on until this morning, when poor Eddie barged in on you and you decided you had a sacrificial lamb you could turn over to Uncle Nick to get the heat off you once and for all."

"What an imagination," Renata said. "A headshrinker would probably say it's because of all the loving you're not getting—oh, yes, Charley told me about you, Miss Knees Together."

Tricia pressed the gun against the base of Renata's spine. "Keep talking. You'll spend the rest of your life in a chair."

"Touchy, aren't we?" Renata burned off some more of the cigarette with another drag, then held it up to show off its rapidly diminishing length. "Sure you don't want to go now? I would if I were you."

It wasn't that Tricia wasn't tempted—what if there really were three gunmen drawing a bead on her right now?—but she shook her head. "Are you telling me," she said, "that you didn't take Eddie to your uncle's earlier today? That you didn't kill him? Because your uncle told me otherwise."

"No, Tricia, I'm not telling you that. I'm telling you I didn't take his money."

"And I'm saying you're a liar," Tricia said. "You lied to your uncle about Eddie, certainly. And why would you have lied about who stole the money if you didn't do it yourself?"

"How do you know Eddie didn't do it?" Renata said. "The man confessed."

"Yeah, he confessed—to stealing both your uncle's money and his photographs," Tricia said. "But I know who stole the photos, and it wasn't him."

"But then—then you must know who stole the money, too," Renata said, "and that it wasn't me."

"Uh-uh," Tricia said. "Not so fast."

Renata fell silent. She was taking no more drags on her cigarette now, Tricia noticed, though it continued to burn slowly toward the filter.

"And," Tricia said, emboldened, "I think you're lying about the three men watching us, too. I don't think there's anybody watching us. I think nothing will happen when you finish that cigarette."

"You prepared to bet your life on that?" Renata said.

"Are you?" Tricia said.

They watched each other in the window. Tricia held the gun without wavering. Steadiest hands in the east.

"No," Renata said briskly. "I'm not." She dropped the cigarette butt on the ground, where it continued to smolder. Nothing else happened. "Let's you and I sit down, why don't we."

°

They sat across from one another at a cafeteria on the corner of Dutch Street. The nearest other patron was five tables away and engrossed in a paperback novel, so Tricia was able to keep her gun aimed at Renata behind a menu without anyone noticing or complaining. Except Renata herself, and her complaints fell on deaf ears.

"Why don't you put that thing away?"

"Why don't you start talking," Tricia said, "so I don't have to use it?"

"As if you'd really shoot me in a public place," Renata said.

"It's been a long couple of days, Renata," Tricia said. "Don't bet on me making good decisions."

Renata poured some sugar in her coffee, stirred it. "You know my uncle thinks *you* have his money. That's what Eddie told him."

"Yes, I know. It's not true—but I don't expect to be able to convince him of that unless I can find out who does have it."

"Well, don't look at me," Renata said.

Tricia pulled back the hammer of her gun.

"I didn't take his money," Renata insisted. "I wish I knew who did."

"If you didn't, why do you care who did?"

Renata seemed to make a decision. "I'm going to tell you something that could make my life a lot more difficult if you repeated it. I'm not just doing it because you've got a gun on me. I'm doing it because if you're serious about finding out who took the money, you might be in a position to make my life a lot easier than it's been for the past month."

"How's that?"

"I didn't steal my uncle's money," Renata said, "but not for lack of trying."

"Go on."

"I took a shot at it," Renata said. "I arranged to get into the Sun after hours, went in all set to open the safe and clean it out. Had an escape route planned and everything. But there was no money for me to get. By the time I got there, the safe was already empty."

Tricia had a powerful feeling of déjà vu. "What are you talking about?"

"I'm talking about an empty safe. Nothing in it. Someone else had already been there, broken in, and emptied the thing out."

"You expect me to believe that? That you tried to rob the Sun but some other thief got there first?"

"You see why I've been lying low?" Renata said. "You see? It's the truth, but you don't believe it. Why would Uncle Nick?"

"Why, indeed."

"I'm not worried that he could have found my fingerprints—I wore gloves, I'm not a complete idiot. But who knows what else he might have found that could lead back to me? And someone might have seen me going in or coming out of the building—I can't swear no one did." Renata gulped some coffee. "So ever since, I've been cooped up in that place on Fulton Street, waiting for the old bastard to catch whoever robbed him and put an end to it. But a month's gone by, he hasn't caught anybody, and according to my father he's been getting crazier and angrier about it by the day, rounding everyone up with the slightest possible connection—"

"Tell me about it," Tricia said.

"Eventually, one way or another, he'd get to me. I had to feed him someone. And then Eddie walked through my door."

"It wasn't Eddie's fault. He thought you'd asked him to come," Tricia said. "You know that, right?"

"Yeah, that's what he said. That you told him I'd sent for him. As he stood there gawping at us. It was awful."

"Well, you certainly paid him back for it."

"That's right," Renata said. "I did."

"Let's get back to the robbery," Tricia said, trying hard to push aside her feelings of guilt over her own role in Eddie's death. "You're saying you just happened to decide to rob your uncle on the same day someone else happened to do the same thing?"

"Not exactly," Renata said. "I didn't choose that day out of thin air."

"Oh?" Tricia said.

"Look, I've been thinking about Sal's safe for years now. I *grew up* thinking about it—about all the money he kept in there, about what the combination might be. I'd made up lists of possible combinations—I know something about how the man thinks, so I was pretty sure one of my guesses would be right. And I knew I could get into the room, I'd just copy my father's keys. But I'd never gotten myself over the hump and actually decided to do it. Because what if I did and something went wrong? If I got caught? He'd kill me. I mean, he loves me, I'm his niece, but if I stole from him? He'd kill me without thinking twice. That's the kind of man he is."

Seeing how he'd treated her husband for a lesser offense, Tricia was not inclined to disagree.

"Then about a month ago I'm sitting in one of the bars my father runs—you know he runs all sorts of businesses for my uncle, right? Bars, a garage downtown, couple of motels in Jersey. Anyway, I'm sitting there, middle of the day, having some lunch and a couple of drinks, minding my own business, and I hear these two guys in the booth behind me talking. And what they're talking about is this robbery they're planning. I mean, they were being quiet, but I was sitting right on the other side of the divider, I could hear every word. And after I'd listened for a few minutes I realized it was Sal's place they were talking about robbing. There was this whole complicated scheme —up a wall, through a window, I mean *crazy* stuff. But I started thinking: This is my chance. All I have to do is go in first, clean the place out, then let these two clowns take their stab at it. They're the ones who'd get caught— no one would ever look twice at me.

"So I waited to hear when they were planning to do it. And they said it very clearly: the eighteenth at 3:30. They said it twice.

"So, fine—I got everything ready for the eighteenth, only I went in at 2:00. Plenty of time, right? Figured it shouldn't take me more than 45 minutes, and I allowed myself twice that." Renata shook her head sadly. "They must have changed the plan. When I got to the counting room, they'd already been. The safe was cleaned out. And *I* was the one left holding the bag."

"You'll pardon me for saying so," Tricia said, "but what a load of crap."

"I swear to god," Renata said, "it's true. May I be struck dead if I'm lying."

"You overheard two guys in a bar. Talking about robbing Sal Nicolazzo."

"Yes."

"A bar run by one of Nicolazzo's main deputies. By his *brother-in-law*."

"Yes."

"And you decided you'd beat them to the punch, take your shot at the money, only they beat you instead."

"Yes!"

"Christ, Renata," Tricia said. "Do you see any hay stuck in my hair? Do I look like some hick you can bamboozle with a crazy yarn about two mysterious crooks who are stupid enough to discuss their cockamamie plot in a place owned by the man they plan to rob, but slick enough to pull it off and vanish without a trace?"

"All I can tell you is what happened," Renata said. "Whether you believe it or not, that's your business."

"So what did these two men look like?"

"I didn't get a good look at them."

"Of course not," Tricia said.

"They were sitting behind me!"

"Naturally," Tricia said. "So what bar was it?"

"Why does that matter?"

"Because we can go there and see if we can find anyone else who remembers these guys."

"It was a month ago!"

"What bar was it, Renata?"

"I don't remember," she said. "It was a month ago. I had a couple of drinks in me. Maybe more than a couple." Tricia kept staring at her and so did the gun. "One of the ones on the west side, maybe Royal's Brew or the Rusty Bucket. Probably the Bucket. I'm not sure."

"You're not sure."

She shook her head. "They pretty much all look alike. My father used the same crew to build them all."

"You know what I think?" Tricia said. "I think these two men in this mysterious bar are like the three men you said were watching us just now on the street, the ones who were supposed to kill me when you dropped your cigarette. You're a liar, Renata, and not even a good one."

Tricia stood.

"Are you going to shoot me?" Renata said.

Tricia put the gun in her pocket, but kept her hand in there.

"Let's see this bar of yours," she said. "Then I'll decide."

41.

Zero Cool

The Rusty Bucket was a wood-paneled bar, inside and out, and at first glance it did look a lot like every other dark, nondescript bar in the city: high stools, low lights, assorted pictures and gewgaws hanging from the walls. But when you walked through the door you realized the place had a certain atmosphere of its own, less the result of its décor than of the people clustered around its tables and in the booths against the back wall. They were young, for one thing, many just a year or two older than Tricia and some of the girls not even that. The men wore striped t-shirts and worn dungarees and tennis shoes or moccasins with no socks; one had kicked his off and was barefoot. Only a few were entirely clean-shaven, the rest sporting combinations of sideburns and goatees and unkempt half beards. The girls wore their hair in horsetails or just hanging straight to their shoulders, with no makeup on and hand-rolled cigarettes burning between their fingers.

There was no jukebox; instead, a small stage had been constructed out of low wooden blocks, and a combo—two men and a woman—sat on chairs there, sluggishly stroking their instruments. The woman pulled a low, slow melody out of her guitar while the men accompanied her on bongos and bass.

"What kind of place *is* this?" Tricia whispered, feeling self conscious.

"It's where the far out crowd gathers," Renata said, her voice rich with contempt. "Especially on weekends, when they're not in the fancy schools mommy and daddy are shelling out for."

"It's different during the week?"

"During the day it is. Then it's just a bar. The rest of the time, it's—well, you can see." She folded her sunglasses and put them away in her purse.

The girl stopped strumming and the crowd gave her performance a light spray of applause, some murmurs of approval. In the silence that followed, glasses were emptied and filled, voices raised and lowered. Tricia heard a match flare and then smelled the cloying odor she remembered from the artists' house in Brooklyn.

"So this is the place," Tricia said, "where you heard your two master criminals plotting?"

"I told you, I'm not sure. You remember every place you've ever been?"

"The important ones I do." She prodded Renata in the back. "Let's see if the bartender remembers anything."

"He's probably not even here during the week."

"We'll see."

The bartender was a slope-shouldered, narrow-faced character with long arms and long skinny fingers and black Buddy Holly glasses perched on the bridge of his nose. Behind them, his eyes were red.

"Can I ask you something?" Tricia said.

"Lay it on me," the bartender said.

"You work here during the week, or only weekends?"

"Only when I need bread," the man said with a grin, "which means I slave all seven, sister."

"Well, my friend here," Tricia said, "tells me she was in a couple of weeks back, saw two guys here, sitting in one of those booths, talking about something pretty important. We're trying to track them down."

"All right," the bartender said. "I dig. What'd they look like?"

Through her pocket, Tricia nudged Renata with the gun.

"I don't know…one was about your height," Renata said, "but a little bigger around, huskier. He had a beard, or the start of one, anyway."

"You just described half the people here," the bartender said. "And the other?"

"A few years older, a little smaller, a little thinner. Less hair—like maybe he was starting to lose it. No beard."

"You're putting me on, right? You want to know if I've seen a couple of guys, one's taller, one's shorter, one's heavier, one's skinnier. Well, sure I have, and so's everyone else who's ever been to an Abbott and Costello picture."

"Thanks, mister," Tricia said. "That's a lot of help."

"Cool down, mama, don't you blow your top," the bartender said. "I didn't say I couldn't help, you just got to give me more than that to chew on. You remember anything else?" he asked Renata. "What those cats were wearing? What they sounded like?"

"They sounded like New Yorkers. The older one might have been from Brooklyn, it sounded like. The other one, the bigger one with the beard…I don't know, could've been from upstate somewhere. Sort of a flat voice, like Warren Spahn—you know what he sounds like? The ballplayer?" The bartender shook his head. "You ever hear Harold Arlen, when he sings his own stuff?"

The bartender nodded this time. "Strictly dullsville—not my scene at all. But yeah, I've heard his sides."

"Well, like that."

He mulled it over.

"You remember what they were having?"

"No."

"What day it was?"

"About a month ago."

"But what day of the week?"

"No."

"What time of day?"

"Lunchtime. A little after noon."

"Two guys a month ago at lunchtime? That's all you've got?"

"That's all."

He mulled some more.

"Strikeout," he said finally. "Sorry, baby. I come up dry."

"Well," Tricia said, "there you go."

"I *told* you—" Renata said.

"You told me lots of things," Tricia said.

The bartender waved at the selection of liquor behind him. "Can I get you wrens anything else? Something to drink?"

"Thanks, but no. We've got another bar to try. My friend's got one more shot to get this right." Tricia started to pull Renata away. But Renata yanked her arm out of Tricia's grip, and sat down firmly on one of the stools.

"Actually," she said, smiling up at the bartender, "I'd love a drink."

He looked from one of them to the other. "Fine," he said, a little uneasily. "What's your kick?"

"Nothing," Tricia said. "We've got somewhere to be."

"I'm staying," Renata said. "You run along. I'll see you later."

"No, Renata, we're leaving."

"Or what?" Renata said. She turned to the bartender: "You won't believe what this one's been telling me she'd do to me if I don't do what she says."

"What's that?"

"See how she's got her hand in her pocket there?" Renata said. "She says—"

"Renata," Tricia said.

"She *says*," Renata said, "that she's got a gun in there."

"Renata—"

"A gun?" the bartender said and laughed. Then he saw Renata wasn't laughing. "Man, that's not cool."

"She's joking," Tricia said.

"I'm not joking," Renata said. "She said she'd shoot me if I didn't do what she says."

"You said that to her? That you'd plug her? That's not cool at all."

"Of course I didn't say that," Tricia said.

"You got a rod in there?"

Tricia smiled weakly. She pulled her hand out of her pocket, empty.

"No rod," Tricia said.

"I've got eyes," the bartender said. "I see it there in your pocket."

Sure enough, the outline was showing, plain as day.

Some of the other people sitting at the bar were looking at her now.

"It's not a real gun," Tricia said. "It's just a prop, from this show we're doing."

"We're not in any show," Renata said. "That's a lie."

"Listen," the bartender said, "I don't know what's going on here—but when you start bringing firepower into it, that's a matter for the Man." He lifted a black telephone onto the bar from underneath.

She didn't know which 'Man' he meant—the police or his employer. Either way, though—

"That's not necessary," Tricia said. "I'm leaving."

"Better believe you are," the bartender said as she backed away, keeping her hands in the air. He kept his on the telephone receiver. "Bringing a piece into the Rusty Bucket. That's way uncool. That's zero cool. That's *negative* cool."

He patted Renata's hand and she put on a hurt-and-frightened face to suit.

"Okay, Renata," Tricia said, "you win. But what exactly do you expect me to tell your uncle?"

"Anything you want, long as it's not about me."

"And why shouldn't I tell him about you?"

"I didn't take his money," Renata said. "That's the truth. I didn't take it and I don't have it. You tell him otherwise and you'll get a *second* innocent person killed."

"Innocent!" Tricia barked. "You're about as innocent as Mamie Van Doren."

The bartender lifted the telephone receiver. They could all hear the dial tone.

He said, "If you're not gone in five—"

She was gone in two.

42.

Shooting Star and *Spiderweb*

"Great," Mike said. "Just great." He turned to Erin. "And you—did you get the call?"

"Like Billy Sunday on a Saturday night." Erin lifted a cocktail napkin from the bar. She'd scrawled an address on it. Mike took one look at it and said, "That's the pier. Where the boat was tied up."

"Well, it's where they want you to bring the money," Erin said, to Tricia. "And the pictures."

"The pictures are easy." She patted her pocket. "The money—that's another story."

"It sure is," Erin said. "But I haven't exactly been sitting on my rump while the two of you went all over town chasing wild geese. I've made arrangements."

"What arrangements?"

"We need three million dollars, right? Or anyway a box that looks like it's got three million dollars in it. You'd think the box would be the easy part, but actually that wasn't so. Hope you don't mind that I emptied this." She dragged a footlocker out from behind the bar.

"Fine with me," Mike said.

"Now for the three million dollars part." She swung the lid open.

No one would have mistaken the contents for money— the hand-cut slips of paper were the right size and shape but they'd clearly been cut out of newsprint or, in some cases, what looked like pages of the phone book. "That's not going to fool anyone," Tricia said.

"Not the way it is now, it won't," Erin said. "But with enough layers of actual bills on top it'll pass inspection."

"You want to tell me where these layers of actual bills are going to come from?" Tricia said.

"By all means," Erin said. "They're going to come from a Mister Reynaldo Bruges."

"And who is mister…?"

"Bruges," she said, pronouncing it like she was clearing her throat. "He's a fine Argentine gentleman who some- times calls Madame Helga to book a model or two for a party he's throwing. For some high roller."

" 'High roller' meaning—"

"The man's a bookie," Erin said. "Takes bets, makes book. Hands over layers of actual bills when one of your bets comes in."

"That's your plan? Place some bets and hope one of them comes in?"

"Who said anything about hoping? I'm talking about a sure thing."

Tricia saw Mike nodding out of the corner of her eye. "What? What am I missing here? What's this sure thing you're so…sure about?"

"The third race at Belmont," Erin said, handing over a copy of the *Racing Form*. There were a batch of bill-sized holes in the front page, but the "Races of the Week" listings on the next page were intact. There were a dozen horses listed for the third race. Ten of the names she didn't recognize. Two she did. She'd briefly shared a stall with one of them.

"Uncle Nick's not going to leave anything to chance," Erin said. "If he's got people sticking around to pick up the purse, he knows there's going to be a purse for them to pick up."

"You're devious," Mike said.

"Why, thank you," Erin said. "I try."

"How much money did you put down?" Mike asked.

"All that Reynaldo was willing to float me, or more precisely all he was willing to float Charley. I told him I was putting the bet on for him."

Tricia said, "And you put it on…"

"Shooting Star and Spiderweb, each to win and then the two of them to win and place, either combination. We'll clear more than eleven thousand dollars if they do. That'll fill the box nicely."

"And if they don't win?"

"Then Charley owes some money he can't afford to pay," Erin said. "It won't be the first time. I'd say he's got bigger worries right now than that." She took Tricia by the shoulder. "But they will win. Nicolazzo's not a gambling man, not with his own horses on his own track."

"You think Belmont's his track?" Mike said.

"His and his friends." She turned the knob on the old RCA Mike kept beside the cash register. With a soft crackle the sound faded in. She tuned it, stations passing in a blur till she got to the far end of the dial. "*…and it's Curtain Call and Rented A Tent, Curtain Call coming up on the outside, Curtain Call taking the lead—no, it's*

Rented A Tent, Curtain Call and Rented A Tent, they're neck-and-neck, I'm telling you, this one's gonna be close, it's—it's—It's Curtain Call, folks. Followed by Rented A Tent, and Brassy Lady coming in to show. Those are your results, folks, coming to you live from the Belmont Race Track, where every race is a winner." A trumpeter played a few notes of "Off to the Races" and the program went to commercial.

"How many more to go?" Tricia asked.

Erin looked at the paper. "Two. That was the first."

They sat impatiently through the second race, which took a while to get started and another while in the post-race analysis afterwards. Then came some more words from the sponsor. But eventually the horses were at the starting gate for the third race. The tension couldn't have been any worse at the track than it was in Mike's bar.

"And…" came the announcer's voice, *"they're off!"*

Tricia found her palms sweating, her nails biting into the flesh as the horses rounded the first turn. You could barely hear the hoofbeats in the background behind the sound of the announcer's yammering, but they were there, like her own thundering heartbeat. The horses' names became part of the general din, a swarm of unfamiliar sounds among which she desperately tried to catch the ones she knew.

"It's Will She Shine in the lead, well ahead of the pack, Shooting Star behind her, two lengths back, King's Ransom and Sun Tomorrow and Spiderweb tussling for the number three spot…it's Will She Shine and will she ever, this race is hers to lose, gentlemen, Shooting Star's coming up but they've passed the halfway mark, there's no way he'll catch her—"

Tricia had never been to a horse race in her life, had never listened to one on the radio before, never watched one on television; she'd ridden, like every other kid in

South Dakota, but this was new to her, and she didn't care for it. It was too frenzied, too loud, too desperate—and there was too much at stake.

"*...the race to place is opening up as Spiderweb pulls out in front, she's coming up from behind...Shooting Star's falling back, it's Spiderweb and Shooting Star, Will She Shine out in front, then Spiderweb and Shooting Star, no, no, Shooting Star and Spiderweb—wait—*" A sudden roar rose from the crowd. "*Will She Shine is down, folks, she's fallen, it's a bad one—*" The announcer was shouting now. "*And Shooting Star takes the lead—it's Shooting Star and Spiderweb, now Sun Tomorrow's making a move, it's Shooting Star and Spiderweb and Sun Tomorrow, Sun Tomorrow's coming up, it's Shooting Star and Sun Tomorrow, no, no, now Spiderweb—*" He fell silent for a moment and you could hear the clatter as the horses hit the finish line. "*My gosh, what a race. It's Shooting Star, Spiderweb by a nose, and Sun Tomorrow, followed by King's Ransom in fourth, and poor, poor Will She Shine out of the action, still lying in the track, the medics are coming over—call her Will She Race now, folks, or Will She Even Walk. The jury's out on what this means for this golden, golden horse. It's a sad day at the Belmont Race Track, listeners, a tremendous upset. Your final results: Shooting Star, Spiderweb, Sun Tomorrow. More in a moment.*"

The trumpets blared, and then a Pall Mall jingle began.

Tricia felt her breath coming fast. Her face felt flushed. "That poor horse," she said. "You think Nicolazzo could possibly have known she'd fall...?"

"Possibly known?" Erin said. "I'm sure he paid the jockey to do it."

"That's sickening," Tricia said.

"Add it to his tab," Erin said, picking up the phone. "Now let's get our money."

43.

The Murderer Vine

The taxi let them out at the foot of the Flatiron Building, just a mile or so south of Mike's place.

"I don't understand," Tricia said. "What are we doing here? Why couldn't we go to his office?"

"I'm sure Reynaldo will explain," Erin said. And indeed, a large man came toward them on the sidewalk, explaining as he neared.

"My dear, my dear, I'm so sorry," he said, gesturing with the walking stick he carried. He wore a heavy, woolen suit—too heavy, given the weather—and a sisal hat whose long brim cast half his face into shadow. "I congratulate you on your victory and look forward to giving you what you're due, but—this much money, I can't pay it off on my own say-so. You understand."

"I don't, actually," Erin said. "You must pay off more than this all the time. We're talking, what, eleven, twelve thousand? Not a million bucks."

"No, not a million, it's true. But still—this much money, on a bet placed so close to post time, in a race where the favorite fell…they won't let me do it. We all answer to someone, my dear, and the man I answer to has said he wants to attend to any noteworthy payoffs on this race personally." He took his first look at Tricia then. "And who is this? A friend of yours? I haven't met her before, have I?"

"No. Trixie, this is Reynaldo; Reynaldo, Trixie."

They shook hands and Reynaldo favored her with a smile. "Do you like parties, my dear?"

"No," Tricia said. "I like bookies who pay off when you win, like they're supposed to."

Reynaldo's expression hardened. "Rather a sharp tongue on this one."

"Who is it we're going to be meeting?" Erin said.

"A man named Guercio. His first name is not important. If he is satisfied that there was nothing untoward about your bet, he'll pay what you're due."

"And if he's not satisfied?" Erin said.

"Why think of such things? Come. He is waiting for us." Reynaldo let them into the Flatiron Building through one of the doors on the side. They took a swift elevator to the sixth floor, where a guard in a rust-colored sport coat gave all three of them a cursory pat-down. He didn't find the gun or the photos in Tricia's pocket, since they were back at Mike's where she had left them lying on the bar. He did confiscate a small derringer from Reynaldo.

"You'll get this back when—"

"—I leave, I know," Reynaldo said. "I've been here many times."

"I'm sorry Mr. Bruges," the guard said, pronouncing it to rhyme with "budges," and Reynaldo winced.

"You're new, aren't you?"

"Yes, Mr. Bruges."

He winced again.

"Follow me." The guard led them down the hall and into an office built into the prow of the wedge-shaped building. Past a sturdy oak coat closet on one side and a pair of filing cabinets on the other, the walls angled toward one another, converging at the far end in a rounded-off point just wide enough for one man to stand; and just one man was standing there, hands in his pockets, staring out at Madison Square Park across the way.

"This was once a lovely park," the man said without turning to face them. "An important park. Did you know, the Statue of Liberty was displayed here, in pieces, while she was being constructed? Her arm and her torch. They stood here for years. Now—"

He turned, walked away from the window.

"Now, it's a place I wouldn't let my sister walk alone." He looked at Erin, at Tricia. He ignored Reynaldo.

"This bet of yours, on the horses that won," he said, speaking slowly, as though he wanted to consider each word carefully before letting it out. "This bet, on horses that would not have won had this unfortunate accident not occurred. This bet...what prompted your Mr. Borden to make it?"

"What do you mean?" Erin said. "Charley thought the horses might win. That's why he made the bet. Why does anyone make any bet?"

"Forgive me," Guercio said. "I understand why bets are made. But this particular bet—it is unusually large for Mr. Borden, is it not?"

"Reynaldo accepted it," Erin said. "If it was too large he should have said something."

"Mr. Borden has an admirable record of losing his bets," Guercio said. "For him to win such a large bet on such an unlikely outcome—it stretches credulity, does it not?"

"You know what they say," Erin said. "Even a stopped clock is right twice a day."

"Ha! This is so. And still."

"Mr. Guercio," Erin said, and Tricia marveled at the straight face she was able to keep as she said it, "I can tell you absolutely for sure that Charley had no inside knowledge about that race. He picked those horses because he liked the sound of their names."

"Will She Shine, that's a fine-sounding name, too."

"What can I tell you," Erin said. "He didn't like it as much."

"Your Mr. Borden," Guercio said. "I have…heard things. On the grapevine, you understand. That he is, forgive me, not long for this world."

Tricia, who'd made a great effort to hold her tongue so far, couldn't contain herself at this. "What are you talking about? What have you heard?"

"Whisperings, here and there. That he has made a powerful man angry. That this man now holds him captive and has no intention of letting him go. The details do not matter."

"What sort of grapevine is this?" Tricia said. "They just got him a few hours ago!"

"I assume you know the business I'm in. Mr. Borden certainly does. In this business, people talk. Thieves talk to thieves, second-story men to other second-story men. Killers talk to killers. They each have their own grapevine, and there are few secrets that can be kept from it for long."

"And which one's talking about Charley?" Tricia said.

"The worst," Guercio said. "He is in the hands of murderers, madam. And the word traveling along the murderer vine is that tomorrow's sunrise will be his last. What's more," he said emphatically, "the particular murderer into whose hands he has fallen is not only a savage fellow indeed but the very man whose horses won this race." He spread his palms as if to illustrate how plain and clear it all was. "So you see, I have to consider the possibility that Mr. Borden somehow gained improper knowledge of the outcome of that race prior to its being run, and that this is why he is now facing the punishment he faces."

"It's not," Tricia said. "That has nothing to do with any horse race."

"That would be most reassuring to hear," Guercio said, "if only I believed it."

"What are you saying?" Erin said. "That you won't pay off on the bet? Because none of the rest of this matters. You accepted Charley's wager, he won, now you have to pay off. That's the way it works."

"Don't lecture me on how my business works," Guercio snapped. He got control of himself again and when he spoke next his voice was measured and careful once more. "A bookmaker is an honorable man and has certain obligations, it's true—but only insofar as he is himself dealing with other honorable men. There is no obligation to pay a man who cheats. There is also, I might add, no obligation to pay a dead man."

"He isn't dead yet," Erin said. "Maybe he will be tomorrow or maybe not—but tomorrow's not today, and today's when you owe him his money. You want word to get out that you welsh on your bets?"

"No," Guercio said, "that would be both unfortunate and false—and doubly unfortunate for being false. Perhaps I can suggest an accommodation."

"Such as?"

"We will hold Mr. Borden's money for now—in escrow, if you will. Safe under lock and key. Should he return, alive and well, from his captors tomorrow, that will be evidence enough for us that he didn't cheat and we will release the money. With a day's interest, of course. We are looking to harm no one."

"That's not good enough," Erin said.

"I'm afraid it's the best I can do. These decisions go even higher up in our organization than I."

Tricia thought of Reynaldo's words: *We all answer to someone.* "How much higher?"

"Enough," Guercio said.

"Then we want to talk to whoever's higher," Erin said. "Whoever's got the power to hand over the money we're owed."

"I don't think that's a very good idea," Guercio said. "All you'll do is make him angry."

"Look," Erin said—and as she said it she reached one arm up under her dress and Tricia heard the sound of tape ripping off skin. When her hand emerged, Tricia's gun was in it. "*Somebody* owes me money," she said, "and somebody's going to pay."

44.

Somebody Owes Me Money

Reynaldo's mouth fell open and Tricia felt her own drop as well. When—? How—?

Erin must have taken the gun after Tricia put it down on the bar at Mike's, she figured. Erin had gone to the bathroom before they left. That must have been when she'd taped it to...what, the inside of her leg?

In any event, she had it in her hand now.

Behind them, Tricia heard the guard grunt and, turning, she saw the man drawing a gun of his own out of a holster beneath his sport coat.

Erin sighted quickly and pulled the trigger, and the man's hand shot back, his gun flying out of his fist. With an expression of pain on his face, he jammed his hand under his other arm. Tricia saw blood slowly soak into his sleeve, turning it an even darker shade of rust.

"Toss the other gun," Erin commanded, and when the guard failed to respond, she repeated it. "Otherwise my next shot goes between your eyes," she said.

Her next shot—

There would be no next shot, Tricia knew; Erin had just used up the only bullet in the gun.

"Erin," she said.

"Not now," Erin said. As the guard threw Reynaldo's derringer away from him and, following Erin's gestures, moved over to the narrow end of the room, Erin swung the gun to cover Guercio, whose hands dutifully rose.

"Erin," Tricia said.

"Not now!"

"It's important," Tricia said.

But Erin ignored her. "Mr. Guercio, we need this money—without it, Charley *is* going to die. What's more, it's ours. You owe it to us. So let's skip to the finish here. Who do I need to see to make this happen?"

"You're making a mistake."

"Maybe so," Erin said. "It won't be my first or my last."

"Don't be so sure," Guercio said.

"The money...?" Erin said.

Guercio took the top slip of paper from a stack on his desk, uncapped a fountain pen, and scratched out a few words, paused for a moment, then scratched out a few more. He screwed the cap back on the pen, laid it down, folded the note in half. Held it out to her. "You can take this to the Satellite Club on Union Square, ask for Mr. Magliocco. If he wants to give you the money, it's up to him."

Erin snatched the paper from his hand.

While she was doing this, Reynaldo stepped forward. He gave the knob at the end of his walking stick a counter-clockwise twist and drew out a slim foot-long blade. He dropped the stick itself and swung the blade up to within an inch of Erin's neck. "Not so fast, my dear."

"Put that thing down," Guercio said. "You're going to get yourself shot."

"Oh, she wouldn't shoot me," Reynaldo said. "We've known each other a long time. Isn't that right, my dear?

I'm sorry to do this—but you can't walk in here with a gun and start threatening people. You are my guest, and I'll have to answer for your behavior."

"I'm sorry, too, Reynaldo," Erin said. "I liked you." She turned the gun to face him and pulled the trigger.

He flinched as the hammer clicked on an empty chamber.

She pulled the trigger twice more with the same result. After a moment of confusion, a smile spread across Reynaldo's face. Another appeared on Guercio's, tinged less with relief and more with malice. The guard had no smile on his face at all—just the malice.

"Ah," Reynaldo said. "My dear."

The derringer bucked in Tricia's hand then as she fired it from just two feet away. The blade spun from Reynaldo's grip to clatter against the wall.

Reynaldo howled in pain, wincing and clutching his hand.

Tricia dropped the little single-barreled gun on the carpet. It, too, only held one shot—but at least she knew it. And fortunately, she'd picked up the guard's gun from the floor as well.

She transferred the bigger gun from her left hand to her right, brandished it aggressively.

Erin backed up without crossing Tricia's line of fire. "Only one bullet," she said. "That what you were trying to tell me?"

"Just go call the elevator," Tricia said.

"What did you do with them?" Erin asked as they rode their second cab of the evening to the north end of Union Square. "Tie them up?"

"There wasn't time," Tricia said. "Or anything to tie them up with."

"So, what, you knocked them out?"

"Do I look strong enough to knock out three men, all of them bigger than me?"

"So what did you do?" Erin said. "You didn't shoot them, did you?"

"Of course not," Tricia said. "What do you think I am?"

"Then what did you do?"

"I apologized to them for what we'd done," Tricia said.

"You...apologized."

"I explained to them that with their help we might be able not only to free Charley but also do some harm to Nicolazzo—Guercio didn't seem to have much love for him. And I asked them please to not interfere with our getting the money we're owed from Mr. Magliocco."

"You asked them please...? They're probably on the phone with Magliocco right now!"

"I don't think so," Tricia said.

"Why not?"

"Because I also ripped the phone out of the wall," Tricia said. "And made them take off all their clothes."

"All their clothes," Erin said.

"And get in the closet," Tricia said. "I locked them in. Then I locked their clothes in the filing cabinet. The phone, too." She opened her palm, where two keys lay, one longer, one shorter.

Erin smiled.

"That's more like it," she said.

"I try," Tricia said.

They showed Guercio's note to the bruiser at the door, who patted them down at length before letting them pass, and then to a crew-cut maitre d' who handed the note back with an expression of surprise. Maybe he was used to the women who came bearing notes from Guercio looking more impressive, less run-down. Or perhaps it was the note's second sentence that surprised him.

The note said, *These women wish to collect Charley Borden's winnings—show them every courtesy. But frisk them carefully first.* It was signed just with initials, *V.G.*

The maitre d' bent to his appointed task, giving Tricia her fourth frisking in 24 hours, and her most thorough yet. Uncomfortable as it was, Tricia submitted to the search with good grace. The guard's pistol was sitting comfortably in a garbage can down the block, so she knew there was nothing for the maitre d' to find.

He didn't find anything on Erin, either, though he worked his way up her body slowly and with obvious relish.

"Touch 'em again and I'll have to charge you five bucks," Erin said.

"I've got my orders," he said.

When he was satisfied they had nothing dangerous on them, he led them through a dark and empty lounge to a leather-upholstered door, where he pulled a braided cord dangling from the ceiling. Somewhere behind the door, Tricia heard a bell chime. Footsteps approached, and the maitre d' said, "It's me—Joey," when they'd stopped.

"Yeah?" came a voice. "What kind of wine we serving tonight?"

"Montepulciano."

The door swung open.

Behind it, a roulette wheel spun at a table surrounded by bettors in wrinkled suits and young women in backless gowns. A croupier stood at a craps table, sweeping the dice along the felt to a waiting shooter's hand. The maitre d' threaded a path between the tables and Tricia and Erin followed close on his heels. A few men looked up as they passed but most remained focused on the money they were losing.

There were tables set up for poker and blackjack, but

with no players at them so far—it was still early, Tricia
supposed. Up on one wall she saw a blackboard listing the
start times of upcoming horse races.

They kept going, past a small stage with a red velvet
curtain and rows of plush seats empty before it, then
down a hallway decorated with framed paintings of naked
women. The door at the far end had no upholstery on it
and no braided cord to pull. The maitre d' knocked.

A voice said, "What's the—"

"Montepulciano."

Tricia watched the doorknob turn and the door swing
to. The room inside was brightly lit and well appointed,
with thick curtains hanging before a wide window and
dark cherrywood furniture buffed to a high gloss. On one
side of the room a low sofa supported the bulk of a black-
haired man of at least three hundred pounds and a slender
blonde coiled up on the seat beside him with a resentful
look on her face. She looked to be about Tricia's age; the
man looked at least two decades older.

"What is it, Joey?" the man said in a voice as husky as a
just-wakened drunk's. "Who are these women?"

The maitre d' passed the note to him. "They had this
note from Vincent, Mr. Magliocco."

He read it, passed it back. "You frisk them?"

"Absolutely."

Magliocco sat forward with his hands on his knees. "I
know you," he said to Tricia. "Why do I know her?"

The man who had opened the door—a little pepperpot
with a tangle of curly hair and a nose you could use to
split logs—came over to them for a closer look. "She's
that dancer you liked, boss," he said. "You remember, at
the Sun. You had me give her your number. She never
called," he added accusingly.

"Oh, yes," Magliocco rasped. "The dancer. I remember.
'Begin the Beguine,' right?"

Tricia nodded.

"And what are you here for now? Borden's money? The man's a cheat, and he's about to become a dead cheat. Why should I pay anything?"

"Because you accepted his bet and it came in," Erin said. "You *owe*—"

"Don't tell me what I owe."

"You've taken his money every time he's lost, haven't you?"

"A man wants to give me money, I'll take it."

"Well, then you've got to pay out when he wins!"

"Ah, get her out of here," Magliocco said.

"Both of them?" the pepperpot asked.

"No, just the loud one," Magliocco said. He licked his lips. "Maybe the dancer and I can work something out."

45.
No House Limit

Magliocco sprang to his feet with more alacrity than his size had led Tricia to expect. He kicked the door shut behind the two men. They'd walked Erin out with a hand on each elbow, and at the last moment she'd looked back at Tricia with more than a little concern in her eyes. Tricia had said, "It's okay, I'll be fine," but it had been a reflex. She wasn't at all sure she was going to be fine.

"So," Magliocco said. "What would you like to drink?"

"I'm okay, thanks. I don't need a drink."

"Who ever needs a drink? A glass of water, maybe, if you're in the Sahara Desert. Other than that, it's for pleasure. So what's your pleasure?"

"A glass of water sounds fine," Tricia said.

"Jesus, Mary and Joseph, you're gonna be a pain in my ass, aren't you?" He said it with some amusement, though. "You're cute, you know. Not what I'd call gorgeous, and maybe you don't got knockers like your friend or like Reenie here, but you've got something, kid."

Reenie was staring daggers at her. Tricia wanted to say to her, Don't worry, he's all yours, I don't want him. But she kept her mouth shut.

"Make us a couple gin tonics, will you?" he said, and since he didn't turn his head when he said it, Tricia briefly thought he was asking her to do it. But Reenie must have been used to this and got up and made her way to a little bar set up in the corner.

"That okay with you?" Magliocco said, and this time he was talking to Tricia, so she nodded.

"Good. Good. So listen, here's the pitch: I want you to come work for me. Dance for me. Ditch that bastard Nicolazzo, forget the Sun, come work here. I'll double your salary and you'll make the same again in tips. More, maybe. Depends what you're willing to do."

"He means will you lay for it," Reenie said. She had a queer high-pitched voice, like a boy who'd swallowed the helium from a toy balloon.

"Tschah," Magliocco said, or something to that effect. "Just make the drinks." And to Tricia: "It's up to each girl what she's willing to do. There's no house limit here, each girl sets her own limits. So, you know, whatever you're comfortable doing, where you draw the line, that says how much money you can make. We got rooms in the back, you want to use them—but a good dancer like you, you could make decent dough without even taking none of your clothes off, probably."

"Mr. Magliocco," Tricia said, straining to keep her tone civil, "I appreciate the offer, and I'll seriously consider it—I mean that. Truth is, I can't go back to work at the

Sun and I've got to work somewhere. But right now I just can't think about myself. Charley Borden's in deep, deep trouble and I'm the one that landed him there. I've got to get him out, and we have a plan, but for the plan to work we need money, and the money Charley won on that horse race is the money we need. Can't you just pay what he won and then we can talk about the job later?"

"No," Magliocco said. "But I'll tell you what I will do. You sign a contract saying you'll come to work for me and I'll pay off that bet the next minute. It's what they call a quid pro quo—you know what that means? It's French for you scratch my back, I scratch yours."

Reenie had come over with the drinks—just two of them, one for Tricia and one for Magliocco—and she said, "That ain't French, dummy, it's Latin."

He took one of the glasses from her hand, dashed its contents in her face. "And that ain't a drink no more, now it's war paint. Make me another and keep your yap shut."

Tricia could see the slow burn the poor girl was doing as the liquor ran down her cheeks and dripped onto her décolletage. She waited with dread for the second glass to go flying. But Reenie turned to her politely and held it out for her to take. What could she do? Tricia took it.

"Excuse me," Reenie said, with great dignity. "I'll be back in a moment." Then she was gone, through a side door.

"You shouldn't have done that, Mr. Magliocco," Tricia said. "It was cruel."

"She shouldn't have mouthed off."

"Still."

"Don't feel bad for her," Magliocco said. "She's a spoiled little brat. I'd have tossed her out on her can a year ago if she wasn't so damn good in the rack." He made a drinking motion with one hand and Tricia reluctantly took a sip. It tasted like licking paperclips. "So, what's it gonna be—you want to come work for me?"

There were probably things Tricia would have wanted to do less, but they weren't coming to mind.

What she said, though, was, "I'll do it—but only if you pay that money out to Erin right now. And I mean now."

"Eager," Magliocco said, "I like that." He snatched up the receiver of a telephone by the sofa. "Joey?" he said. "Yah, it's me. The redhead still there? Good, good. Hold on." He waved Tricia over to a desk on the far side of the room, beneath the window. "There's paper and pens there." There were. "Sit down. Write. 'I—,' whatever your name is, '—being of sound mind and body, do hereby solemnly swear to come work for Alessandro Magliocco starting tomorrow and continuing for as long as Mr. Magliocco says I should. Yours truly, et setra, et setra. You got that? Read it back."

"I didn't get it all," Tricia said.

"That's all right, just sign the bottom, I'll fill it in later."

She signed. It wasn't her name that she signed—not even her fake name—but ink went on the paper, and that seemed to be good enough for Magliocco. As far as he was concerned, a deal had been made. He returned to his phone call. "All right," he said, "give her the money. What? Yes, the money. Borden's money. Yes, all of it. What? I don't care, hundreds, fifties, whatever you've got. What's that? Yeah. Yeah, she did." He hung up.

"You won't regret this," he said. "It's much better here than at the Sun. A much better class of customer."

"I can see that," Tricia said.

The side door opened then and Reenie came through it, pulled it shut quietly behind her. She'd changed out of the dress and was wearing slacks and a blouse under a blue raincoat. In one hand she held a cardboard suitcase.

"What the hell's that?" Magliocco said.

"I'm leavin'," she said. "I've had enough of you."

"Like hell," Magliocco said. "You don't leave till I say you leave. You signed a contract."

She came over, buttoning her raincoat as she came. "Here's your contract," she said, reaching into the pocket of the coat. At first Tricia couldn't see what she pulled out. Then it went *thump* into his massive chest and she could see half of it, the half that was sticking out. It looked like the wooden handle of a chef's knife.

Magliocco staggered forward, groping for the knife, spraying blood. Most of it went on the raincoat, which Tricia realized she'd probably worn for that very reason.

"It's like you said, Al," Reenie said. "Every girl's got to draw the line somewhere. Well, this is where I'm drawing it."

The big man went down on his knees. He was gasping for breath, trying to say something. Whatever it was, it didn't come out. The only sound he made was the impact when he hit the floor, driving the knife in deeper.

"Everything okay in there?" came a voice from outside.

With one fist, Magliocco was pounding against the floor. But after the first couple of blows, his fist fell slower, then slower still, and then stopped altogether.

Reenie unbuttoned the raincoat, stripped it off, and held it by the collar, careful not to get any blood on her clothes.

"Hey, you," she said. "Here. Catch."

She flung the bloody raincoat at Tricia and, while it was flying toward her, screamed.

46.

Baby Moll

"She killed him!" Reenie wailed. "She's killed Al!"

While a scrambling began on the other side of the door, Tricia watched the raincoat loft toward her. If she caught it, she'd have Magliocco's blood all over her—her hands, her clothes. Of course, it wasn't her raincoat and she could prove it; they'd all seen her come in without it on, and it's not as though she could've been hiding it somewhere while being frisked to within an inch of her life. But seeing the big man's blood on her might be enough to set them off without thinking—his lieutenants might not pause before whipping out their guns and blasting away.

So Tricia hurled herself to one side and let the coat land in a ruinous heap on the rug. She regained her feet as the door banged open, slamming against the wall, and two men rushed in, the pepperpot and another she hadn't seen before. "My god!" Reenie screamed. "He's dead!"

"I didn't do it," Tricia said, her hands going up as they trained their guns on her. "She did. Look at her, she's got some in her hair, it's all over her coat. Look—see her suitcase, she said she was leaving him and he tried to stop her. Honest to god, it wasn't me. Take her fingerprints— they'll be all over the knife. I mean, assuming wood takes fingerprints, I don't know if it does—"

"Quiet," the new man said. He unclipped a radio from his belt and spoke into it: "Joey, Joey, you there? Lock the place down, don't let anyone leave. You hear me? No one in or out."

After a second's delay, Joey's voice crackled out of the radio: "You're too late, that woman just left, with Borden's money. Should I go after her?"

"No, stay here, I need you to lock the place down."

"Roger," Joey said, sounding for the first time like his military haircut might once have suited him.

"Roman," the new man said, "go get the doc."

"But if he's dead—" the pepperpot said.

"If he's dead it won't matter, but if he's not it will. Go."

Roman darted off.

"Now, you." He went up to Reenie, shook her by the shoulders till she stopped wailing. "What happened?"

"That little bitch," she said, her chest heaving, "she pulled out a knife and stabbed him right in the chest."

"Where'd she get the knife?"

"I don't know, ask her."

"I did ask her. She said you did it."

"Who're you gonna believe, her or me?" The guy didn't answer quickly enough. "Tony! I *loved* him!"

"Sure—the true love of a woman for a pile of dough."

"Don't say that."

"Why not? You pocketed plenty."

"Of course he took care of me, Tony. I was his woman."

"You were his *moll*, baby—not even, you were just some teenage tail he kept on hand for when there were no grown-up women around."

She slapped him, hard, the crack ringing in the air. "Don't you ever say that," she said.

"That one's going to cost you," Tony said. "Later. First we've got to—hold on, where'd…?"

Tricia, who could only hear his voice faintly at this point, figured he must have noticed now that she was gone and begun searching the room for her. She hastened

along the passageway on the other side of the door Reenie
had used for her earlier exit and entrance. She'd snuck
through it while Tony was occupied with Reenie, and she
heard it swing open behind her now.

"Hey!" he shouted.

Fortunately she was already at the end of the corridor
and was able to make a turn before the pair of gunshots
he fired reached the spot where she'd been standing.

He ran; she ran faster. Pulling open a heavy door, she
found herself in the wings of the stage, behind the velvet
curtain. On the other side of the curtain, she heard people
milling about, a confused murmur of voices, Joey's rising
above them: "People! People! Calm down, I'm telling
you, this is a routine security matter..." She didn't stick
around to hear the rest of his explanation, though she'd
have been curious to. Did the maitre d' even know his
boss was dead?

Tricia dashed through the cluttered backstage area to
a service exit, but Joey had gotten there first and the door
was locked and barred. She rattled the bar briefly out of
sheer frustration and moved on.

But to where? The front door was out, obviously; and
she didn't know enough about the layout of the place to
guess where the other exits might be, never mind which
one Joey's lockdown would reach last.

She shot blindly past several doors, all of them internal
ones, not ones that would lead to the outside. Then,
struck by a momentary inspiration, she doubled back.

Where would Joey's lockdown reach last? Probably
this room. She pushed through a door marked LADIES.

A window, she told herself on the way in—that's what
she needed. She said a little prayer: Let there be a window.
Please, any window. Even a small one.

And there was—a very small one. It was high enough
up on the wall that she had to drag over a trash can to

reach it, and then, once she had, it took all her strength to force it open even half a foot. Wriggling through a half-foot opening was a painful process and twice she thought she'd gotten irretrievably stuck. But a combination of inhaling deeply, straining like a woman in labor, and kicking like mad eventually deposited her headfirst in a litter-strewn alleyway behind the club. She didn't bother dusting herself off, just hobbled to the mouth of the alley, looked this way and that, and ran out onto Park Avenue South. A taxi screeched to a halt inches from her shins. Apologizing profusely for nearly getting run over, she tumbled into its back seat.

"Where you going, lady?" the driver said, glancing in the rearview.

She gave him Mike's address.

"You look like you left that place in a hurry," the driver said. "Anything the matter?"

"Just some men trying to kill me," she said. "It's been like that a lot lately."

"You want me to take you to the police?" he asked.

"God, no," Tricia said. Then, seeing his expression in the mirror, she said, "They're so busy. I wouldn't want to bother them."

Ten minutes saw them to the door of Mike's building. Tricia had just enough money to pay the fare with a few pennies left over for a tip.

"You sure you're okay?" the driver said.

"I'm fine now," Tricia said. "Just as long as no one followed us here."

"Followed us?" the driver said. "The way I was going? Not a chance."

It was true—he'd gone at top speed, weaving between cars and taking corners recklessly enough that more than one pedestrian had jumped back cursing. She'd certainly seen no sign of pursuit out the back window, despite checking repeatedly, and she saw none now. As the cab drove off, Tricia finally found herself breathing a little easier. With any luck, Erin and the money would already be upstairs, and Mike, too; they'd get everything ready for the morning and even have time to grab some sleep.

She climbed the stairs, knocked on the door, entered when it swung open.

And there was Mike, behind the bar, and Erin in front of it, a bulging paper grocery sack by her feet. There was the little leather box of photos sitting on the bar, where Tricia had left it. There was the footlocker, standing open, with its stacks of cut-up newspaper inside. There was only one thing wrong. If Mike and Erin were at the bar, who'd opened the door?

She turned to see. What she saw was the barrel of a revolver.

"Don't even think of running," O'Malley said. "You're under arrest."

47.
The Max

There they sat on the scarred wooden table in the drab little interrogation room: the bulging paper grocery sack, the leather box of photos, and the footlocker filled with stacks of cut-up newspaper. They looked lost there, and a little embarrassed. The tabletop was covered with random gouges and scratches, with cigarette burns, and with faintly shiny rings left by countless cups of coffee. A few hardy souls had tried scratching their initials into it. They mostly seemed to have been interrupted before they could finish. Beneath Tricia's wrist was another vague cloud of scratches. She knew how these had gotten there: from the sharp edges of handcuffs like the ones she was wearing. Her mouth still seemed full of the paperclip taste of Magliocco's gin. There seemed to be some kind of fine grit under her eyelids. It seemed to cover her skin. She touched her face lightly with her manacled hands; it was abnormally sensitive, as if she were sunburned. She wondered what time it was. She wanted another glass of water, but it seemed too much trouble to ask. She was very, very tired.

There were two men across the table from her, O'Malley and a very fit-looking young man in a pale gray suit. The man in the suit was looking at her attentively. O'Malley was ignoring her, riffling a stack of bills from the grocery sack with an abstracted air.

"My, my, my," he said. He dropped the stack of bills into the bag and looked at Tricia. He still wore a thick cap of bandages on his head, and his nose and one eye were a few shades purpler than when she'd seen him last. "Let's talk about your situation, Miss Heverstadt."

"Can't we talk about something more pleasant?" she said.

"I'd love to talk about pleasant things, Miss Heverstadt. But I'm afraid I'm out of practice. Now. Just to get it out of the way, I'm not going to charge you with assaulting a police officer in the execution of his duty."

"Good. That wasn't me."

"I'm not charging anyone. I don't need it. Or with attempted murder, reckless endangerment, kidnapping—"

"*Kidnapping?*"

"You tied me up, didn't you? But forget it." He waved a hand airily. "What do I need with chicken feed like that, when I've got two, maybe three actual, honest-to-God charges of murder? A Mister Roberto Monge, with a knife. A Mister Mitchell Depuis, gunshot. And we understand

Al Magliocco got himself done earlier this evening, and that you were in attendance."

"I wasn't the one who—"

"No, of course not. What else've we got? Illegal possession of a firearm. Four counts of resisting arrest. That was somebody else, too? Breaking and entering, I forget how many counts. Grand larceny—let's not forget that little item. Three million smackers, which you wrote a whole book about stealing. And of course these very interesting photos. Can I add blackmail to the list?"

"Do I look stupid enough to try and blackmail Salvatore Nicolazzo?"

"You'd be surprised, Miss Heverstadt. I don't look stupid myself, and just look how stupid I've been over the past few days." He leaned across the table, brought his face close to hers. "Listen, girlie. You're looking at the max."

"The hell I am," Tricia said. "You're bluffing."

The man in the suit looked pained when Tricia said *hell*. "Miss Heverstadt," he said, in a smooth, authoritative voice, "I'm afraid your attitude is not helpful. I can assure you that what Captain O'Malley says is correct." He had a glistening crew cut, a wide, squarish jaw, and a short and very straight nose. He would have been handsome as a movie star if his eyes hadn't been so close together.

"You sound like a radio announcer. Who is this guy?" Tricia asked O'Malley.

"Now *that* is a question I was asking myself not so very long ago. Miss Heverstadt, may I present Special Agent Houghton Brooks..." He turned to Brooks. "I'm afraid I keep forgetting. Are you Houghton Brooks the Third, or the Fourth?"

"Just Junior, Captain," Brooks said with a strained smile.

"Agent Houghton Brooks, Jr. of the United States Federal Bureau of Investigation. The federal authorities have been kind enough to interest themselves in our little case, Miss Heverstadt. They are *very* interested in you. And you still don't think you're looking at the max?"

"I don't know," Tricia admitted. "What's the max?"

"The maximum penalty permitted under New York State sentencing guidelines, Miss Heverstadt. In your case, several consecutive sentences that'll add up to life without parole." O'Malley stood, leaned forward on both hands and looked down at her. "How old are you, Miss Heverstadt? Eighteen, nineteen? You haven't done much living yet, have you? How'd you like to do the rest of the living you'll ever do, spend the rest of the years you've got to spend, in the slam? How'd you like to grow old in a cage?"

"Right now, Captain, growing old anyplace at all sounds pretty inviting."

"And how about your friends? Your bartender friend we don't have much on except operating illegally after hours—but Miss Erin Galloway, now there's a piece of work. Of course you'll probably tell me she didn't try and fracture my skull, either." Tricia shrugged. "Well, never mind that. We're charging her with Murder Two—an employee of Uncle Nick's named Celestino Manzoni, by means of another firearm she wasn't legally entitled to possess. Grand larceny again—a racehorse this time. And as an employee in good standing of Madame Helga's organization, I'm sure she's been up to a few things that might interest the boys in vice.

"And your friend Borden, now, where do I begin? He likes to assault cops and impersonate officers and steal cop cars. That's when he isn't publishing smut or running Madame Helga's himself. Some breaking and entering for Mister Borden, too, as well as—"

"All right," Tricia said. "All *right*."

"I'm sorry, Miss Heverstadt. Am I boring you?"

"I'm tired. I'm very tired, and it's—late. And I would like you to get to the point."

O'Malley turned to Agent Brooks. "You see? She's a pain in my thigh, and she's rotten straight through, and she lies like a hundred-dollar Persian rug, and she's keeping company with big piles of newspaper cut up the same size as money, God knows why. But like she says, she's not stupid. She knows there's a point." He turned back to her and his eyes, shadowed by bandages, were suddenly savage. Very softly he said, "I don't care about any of this crap, girlie, and I don't care about you. I don't care about you or your whore friends or your piss-ant smut-peddler boyfriends. You're not even annoyances to me. You're gnats. You're something I've got to brush away from time to time so I can go about my business. And my business is Sal Nicolazzo. And you are going to bring him to me."

Tricia stared at him.

"Permit me," Agent Brooks said. "Captain O'Malley expresses himself a bit—"

"That's right," O'Malley said. "I expressed myself. You've got a way about you, sister. You seem to wiggle your little butt into and out of Uncle Nick's place easier than anybody I've ever seen. He's interested in you."

"He's interested in his three million dollars, Captain O'Malley. He thinks I've got it. He's wrong—but that's what he thinks. He's also interested in those photos. And he's given me until six AM tomorrow—six AM *this morning* —to get them to him, on that boat of his. That's why the piles of newspaper. They're going to pick me up at six at a pier in Brooklyn and I've got to have it all with me, or Charley and my sister…he's got them out there, and he's said he'll kill them. They'll die."

"Well then," O'Malley said. "That gives us something to work with."

"To *work* with?"

"Yeah. You're going to go out there to Uncle Nick's boat. You're going to bring—" He shouted toward the door. "Nevins!" A balding head appeared. O'Malley pointed to the leather case of photos. "Get Levitas out of bed. Now. Get him to copy these photographs. I want negatives by three this morning, and I want a set of dry prints on my desk at nine, and whatever fingerprints are on these photos and this case better still be on them and nobody else's. Clear?" Nevins nodded and disappeared, and O'Malley turned back to Tricia. "You're going to bring these photos, and your case of funny money, to that boat, and you're going to bring a story with you, and that story, when you tell it, is going to bring Uncle Nick back to dry land where Agent Brooks and I can get at him. That's what you'll do, and that's all you'll do. And when you're done, you and your whore friend and your smut-peddler sweetheart and your sister can all walk. The bartender, too. Understand? I'll wipe the slate. You give me Nicolazzo, and we're quits."

"And what's this story I'm going to tell him?"

"That's up to you," O'Malley said. "Just as long as it works."

There was a moment of silence.

"Jesus," Tricia said. "You must be desperate."

Agent Brooks said, "It may sound to you like a desperate idea, Miss Heverstadt—"

"No. The idea sounds loony. *You* two sound desperate."

"Captain O'Malley and I have been reviewing your case, and as he says, you seem an exceptionally resourceful and ingenious young woman. We have a good deal of confidence in your ability."

"*You* may have a good deal of confidence in my ability, Agent Brooks. Captain O'Malley just thinks I'm worth a try. If I succeed, he wins big. If I don't, I save the City of

New York the expense of a trial and a jail term. Hell," she said, and Agent Brooks winced again, "the city probably won't even have to pay for a burial since if anything goes wrong Nicolazzo will do the honors himself with a good old-fashioned burial at sea. Do I understand you correctly, Captain?"

O'Malley smiled beatifically. "You see, Agent Brooks? Not a bit stupid. Yes, Miss Heverstadt. You understand me correctly. I wouldn't gamble a nickel on you succeeding, but as it happens, a nickel's about five cents more than you mean to me. So what the hell? Sometimes a long shot comes in. And Agent Brooks here thinks it's a dandy idea, don't you, Agent Brooks?"

"I understand your skepticism, Captain, but in fact I do think so. Miss Heverstadt, I think I'm a pretty good judge of men—and, ah, women, in this case. And I think you've got that certain something it takes to see a highly sensitive and perilous mission through. You also appear to be quite well connected in the underworld, something the Bureau finds most valuable. In fact, if you do well enough with this assignment—with your first quarry, if you will—the Agency might like to talk to you about other assignments."

O'Malley was mouthing the word *quarry*.

Brooks opened a briefcase and removed a small box covered in pink satin with a brass clasp, crudely embroidered with the initials *TH*. "Here's what you'll use to communicate with us once you've brought Nicolazzo back to land. Now, this may look like an ordinary makeup case…"

"It looks," Tricia said, "like nothing on earth. Have you ever *seen* a woman's makeup case?"

"I believe Agent Brooks Junior is a bachelor," O'Malley said to the ceiling.

Agent Brooks' eyes seemed to be getting closer together. "But inside," he said doggedly, "under this hidden panel containing the little pots of powder and so on, there is a Regency TR-1, the most advanced miniature transistor radio on the market today, which my colleagues have modified to send a homing signal with a radius of twenty-five miles. When you've succeeded in luring Mr. Nicolazzo to a convenient location, all you need do is switch this beacon on, and our men will be there within minutes."

"That's all I need do, huh?"

"You don't need to do a damn thing, girlie," O'Malley said. "You can call your lawyer, or have us call one for you. We've already got a nice cell waiting for you. And at six thirty or so, your sister and your friend get the chop, like you said. But *you* don't have to do a damn thing but sit in a nice warm cell, if you don't want to."

Tricia looked at him meditatively for a minute. Then she held out her shackled wrists.

She said, "Take these damn things off of me."

48.

The First Quarry

Dawn wouldn't break for half an hour still, but the piers were already busy with dockworkers walking to and from the ships, deckhands loading supplies and unloading cargo. The few birds that were awake were circling overhead, cawing lustily and diving when they spotted a bit of breakfast swimming near the water's surface.

Tricia sat on the footlocker, legs crossed at the ankles, and waited. She'd lugged the thing this far, dragging it from where the taxi had left her, and that was far enough. Nicolazzo had promised that two men would pick her

up—well, they could pick up the footlocker while they
were at it.

She rubbed her wrists where O'Malley's cuffs had
chafed them, or anyway where she imagined they had.
You couldn't see any marks, but it felt to her like she still
had them on.

Her first quarry. Jesus Christ. Brooks had made it
sound like he was making her a Junior G-Man or some
sort of secret double agent out of the movies. When what
he really was doing, most likely, was sending her off to get
herself killed. What were the odds that she'd be able to
bring Nicolazzo back to shore and into their hands? Bad
enough when all she'd had to worry about was getting
Coral and Charley off his boat alive.

O'Malley had ridden with her back to Mike's, had
turned the leather box of photos back over to her, and
had directed the junior cop who was driving them to
unload the footlocker from the trunk. The cops had help-
fully prepared the money inside, even adding paper
bands just like the ones you'd get from a bank to hold the
individual stacks closed, and making sure the stacks on
the first two layers all had at least two real bills on top and
one on the bottom. The driver had proudly described
the process, like a hobbyist talking about painting lead
soldiers. They'd stayed up all night working on it, he'd
said.

When they were out on the street, O'Malley had
handed her the radio-cum-makeup case, tucked into a
blue, beaded purse that matched her dress only a little
better than a feather headdress would have. She'd accepted it. It wasn't like she had a variety of purses to
choose from or any place to get a better one at five in the
morning.

She'd made them wait on the sidewalk while she went
upstairs. Her stated purpose was to use the bathroom

and she did that, but she also stopped by the back room and fished through the pile of old newspapers and pawn-shop tickets till she found one of the latter on which the merchandise being pawned wasn't a set of flatware or a watch but "one (1) valise—large—brown leather." Taking the ticket into the bathroom, she opened Mike's safety razor, slid out the blade, and used it to scrape the date and the name and address of the pawnshop off the ticket. She slipped the ticket into her pocket; the razor blade, too, for good measure.

Downstairs again, O'Malley had put her into a cab, loaded the trunk into the trunk, and patted the car's side the way you would a horse's when you wanted it to go. The driver had sped off toward Brooklyn and arrived at the Gowanus piers a few minutes before the deadline. There'd been no traffic. Tricia hoped that hadn't used up her quota of good luck for the day.

She waited, wishing she had worn a watch. It had to be after six, but just how much after, she couldn't be sure. She felt a little nervous, sitting by herself on a box of money—true, it wasn't the three million dollars it was pretending to be, but eleven thousand was still more money than she'd ever found herself sitting on before. And if someone wanted to take it, she wasn't sure she'd be able to prevent—

"Hey," a voice called. "You Tricia?"

Looking up, she saw two men walking toward her. They ran to type, as if Nicolazzo went to the same casting of-fice Hollywood used when picking heavies. One could've been Bruno's twin brother: same build, same pink dome, same glowering expression. The other—the one that had spoken—was smaller, though not by a lot, and looked very much like pictures she'd seen of the current resi-dent of Gracie Manor, Mayor Wagner: jowly, big ears, receding hairline. But she suspected the resemblance ended there. For one thing, she doubted this one had gone to Yale.

"Yes," she said. "I'm Tricia."

"We've been waiting for you," Mayor Wagner said. "Over there." He pointed at a little launch bobbing at the end of the pier.

"Well, I've been waiting for you, right here."

"Why?"

"Because this thing weighs almost as much as I do," Tricia said. "Your boss wants it, you can carry it."

"All right," he said, "no need to get huffy." He snapped his fingers at his cohort. "Now, howsabout you get up and put your hands out to the side?"

She stood, lifted her arms, and suffered through her first frisking of the morning. She was getting to be quite an old hand at it, no longer even flinching as a stranger's hand brushed over her backside.

While the smaller man took care of patting her down, the larger one bent, gripped one of the footlocker's handles in each hand, and lifted the thing effortlessly into the air.

The smaller one plucked the box of photos out of her pocket. "What's this?" he said.

"Those are Nicolazzo's photos," she said. "Feel free to take a look if you don't believe me." But an expression of horror crossed his face and he handed the box back to her.

"No, thanks," he said.

"Why not?"

"Kagan and me, we're not allowed to see them," he said. "Uncle Nick made that very clear. His eyes only."

Kagan nodded forcefully. He'd given the impression of paying only cursory attention to what was going on around him, but this point he clearly felt was important.

"Okay," Tricia said. "Suit yourself. How about the money, you want to take a look at that?"

He laughed. "What, to make sure it's not just a lot of cut-up newspaper? Come on. Nobody'd be that stupid."

"No, I guess not," Tricia said.

"Let's get a move on. We're already running late." He gestured for her to walk ahead of them down the pier.

She walked. "What should I call you?" she said as they neared the boat.

"Mr. P," he said. "It's short for Pantazonis."

"Greek?" Tricia said.

"No, Zulu," he said.

They boarded the boat, Tricia first, then the two men. There wasn't a huge amount of room, and Tricia found herself sitting on the footlocker again. What the hell, she figured. Maybe it'll hatch.

Kagan fired up the engine and they cruised out of the dock, heading for open water. As they hooked around toward the mouth of the bay, they passed a large wooden billboard proudly proclaiming this the future home of the Verrazano-Narrows Bridge, courtesy of a list of public servants that started with City Construction Coordinator Robert Moses.

Where Moses wants a bridge, Tricia thought, he gets a bridge.

Apart from the spray flying in her face and a bit of seasickness that kicked in when the waves got choppy, the ride wasn't too unpleasant. Neither man spoke to her, nor did they talk much to each other. Pantazonis spent most of the time hunched over, trying to stay dry, while Kagan stood straight and tall in the front like a bald Viking and steered with his eyes on the horizon.

It felt like it had been at least half an hour before Tricia got her first glimpse of Nicolazzo's yacht. It looked deceptively small until they drew closer, and then suddenly revealed itself to be many times the size of the boat they were in, more like a small cruise ship than like anything one man should have for his own use. Kagan cut the power and they coasted in gently, bumping hulls as they arrived. Several heads appeared at the railing above them and a rope ladder was thrown over the side.

"Go on up," Pantazonis said. "We've got a winch for the box." And sure enough, while Tricia carefully climbed the ladder, trying hard not to lose either the purse looped around her wrist or her shoes along the way, she saw a cable being lowered beside her toward the launch. As she stepped off the ladder onto the deck of the ship, she saw the cable begin retracting, hauling the footlocker on board.

She looked around. There were five men there, all of them unfamiliar. "Where's Uncle Nick?" she said.

"Right here," Nicolazzo said. She turned around. He was standing at the midpoint of the deck, one hand on an open door. "Won't you join me?" he said. "I've got some people downstairs who are dying to see you again."

Two of the men pushed her forward, gripping her tightly by the arms. A third pulled her purse out of her hands, and turning she saw it was Pantazonis.

"Wait, I need that—" she said, but it was already gone, and he with it.

So much for the plan, she thought. Now what?

At Nicolazzo's insistence, she preceded him down a narrow staircase and along a low-ceilinged hall to an open doorway. She ran inside when she saw Coral, her arms tied behind her around the back of a wooden chair. Her face was bruised, but that could have been a remnant of her fight with Stella; she didn't seem to have any new monograms on her cheeks. But her hair was tangled and there were pouches under her eyes and even when she saw Tricia she was slow to respond. The last few days clearly hadn't been good ones for her.

"Cory," Tricia said, hugging her tightly, "are you okay?"

Coral didn't say anything, just nodded as Tricia stepped back.

"I'm going to get you out of here," Tricia said.

"You shouldn't have come," Coral said softly. "You should've taken Artie back home."

"Don't talk like that. The only one going home is you."

"I hope you don't mean that," Charley said from behind her.

She turned. His black eye was as richly colored as it had been the last time she'd seen it, though the swelling had gone down a bit. Otherwise he seemed not too much the worse for wear—except, of course, for the tape wrapped around his right index finger. It looked like they'd splinted it with a Popsicle stick.

"Oh, Charley, I'm so sorry. I wish I'd never—"

"Sure," Charley said. "We both do. But you can still make it up to me by giving this guy what he wants."

"That is excellent advice, Mr. Borden," Nicolazzo said. "I am glad you've come around to my way of thinking. You, too, Miss Heverstadt."

At a gesture from Nicolazzo, Kagan carried the footlocker in and deposited it heavily on a fold-down counter bolted to the wall.

"You want me to open it?" Kagan said.

"One thing at a time," Nicolazzo said. "My pictures...?"

Tricia handed over the leather box. He slid the cover off and flipped through the photographs one by one. He nodded when he reached the last one. "Very good." The box vanished inside his jacket pocket.

"Now the money." Nicolazzo shooed Kagan away and lifted the two spring latches holding the footlocker closed.

He eyed the money inside with a combination of satisfaction and wariness. Choosing a stack of bills from the middle, he riffled through it. His expression didn't change, but even from where she was standing Tricia could see at a glance when the real bills ended and the newspaper began. Without saying anything, he picked up another stack and riffled through that one, then a third. He put them back in place.

"Kill the sister," he said.

"Wait!" Tricia shouted. She yanked the pawnshop ticket out of her pocket, waved it overhead.

"What's that supposed to be, Miss Heverstadt?"

"The rest of your money," Tricia said. "You didn't really think I'd bring it all here, did you?"

"I did expect that, yes. It's what I told you to do."

"If I had, what would have prevented you from killing all three of us and just dumping our bodies over the side?" She walked up to Nicolazzo, handed the ticket over. "I needed a way to ensure you'd let us go. You'll get your money, every penny of it—but only once we're safe on land."

"You left my money at…a pawnshop?"

"Some of it," Tricia said. "Some is in that footlocker. I'm afraid most of it is at the pawnshop, though."

"And how am I supposed to find this pawnshop? The name's been scratched off."

"Oh, has it?" Tricia said. "It's a good thing I remember which one it is, then. Or I suppose you could try going to every pawnshop in New York one at a time asking to see every brown valise they've got—that shouldn't take more than a month or two, if you work hard at it."

She could see him struggling with conflicting emotions, the hunger to lash out warring with his own self-interest. Before he could settle the matter, Pantazonis rushed in, knocking on the doorframe as he entered. He had the beaded purse in one hand, the pink satin makeup case in the other.

"Sorry to interrupt, boss—"

"*Uncle Nick,*" Nicolazzo growled.

"I'm sorry, Uncle Nick." Pantazonis started over again. "I thought you'd want to see this."

"Why would I want to see a purse?"

"Not the purse," Pantazonis said. "This thing. Look what I found in it." He swung open the hinged top of the makeup kit and lifted the false panel, revealing the transistor radio inside. "It's a radio," he said unnecessarily. "Only when I turn it on, it doesn't play any music. It doesn't play anything—but the little light goes on."

Nicolazzo snatched it out of his hands, turned it over to look at the back, then waved it in Tricia's face. "You think I don't know what this is? After I've had the federal boys on my back for seven years?" His eyes blazed. "Pawnshop, my eye. This is a set-up. They want you to lure me back to land, don't they? And when you get me there you're supposed to flip the switch on this thing and it'll send out a signal: *Here's Nicolazzo, here's Nicolazzo. Come and get him.* Well. Here's what I think of that." He strode to a porthole in the wall, opened it, and pitched the radio out. They could all hear the splash a moment later.

He slammed the porthole cover shut.

"Now, Miss Heverstadt, you are going to tell me where my money really is. And then you're going to take me to it, or I swear I *will* kill all three of you. For now, one will do." He turned back to Kagan. "Like I said. Kill the sister."

"No, don't—" Tricia said.

"You're not taking me seriously, young lady, and you won't unless I give you a reason to."

Kagan pulled out a gun.

"Please," Tricia said to Kagan, "don't do it."

"Oh? You'd rather he kill your boyfriend here?" Nico-lazzo grabbed Charley's chin in one hand, shook it roughly. "That's fine with me. Your choice. Which one?"

"Neither," Tricia said.

"That sounds good to me," Charley said.

"You shut up," Nicolazzo said, wheeling on him. "You, you *imbroglione*, with your goddamn cheating cards—you know what, I think maybe *you* should choose, how about that? Huh?"

"I'd rather not," Charley said.

"Ah, but you will," Nicolazzo said. He snapped his fingers at Pantazonis. "Get me a deck of cards. Now!" Pantazonis scurried out of the room.

"I've wanted to do this ever since you walked out my door," Nicolazzo said. "A little rematch. A hand of Fifty-to-One—only with my deck this time, not yours. You want to know what the stakes are?"

"I doubt it," Charley said.

"If I win, my man here shoots you—in the head eventually, but not right away, he'll take his time. He's got plenty of bullets and you've got plenty of other places to get shot in first. Painful places."

"And if I win?"

"If you win, I spare your life—for now," Nicolazzo said. "And kill her instead." He jabbed a finger in Coral's direction.

"You're insane," Charley said, and it earned him a punch in the head.

Pantazonis came back through the door, a deck of cards in his hand. Nicolazzo peeled the top card off, threw it in Charley's face. It bounced off and landed on the floor. Eight of hearts.

"What's the next one, Borden?" Nicolazzo said. "Think hard. There's a lot riding on it." He waved Kagan over. The big man positioned himself at Charley's side and pressed the barrel of his gun against Charley's neck.

Charley looked over at Tricia, past the gun. There was something in his eyes—sadness? Regret? Resignation? Maybe a little of all three.

"Name a card," Nicolazzo said. "Or I tell him to start pulling the trigger right now."

Charley closed his eyes. "I don't know," he said. "Queen of spades."

"There you go," Nicolazzo said. "Was that so difficult? *La donna nero.* Well, let's see if this fickle lady, she comes to your rescue."

With a nasty flourish, Nicolazzo turned over the top card. His face paled, and he looked from the card to Charley and back again. It was the queen of spades.

"What did you…?" Nicolazzo threw the cards down, scattering them everywhere. He grabbed Charley's throat in both hands and started throttling him. "How did you do that? I demand that you tell me!"

"I didn't do anything," Charley croaked. "It was just a guess—"

Tricia ran to Nicolazzo, started battering his back with her fists, but it had no effect.

"You lie!" Nicolazzo roared. With one arm he swatted Tricia away from him and she went sprawling among the cards. "You," he said to Kagan, "kill the sister—now! How many times do I have to tell you?"

"Yes, sir," Kagan said. He crossed to the other side of the room, pointed his gun at Coral.

What happened next Tricia didn't see clearly. There was a blur of motion as Coral stood up from the chair and slapped Kagan's arm aside; his gunshot went wide, punching a hole in the wall. The rope that had bound her hands and legs fell to the ground, neatly sliced through.

Coral swung at the big man's chin, a bare-knuckled uppercut that cracked, bone against bone, like a second gunshot. Kagan staggered back. Coral closed again and gave him another brutal right, then slashed at his arm with her left hand. A spray of blood shot into the air and his gun tumbled to the floor, just inches from Tricia's face. A moment later a razor blade landed beside it—the one Tricia had passed Coral when she'd hugged her, the one Coral had just used to draw blood.

Tricia grabbed the gun and got to her feet. She also—carefully—picked up the blade. Above her, Coral was raining jabs and body blows on Kagan. He had his hands up protectively, but she kept sneaking punches in below his guard and to either side, vicious kidney punches and below-the-belt combinations.

Nicolazzo looked on, furious, shouting something in Italian to Pantazonis, who looked like he only understood every third word.

But he understood enough to whip out a gun of his own.

He leveled his at Coral and Tricia leveled Kagan's at him. They both pulled the trigger at the same time.

49.
Gun Work

The dual explosion in the small room deafened everyone and the choking cloud of gunsmoke added to the confusion. Pantazonis lay at Charley's feet, leaking blood like a punctured water bottle. Kagan and Coral were both upright; Pantazonis' bullet had missed them.

Nicolazzo released Charley's neck as Tricia swept her gun up toward him. He jumped over Pantazonis' body and shoved her aside, continuing on through the door.

Tricia heard him running down the hallway, shouting for his men.

She raced to Charley's side. Her hands were shaking; her breath was coming rapidly. She fought the nauseous feeling rising in her gut. Had she just killed a man? She pushed the question from her mind. She could think about that later. If there was a later.

She started working on the ropes around Charley's hands with the razor blade, trying not to slit his wrists in the process. At the other end of the room, Kagan and Coral were still standing toe to toe, fists raised like contenders in a boxing match. They looked at each other, smiled. He shrugged his shoulders; she stretched her neck, bending it this way and that; he cracked the knuckles on both his fists. Then she drove a right cross into his face. He swayed for a moment and fell like a tree. He didn't get up.

"My goodness," Tricia said.

"I don't mean to be selfish here," Charley said after a moment, "but do you think you could...?"

"Oh, yes—sorry." Tricia finished slicing through the rope.

Coral, meanwhile, bent to grab Pantazonis' gun.

"Is there any other way out?" Tricia said.

"Not unless you can fit through that porthole."

Tricia thought she might—it wasn't that much smaller than the bathroom window at the Satellite Club. But there was no way Coral or Charley could, and anyway none of them could swim to safety from wherever they were, somewhere outside U.S. coastal waters. The nearest land was probably miles away.

"Then let's get out of here," she said, just as a pair of Nicolazzo's men burst through the door with guns in hand.

Before Tricia could react, Coral had dropped them both, one with a bullet to the gut, the other with a pair in his leg, the second shot blowing out his kneecap. Both fell to the ground moaning. Coral threw away the gun she'd used and pried theirs out of their hands. "Here," she said, handing one to Tricia. "These'll be fully loaded." Tricia had only used one bullet from Kagan's gun; she held onto both.

They went cautiously out into the hall. There was no one there at the moment, but halfway to the stairs they saw a pair of legs coming down. Coral didn't wait, just took aim and fired, and the possessor of the legs slid to the bottom in a heap.

"Where'd you learn to shoot like that?" Tricia said.

"You pick things up," Coral said.

"Sure," Tricia said, following her up the steps to the deck, "but not things like that."

"You do if you have to," Coral said.

A bullet caromed off a metal railing beside them and they dropped to their hands and knees, crawled behind the nearest bulkhead. Coral poked one arm around the side to blindly squeeze off a shot, then fell back.

"How many of these guys are there?" Tricia said.

"I'm not sure. Fewer than ten, I think. Maybe it's ten with the ones that brought you."

"Then we've already gotten rid of half of them," Tricia said.

"You always were an optimist," Coral said, and rose from her crouch to take another shot.

Behind them, Tricia heard Charley crawling away. "Where are you going?" Tricia said.

"I have an idea."

"How about not getting shot? I'd think you'd like that idea."

"I love that idea," Charley said, "but I'm not convinced sitting here waiting to run out of bullets is the best way to accomplish it."

"We should stick together," Tricia said.

"With Annie Oakley there on your side? You don't need me."

"At least take a gun," Tricia said, and tried to hand him one.

He held up his taped hand. "Broken trigger finger. Thanks, anyway."

"Be careful, Charley," she said.

"Always." He hesitated a moment, then leaned in and kissed her. "In case I don't get another chance," he said. Then he scurried away, around the corner, chased by gunfire.

Someone patted her roughly on the shoulder.

"Hey," Coral said, "are you listening? I said give me that gun."

"Sorry," Tricia said, and passed Kagan's gun to her.

Coral pointed across the way, the opposite direction from the one Charley had gone. "When I say go—"

Tricia nodded.

"Go!"

Tricia scuttered through a wide open No Man's Land while Coral laid down protective fire and followed her. Return fire plowed up the wooden deck at their feet and one splinter caught Tricia in the calf. She could feel the bite and the blood running down her leg.

"You okay?"

"Yeah," she said, grimacing. She hunched behind a broad wooden bitt with a hawser coiled around it. Coral crammed in beside her.

"Ladies," came a booming voice, Nicolazzo's, "if you put your guns down right now, I won't kill you."

"You think we'd fall for that?" Coral shouted back.

"Your sister's got a lot of money that belongs to me," Nicolazzo said. "Much as I would enjoy killing you both, I wouldn't pay millions of dollars for the pleasure."

" 'Kill the sister,' " Coral said. "I heard you three times."

"Clearly the situation has changed."

"Yeah," Coral said, "it's changed because I've got a gun. How about *you* put *your* guns—"

The boat lurched before she could get the rest of her thought out. Tricia felt the engines turn on belowdeck and over the side she saw the water churning as they got underway.

"What's going on?" she asked.

"I don't know," Coral said.

The men on the other side of the deck seemed confused as well, judging by the argument being carried out in yelled Italian. Tricia glanced up, over the side, toward the horizon. "Look!"

She pointed.

There was another boat in sight, headed their way, bouncing in the spray as it chewed up the distance between them. Nicolazzo's boat was trying to get away, it seemed, powering in the same direction but more ponderously, a wildebeest being chased down by a cheetah.

A red light mounted on the other boat's fly bridge went on and began spinning. A harsh voice amplified through a bullhorn said, *"Cut your engines. This boat is operating under the authority of the Federal Bureau of—"* The voice went silent for a second. *"—under the joint authority,"* it resumed, *"of the Federal Bureau of Investigation and the New York Police Department. Prepare to be boarded."*

Nicolazzo's yacht was gaining speed, grinding angrily through the waves. Off in the distance, through the early morning haze, Tricia thought she could just make out the outline of the coast. They were making headway. But the police boat was making more, growing larger and louder— a siren went on, to go with the flashing light—and pulling up alongside them.

Nicolazzo's men ran to the railing, Tricia and Coral forgotten, and began shooting down over the side. More sounds of gunfire came up from below, and one of Nicolazzo's men fell backwards, clutching his throat.

"You are firing on agents of the United States government, a federal offense punishable by life in prison. Drop your weapons and allow us to board."

The ships kept racing, jostling each other for position, the big yacht pulling away in one direction, then the other, only to find itself headed off by the more nimble boat. Finally, Tricia felt the engines cut out and they slowed to a dead stop with the police boat out of sight on the far side of the pilot house. Nicolazzo and his men ran down that way; once they were past, Tricia and Coral followed.

By the time they arrived, O'Malley and two uniformed cops were standing on the deck alongside a half dozen federal agents, thick flak jackets protecting their torsos, steel helmets covering their heads. The feds had machine guns cradled at the ready in their arms and Nicolazzo's men had their hands up, guns littering the deck at their feet.

Tricia dropped her gun. When one of the feds looked Coral's way, Tricia nudged her with an elbow and Coral reluctantly released hers as well.

Two of the feds cleared an opening at the rail and Special Agent Houghton Brooks, Jr. climbed up through it. He wasn't wearing any armor or protective gear, just the gray suit he'd had on in the interrogation room. But he walked blithely into the middle of this deadly crowd as if he'd been taking a stroll down Fifth Avenue.

He located Nicolazzo and marched up to him.

"Salvatore Nicolazzo," he said, "you are under arrest."

Nicolazzo chuckled, looked at the men on either side of him. "You can't arrest me here. You can't even be on board my ship. We are in international waters. You have no jurisdiction here."

"You were," Brooks said, "in international waters. Until about five minutes ago. You're in U.S. waters now, mister."

"That's ridiculous," Nicolazzo said calmly. "Check the instruments. I assure you my captain knows perfectly well where international waters begin and end."

Tricia tried to see through the window of the pilot house, but the glare from the morning sun prevented it.

"Very well, let's check the instruments," Brooks said. He strode up to the door to the pilot house and swung it open. A man trussed hand and foot rolled out. He'd apparently been leaned up against the door. This was the captain, Tricia presumed, judging by the nautical cap on his head. A gag of some sort prevented him from making more than soft mewling sounds as he squirmed about.

Past him, inside the pilot house, Charley stood at the ship's wheel, his hands gripping it tightly at the two and ten o'clock positions. His taped finger stuck out accusingly.

"What have you done?" Nicolazzo said. *"What have you done?"* He would have leapt at Charley but one of the feds, coming up behind him, restrained him.

Brooks checked the instruments, nodded. "U.S. waters. I assure you, Mr. Nicolazzo, we wouldn't have come after you otherwise. The Bureau always operates by the rules." And to Charley: "It's just as well that it took us a little while to pinpoint Miss Heverstadt's signal underwater. That gave you enough time to steer the ship here. Your government is grateful to you, mister…?"

Charley looked at Tricia.

"Stephenson," she said.

"Borden," he said.

50.

Fifty-to-One

The man the glazier had sent over was kneeling in the corridor, fine brush in hand, carefully painting gold letters onto the new pane in the door:

HARD CASE CRIME
CHARLES BORDEN, PROP.

"I might ask him to change that," Charley said. "Borden, I mean."

"Why?" Tricia asked.

"Now that the feds are keeping an eye on me, it feels like maybe it's time for a fresh start," Charley said. "Anyway, too many people who know me by that name would like to do me harm."

"Or you owe them money," Erin said.

"That, too."

"So what'll you change it to?" Tricia said.

"Why?" Charley said. "You think you might have a personal stake in the matter some day?"

She found herself blushing again, damn it. "Anything's possible," she said.

He kissed the side of her head. "Don't worry, I'll pick something that sounds similar to Borden. Keep it easy to remember."

"Gordon?" Erin said. "Arden?"

"Something like that."

He opened the door to the chateau. Four faces turned

their way. "That's okay, don't get up, girls. I just wanted to let you know I'm back."

"You ever hear of knocking?" Annabelle said. She had nothing on but a towel—wrapped turban-style around her head.

"What, and miss seeing you like that? Never." He pulled the door shut and they went on to Madame Helga's at the end of the hall.

"What happened to you?" Billy Hoffman said as they entered, gesturing toward Charley's black eye and taped-up finger.

"Long story," Charley said. "Let us use your office, will you?"

"Of course."

They went inside.

Charley handed the phone over to Tricia, who sat behind Billy's desk. How long had it been since she'd walked through that door for the first time? Since she'd seen Hoffman sitting right here and Robbie Monge staring at her as she danced. Poor, unfaithful Robbie Monge.

She picked up the receiver and placed a call to Aberdeen. The phone rang and rang and she let it—mama might easily have been at the other end of the house when the ringing started, and she wasn't as young as she used to be.

"Hello...?"

Tricia's face lit up. "Mama! It's me, Patricia."

"Patricia? Are you coming home?"

"No, mama, I'm not. But guess what? Coral is."

There was silence on the other end. Then: "Coral?"

Tricia thought about the scene down on Cornelia Street earlier that morning, when she'd accompanied Coral to her room. She'd finally gotten to see Artie. Damned if he didn't have his father's chin after all, and no doubt at all who the father was.

What are you going to do? she'd asked Coral, who'd had to think about it.

I'm going to go home, she'd said finally. *Not for good— but for now.*

"Yes, mama," Tricia said. "Coral. And she's bringing someone with her."

"A man?" her mother said coldly.

"After a fashion," Tricia said.

Charley got up then, waved at Erin to do the same. "We'll be outside," he said. "Take your time."

When her call with her mother was finished, Tricia didn't hang up the phone, just depressed the hooks with her forefinger and then released them. She placed another call, to a number written in a neat, straight hand on the back of a business card whose front only contained a man's name, not the name of his employer.

"Brooks here," the man answered. Over the phone he sounded, if anything, even more stiff and formal than in person.

"This is Tricia Heverstadt."

"Oh, Miss Heverstadt," he said, warming up just a little. "I want to express our thanks once more. You did an outstanding job this morning. And now with Royal Barrone turning state's evidence against Nicolazzo—"

"I can't take credit for that."

"You put us in touch with him," Brooks said.

"I made one phone call," Tricia said.

"You did an *outstanding* job," he repeated. "And that is the reason I asked you to call me. So that we might discuss in private the matter I alluded to in our first conversation."

"What matter is that?"

"Your skills, Miss Heverstadt, could be of considerable service to your government. Salvatore Nicolazzo is not the only criminal who has eluded us for years. If you were able to get close to him and his confidants, perhaps you could do the same with others."

"I don't think—"

"Simply by way of example," Brooks said, and she heard some pages flipping on his end of the phone, "there is a mister Jorge Famosa, living in New York now but a native of Cuba originally. He peddles narcotics in the northeast, smuggled in from his homeland. His operations have been disrupted recently by the fighting down there—you have heard of this rebel, Castro, and his guerilla forces?"

"I think I've seen the name," Tricia said, "but—"

"Well, Miss Heverstadt, we have word that Famosa is recruiting criminals from New York's Cuban community to travel to Cuba and kill Fidel Castro. And once they've done that, they intend to back a bid for power by the dead man's brother, Raul Castro, whom they believe will be more sympathetic to their operations."

"What does this have to do with me, Agent Brooks?"

"We thought you could infiltrate Famosa's organization and help us bring these men to justice before they create an international incident."

"Do I look to you like I could pass for Cuban?"

"No, ma'am," Brooks said, "but then you don't look Italian, either."

"I'm sorry," Tricia said, "I'm just not comfortable—"

"That's all right," Brooks said, and she heard some more pages flipping. "If you're more comfortable with our Sicilian friends, we have no shortage of assignments there, especially now, with Nicolazzo and Barrone out of commission. That creates a power vacuum and we have already heard this morning—on the QT, you understand—that certain men at the next level down are trying to fill it. There's one fellow, for instance, who has been operating a brothel out of the Statler Hotel—he's employed there as their house detective, if you can believe that."

"Agent Brooks—"

"Then there's another gentleman, Paulie Cusumano, a.k.a. 'Paulie Lips.' He runs a club called the Moon and word is he intends to turn it into a casino—"

"Agent Brooks!" Tricia had to shout to get his attention. "Agent Brooks. I appreciate what you've done for me, you and Captain O'Malley. You've given me a second chance and I won't forget it. But I've had my fill of this sort of thing. I just want to lead a simple, quiet life from here on in. No criminals, no gunfights, no undercover assignments. Just working in the book publishing business with Charley—where at least in principle all the danger stays on the page."

"I'm sorry to hear it," Brooks said. "You have the makings of an excellent field asset."

"Thank you," Tricia said, "I think. But I assure you, my mind's made up."

"Very well. The government does not pressure its citizens. I'd like to think you might reconsider someday— but that's entirely up to you. In the meantime," Brooks said, "there are just a few loose ends I'd be grateful if you could help us tie up. For example, the matter of the stolen three million dollars. Are you quite certain, Miss Heverstadt, that you don't have any idea who took it?"

"Quite certain," Tricia said. And before he could say anything else she added, "Would you look at that? I'm so sorry, Agent Brooks, I just realized it's almost noon and I have to be somewhere."

"But Miss Heverstadt—" Brooks said.

"Goodbye, Agent Brooks." She hung up.

Outside, Erin was seated at her desk, going through the mail that had piled up. She said, "Everything okay?"

"Fine," Tricia said.

"Want to get some lunch?"

"Actually," Tricia said, "all I want to get right now is

some sleep. Could you let Charley know I'll see him a little later?"

"Sure," Erin said.

And Tricia headed out. But instead of going across the hall to her cot, she took the elevator downstairs.

Down the block, where it had once said "Red Baron" in Gothic letters, the sign now said "O.J.'s Bar and Grill." Inside, the propellers and framed aviation pictures had been removed from the walls. The place looked unchanged otherwise, though, and was every bit as barren of customers at noon as it had been any of the previous times she'd come here. She ordered a coke from the bartender, who served it to her unenthusiastically. She carried it to one of the dark, anonymous booths against the back wall. Renata was right, she thought. These places did all look pretty much the same.

She didn't have to wait long—maybe ten minutes. Don was the first to show up, coming in through a doorway labeled EMPLOYEES ONLY behind the bar. Larry appeared a few minutes later, walking in off the street. Larry's beard had come in a bit more in the months since she'd seen him last. Otherwise, the two looked much the way they had, though she thought maybe their clothing seemed a little improved.

"Boys," Tricia said, raising her glass and waving at them with it. "Want to come over here for a minute?"

"Why, it's our authoress," Larry said. "Our mystery writrix. What brings you here? Are you working on another book?"

"You'd like that, wouldn't you," Tricia said, and there was something in her voice that stopped them dead.

Larry exchanged a glance with Don, who shrugged expressively. Without another word they came over to her table, Don drawing two glasses of beer along the way.

"You want another drink?" Don said, pointing at the finger of coke left in her glass.

"I still have some," Tricia said.

"You know what they say, Don," Larry said, "some people look at a glass as ninety percent empty, while others prefer to see it as ten percent full."

"How did you know you'd find us here?" Don said.

"I didn't," Tricia said, "but I figured it was worth a try. This is the time we always used to meet when we were working on the book. Remember? Ten past noon."

Larry took a long swallow of his beer. "Some people see it as ten past noon," he said, "while others prefer to see it as fifty to one."

She gave him a funny look.

"What?" he said.

"Nothing," Tricia said. She turned back to Don. "You seem very much at home there behind the bar. You get a job here?"

"Not exactly a *job*," Don said.

"What my friend is too modest to say," Larry said, "is that he owns this place now. Bought it fair and square from the previous owner. Tore down that wretched bric-a-brac from the walls, turned it into a proper establishment one isn't embarrassed to be seen in."

"Really," Tricia said. "And where, might I ask, did you get the money to buy a bar? You'd have to write a lot of travel guides to make that kind of dough."

"My beloved aunt," Don said, "passed away."

"Ah," Tricia said. "I'm sorry to hear it. And you, Larry? What are you doing these days? Still writing?"

"Of course—we both are," Larry said. "We're writers through and through. We will never stop."

"That's so," Don said. "But what *he's* too modest to tell you is that he has also opened a bookstore. Down in the Village. Sells used books. Some rare, some not so rare. A real addition to the neighborhood."

"And where'd you get the money to do that?" Tricia asked.

"My beloved uncle," Larry said.

"Dead?"

"The poor man."

They all took a drink in silence.

"One of you want to tell me about it?" Tricia said.

"Not particularly," Larry said.

"You know," Tricia said, "all along we kept asking ourselves, who could possibly have read the book before it was published? It never occurred to me to ask, what about the guys who helped come up with the plot in the first place."

"What finally made you think of it?" Larry said.

"You were overheard," Tricia said. "Making your plans. This woman said she'd seen two men, one with a beard, one without, both New Yorkers by their voices, around noon in a back booth in one of her father's bars. At first I thought she was just making it up to save her skin. But then it dawned on me about the names of the bars."

"The names?" Don said.

"Her father's name is Royal Barrone, and he's in the habit of naming all his bars after himself: Royal's Brew, the Rusty Bucket. The same initials. And then I thought about where we'd met to do all our plotting. The Red Baron."

"I see," Larry said.

"Why did you do it?" Tricia said, and she couldn't keep her voice from quavering as she did. "Do you have any idea what sort of trouble you caused me? I almost got killed. My sister, too. Quite a few people did get killed. And for what? So you could run a bar?"

"And a bookstore," Larry said.

"You risked your own lives, too," Tricia said, "and on the basis of what, a crazy plot cooked up for a crime novel?"

"Not a crazy plot," Larry said. "A brilliant plot. You remember I asked you at the time, why should we come up with a perfectly good plot and hand it over to you, when we could use it ourselves?"

"For a book! Not in real life!"

"And why not? After you left that day, when we finally put the last pieces in place, Don and I sat here a while longer, talking, and it dawned on us that this was much too good a premise to waste on mere fiction."

"But the combination to the safe—that was just a guess on my part! Didn't you realize that? It could've been completely wrong!"

Larry shrugged. "But it wasn't. And I had a feeling it wasn't going to be. It just made too much sense."

"You climbed up the side of a building, broke in through a window, sawed and chiseled through a door, and braved angry mobsters on the way out, all on the basis of a *guess*, just because you thought it made sense?"

"Well, when you put it that way, it sounds foolish," Larry admitted. "But here we are, owners of a bar."

"And a bookstore," Don said.

"Aren't you afraid the man you robbed will figure it out?"

"Why? He hasn't yet."

"Well, for one thing, directly or indirectly, he's the man you bought the bar from. Royal Barrone works for Salvatore Nicolazzo. He used to until today, anyway."

"You're kidding," Don said.

Tricia shook her head.

"You mean I used the man's own money to buy his bar from him?"

"That's what it looks like."

The smile that broke out on Don's face was a thing of

beauty. "That's just perfect. You couldn't make something like that up. You put that in a book, no one would believe it."

"Not in a million years," Larry agreed.

"Just be glad that Nicolazzo got arrested today," Tricia said, "and that the people under him are going to be too busy fighting for control of his empire to bother paying attention to the two of you."

"That does sound good," Larry said.

"I'm sure it does," Tricia said. "But remember, there's one person who does know what you did."

"Oh?" Don said. "Who's that?"

"Me."

They all took another swallow. It was the last one for Tricia. She pushed her empty glass aside.

The two men eyed her balefully.

"You wouldn't turn us in, would you?" Larry said.

"You mean to the cops? Or to the gangsters?"

"Either."

"Of course I wouldn't," Tricia said, and instantly the atmosphere around the table lightened noticeably. "But," she continued, "there's something I want in return."

"What's that?" Don said.

"I'm going to be working for Charley now," she said. "I'll be working with him on his books."

"Presumably not the pornography," Larry said.

"No, Hard Case Crime," Tricia said. "And it occurs to me that the day may come when Hard Case Crime might need to ask one of you for a favor. Maybe it'll happen tomorrow, maybe it won't be for a year. Maybe ten years. Maybe *fifty* years. But when that time comes, and we ask for your help in some way—maybe we'll want to publish one of your books, or maybe we'll ask you to make a personal appearance somewhere to help us out—I want you to do it, no questions asked."

"No questions?" Larry said.

"No questions."

"And if we agree to this, you won't tell anyone about…?"

"About anything. Hell," Tricia said, "I'd rather see the money in your hands than the bad guys'."

"I'll drink to that," Larry said.

"So," Tricia said, "do we have a deal?"

The two men nodded and they shook hands three ways.

With that behind them, Don said, "But Trixie, tell me honestly—it's great that you're going to be working there, but what do you think the odds are that Hard Case Crime will be around in fifty years? Seriously. A hundred to one?"

"Oh, I don't know," Tricia said, and she reached over, picked up Don's glass and downed the rest of his beer. Then she did the same with Larry's, wiped her mouth on the back of her hand and spread a companionable arm over each man's shoulders. "I bet it's no worse than half that."

Author's Note

When we set out to celebrate the publication of Hard Case
Crime's 50th book—quite a milestone for a series Max
Phillips and I originally thought might never make it past
its fifth—a variety of ideas got bandied about. Maybe
we'd do a collection of short stories, with each of our
living authors contributing a yarn. Maybe we'd uncover
some important lost novel from a true giant of the field,
something along the lines of a never-before-published
Sam Spade novel by Hammett, or perhaps the long-
rumored "black McGee" novel by John D. MacDonald.
(Alas, neither exists.) Maybe this, maybe that. None of
the ideas seemed quite right.

Then I hit on the notion for *Fifty-to-One*.

Not the title, that came later—and my thanks to author
Amy Vincent for suggesting it. Just the concept. But the
concept was enough to get my blood pumping.

Of course, in retrospect the concept was insane: to
write a 50th book that would commemorate the (fictitious)
50th anniversary of the founding of Hard Case Crime,
set 50 years ago, and to tell the story in 50 chapters, with
each chapter bearing the title of one of our 50 books, in
their order of publication. Our books' titles hadn't been
chosen along the way with this sort of project in mind—if
they had, I'd never have agreed to let Lawrence Block re-
title his fourth book for us *A Diet of Treacle*, or published
both *The Last Quarry* and *The First Quarry* (especially
not in that order), or published books with titles as un-

yielding to the repurposer's art as *Zero Cool* or *Lemons Never Lie* or *The Murderer Vine*.

But these things take on a life of their own, and as soon as I'd had the idea I couldn't resist the challenge. In fact, the trickier the challenge appeared, the keener I became. (Keep in mind that I'm someone who loves books like Nabokov's *Pale Fire* and Calvino's *If on a winter's night a traveler* and Perec's *A Void*. If you have a taste for trickery on a grand scale and haven't read those books, you must. Stop reading now, put this book down, go to your local bookseller, buy all three, and read them. When you're done, come back and we'll continue.

[Taps fingers. Whistles a bit. Checks his watch.]

Done? Very good. Onward.)

The project began taking shape in the second half of 2007 and I began writing seriously at the start of 2008, with a mid-year deadline to hit a year-end publication date. The time pressure was part of the fun, of course: No better way to write a pulp novel than to have a deadline hanging over your head. (I kept picturing myself hammering out pages on a manual typewriter, then yanking them out and passing them to a copy boy to get them set in hot lead. Sort of like Stephen J. Cannell at the end of all those old TV shows he wrote.)

Along the way, several things occurred that heightened my excitement even further. First, Glen Orbik painted his gorgeous cover painting. All of Glen's covers for us have been spectacular, but he really outdid himself with this one. The original is now hanging in my living room at home, and it fills me with delight every time I see it.

Then Max Phillips, who not only founded Hard Case Crime with me but also wrote one of the series' most celebrated titles, the Shamus Award-winning *Fade to Blonde*, agreed to pen one of the book's 50 chapters. (I'll leave it to you to figure out which chapter was the one Max wrote.)

Then Dorchester Publishing, the publisher that has done such an extraordinary job of producing and distributing our books and getting them into the hands of hundreds of thousands of readers, agreed to let us include in the book a full-color insert section showcasing our first 50 covers, something I knew long-time readers would relish.

And finally I had the idea for putting Don and Larry (or at least heavily fictionalized versions of them) in the book, and when I ran it by them, they didn't put the kibosh on it. Far from it, actually. Larry riffed on it a bit, suggesting one of my favorite jokes in the whole novel. (Again, I'll leave it to you to guess which one. You can just pick your favorite and assume that one's Larry's. He's much funnier than I am.)

Plotting the book out was, as you can imagine, a bear, and I want to thank my wonderful wife, novelist Naomi Novik, for putting up with many a dinner conversation in which I bent her ear about one knotty plot problem or other. Like Max and Larry (the other people whose ears I bent), she made a number of suggestions that wound up in the finished book and improved it greatly.

A few other thanks:

Tim DeYoung of Dorchester was the person who originally decided to take a chance on Hard Case Crime back when it was no more than an idea; without him, the series might never have launched, much less lasted as long as it has. I can't thank him enough—and if you like our books, you can't either.

I also want to thank our very talented art director, Steve Cooley, and typesetter, Leigh Grossman, for work above and beyond the call, not just on this book but on all the books in our line. There wouldn't be any Hard Case Crime books without the work they do, month in and month out.

I want to thank Sarah Nicolazzo for supplying a sur-name for my gangster. (I hope she doesn't mind.)

I want to thank our forthcoming 51st book, *Killing Castro*, for not being one of our first 50, since (Agent Brooks' desperate final sally notwithstanding) that title would just have been the straw that broke the camel's back.

And I want to thank all of you, our readers, especially those who've been with us from the start, for supporting this crazy labor of love. Hard Case Crime has always struck me as close kin to the coyote in those old cartoons, who could only keep running on air as long as he didn't look down and spot that he was doing something impos-sible. You've kept us looking up, and airborne, all this time, and with our feet pedaling madly in space we've somehow managed to make it this far.

Fifty books. Dear god.

It was the winter of 2001 when, over drinks on a blus-tery day (at a Japanese restaurant called Azusa, no matter how many times I've told the story wrong and said it was the Algonquin), I said these fateful words to Max: "Why doesn't anyone publish books like that anymore?"

Thank you, all of you, for making it possible for us to publish books like that again.

—Charles Ardai
New York City, July 2008

Get Hard Case Crime by Mail...
And Save 43%!

☐ **YES! Sign me up for the Hard Case Crime Book Club!**

As long as I choose to stay in the club, I will receive every Hard Case Crime book as it is published (generally one each month). I'll get to preview each title for 10 days. If I decide to keep it, I will pay only $3.99* — a savings of 43% off the cover price! There is no minimum number of books I must buy and I may cancel my membership at any time.

Name: _____

Address: _____

City / State / ZIP: _____

Telephone: _____

E-Mail: _____

☐ **I want to pay by credit card:** ☐ VISA ☐ MasterCard ☐ Discover

Card #: _____   Exp. date: _____

Signature: _____

Mail this page to:
HARD CASE CRIME BOOK CLUB
20 Academy Street, Norwalk, CT 06850-4032

Or fax it to 610-995-9274.
You can also sign up online at www.dorchesterpub.com.

* Plus $2.00 for shipping. Offer open to residents of the U.S. and Canada only. Canadian residents please call 1-800-481-9191 for pricing information.

If you are under 18, a parent or guardian must sign. Terms, prices, and conditions subject to change. Subscription subject to acceptance. Dorchester Publishing reserves the right to reject any order or cancel any subscription.